WHAT REVIEWERS SAY ABOUT *THE COLOR OF LIES*
FIRST PLACE, ROYAL PALM LITERARY AWARDS, 2010, WOMEN'S FICTION (UNPUBLISHED)

"In this complex tale of deception, love, and race, Meredith blends cringe-causing moments of fear with scenes of tenderness and connection to explore how lies are interwoven with the deepest truths of our lives. But while dishonesty grips the characters, you'll find none in Meredith's writing, a shoot-from-the-hip style to match her storytelling gifts."

-Ron Cooper, author of *Purple Jesus*

"Though there is a Cassandra King/Connie May Fowler flavor, *The Color of Lies* shines with Donna Meredith's own strong voice. Meredith's respect and love for her characters resonate as she spins this story of small town webs of connections that transcend color."

-Claire Matturro, author of *Skinny-Dipping*

WHAT REVIEWERS SAY ABOUT *THE GLASS MADONNA*
ALSO BY DONNA MEREDITH

"A masterful blend of history and fiction . . . transports the reader to an earlier time, yet reverberates with themes still current . . . abuse, healing, and renewal."

—*Southern Literary Review*

"An action-packed page turner . . . an expansive and generous novel."

—*Tallahassee Democrat*

"The story reveals the daily home life, customs and beliefs of the glass workers: women in the work force, the availability of the birth control pill, the effects of the women's liberation movement, the proliferation of day care centers, and the impact of wars this country engaged in . . . the author skillfully intertwines the lives of the German ancestors with the lives of their modern-day descendants to show the changing roles of men and women."

—*West Virginia Book Festival*

The
Color
of Lies

The
Color
of Lies

DONNA MEREDITH

Wild Women Writers
An Independent Publishing Company

The Color of Lies

ISBN: 978-0-9829015-5-7
Library of Congress Number: TX0007415312
Published by Wild Women Writers, Tallahassee, FL
www.wildwomenwriters.com
First Publication: October 2011

Logo design by E'Layne Koenigsberg of 3 Hip Chics, Tallahassee, FL
www.3HipChics.com

Cover Art by DeDe Harter, who creates drawings, paintings, and sculpture from her home-based studio in Tallahassee, Florida. She teaches art at Florida State University and Valdosta State University.

Printed in the United States of America

Dedication

For every teacher with the idealism to stand in front of a classroom believing she or he can make a difference.

Especially
- Mildred Nicholas, who cautioned me to do noble things, not dream them all day long

- Virginia Nutter, who taught me structure

- Genevieve Broughton, who encouraged creativity

- And these college professors, each of whom left an imprint on my life: Jane Dumire, Marilynn Jones, Frederick Pudsell, Jack Wills, and Sheila Ortiz Taylor

And for my colleagues at Grafton, Washington Irving, and Thomasville High Schools, who remain some of the finest people I have ever met.

Acknowledgements

Thanks to

• Early readers for their suggestions and encouragement: Rhett DeVane, Marie Eckberg, Laura Garrison, Liz Jameson, Shirley Jones, Peggy Kassees, Anne Lewis, Sylvia Livingston, Hannah Mahler, Harriet McDonald, Pat Murphy, Leslie Patterson, Mary Jane Ryals, Karen Schneider, Patricia Stephens, Michael Whitehead, and Susan Womble.

• Paula Kiger and Liz Jameson for their careful editing.

• My husband John, for tolerating the myriad ways my writing disrupts our lives.

• My daughter, her husband, and my grandson, for the joy they bring.

• My mother, for her unconditional love and unfailing support.

A Word from the Author

Teachers have one of the hardest jobs imaginable, but most of you already know that. You remember how you and your classmates squirmed, fidgeted, doodled, daydreamed, procrastinated, passed notes, and chattered when you were supposed to be focused on the day's lesson. It's only gotten worse since you were in school. The teachers I had and the ones I worked alongside rank just short of sainthood for their dedication to young people. They cared. The job meant much more than a small government paycheck and pension.

I want readers to know from the outset the racist incidents described in *The Color of Lies* don't reflect my experiences in these schools. I believe most of my fellow teachers and principals had genuine love for their students, the kind my protagonist Molly Culpepper and her crew in the lounge have. My characters are fictional, though a few of the quirkier traits are drawn from teachers I had in school myself, and the students are often amalgams of the many wonderful young people I taught during my career.

Some readers will object to this novel because it addresses racism, but skin color is not a dead issue in the United States, no matter how much we wish it were. The election of our first black president marked a high point in erasing barriers of the past, but it also engendered backlash and resentment. Division in our country today may be based more on wealth and class than race alone. Yet ugly incidents like the one that begins this novel are still happening today. And without question, our education system can and must do more to meet the needs of all students, regardless of ethnicity or family wealth. Programs based only on the classroom are likely to be less successful than those embracing the whole child and the whole community.

Small towns have intricate webs of connection, an almost palpable love of community and tradition. I tried to capture this devotion in my fictional town of Alderson. But Alderson isn't perfect. Like real small towns, Alderson can be slow to change. Sometimes that is a good thing. Sometimes it is not. I've tried to construct nuanced characters and a nuanced community, neither wholly good, nor wholly bad, characters and a town that are loveable, even though flawed. I love the town and characters I created. I hope you do too.

~~~

For more information about Donna Meredith and her writing, visit www.donnameredith.com. Recipes for most dishes mentioned in the novel are available on the website.

One

Ten minutes into my scintillating lecture on interview techniques, my newspaper editor Tameka Coakley hollered, "Y'all gotta see this. Mr. Brown called out Barack Obama right on the blackboard." Any illusion that my students had been spellbound by my words or that I even could control my classroom crumbled. Tameka scrambled across the hall, pulling my entire fourth period class in her wake, my commands to get back into seats ignored.

I elbowed my way through the bodies so I could see the words for myself. I couldn't believe Tameka was telling the truth. No teacher could be that stupid, not even Francis Brown. But the evidence stared back at me and for a second I couldn't breathe. Six little words chalked on the blackboard. The equivalent of a bomb.

"Holy shhii—" I trailed off, my eyes darting side to side to see if anyone had heard. I didn't think they had. They were too busy cussing as well, a violation of rules I normally would correct. Under the circumstances, I let it go. I don't swear. Ever. Well, hardly ever, and never in front of my students. But right now I wanted to. I could feel the ground shifting beneath Alderson High School, could feel cracks radiating out from Brown's room. Seismic cracks guaranteed to divide our community.

I didn't know whether to cry or scream as I stared at Mr. Brown's block-style lettering. What had he been thinking? No one with a modicum of intelligence or sense or courtesy would have written "HOPE: Help Overthrow a Pickaninny's Election" on the board in a room full of mostly black teenagers. The phrase felt like a ten-ton weight pressing against my eyes. I became acutely aware of the fluorescent lights glancing off the white letters. I could smell the accumulated chalk dust in the magnetic tray that clung to the board at a downward angle, symbolic of a classroom gone horribly awry.

I had never much liked Francis Brown. He showed up in Alderson a year ago after he was laid off from NASA. Gossip said he was about to lose his second wife as well. The former engineer strutted down the hallway, scratching his bald head, muttering insults under his breath. Sometimes I could catch a word or two. "Natives." "Ghetto." His bushy gray mustache seemed to quiver with indignation that his life had come to this. He stood only four inches taller than my five-foot frame. Francis compensated by swelling up with his own importance, a trait which earned him the nickname "Napoleon" in the faculty lounge. He didn't like the kids in his math classes and they knew it. This time he had crossed a line you just don't cross.

I took a deep breath and gathered my wits. Students usually only got this riled up when a fight broke out. I grabbed the first forearms I could reach and turned those kids around.

"Y'all get back to class. Now!"

"Ah, Miz Culpepper!" several protested.

"Come on. Class time is precious." My voice rocked with mother-teacher authority and they filed across the hall in an orderly fashion. Okay, a snail could have crossed faster and the exodus wasn't quiet and it wasn't tidy, but at least they eventually obeyed.

I turned out the lights and closed the door. That Brown's class-room echoed with emptiness when it should have been occupied slowly dawned on me. "Where are Mr. Brown's students?" I asked no one in particular.

Tameka turned to me in the hallway, eyes glittering with her scoop. "Crammed into the office conference room. That new guidance coun-selor is giving them the big talk. How to hang on to your self esteem in the face of haters. Mr. Brown's in the principal's office. I wouldn't want to be in his shoes right now." The giggle that rumbled deep in her throat was tinged with glee.

"How do you find out these things?"

"Angela texted me."

"You better put that cellphone away. I see it out, it's gone."

"Yes, ma'am, I know."

I chided myself for not noticing her thumbs mashing keys furi-ously during this back and forth. She probably had cradled the phone in her lap, but you'd think I would have seen her chin digging into her neck, her eyes cast too far down rather than on the handout on her desk. You'd think after a dozen years I'd have this teacher game down better, but no, I was a loser, outwitted by these kids time and again. I herded everyone back into my room and resumed the journalism lesson. I persevered, even though my mind wasn't on how to phrase strong questions. Neither was anyone else's. One girl tore little slits in the sides of the handout. Others stared blankly into space. Tameka sucked her bottom lip in and out as if she were swallowing sounds she yearned to unleash.

We liked to think of Alderson as an All-American town and AHS as the ideal school. Rah, rah, rah and all that. We swatted away any evidence to the contrary as persistently as the mosquitoes and no-see-ums that dogged us in South Georgia year-round. We prided ourselves on restored Victorian homes painted in shell pink and buttercup with elaborate white gingerbread trim. We fought off the incursion of a mall and preserved the mom-and-pop businesses lining our brick-paved downtown streets. At AHS we all got along, more or less, no matter which category of the sixty-nine percent black, twenty-five percent white, and four percent other we belonged to. Two percent refused to be categorized.

We were Alderson. Camellia Capital of the South. Four-time AA state football champions. Home of the Marching Patriots Band. Those hip-hopping steppers were invited to prestigious venues every year. Macy's Thanksgiving Day Parade. Disney World. I'd heard the Obama campaign had already formed a transition team in anticipation of victory. Thanks to Francis Brown, they were probably testing their shredder on our band's invitation to the inaugural parade.

A clear image of Brown's blackboard jumped into my mind again: "HOPE: Help Overthrow a Pickaninny's Election." I shuddered.

With certainty, I could pinpoint five defining moments in my life. The day I began my dream job at AHS with high—and unsustainable—ideals. The day David, a man of substance and character, asked me to be his wife, putting a welcome end to my father's attempts to set me up with his charming bar mates. The morning David died. The night my son Graham was born and clasped my finger for the first time, and I was crushed equally by the weight of joy and the desire to insulate him against the pain that inevitably descends on us all. The day my beloved mother died, thrusting me into the role of family matriarch, long before I felt ready for that responsibility.

In the midst of these moments, I felt the path shifting under my feet, knew my world would never be quite the same again.

On September 17, 2008, when Francis Brown unleashed those hateful words, they didn't change my world. But they began to change the way I saw it.

I knew Alderson in the way you can only know a town when you were born in its two-floor hospital and grew up running freely through the neighbors' back doors without knocking. My blood was colored by its camellias, my bones informed by its white picket fences. I knew whose pecan trees produced sweet nuts and which ones were too bitter to eat. I knew the Murphys down the street were cousins who had to get special permission to marry, knew which deacon resigned when his church sponsored a teen dance, knew which bank president did the horizontal rumba with his secretary while his wife chaperoned students touring Italy and Greece. As a native, I was connected to Alderson by a special umbilical cord. Our hearts beat to the same rhythm.

Brown's words severed the cord.

When you live in a house long enough, you stop noticing the chips and nicks in the baseboards, the fingerprint smudges on the kitchen cabinets, the dirt furred along the ridges of the microwave's fan vent. Then one day company's coming and you look at everything with the eyes of a stranger. There it is, and it's been there all along. All that dirt.

On September 17, I started to look at my town through different lenses, and was shocked to discover the nicks and the smudges. All that dirt.

For two weeks, not only the front pages of the *Alderson Herald*, but also every national TV talk show vented outrage over Brown's slur. Pundits questioned whether Alderson was just another Southern town that couldn't get over the Civil War. They speculated that if Obama were elected some wing-nut like Francis Brown might assassinate him rather than allow a black man to be president. Fortunately for us, the nation's attention span was as about as long as my students'. Reporters soon packed up their camcorders and moved on to other conflicts. Alderson was slowly returning to what passed for normal. My sophomores resumed debates over the relative merits of

Alicia Keys and Usher, and the chances of our football team to win the regional championship.

In early October a six a.m. phone call from my father's boss sent me hurtling across town in my SUV because Daddy hadn't been to work in three days. The streets were dark and mostly deserted. My sons slouched in their seats, Graham in front, Quinn in the back, both grumpy because I'd rushed them out of the house. My tires blew out gravel on my father's driveway. I bolted past his rusted-out truck, my jaw tightening over the "NObama" sticker on the rear window. I unlocked the kitchen door. Crusty dishes towered in the sink and the trash can overflowed. Mama would have taken one look at the mess my father had made of their kitchen and torn him a new one. She tolerated no outward signs that anything was wrong with our family. We were *Family Circle*. We were *Southern Living*. We were better than *Better Homes and Gardens*.

I thumped up the stairs to their bedroom. Mama's floral overstuffed chair was strewn with filthy clothes. Even the reproduction of Renoir's *A Girl with a Watering Can* hung askew on the wall. Straightening out my father's sorry butt fell to me since Mama was no longer around to do it.

Woodson Trask sprawled across the quilt in boxers and tube socks, one leg cocked at an impossible angle, the foot dangling almost to the floor. My father possessed an alcoholic's scrawny body and a workingman's tan—arms dark and leathery from the elbows down, and neck from the collar up. With his gravelly voice stilled by sleep, he appeared vulnerable—a broken old man who had the same rotting potato smell as the homeless guys who hung around Winn Dixie dumpsters. I sniffed the room, puzzled less by the overly sweet scent of bourbon than the trace of acrid chemicals. Ahh—the likely culprit lay on the floor by the wastebasket: a cigarette stub, with an inch of singed blue carpet fibers radiating from the tip. Frigging idiot was going to kill himself someday. Thank God I'd left my sons in the car, Graham texting his friends, Quinn playing a game on his cellphone. They didn't need to see their grandpa like this.

Despite the clamor of my running up the stairs and the overhead lights glaring down on his face, Woodson still hadn't moved. An overwhelming fear stole my breath. He was dead. Here I was, wanting to kick his butt, and the old man was dead. Maybe I had lost both parents in less than a year. I was an orphan.

"Daddy?" The voice, high-pitched and tentative, didn't sound like me at all. This voice belonged to a seven-year-old girl whose father was teaching her sharps, flats, adagio, and fortissimo. A girl who still adored him. My fingers whispered against his bare shoulder, against the sparse gray hairs sprouting from his collarbone. "Dad?"

His eyes slit open, and I jumped as if a corpse had moved. My sorrow over his imagined death evaporated. "Daddy, you should have been up an hour ago, an hour! Why are you still in bed?"

The slits shifted toward the alarm clock. "What the devil are you doing here?"

I hadn't expected him to say, *Gee thanks, Molly, thanks for caring enough to take time out of your busy morning to make sure I was still alive,* but he didn't have to sound as if I were the last person in the world he wanted to see.

"Mr. Kelso called and said you haven't worked in three days. You didn't even call in sick or answer the phone. What's the matter with you?"

"You got two boys to look after—don't you have enough to do without bothering me?" He groaned. "Where are the boys, anyway?"

"In the car." I'd told them Grandpa needed to sign papers concerning Grandma's estate. Papers that had to be postmarked today. Once Woodson knew his grandsons weren't observing him, he slipped back into a stupor. I grabbed a pillow and whacked him in the chest.

"Just look at you! When's the last time you had a bath?"

"What pope nominated you for sainthood? If I disgust you so much, don't come over no more."

"You'd better haul your tail out of bed before Mr. Kelso fires you."

"Jack wouldn't do me the favor."

We both knew he didn't mean it. He levered himself up with his elbows and swung his other foot to the floor. His fingers kneaded his eyes, then dug through the stubble on his cheeks. "All right, I'm up. Satisfied?"

Hardly. One morning Mr. Kelso would decide he'd had enough of Woodson Trask and fire him from the cable company, and then what? It didn't bear thinking about.

"My house for dinner tonight," I said. "Six-thirty, don't be late, no excuses. By the way, I told Mr. Kelso you had intestinal flu."

My father barked out a laugh. "What'd you go and tell Jack that for? I been working for him twenty-seven years. I reckon he knows my ways by now. Better hurry on 'fore you're the one who's late, Miss School Marm."

I hated it when he called me that. On the way out, I left him a present on the kitchen counter: a manila envelope filled with AA information. The Lord only knew how he would cuss and fuss when he read the contents.

Short of breath from running, I shouldered my book bag and pushed through the red double doors leading to the cafeteria. An ocean of angry voices pitched and swelled. I expected to find two girls, necks craned, lips bared, ready to scratch and slap. Typical scene: "Wanda tole me you said I looked like a whore at Dexter's last night. That what you said, bee-otch?" Or two guys on the brink of a punchdown over an insult to either one's a.) clothes b.) game c.) mama or d.) all of the above.

But there was no discernible cluster of teens spitting words and stabbing fingers, just general chaos throughout the room. Eat your rubbery scrambled eggs, I thought. Too early in the morning for all this fuss. I hustled on to the teachers' lounge, half an hour behind schedule. I tossed my lunch into the refrigerator and was about to race down the hallway to my room when Betsy Mulharin waved the *Alderson Herald* under my nose.

"Can you believe this story, Molly?"

"Didn't get around to the paper this morning." I'd been lucky to find time to brush the moss off my teeth.

I absorbed the lead headline. "A lawsuit—filed against us?"

The first few paragraphs complained about the school letting students choose among three tracks of study: honors courses, a more moderately paced track for most students, and a remedial track. Yeah, yeah, yeah. Those tracks had been in place forever. Occasionally someone complained. Old news. They'd fuss even more if we took a kid who could barely read and expected him to write analytical essays on Macbeth. Besides, parents and students chose the track, not the school system, so where was the gripe?

The third paragraph of the story made me want to roll up the newspaper and whack someone:

> "Practices at AHS are holdovers from the days of segregation," said the Rev. Josiah Bolden, founder of Blacks For Progress.
>
> One key area the lawsuit asks the court to examine is disciplinary policies.
>
> "A careful analysis of statistical data reveals black students receive harsher punishment than whites," said Bolden. "For example, more than twice as many blacks are assigned to In-School Suspension as whites."

I exploded. "We're three-fourths black! Of course more black students get discipline referrals."

Betsy nodded, lips pressed together. "Keep reading."

I scanned further:

> "In a school where three quarters of the students are black, every year each of the big scholarships go to white students," Bolden said. "You know the ones I'm talking about. Lots of token scholarships go to black students, the ones for $100 or $150. Those wouldn't even pay for textbooks."
>
> Bolden also claimed most extra-curricular activities are subject to race-based policies. "The school always chooses to produce a play requiring a mostly white cast when they could choose one like 'A Raisin in the Sun.' Or they could choose to ignore race completely when making casting decisions."
>
> First year drama instructor Betsy Mulharin said she is willing to consider a play with more black characters. "But the choice of a play has to be approved by the principal and the school board," she said. "I don't get to choose it by myself."
>
> The golf team also came under fire for its all-white members. "The school has to go along with Alderson Country Club's policies," said Superintendent Mark Rice. "That's the condition

of the school's being allowed to use club facilities for practice and matches."

"Then it's time to stand up for AHS students—all of them— and force the club to change," Bolden said.

Another of Bolden's complaints is the scarcity of black students selected to attend the state honors camp. The Herald verified that only two blacks have been chosen to attend, one in 1999 and another in 2005. The school can send three students each year to the prestigious camp for gifted students.

"We select students based on a strict set of criteria," Superintendent Mark Rice said. "Standardized test scores, grade point average, and extra-curricular participation are all part of the process. I have appointed a committee to reexamine our criteria to insure there is no racial bias."

When informed of the superintendent's comment, Bolden asked, "How can we trust a man who lied to everyone about firing Francis Brown?"

Bolden referred to the Alderson High School teacher who last month wrote HOPE on the blackboard as an acronym for a slogan that employed a racial slur.

Rice first said he'd fired Brown, but after CNN reported Brown was now teaching at the alternative school, Rice insisted he couldn't dismiss an employee based only on the word of students.

"All I can say is the matter is being reviewed. I can't comment on personnel matters publicly," Rice said.

Brown's attorney, Alex Young, claims his client was joking.

"There's nothing funny about making racist remarks to impressionable young people," Bolden said.

"I welcome our day in court and am sure the school system will be fully vindicated," said Alderson City School System attorney Katrina Cromartie.

First hearings will take place in front of the Honorable Tim Crutchfield in January.

So that's what this was really about. The whole country was going to judge everyone in Alderson, all 21,300 of us, by the actions of one ignorant teacher. The other 21,299 were mostly good people. Really we were. At least no worse than anyone else.

The newspaper crackled in my hands as I folded it. "I can't believe the superintendent didn't fire that moron Brown, even if he is his wife's cousin."

"Yep. Looks like we're all going to suffer for it," Betsy said.

"Hearings. Geesh!" The United States was poised to elect its first black president in another month. Hadn't we moved past this? Francis Brown should stand trial. Not the rest of us.

Betsy tucked her Alice-in-Wonderland hair behind one ear. "Who is this Reverend Bolden?"

I had never met him, but I'd heard of him often enough. "Liz Powell's pastor."

"This lawsuit will stir things up, make these kids impossible to teach," she said.

Funny she should choose that phrase. When Betsy had arrived at Alderson two months ago, I thought her youth and looks would make it impossible for her to teach anyone. Especially the boys. More than once I'd heard them refer to her as a hottie. But I was wrong. My son Graham was stretching his mind in new directions in Betsy Mulharin's freshman English class, though I had no illusions about him. He drooled over her long blonde hair and even longer legs like all the other boys.

Just in time to overhear Betsy's worries, my department chair, the inimitable Miss Baker, charged in. Even though she weighed all of ninety pounds, she somehow managed to make any room feel crowded. We shifted away from the refrigerator so she could get by.

There was a sucking sound as Miss Baker opened the fridge door and threw her lunch sack inside. "Don't be ridiculous. The lawsuit is baseless—that goes without saying. Everything will go on the same as always. At least in *my* classroom it will." Her hip bumped the door closed. In Miss Baker's classroom, everything went on the same as always, and had been going on the same as always since way back when I was her student.

As soon as she left, I returned the newspaper to Betsy. "The lawsuit may make things tough for a while."

"All the kids were yakking about it in the cafeteria. Way too loud.

The cafeteria manager had to come out to settle them down."

"I heard the ruckus. This assumption that we're all a bunch of prejudiced pigs makes me so—" I let my voice trail off as Liz Powell walked in. My lunch buddy since we had started together as new teachers at AHS a dozen years ago. We toted casseroles to each other's homes when a family member passed. Liz and I had discussed what made our children stick rocks up their nose and what men really wanted from life besides the obvious—cold beer and hot sex. We talked about bad hair, big thighs, and getting our boobs smashed between mammography plates. Once, when I found a lump, Liz had been the first to dismiss it as a cyst. The mammogram proved her right. But here I was cutting off a conversation because it centered on the one thing we never acknowledged. The Big Taboo. The Absolute Don't-Go-There. The difference in our skin. Mentally I reviewed every word I'd said to Betsy, hoping nothing could have been offensive to Liz.

"Morning, y'all." Liz didn't meet our eyes. "Excuse me for running off but I've got to get some notes on the board. Running behind."

True or an excuse? The question never would have entered my mind until this morning.

Minutes later I slouched against the wall beside Room 104B, keeping the hallways safe from shoving, fist fights, malingering after the tardy bell, and unseemly displays of affection. Down the hall Alderson High School's new principal, Mr. Van Teasel, pressed a clipboard against his crisp white shirt and red striped tie. I jerked away from the wall. Mr. Van Teasel jetted toward us, cutting between students, his body inserted into the middle of conversations. He barely acknowledged me with a flick of his eyes as he blew past and settled into a desk near the back of my room. Students gave each other sidelong glances and nudges that halted vehement discussion of the lawsuit, flirtation, and homework-copying.

I couldn't imagine what he was doing. Since school had started in early August, he had shown a clear preference for his office over the front lines of education. Some days I couldn't blame him.

His head slowly rotated as he surveyed the room, those close-set eyes taking everything in. He scribbled something on the legal pad attached to his clipboard. Then I knew. Of all mornings, he had chosen this one to observe my teaching for the first time. Geesh! The one morning, thanks to my father and the lawsuit, I hadn't arrived at my desk forty-five minutes early to ensure every detail of my lesson plan was ready to execute, every handout laid out in precise order. A morning when students were unpredictable. My mind went blank. I couldn't even remember what my lesson plan said.

Orville Chidester hurtled his linebacker's body down the hall to beat the tardy bell. On the threshold of my room, he whirled around and whispered, "What's The Weasel doing here?"

Even Orville's whisper boomed like a canon, and I feared Mr. Van Teasel would think I encouraged such disrespect. "Shhhh. Move it, before you're—"

The bell began its ear-shattering ring and Orville sprinted to plant his backside before the sound ebbed.

Mr. Van Teasel required all teachers to post an Essential Question on the wall to help students focus on unit instruction. His narrow face constricted even further as he observed mine. In eight-inch high arrest-me-red letters, I had written on a long rectangle of newsprint, "Nature or nurture: how and why do males and females differ from each other?" My students found it intriguing, but from the way Mr. Van Teasel's cheeks twitched, I didn't think he cared for it.

Even though his presence caught me off guard, I was relieved he had chosen first period. A class develops a personality as distinctive as any individual's: eager or apathetic, accepting of leadership or rebellious, playful or humorless, competitive or cooperative. The addition or subtraction of one student can change the whole group personality. In August when another school year launches, I love all my classes equally, but by October favorites emerge. This year first period kept polishing a shiny place in my heart until it shone like red glass.

As Brian Jones and Marissa Powell pushed the big screen TV toward the center of the room, my lesson plan came back to me. A student-made video of Act IV, *The Taming of the Shrew*. I sighed with relief. Mr. Van Teasel couldn't have selected a more auspicious time to observe my room if he had sacrificed a goat and studied its entrails for good omens as the ancients used to do. From the bookshelf beside my desk, I pulled out my lesson plan notebook and presented the appropriate page to the principal. A sacred offering. I hoped it would please him. We settled in to watch the show.

The video wound into its final moments, delivering an extreme close up of Marissa Powell—my friend Liz's daughter, whose elegance reminded me of Whitney Houston before drugs, time, and Bobby ravaged her looks. Slowly, exquisitely slowly, the camera lens widened to reveal more of Marissa preening before a cheval mirror. Her character, Kate, was seeing herself in a red-beaded flapper dress for the first time. I wondered where Marissa had gotten it. "Washboard Wiggles" jazzed softly in the background. The camera dollied back and we glimpsed sophomore class president, Brian Jones, in a double-breasted suit and Panama hat, his dark skin gleaming like an eggplant. I realized with appreciation that they had used some kind of fill light on the left to illuminate his face. Their cameraman was taking TV Production and it showed.

"It's a dress for a bug-eyed Betty, you foolish woman!" Brian shouted at the seamstress. "Nowhere close to being good enough for my doll Kate!"

Marissa turned to face him. "Aw, Petey, I want the dress. It's the bee's knees, that's for sure." She pirouetted in front of the mirror, the fringed hem of her red dress flaming away from her legs and igniting every male in the class.

I risked a glance at the principal. Chuckling. So engrossed in the video, he wasn't writing a thing on the evaluation. He *would* realize this was part of teaching, wouldn't he? The buzz word for it was student-centered learning. I tried to remember the checklist of behaviors he had to observe, got to three, and gave up. I had an evaluation of my own to finish and awarded ten points for variety of camera shots.

The camera zoomed tight on Brian's face. "Baloney," he scoffed. "I say the dress is a rag, a plain Jane, a—"

Cut to a wide shot of Ceci Barnes as the seamstress. Her light brown hair had been rolled into old-fashioned curls, held back from her face with tortoise shell combs. "That's a bunch of hooey. She looks swanky in that getup, yessiree. I want my clams now, Pops. Pay up."

As the credits rolled minutes later, the camera operator, Orville Chidester, roared over the clapping, "That was the best one yet. Admit it!"

"For sure!" Ja'Neice said. "Y'all Hollywood!"

I grinned, then cringed. Their voices probably carried right through the wall into Miss Baker's room, and Miss Baker didn't approve of noise. Mr. Van Teasel probably didn't either. His pencil scrawled across his tablet now. What was he writing? I imagined, *Your classroom is nearly as quiet and controlled as a soccer stadium riot.*

I stood in front of the group and held my palms up. "Shush now. Let's discuss what the video accomplished. What did you like best?"

Ja'Neice raised her hand. "The slang and costumes rocked. Y'all really translated Act IV into the 1920s." She turned to Brian. "Where'd you get those clothes?"

"Thrift store. Go on; tell me I looked good in that hat."

Vashawn cut in. "Nah, Marissa's the one that looked good. She looked real good. Miz Culpepper, Shakespeare's language doesn't make much sense. I don't get into this play when we read it out loud. But in the video I could see what kind of game Petruchio was running. I liked the way they changed Petruchio into Petey, too."

Vashawn was trying to make me look good in front of the principal, and that shine I had for first period glowed even brighter. Once or twice Vashawn and I had clashed in minor ways, so it was comforting to know we were still on the same side when it counted. What he said was exactly what I wanted Mr. Van Teasel to hear—in case he hadn't figured out the purpose of the assignment.

We talked a while longer, Brian dominating more than he should have, as usual. His assurance came naturally from having a doctor for a mother and a father who was a colonel in the National Guard. Brian went too far when he interrupted Ja'Neice.

"Brian, my mama always said there's a reason you have two ears and only one mouth: so you can listen twice as much as talk," I said.

The class burst out laughing.

Brian was able to laugh at himself, too, a trait I loved in him. "My bad," he said.

I gave the class ten minutes to journal reactions to the video while I took attendance.

Mr. Van Teasel leaned over my desk on his way out. "Interesting lesson. Your evaluation will be in your mailbox by the end of the day."

Interesting—that was positive, wasn't it, even if he hadn't been smiling? One of the criteria he had to check off was that all students were engaged. They had been. The video had been so entertaining I hadn't thought once about my father. The lawsuit had the kids stirred up, but maybe Miss Baker was right. Things would go on as usual. I might have difficulty controlling certain members of my family, but I was a frigging genius in the classroom.

Before I could stifle that little explosion of vanity, J.D. Marshall pimped into my room.

Two

From the beginning, everything about J.D. irritated me. The way he slow-rolled from the outside of one foot to the other. The way his chin flicked upward to the right while his eyes cut down to acknowledge his classmates, expecting them to fawn over him as if he were some kind of celebrity.

I noticed the blue schedule in his hand and raised my grade book to hide my face as I mouthed, "Shhii-ugar!" For crying out loud, this class had grown, a student here, a student there, until thirty desks packed every square inch of floor space. It was impossible to turn around without tripping over somebody's back pack. A new student couldn't arrive at a worse time. We had almost finished reading the play. I would have to conjure up activities to keep him busy while the class wrote papers on it. The office could have given the boy to Miss Baker. She only had fifteen in her first period. Still, none of this was the boy's fault.

J.D. dressed in the baggy style preferred by most boys at Alderson High. The crotch of his pants hung so low he looked like a toddler carrying a load in his britches. I knew it was uncomfortable because my pantyhose were riding in the same region, though not by choice. J.D. took five steps into the room, then paused, grabbed his waistband through his tee-shirt and hitched his pants upward half an inch. All the guys had mastered this move. Seemed like a waste of time. One wrong twitch and those pants were going down.

I set my grade book aside and smiled up at him. "Good morning. May I help you?"

He smiled back, revealing a gold-capped front tooth with a star cut-out. "Whaz up, dawg?" Pencils stilled across the room and I could feel all eyes on me. I willed my lips to maintain the smile. "You Miz Culpepper?" he asked, one hand hitching his pants up again.

"I am." Our new guidance counselor leaned against my door jamb, telegraphing a request to join her in the hall, but I couldn't leave the kid standing there. "Delighted to have you in my class." I pointed to the third row, sixth desk. "You can sit right there."

He strolled down the first row, plunked himself into the last seat, leaned back, and crossed his arms. "This one looks good to me."

Students craned their necks to watch my reaction. I narrowed my eyes, drew my brows together, and compressed my lips into a severe line. Back when I was a rookie, I had perfected this expression in front of a mirror. Their eyes dropped back to their journals. Not that I was fooled. Their antennae homed in on every nuance of this exchange. Thank heavens Mr. Van Teasel wasn't in the room now.

"You can sit there today, but that desk belongs to someone who's absent. Tomorrow you need to sit where you were assigned."

J.D. didn't acknowledge that he'd heard. I handed him a folder I kept for new kids: class rules, school handbook, syllabus, plus a laminated bookmark I made over the summer for each student. J.D.'s had Robert Hayden's poem about Malcolm X printed on it, along with a photo of the black author.

"Writing topic's on the board. Back to work, folks."

Everyone complied except J.D. He made a performance of slow-walking the bookmark up to the trash and dropping it from head height. It clunked into the can. Someone sniggered. When J.D. returned to his seat, he fingered a rhythm on his leg. His neck bobbled like one of those Russian dolls, his lips moving without sound. At least without any sound I could overhear from my desk. I wanted to go back to bed and start this day over.

"Mrs. Culpepper, can I see you a minute?" Tessa Kaufmann, the new counselor, held a yellow schedule card in her hand. My copy. Tessa's voice rang out with a nasal quality that grated on the ear. That New Jersey accent marked her as an outsider. Our department chair would have found it necessary to tell our new counselor she should have used "may" rather than "can," but I am not that kind of person.

I sighed. In minutes, journal writing would end and we would read the last act of the play. Leaving students idle even for a moment was asking for trouble. I thumped toward Tessa and, after making sure no student could see, did my best imitation of Munch's *The Scream*. (Bet you ten bucks that painting's model was a teacher.)

I closed the door partway so students couldn't overhear. "What's with this kid?"

Tessa puffed out air smelling faintly of mint and raked her fingers through short brown hair streaked with gray. "J.D. just moved to Alderson from Atlanta."

She didn't need to say another word. Everyone knew Georgians came in two types: the crazy people who lived in Atlanta and risked their lives with all that traffic and crime, and the rest of us normal humans.

Tessa continued. "As you've already figured out, J.D.'s a special case. Requires careful handling. He comes from a really rough background—I'll fill you in later, maybe at lunch." A beat of silence ensued. "I have an appointment today, but could I join your table tomorrow?"

I assured her it would be more than okay. We assumed her workload kept her chained to her desk during lunch, but now I wondered if we had made her feel like an intruder. Although the faculty joked about it, we didn't have assigned seats in the lounge. Not really, though I will admit when a substitute usurps my place, my esophageal sphincter malfunctions. Feels kind of like a pile of stones crushing my chest and throat.

Tessa studied my new twin set and matching black and garnet flowered skirt. They were terrific yard-sale finds, dirt cheap with tags still attached.

I inched my shoulders back and stood up straighter. Twelve years of experience told me J.D. Marshall could change the class chemistry completely. "Why this class?"

"The kids say you work with them more than anyone else, are more flexible."

My eyes held the counselor's. Silence can be a most effective tool in winkling out the truth. Several students slipped by behind us, carrying attendance forms to the office.

Tessa crumbled. "Look, Miss Baker kicked him out yesterday. He called her seating system 'lame.' Didn't last a whole period."

My breath caught. "No one calls Miss Baker's seating system 'lame.'"

"Why not? Kids call everything 'lame.' Anyway, what's the big deal? Most teachers have seating charts."

It was easy to tell Tessa was new to Alderson. "Not like Miss Baker's. She reseats the whole class several times a week based on points. Once in a while she even reseats everyone twice in the same period." Her system hadn't changed since I was her student more years ago than I cared to count. We earned points for everything: tests, quizzes, homework, good behavior. Feigning interest in Emily Dickinson's life while wondering if Jerry Griffin's kiss would feel more like the fuzz or the flesh of a peach. (I never did find out. He and I competed for first seat.)

I tried to set Tessa straight. "I guess J.D. didn't like starting out in last place. After his comment, he would have stayed there for a while. Probably until he graduated. No one talks like that to Miss Baker."

Tessa shook her head. "Why does everyone around here act like she's the Queen? Anyway, Mr. Van Teasel said to give J.D. to you."

Through the glass-paneled door, I watched J.D. scoot his chair into the aisle so he could prop his feet on the desk in front of him. Talking erupted throughout the room.

Tessa handed me the yellow schedule. On top of a thick smear of white-out, she had hand-written "Culpepper" into the eight o'clock slot. Long ago I had resigned myself to inheriting rejects from the legendary department chair.

"All right, that's it—no Christmas present for Miss Baker, she's off my list." Even after twelve years of teaching in the room beside hers, I couldn't bring myself to call her Jolene.

Tessa grinned. "Alrighty then, let me know if you have any trouble, Molly."

I needed to stop the hoo-ha in the classroom. I grabbed the doorknob. "*If?*"

Tessa's lips flattened into a thin, wide line. "Yeah, well, he plays football, so you can talk to the coach. I bet he'll help you."

I winced. Sonny Haswell taught social studies in my room during my planning period. Though I resented having to give up my space, I would have been polite if he hadn't developed a nasty habit of hiding a foam cup full of spit-laden tobacco inside my bottom desk drawer. Tobacco in any form was illegal in school, but that didn't stop Sonny from indulging his addiction. Administrators surely knew but they let almost anything slide in a head coach who won championships.

One day brown specks trailed across my desk calendar. I ripped off the ruined page and stuffed it and his nasty cup into Sonny's office mailbox with a note. I don't remember exactly what it said. Something about not being his mother and his needing to clean up his own mess.

Tessa's eyes flitted over my outfit again. I did look pretty good despite the twenty pounds super-glued to my middle since Quinn's birth. I sensed that any minute now the counselor would compliment me: *What a lovely outfit—where did you get it?* I couldn't wait to share my tale of shopping prowess.

Finally Tessa gestured toward my bottom. "You might want to wipe that chalk dust off your behind before you go in there. See you at lunch tomorrow."

After school I stopped by the front office to see Mrs. Alford. The secretary held a compact in front of her nose while she applied lipstick.

"Red Zin—do you think it's too dark?" She rubbed her lips round and round, up and down, to press the waxy concoction into every crack and crevice. It took a while. She had long since passed the age when red looked good on a woman. The lipstick was ghastly where it bled into the pale wrinkles around her mouth.

"Perfect shade. I was wondering if I could get some staples."

Mrs. Alford grabbed a collection of keys from her desk drawer, and we trooped into the supply room. She unlocked a cabinet and withdrew two sticks from a box.

"I hoped this once you could let me have a whole box," I said. "I was in here a couple of days ago and I hate to keep bothering you."

"No bother."

"Are you sure it wouldn't be easier to let me take a box?"

"You know as well as I do, the rule this year is two sticks at a time. We have to conserve our resources. Everybody has to tighten their belts."

I accepted my allotment. Local funds had dried up like Mrs. Alford's skin because someone at the city tax office had made a mistake in setting the millage rate for property taxes. That on top of worsening recession devastated our funding. Consequently, Alderson High had to muddle along without a school resource officer or a reading specialist, and the office staff rationed consumable supplies. I taught 136 students a day and three different subjects. There were 210 staples per stick, enough for two handouts or tests per student. Two sticks weren't squat. At this rate, I'd wear a path between Room 104B and the secretary's desk.

She smiled a Red Zin smile. "Use the chalkboard more often, dear."

I refrained from telling her where she could stick a piece of chalk.

On the way past my mailbox, I noticed yellow and pink carbonless paper protruding: my evaluation. I snatched it out and held my breath. All "meets or exceeds expectations" check-marked. No "needs improvement." In the comments section, I scanned through complimentary phrases: "incorporation of technology," "fully engaged in learning," "stimulating environment," and "high degree of motivation." The tension eased from my shoulders and an orgasmic glow spread through my whole body.

Then I read the last sentence: "Teacher should do more to control noise levels in classroom."

I sucked.

Three

First words out of my father's mouth: "So what do you think about this lawsuit?" Woodson didn't read the papers, so I knew he'd heard talk around town. I handed my sixth grader, Quinn, a stack of plates to set the table.

"Makes me sick," I said. "I hoped having a black man a month away from winning the presidency would put all this divisiveness behind us."

"Fat chance—things will be worse than ever. Francis Brown just said what the rest of us are thinking. Anyone with sense would vote for McCain. A real American hero. Way more experienced, too." Woodson cracked the tab on one of the beers he'd brought along. "You ought to take down that Obama sign in the front yard. It'll just cause trouble."

"Don't you like our sign?" Quinn asked.

"Go get your brother for dinner," I said. When Quinn was out of earshot, I explained the boys and I had designed the sign ourselves. After our second standard-issue campaign sign was stolen, I went to the lumber store and bought plywood and two posts. With leftover wall paint, Graham designed the first letter, "O," as a soccer ball, his passion. The "B" became the two books Obama wrote, my idea. The "A" was a robot, since Quinn was in the middle of building one and Obama backed scientific research. The "M" was a bunch of pencils pointing in different directions, and the last "A," a rocket ship blasting off. I nailed the sign to the posts, and the boys buried them deep in the sod.

"It won't be so easy to make off with it this time. If I catch anyone out there, I'm going after them with a baseball bat." Something about the way my father blinked made me wonder if he had stolen the first two signs. Nah, he wouldn't have—would he?

Woodson scraped his index finger around in his ear. "This county will vote Republican, same as always. America's never going to put a Muslim in the Oval Office."

"He's not a Muslim, never has been, and he's going to win. Read the polls."

"You better hope he doesn't or there will be more of this Black Nationalist stuff. Coloreds will think they can get by with anything."

I wanted Atticus Finch for a father. Instead I got stuck with Woodson. What had my mother ever seen in him? "You're impossible. I refuse to have this conversation with you. What did Mr. Kelso say to you this morning?"

"Now, *that's* a conversation I refuse to have with you."

The boys came in, so I let it drop. While Woodson shared our chicken and black bean enchiladas, he entertained us with a wild tale about his youth. After he'd gotten his draft notice and knew he was headed to Korea, he hitchhiked all the way to Daytona Beach during spring break with a six pack, two bunches of bananas, a bag of those spongy orange marshmallow peanuts, and $15 in his backpack. For five days he'd managed to party all night and sleep on the beach during the day. By then, he was flat broke and grungy as any bum.

My father lit his after-dinner cigarette. "So a policeman rousts me for vagrancy. 'Go home,' he tells me. I say, 'Wish I could, officer, sir, but Uncle Sam has other ideas. Like boot camp.' Well, that fella took me out and bought me a couple of brewskis. Says to stay on the beach long as I want. Wish I'da left when he'd first told me to. Next day I forgot to roll over and got the nastiest sunburn you ever did see. I'm telling you, I was redder than the head of a dog's—"

"Dad!" He had no sense of what was proper to say in front of children. Graham snickered and flipped his head to shift corn-colored bangs out of his eyes. Guess he'd heard the crude expression before. Quinn was laughing, too, his eyes darting from one to the other of us, trying to figure out what he'd missed. With a certain amount of irritation, I felt sure Graham would fill him in later. Quinn would grow up soon enough. Too soon.

Woodson laughed and flicked an ash onto my tablecloth. "All those sit-ups about killed me before the Gooks got a chance to try. Just imagine what it was like rolling up and down on those blisters. I can tell you it hurt like a son of a—"

"Language!" How many times had I asked him not to cuss in front of the boys? Yet they loved his stories. I wondered if half of them were true. When dinner was over and I could hear strains of Kenny Chesney's "Better as a Memory" knife from Graham's Ibanez guitar with Quinn thumping away on the drums, I brought up the contents of the manila envelope.

Woodson set down his coffee mug harder than necessary. "I almost didn't come over here tonight because I knew you were going to bring that crap up. I adjust my attitude a little after work, so what? Everybody does. I don't drink no more than anybody else."

I fumbled for the words I needed. All my life, Woodson had alternated between bingeing followed by months when he seemed relatively under control, yet in our house we never mentioned it. My mother fetched him another glass of "pop." He was "sleeping" on the couch and my brother and I needed to play outside so we wouldn't wake him. The bartender would call my mother to pick Woodson up after "happy hour" when he got a little too happy.

I cleared my throat. "Dad, it's gotten worse since Mom died."

"Bull. Just so you know, I threw your whole pretty little package in the trash. Save your paper next time, Miss Recycler."

I hated it when he called me that. "Mr. Kelso said you missed work five times in September."

"I was sick, for real. Stomachache."

"Have you seen Dr. Roberts? Could be—"

Woodson snorted. "Day I can't handle a stomachache will be a cold day in hell."

Men were a pain in the patoot, the way they needed to see themselves as tough. "You still should get it checked out. If you can't stop drinking on your own, you should join AA. I hear they meet over at—"

He scraped his chair away from the table and shot to standing. "You think it's such a good thing, you should join. You're the one with an addiction. You eat too damn much."

I recognized the defensive tactic for what it was—the deflection of blame onto someone else—but his criticism still wounded. Too much truth in it.

You eat too damn much.

My thoughts scattered like mercury from a broken thermometer. And the more I tried to rein them in, the further they skittered apart into dozens of tiny negative fragments.

Teacher should do more to control noise.
Black students disciplined more often than whites.
What Pope nominated you for sainthood?

It had been one of those days, starting with Mr. Kelso's pre-dawn phone call. Too much input. No off switch and I was ready to burst.

The porch swing undulated gently. I inhaled deeply and let the heavenly fragrance of the eight-foot tea olive at my back ease my father's exit line from my head. Aromatherapy. From the garage, Graham's baritone rang out for the hundredth time on the line "My only friends are pirates, it's just who I am." My oldest son approached music the way he did everything else, practicing until he achieved excellence. His fretwork wasn't quite there yet, but the vocals sounded pure and clear from years of singing in the church choir. For now, he was rehearsing alone while his drummer reviewed for a vocabulary quiz.

"Awry," I read aloud from the flashcard. Slouched beside me on the swing, Quinn spelled and defined the word correctly.

"Now a sentence," I said.

He jerked up straight. "What's that?"

"What's a *sentence?*"

"No, you're so silly, Mom. That whining."

I heard it then. Probably a cat.

The sound shivered through the air again, more whimper than whine, more fear than complaint, and it was coming from under my Debutante camellia. The leaves rustled. Quinn bounded down the steps and picked up a fuzz ball that barely filled his cupped hands. The puppy weighed maybe four pounds—and two pounds of that was well-groomed red fur. Hadn't been gone from its owners long. I was no expert on dog breeds, but it looked at least part Pomeranian. I bent over the porch railing to pet the puppy, catching the combined aromas of warm milk, dried urine, and animal musk. The puppy quivered. Understandable, after finding itself in an unfamiliar environment. He must have wandered through the open gate in our picket fence. I always left it open—seemed more friendly that way.

I scanned the street to see if any neighbor might be searching for a missing puppy. The only sign of life was the recluse who lived across the street in a two-story with a shingle hung on the side door:

C. Lodge Piscetelli, Attorney at Law. He was shifting boxes around in his van, a commercial vehicle with "C. Lodge Piscetelli, Computer Design and Repair" written on the side. He was C. Lodge. Guess he couldn't decide what he wanted to be when he grew up. I always waved to him, but he had kept pretty much to himself since moving in two months before. Although I had carried over one of my orange juice cakes as a house-warming gift, the melt-in-your-mouth confection hadn't induced an invitation to sit down and share life stories the way it usually did. I asked what brought him to town and all he'd offered was "Business." He'd practically shut the door in my face. No Mrs. Piscetelli was in evidence, but a pony-sized black Lab kept him company. Several times I had caught Quinn playing with the dog and asked him to make sure our neighbor didn't mind.

"Mr. Piscetelli, you missing a puppy?" I asked.

He shook his head and surprised me by coming over. As always, he wore jeans and secured his long hair in a skimpy braid. I figured him for a throwback to the seventies, one of those dope-smoking hippie types.

He held his fingers near the puppy's snout so it could sniff, and after he'd won approval, massaged those little clefts behind its ears.

A smile animated my neighbor's face and his eyes shone with a lively intelligence. "Hey, he's a cute little guy, isn't he? Pomeranian?"

Ah, so it was male. How could he tell under all that fur?

"I think so. Do you know who might be missing a dog?"

"No, ma'am, I don't."

"Molly, please. 'Ma'am' makes me think you're one of my students." Besides it made me feel old, and I was certainly no older than Mr. Lawyer-Computer Repairman. My hair didn't yet have the gray that sprung out like fine wires from the sides of Mr. Piscetelli's braid. My husband had once told me my hair was the color of pecans. Still was.

Quinn murmured soothing sounds to quiet the puppy. Strange, how everyone adopts a syrupy tone with babies, no matter what the species. Something instinctual.

"You sound just like your father," I told Quinn. "I remember him cuddling you when you were a little baby. You were crying up a storm, and he crooned, 'There now, widdle guy.' Your daddy sure loved you."

A huge smile lit Quinn's beautiful brown eyes. "He did, didn't he?"

Then his face crumpled, and I wished I'd kept my mouth shut. David's death had left a cavernous hole in our lives. We all tried to keep our distance from the edge. I ruffled Quinn's hair and shifted attention back to the puppy. A bit of pistachio green, mostly buried in fur, flashed at its neck. "Is that a collar?"

Quinn's fingers dug into the rusty fluff. "Look, there's a piece of paper attached with a paper clip."

"Tear it off," Mr. Piscetelli said. "Maybe it's the owner's name and address."

I snatched it from the collar. "'Hi, I'm looking for a good family.'" I lowered the scrap of paper. "What kind of person would abandon a puppy? It's downright criminal."

Mr. Piscetelli agreed. Two houses up the street from Mr. Piscetelli's, Eileen O'Halloran was watching us, half hidden behind one of the columns that supported her porch roof. I waved. She pulled back as if to hide, then must have realized it was too late. She returned my wave and went inside. No doubt she was peeping at us from behind her curtains now.

I turned to Mr. Piscetelli hopefully. "You want a puppy?"

He threw up his hands. "Already have a dog. I'm sure you've noticed Baxter; he's hard to miss. Why don't you keep it? Every kid needs a dog, and this one looks purebred."

"Looks like trouble to me. Quinn, get your shoes on. We'll have to take it over to the shelter and see if they can find the owner."

My son cradled the puppy even closer. "Can't we keep him, Mom?"

I puckered my lips in the shape of "no"—should have said "no." The last thing I needed was another mouth to feed and something else to clean up after. Quinn's pleading expression turned my brain to jelly. Mr. Piscetelli looked relieved when I relented and let Quinn take the dog inside.

As soon as my son set the puppy down, it peed on the carpet. I got a wet rag to clean up the mess. The puppy explored the underneath of the coffee table, sunk sharp teeth into a Persian rug—I quickly disengaged him. As he licked crumbs off the kitchen linoleum, I could see his potential to replace our vacuum cleaner. He even looked a little like a feather duster. Maybe a puppy wouldn't be so bad after all. His excited yapping brought Graham out of his room—would wonders never cease? When he stayed home, he spent the evenings holed up in his room texting his friends and doing homework. More often, though, he left for choir practice or a soccer match or football practice or a game of pick-up basketball and he didn't want Quinn tagging along.

Graham caught the puppy as he was about to head down the hallway to the bedrooms. "Where'd you come from?"

"We already asked, but he isn't talking," I said. "You two keep him corralled in the kitchen so he can't cause too much damage."

Graham put the puppy down and knelt beside it

The puppy nibbled on Quinn's finger. "Hey, cut that out! What are we going to call him?"

I grabbed my purse and car keys. "You think of something while I'm gone."

"Where you going?" Quinn asked.

"If we're going to keep him, he'll need food, bowls, and a leash." For starters. Gloom descended on me as I mentally assessed the reality of pet ownership. There would be shots and vet bills. Chicken wire to block the gaps in the picket fence. No such thing as a free dog. Halfway out the door, I heard Graham address the puppy.

"Hey, you widdle wascal, where you twying to go?"

From the porch I watched my boys sitting on the kitchen floor, their legs splayed out to trap the puppy between them. The puppy bent his head down and stuck his rear end up.

Graham lost the surly expression he had worn at home since David's death. "Ha! The little furball wants to play."

"He looks like those gobs of hair and dirt that scoot around under Mom's furniture," Quinn said.

Graham laughed. "Dust bunnies, you mean. You're right. Last week I was hunting for my tennis shoes under my bed and found a killer one the size of two fists. Hey, that'd be a cool name for him."

Quinn tried it out. "Come here, Dust Bunny." The puppy came right over.

"I meant Killer—that'd be funny. Here, Killer!" The puppy ignored Graham. "Okay, here Dust Bunny! Dusty, boy, come here Dusty!" The puppy jumped onto Graham's lap, and chose his own name.

When the phone rang, I set down the papers I was grading and craned my neck to look at the clock on my living room wall. Eleven thirty. Way later than the boys could receive calls. They were already asleep. I prepared to chew out whoever dared break the well-known Culpepper house rule. But the call wasn't for the boys. It was my husband's former partner.

"I tried to reach you earlier," Roosevelt Pitts said. "Didn't Graham tell you?"

He hadn't. The puppy had pretty much turned our lives inside out all evening. Mercifully, Dusty had finally curled up beside me on the couch and fallen asleep.

"It's your dad," Roosevelt said. "We picked him up on a DUI after he backed his truck into the side of the Save-More. He said not to call you, but I thought you should know. He's passed out in a cell right now. Woody was pretty drunk, Molly, worse than I've ever seen him."

All the material I'd left him about damage to the brain, heart, and liver had been really effective. *Way to go*, Molly, I chided myself. *You made him so mad he went out and smashed up his truck.* Yet without my mother as a buffer, it was only a matter of time until the outside world and Woodson collided. Thank God he hadn't hurt anyone else.

I found my voice again. "Be right there."

"Might do him good to wake up here in the morning. Make him think about the situation a little—you see where I'm coming from?"

Maybe he was right. "But I have school in the morning. I can't come down to bail him out."

"We'll get him a bondsman, don't you worry about that."

"What do I need to do?"

"Probably nothing. Truck's impounded. A court date will be set, a fine assessed, community service likely. He doesn't have prior DUIs so he won't lose his license. This time."

"Can you make sure he gets to work tomorrow even if it's late? I don't want him to lose his job."

"Give it my best shot." He hesitated, then offered a warning. "It'll be in the papers, Molly, a mention in the police record. I didn't want you to be blind-sided. You know how people talk."

I thanked him. The man was a prince. He never forgot my boys' birthdays, arriving with gifts like the World's Largest Squirt Gun or a giant bubble machine. Once when he'd stood on my porch delivering a door knocker he'd made in his wood shop, my nosy neighbor Eileen O'Halloran had phoned to see if "that huge black fellow" was threatening me. I suppose people often reacted to Roosevelt's size that way. At six-four, he was built like a bachelor's chest of drawers, thick and sturdy, but he was as much a puppy as the Pomeranian we'd taken into our home. A transparent man, whose whole face and body language told you he liked you. But once, out at the strip mall, I'd seen another side to Roosevelt when he wrestled down a man slapping his wife around. There'd been no mercy, no pity in his expression then, and he had used his mammoth size to full advantage. He was a good friend to have.

Four

The puppy book's best advice on house-training was to be alert to when the dog begins to squat. It said to pull up his back end and carry him outside. Since Dusty was only four inches tall to begin with and his fur hung all the way to the floor, it was hard to distinguish between sitting, standing, and squatting. I only noticed the puddle left afterwards.

Dusty cried off and on all night. I wouldn't have slept much anyway because I was mentally rehearsing my speech about Woodson to the boys. Twice I dragged myself from bed to take the puppy outside to potty. Dusty romped around and attacked my shoelaces as if they were snakes. As soon as we came back inside, the dog peed. Before I went to work, I shut him in the laundry room and said a prayer he wouldn't do too much damage to the house or himself. I worried he could squeeze behind the dryer and get stuck, or chew through the electric cords.

Once everyone was loaded into the SUV, I cleared my throat. "Your grandfather was arrested last night for driving after he had one too many. It was in the Police Report in this morning's paper, so other people might mention it. You might just say, 'Yes, it's too bad,' if anyone asks about it."

"Is Grandpa going to be okay?" Quinn asked.

Woodson hadn't been okay for years. "Of course."

Graham didn't comment, but his thumbs missed a few beats. I wondered who he was texting. Probably that Marcinek girl.

Quinn's expression in the rear view mirror looked troubled. "Will Grandpa be home tonight?"

"Oh, even before that, I should think." I was proud of myself for having muddled through without calling Woodson any forbidden words: alcoholic, drunk, rummy, boozer, lush, or wino. Nor had I referred to beer, whiskey, bourbon, scotch, hootch, or liquor. In the house where I'd grown up these words were never spoken. My mother would have been proud.

The boys seemed to handle the news well, not that I could interpret Graham's silences anymore.

We turned onto Madison, the brick-paved main street that ran through Alderson's business district. In barrel-sized concrete planters on each street corner, lavender loropetalums were putting on their second show for the year. I'd heard the city was going to replace the Bradford pears that lined the sidewalks because the trees had developed some kind of blight. I hoped they put in crape myrtles. On the other hand, if their budget was as tight as they claimed and we couldn't afford staples and paper in our schools, I didn't know how they could afford to landscape downtown.

We turned onto Jefferson and stopped at the light in front of the jail.

"Could we run in real quick and check on Grandpa?" Quinn asked.

"I don't think so, honey. He's probably still sleeping." Sleeping it off, anyway.

Before first period began, I reminded myself I started every school year with one goal: no child would fail my class. No throw-aways. That now included J.D. As we discussed the play, I was thinking there must be some way to reach him when he whispered in a voice he meant me to overhear, "The teacher is kind of cute, kind of like the Pillsbury Doughboy." Surely there was some way to connect with him besides the one that rolled through my mind right then: slapping him up the side of the head.

Later I asked the class if they thought Petruchio's treatment of Kate at her sister's wedding reception was justified. J.D. raised his hand. I was delighted he wanted to participate, even though he hadn't read the play.

"Hey, Miz, do you think Tupac is really dead?" he asked.

I spied a black wire snaking from under his shirt to his head. My face grew hot enough to melt ear wax. IPod's, CD players, radios—these were banned in every school classroom and he knew it.

I assigned detention and recited school policy requiring me to confiscate his tunes. He tucked his iPod under his arm like a football. "That's bootleg!"

I didn't want to—and probably couldn't—take it from him in a physical struggle. Couldn't back down either. He finally handed the iPod over and dropped the f-bomb on me. We had all heard the word before, of course, but there were boundaries, things you didn't say in class, not at Alderson High School. South Georgia was not New York City or Atlanta, and he'd better wise up to it fast. I doubled his detention.

The department chair, Miss Baker, wouldn't have lost control the way I did. She never raised her voice. Didn't have to. Wouldn't let boys like J.D. stay in her class. Why couldn't I be more like her?

The only thing J.D. did right was sit in his assigned seat without being asked. I had to be thankful for that. The rest of the morning passed without incident though it seemed as if all the students were squirrelier than usual, less focused. By noon, when Brian Jones came in, my chin was about to drag the floor. He swung his back pack onto a desk.

"What've you got in that thing—rocks?" I asked. "You're bent over like an old man."

"Hmmph. I think you teachers had a contest last summer to see who could find the heaviest book. English won, but social studies is a close second."

He had on a Serena Williams tee-shirt I hadn't noticed in first period. Once he had confessed he dreamed of winning Wimbledon himself or becoming the second black president. He and I were both sure Barack Obama was going to be the first.

"Nice shirt."

"Thanks. So whatcha gonna do about the new kid?" Brian asked.

"Teach him English, what else? Strap that bag back on. I'm heading out to lunch."

I felt a little guilty. You would think the sophomore class president would have lots of friends but Brian didn't. He dressed respectably and got good grades, qualities that won elections but few male friends. Every free moment he hung around my room. Though I usually didn't mind, the morning had completely drained my energy. I wanted my lunch. I wanted my twenty-five minutes of quiet with no one bellowing "Miz—Miz!" I wanted to get to the lounge before Tessa Kaufmann could sit in my chair.

Brian fell in one step behind me as I squeezed through the throng of students rushing to lockers and lunch. We followed the red and blue paint that striped the walls toward the cafeteria.

Brian projected his voice over clanging locks and slamming books. "You know what I mean. J.D.'s a pain."

He thought I hadn't noticed? "I'm sure he'll adjust to Alderson in time."

Brian and I dodged between two bodies hurtling down the hall. We neared the cafeteria where the forward press became a notch less civilized than a stampede. "We having a pop reading quiz tomorrow?"

I glanced over my shoulder at him. "It wouldn't be a pop quiz if I told you ahead of time, now would it?"

He shrugged, grinned. "You can tell me. I'm your favorite student."

I whooped, the only answer he deserved. I pushed open the door to the lounge, still laughing because he was right. He was a favorite. I understood why Miss Baker took an instant dislike to J.D.—he would present a challenge to anyone—but she didn't care for Brian either. Said he was conceited and greedy for attention. I couldn't help liking him. He grasped new material quickly, he was determined to be valedictorian, he was witty, charming, and yes, an attention hound, but I never regretted signing the schedule change allowing him to get out of Miss Baker's class.

All the students in first period were my favorites. I liked them and they liked me. I came to a complete halt in the lounge. Maybe that was all J.D. needed. To feel one teacher liked him. Probably hadn't happened often—a wild guess. I would bestow compliments on him like undeserved gifts. Hold up a mirror to show him what he could become, the way Petruchio did for Kate in *Taming*. Kill him with kindness. Praise his papers, his shoes, his jacket, his bling. Trust him to take messages to the office. He would live up to my expectations.

Happy with my plan, I proceeded through the lounge. A round metal tray filled with cookies sat like a bulls-eye on our lunch table. I needed to visit the bathroom so badly my eyeballs were turning yellow, but I couldn't resist. Still warm, the cookie sagged when I lifted it to my lips. I closed my eyes and came within inches of an orgasm over the crumbly texture, the velvety bits of chocolate, and the rush of brown sugar. I'd been so long without. Six days and counting. (Sweets, that is. Sex, much longer, since David's death.) Before dashing to the restroom, I parked my purse on my customary chair to stake my claim. The line to the bathroom extended out the door. Served me right for ruining my diet.

I fell in behind Miss Baker. Since it was Tuesday, she wore her gray suit with a white bow-neck blouse. She rotated her clothing with the same predictability as her seating chart. The gray suit would appear again on Thursday with a different blouse, bay blue or if she felt particularly frisky, garnet. On Mondays, Wednesdays, and Fridays she wore a navy suit, same style, same blouses.

"Pretty sweater, dear," Miss Baker said. "You've got something on it, though."

I looked down. Crap. Fishing a tissue out of my purse, I began to rub the chocolate. The tiny spot spread to twice, three times its size.

"Stop that." Her voice forbade argument.

The line of waiting teachers parted like the Red Sea once they saw it was Miss Baker who wanted through. She returned, holding a napkin sudsy with hand soap.

"Rub this on. It'll keep the stain from setting."

I did as I was told.

The lounge contained two round formica-topped tables, each ringed by eight plastic chairs. Against one wall were a frumpy orange plaid couch and a stuffed chair with uneven legs that wobbled whenever a new sub sat in it. In the corner stood a bookcase filled with education magazines and single copies of textbooks used in the '80s and '90s. Judging by the dust furred along the tops, no one ever picked them up. The middle shelf was crammed full of grease-stained paperbacks. On the opposite wall yellowed tape held up an Armed Forces recruiting poster and a promotion for an employee mental health program.

Liz, I was happy to see, sat in her usual chair. She had skipped lunch the previous day when news of the lawsuit had broken. I spooned sugar-free peach yogurt into my mouth and listened to her describe a fight in third period. Two girls, best friends until today, had attacked each other with slaps and fingernails and teeth and hair-pulling and spit.

I was relieved to find things back to normal. "Over a boy, no doubt."

"Of course." Liz's voice was as soft and warm as a flannel shirt. "Not likely the class was going to learn much about the phylum Annelida after that. I tried though, honey, you know how I tried. I kept telling them to move away from my little friends, but those girls were too busy cussing and fussing to hear a word I said." The friends she referred to were a menagerie of small snakes and mice she kept in her lab, and a boa her sophomores called Hairy.

An office aide came in and handed Liz a note. She skimmed it and with smooth brown hands pocketed it in her denim jumper before continuing her story. "Somehow they knocked the latch on Hairy's cage loose, and he disappeared in all the hoopla."

"What!"

"Don't worry. He'll come back when he gets hungry enough."

"I'm not worried about your snake." Only about thirty yards separated her hall from mine, and I knew that monster better not get within a mile of me or I wouldn't be responsible for what I said or did.

Betsy, who was pale anyway with a natural blonde's complexion, blanched even more and looked as if she might pass out. "The kids are hunting for him, aren't they?"

"Sure, but Hairy won't hurt anyone."

"Does Mr. Van Teasel know?" Betsy asked.

"No, but I told the custodians. They'll keep an eye out for him."

They'd better. My skin crawled just thinking about that nasty creature. How did a five-foot boa hide in a classroom full of kids anyway? With all the food it could find around AHS, he might grow longer than Jack's beanstalk. There were cockroaches, there were mice, and right now there were even birds that got into what I guess you'd call an attic. We'd hear them fluttering above the ceiling tiles occasionally. They must have come in through the air vents and nested up there.

The lounge door squeaked open. Tessa Kaufmann's eyes slid over the occupants, her hand never relinquishing the doorknob. Her eyes rested on the only empty chair beside Miss Baker at the other table. Tessa turned halfway, as if to leave.

I pulled the empty chair beside mine and patted it. "So, give me the scoop on this new kid."

Tessa sent a grateful look my way, eased into the chair, and began to slice into an apple with a small paring knife. As she spoke, I noticed again that her breath smelled like mint. Pleasant—unlike her Yankee voice.

"J.D. tests gifted, so we want him in a college prep class, but he's moved around so much his skills leave a lot to be desired. This past year he's lived with an aunt in Atlanta and gotten into some trouble, but he's back with his mother now." She hesitated the way someone does when she's going to filter out the real dirt. I wondered what it was. "His mother's very concerned. She knows he can be difficult, but she's trying to work with him."

"Difficult? Tessa, algebra is difficult. Losing weight is difficult. J.D.'s a real pain in the patoot."

"Give him a chance, Molly."

"Don't worry; I'm not giving up yet. I have a plan for J.D." It sounded good, but visualizing the insolent-eyed fifteen year old gave me heartburn.

I finished the yogurt and ignored the tray of cookies, choosing instead to crunch into a celery stick. The strings stuck between my teeth like frayed dental floss. They ticked me off. The chocolate on my sweater ticked me off. Jolene Baker ticked me off for dumping yet another problem child on me. Worst of all, I was mad at myself. I let J.D. push my buttons too easily. Today the class stood by me, but their loyalties would shift if I couldn't win J.D. over. When twenty or thirty teenagers cornered you in a classroom, you had to fight back with all the weapons you could muster. You had to be smarter, funnier, and more imaginative than they were, or they'd figure out there wasn't really a lot you could do if they revolted.

"Enough about J.D. What about you—where you from?" The women in my Sunday school class had already told me she was from up North, but the question seemed like a good starting point.

"New Jersey, originally," Tessa said.

Ahh! That explained the too-loud nasal voice.

"Then my husband got transferred to Ohio for two years. He's with Jameson Plastics. We hope this is the last move we have to make since Noah is a freshman, and I'd like for him to have all four years in one place."

"You have a freshman?" I'd have remembered if the Sunday school class had mentioned that. Maybe Graham could keep an eye out for Noah. Alderson High could be cliquish. "My oldest is a freshman. He plays soccer, football, and messes around with a guitar in our garage.

My boys think they're going to be the latest American Idols."

"Hey, my son plays guitar, too."

We made arrangements for Noah to join my boys on Saturday. Right after Graham had gotten his guitar, I had considered not paying the electric bill so I wouldn't have to hear the whine of those strings anymore, but he was improving. And Quinn was pretty good on drums. They inherited their musical talents from me. I played piano quite well and earned spending money in college doing weddings. Neither Graham nor Quinn continued piano lessons beyond early years of grade school, but the love of music had gelled.

"So, how do you like it here?" Liz asked Tessa.

"We love it—exactly the kind of place we were looking for to raise the kids. The atmosphere in Noah's last school was—how should I put this?—conducive to trouble. I can already tell Alderson's going to be better. And Larry loves his new job. What does your husband do, Liz?"

"He owns a small business."

Actually, Lem Powell owned and operated what a local billboard boasted was the "number one business in number two." Septic systems. His customers lived outside the city limits, and they must have liked him because his business had expanded to cover three counties. Lem was also the first black elected to the County Commission, but Liz wasn't one to brag.

Tessa inclined her head toward me. "What about your husband?"

I couldn't say anything for a few seconds, and no one else did either, but I could imagine the looks they were giving each other. David had been a police officer. Every day I lived in fear that blue-uniformed men would come to my door and tell me he was dead. Maybe it would be his partner, Roosevelt Pitts, cap cradled between big brown paws, and he wouldn't have to say anything, I would just know by his expression. Chief Jim Bob Lester would accompany him, a burden that came with authority. I had imagined all kinds of ways it could happen—an abusive husband, a crackhead, an ordinary traffic stop gone awry.

What I least expected was my neighbor, Eileen O'Halloran, her hair still in curlers, a gray-tinged bathrobe clutched around her body, ringing the doorbell at 6:30 a.m. She told me David was lying in the street down the road from her house. Her husband was administering CPR. A siren already moaned in the distance as I pushed past her and ran toward David.

"He's dead. Hit by a car while jogging." I couldn't talk about it, not to anyone, without getting teary-eyed. Everyone expected me to be over it by now. He had died one year, nine months, and twenty-three days ago. I clamped my teeth together while Tessa murmured condolences.

Liz, a true friend, changed the subject. "You still on that diet?"

I nodded. "They say you can lose ten pounds in two weeks." Yogurt for breakfast and lunch, celery sticks any time, boiled or grilled chicken for dinner with salad, squash, or green beans. This time I was going to do it. Memories of the grapefruit and hard boiled egg diet, the green tea diet, the cabbage soup diet, and blood type diet surfaced, but I pushed them aside. This time I was going to succeed.

"Any of y'all been evaluated yet? Mr. Van Teasel dropped in on me yesterday morning."

"Really? You must be the first," Liz said. "What a morning to choose, what with the . . . lawsuit." The last word trickled out as she realized she was about to mention the topic we were all avoiding. For a minute it was as quiet in the lounge as a classroom in the midst of final exams. At last, Liz broke the silence. "Things go all right?"

"I guess. Hard to tell with him." Even with friends, I couldn't share his criticism of my noisy room.

Tessa leaned in closer and lowered her voice. "Van Teasel's a strange little man. When he interviewed me, he asked what church I attended, and before I could sputter out none of your beeswax, he said I needed to join one right away and highly recommended First Baptist. When I finally found my voice, I told him we were Methodist, thank you very much. Can you imagine?"

We could. Some counties had restaurants or used car dealerships lined up along the road to the county seat. Mason County had a row of churches instead, nine different denominations. Downtown the mega-churches gobbled up whole city blocks. Even though Mr. Van Teasel hailed from Alabama, he had quickly assessed the importance of religion in this community. Not that we approved of his ordering new teachers to join a church.

Tessa sliced the last quarter of her apple. "He said if my husband or I partook—partook, that's the funny old word he used—of alcoholic beverages, he expected us to buy them over the county line."

The lounge filled with more snorts than a pig pen. Liquor consumption had entrenched itself as firmly as Jesus in Mason County.

Miss Baker thumped her thermos onto the table. "I believe in supporting our local stores." Everyone knew her brother tipped the bottle heavily.

David and I certainly had consumed a few beers at backyard barbecues. My father—well, the local liquor stores might go bankrupt if Woodson Trask ever followed my advice and stopped drinking. Mr. Van Teasel still had a lot to learn about Mason County.

The bell rang, and Liz jumped to her feet. "Okay, y'all, we can't let the lunch ladies think we don't appreciate these cookies." She distributed napkins. "Wrap some up for your kids."

A fine idea since the boys didn't get many sweets when I dieted.

As Liz and I walked back toward our rooms, I repeated what J.D. had said about Miss Baker's seating plan.

She stopped so abruptly a student bumped into her from behind. "Uh-uhn, he didn't! I sure never had the nerve to talk back to Miss Baker."

We moved to the side so students could flow around us. "No one would. At least no one who grew up in Alderson."

"I was one scared little junior when I walked into her classroom for the first time. Shoot, that woman still scares me."

"Me, too." That made me wonder about J.D. even more. What kind of kid didn't feel intimidated by Miss Baker?

By the time I left school, it was 4:30. I stopped by the office supply store to buy staples and missed most of my youngest son's scrimmage. Quinn had joined the YMCA soccer league this year because his big brother had played in sixth grade, but where Graham was lean and graceful like his father, my youngest lumbered instead of leaped.

An older kid, an eighth grader I recognized though I couldn't remember his name, banana-kicked the ball, delivering it right to the front of my son. Quinn stumbled a fraction of a second, and then recovered, but not quickly enough. The ball scudded out of bounds. His shoulders slumped, and an ache grew in my sternum.

"Good effort, Quinn!" I called out. He didn't acknowledge he'd heard me, but maybe his shoulders straightened a fraction. I hoped the scrimmage hadn't all gone badly for him.

Teacher should do more to control noise. The words rolled through my mind. *Stimulating. Motivated. Engaged*—I reminded myself. Concentrate on those. Accentuate the positive.

On the field, Quinn launched his body into the air in an attempt to chest trap a chip shot. If he had connected, it would have been a brilliant move. Instead, a second too late, he thudded into the ground, his hip taking the worst of the blow. The ball sailed past the sweeper and the goalie. When Coach Freeman whistled the play to a stop, the boys gathered around him. My eyes slid over Russ Freeman's body and I was wishing my hands could travel right along with them. Broad shoulders tapered to a thin waist, firm biceps under a neat polo shirt, solid glutes rippling under khaki slacks. Thick chestnut hair. Russ Freeman was a hunk by anyone's standards. As the boys trotted off the field, he slapped their shoulder blades or shook their hands. Made every boy feel special.

If only Quinn could make one big play, it would make such a difference in his confidence. I imagined Coach Freeman surveying his team at the end of a tie game. Tired, beaten boys. But he sees something in Quinn's eyes, sees he still has what it takes. The coach sends Quinn in for the single elimination kick. The other side kicks first, misses. Quinn takes the field, the whole team high fiving him on the way in. The stadium collectively holds its breath, and I have to put my hand over my mouth so I won't squeal and—

Quinn waved his arm in front of my face. "Earth to Mom, where are you?"

I withdrew my hand from my mouth, smiling sheepishly. "Hey, Goober, you looked good out there."

Quinn shrugged and gathered up his gear.

"Lots of grass stains. Shows your effort."

Mr. Martin was yelling at Coach Freeman. As Quinn and I headed for the parking lot, I overheard enough to know it was about Martin's boy not getting to play enough during the real games. If Russ Freeman had a flaw as a coach, it was that he didn't put sixth graders into the games, with few exceptions. It didn't hurt the boys to wait a while to get playing time. They would learn patience and persistence.

Wally Martin stood at his father's side, head down, kicking at the dirt with his right foot, watching his shoe as if it were of paramount interest. I felt sorry for Wally and for Coach Freeman. Only a really nice man would volunteer to coach when he didn't even have a son on the team.

I slid into the bucket seat of our hunter green hybrid. Still had that new-car smell. The boys had tried to steer me toward an SUV rated a measly twelve miles a gallon, but I resisted. I remembered my words: *We're supposed to be good stewards of the earth. Besides, it makes political sense. We gotta reduce our dependence on Middle Eastern oil.* I wanted to lead my boys through example.

Quinn hooked up the seat belt. "What're these?" Quinn held up two greasy, chocolate-chip stained napkins sitting on the console.

"Just some trash I picked up in the parking lot." I felt certain my mother heard my lie from her grave, knew I'd eaten the cafeteria cookies, and she wasn't smiling.

Five

W hen I arrived at my classroom, Ceci Barnes already sat cross-legged on the dingy carpet in front of my door doing homework. A clip with huge teeth gathered her long hair into sort of a loose ponytail. She unfolded coltish legs to stand, a Keira Knightley kind of girl, towering over me by nine inches. I felt like a hobbit beside her.

I opened the blinds to admit the faint morning light. My window faced the large open-to-the-sky grassy area students called the Quad. It was surrounded on four sides by L-shaped rectangles that formed the main building of Alderson High. Early arrivals gathered around the picnic tables in the Quad to socialize or copy each other's homework. Students also ate lunch there when weather permitted. I spotted Graham at one of the tables. A girl with long caramel hair latched onto his arm and slid onto the concrete bench beside him. That Marcinek girl, most likely, though it was hard to be sure from behind. I hoped he wasn't getting too serious about her. They were way too young for that. I turned back to Ceci.

"I know you're not here this early because you love English so much. What's up?"

"You gotta help me, Miz Culpepper. I'm never going to get into college." Those words brought on snuffles. "My mother was ready to kill me when she saw my SAT scores."

"I've known your mother since high school, and far as I know, she's never killed anyone." I could imagine how upset the family was, though. Yesterday when I had distributed the scores from a practice Scholastic Aptitude Test, Ceci had glanced at the dismal 320 on her verbal section, then folded pale arms on her desk and burrowed into them until class ended. Her performance ranked far below the 780 verbal score of her sister, who was now an engineering major at Georgia Tech. One of the brightest students I'd ever taught.

I handed Ceci a roll of toilet paper so she could blow her nose. "Let's talk about what we can do to improve your scores. I'll loan you some SAT preparation books."

More snuffling. She had inherited several of those books from her perfect sister. They hadn't helped. A tear striped her cheek with mascara.

"I can coach you if you're willing to come in before or after school."

Like magic her tears dried up.

"Don't expect miracles," I cautioned. "Some students improve dramatically through coaching. Everybody's scores go up anyway as they advance in school. You'll do better next year, and even better your senior year whether you are coached or not."

Back in the days before the No Child Left Behind Act and Mr. Van Teasel, I taught a unit on improving SAT scores, but this new principal focused like a laser on the graduation exit exam. Students' scores on the grad exam were the main measure for achieving adequate yearly progress under NCLB. So I had to slash units on SAT preparation and modern drama. All my college-bound students would pass the graduation test without intervention. The test only covered basic skills, for heaven's sake. But no matter. Van Teasel = The Boss.

Ceci wrote out a schedule of mornings to come for tutoring.

"Morning, Miz C." Brian Jones's book bag thudded to the ground. He dug out his geometry text and began working problems.

When Ceci closed her notebook, I noticed a finely detailed sketch of a Tennessee Walker on the cover. The horse's muscles were penciled in so realistically it almost loped away as I looked at it.

"Did you draw that?" I asked.

"It's nothing, something I did last night."

"It's not nothing—it's beautiful."

Ceci's face lit up.

"Let me see," Brian said.

She oriented the notebook toward him.

"Wow. I wish I had talent like that!"

Ceci pouted. "You have all A's. You're talented at everything. You gotta let the rest of us be good at something."

"Why don't you join the newspaper staff next year?" I said. "We always need good artists."

She looked as if she was ready to answer, but Brian began talking first. "I'm entering an essay contest, Miz C. If I win, I get to go to Washington, D. C., and meet with congressmen and maybe even President Obama. Think you could proofread my entry before I send it in? Give me some pointers?"

I deviled him. "What if John McCain wins?"

"He won't."

Six

Sunday after church, the boys and I visited the cemetery, navigating between the headstones until we reached the back section where David was buried. My family owned five adjacent plots. In my early thirties, I had been skeptical when my mother told me she was buying them. There's such a thing as too prepared, I thought. Better to spend your money on current needs or college funds for the boys. How quickly my perspective changed when my mother offered one of the burial sites for David. One less thing to worry about in the haze that followed his death. None of us had any way of knowing when we buried David that my mother would lay a few feet away less than a year later. I set a planter of pansies beside her headstone while the boys arranged potted mums on each side of their father's grave.

My mother had chosen the gravesites because they backed up to the old Blankenship plantation, not out of any fondness for the Blankenships and certainly not for plantations, but for the lovely hundred-year-old camellia garden you could see from these plots. The japonicas weren't blooming this early in October, but a hedge of sasanquas set little puffs of pink cotton-candy blooms on the end of every branch.

I remembered my father's words as we stood around after the minister finished my mother's service: *Every year when they bloom, they'll be a tribute to Alderson's most beautiful Camellia Queen. She'll have flowers even after we're all gone and there's no one left to put them on her grave.*

June Sullivan had reigned over all of Alderson the year she turned twenty. Every January the Camellia Festival drew in thousands of visitors and gave the local economy a much-needed boost. Preserved in a photo album, my mother, a wisp of a girl, waves from a flower-covered float, chestnut hair ruffling around slim shoulders. The band is coming up right behind her and crowds line the street. Even in pictures of the talent competition, her hazel eyes convey a bit of impishness as she swings beads and flips her feet up in a rendition of the Charleston.

No wonder my father adored her.

He wasn't handsome, my father. I guess you'd call him a decent provider, a hard worker, a blue collar kind of guy. I never could fathom what drew them together. She read the Brontes and Austin; he thought books were for sissies. She folded afghans into neat triangles; he threw wet towels on the floor. She was devout; he was anything but.

One day I happened to return a borrowed casserole dish, and I got an unexpected glimpse into their relationship. My mother had walked me to the driveway, when my father pulled up in his truck and unloaded a parking meter. He plunked it down beside their outdoor hot tub. My mother gasped, her hands flying to her mouth to hold something in—shock, certainly, but a shiver of excitement too. Obviously she had reservations about how he had acquired it— but she couldn't hide the laughter in her eyes.

I didn't see anything funny about it. "What on earth is that for?"

"Well, see, I put in two dimes before I get in the hot tub," my father said, "and when the red flag pops up, I'll know I'm about cooked."

"Wouldn't it be easier to buy a timer?"

He looked at me as if I'd completely missed the point. "It's like having my own bank. Answer me this: can you think of any better way to accumulate beer money?"

Truth was, Woodson liked being a bit of a character. I never asked how he had gotten his meter. Maybe my mother did, but I'd learned long ago that where my father was concerned, you were better off not knowing. If the police—and I lived with one of Alderson's finest—ever asked questions, I could honestly plead ignorance, but sooner or later David and I and everyone else in town surely noticed the absence of a meter over on Symonton Street. Right in front of Big Fred's Bar and Grill. My father probably had gotten tired of paying parking tickets.

For some time after my father retreated inside the house, my mother and I stared at his new acquisition. Finally, she shook her head, her hands planted on her hips, and allowed herself to laugh. "I wish I could be more like him. He gets such a kick out of life. Woody does these crazy things—outrageous things—I'd never have the nerve to do. I'd worry myself sick about getting caught or hurt. I'd think about the consequences until, even if I did decide to do it, I would have stripped the fun right out of it. You're the same way. But Woody just bulldozes ahead and does whatever he feels like doing, and somehow it turns out okay."

She never seemed to mind that he'd littered her yard with a second-hand hot tub covered in tattered brown vinyl, a parking meter, an old truck with see-through rust elevated on concrete blocks, and a collection of rotting tires and old oil cans. As long as he kept his junk to the left side of the gravel driveway. The right side was her space: the flower gardens and the house, a Victorian with gingerbread trim.

Kneeling down to pull some crabgrass away from her marker, I wondered if my mother had been happy. Probably was, as much as anyone could be. Content, at least. She seemed to take Woodson's eccentricities and his periodic drinking in stride. Unlike my mother, my brother Sam and I couldn't deal with Woodson. He embarrassed us. Angered us. Frightened us. My mother carried one ache with her every day of the last twenty years of her life: Sam's absence—and that was all my father's fault.

When we left the cemetery, we stopped at Mrs. Haswell's General Store. It was painted in happy colors, its aisles crammed with merchandise. One wall had stacks of old-fashioned grocery and drug store items like Clabber's Baking Powder, Hodgson Mill Whole Wheat Flour, and Williams shaving soap. On the other side, shelves beckoned with toys: wooden benches with colored pegs and a hammer, balsa wood airplanes powered by rubber bands, green rubber snakes, whoopee cushions, special edition pop-up classics like *The Wizard of Oz* and *Alice in Wonderland*, comic books, sock monkeys, yo-yos, jacks, and pick-up sticks. The back wall offered basil and zinnia seeds, welcome signs for the yard, herbal potions and lotions, and garden tools for children and adults. By the register you never knew what you would find: red wax lips to chew, giant chocolate kisses, jars of windmills or stick candy or glitter pens, pralines, stuffed animals that fit in the palm of your hand, finger skateboards or finger puppets. On a good day maybe all of the above. The meat locker in back contained homemade sausage. Mrs. Haswell always waited on us personally.

Her hands full of faux pearl dog collars and canine clothes, Mrs. Haswell bustled by to arrange a display. "Hear tell that new principal of yours is going to crack down on what you wear over there at the high school," she called over her shoulder.

"That's okay with me, long as he's the one who does the cracking down on those kids. We teachers don't need one single extra thing to do. Last week the federal government made us administer a drug use survey—took two hours out of class time, and on our last teacher planning day a nurse lectured us on how to spot abuse. We can go to jail if we don't recognize and report the abused kids in our classes—now isn't that something? We certainly don't want to become clothing police on top of everything else."

"Oh, I don't mean the kids. Hear tell he's going to make you women teachers wear dresses and hose and shoes with closed in toes and heels, and the fellers have to wear coats and ties. Sonny's having a fit. Said he draws the line at wearing a suit."

I could see his point. Chewing tobacco wasn't the best accessory for a suit, and I'd never seen him without a can. I wondered if Sonny ever told his mother about the nasty note I'd stuck in his mailbox about his spit cup. If so, she didn't appear to hold it against me.

Mrs. Haswell separated the dog clothes into two piles: pink tutus for the girls and black tuxedo tee-shirts for the boys. "Principal's wife told my cousin Anna—you know her, married to that Keefover boy from over in Coolidge—if y'all want to get paid like professionals, you ought to have to look professional. I'm surprised you haven't heard about it, living next door to them and all."

I rarely saw the Van Teasels outside of school or church. They weren't neighborly types who came over and chatted while I was deadheading chrysanthemums or bringing in the newspaper. The Mrs. was a hospital administrator.

"Hope they don't expect us to dress like a bunch of CEOs because the pay isn't nearly that professional."

Mrs. Haswell nodded sympathetically. She showed Quinn a new anime book and pointed out a collection of red, white, and blue school spirit buttons to Graham. "That little Mary Wade Marcinek was in here and bought one of those buttons yesterday."

Graham probed Mrs. Haswell until she remembered which one Mary Wade had bought, and he purchased the same one. Quinn chose an anime, and I selected a bandana for Dusty.

We usually didn't buy a lot when we visited the General Store, but we always took home more than we came in with.

That evening in the bottom of the freezer, I found a box of Girl Scout cookies that somehow had escaped attention. The perfect accompaniment to a cup of chamomile tea. Woodson's accusation replayed: You eat too much.

I silenced his voice. Since when did I listen to Woodson, anyway? Eating helped me think. Built up my courage. Besides, I could resume my diet after this family crisis was resolved. As Woodson's only children, Sam and I should confront our father together about the way his drinking had spiraled out of control. It wasn't something I should have to do alone. When we were growing up, my brother Sam and I had been close, but time and distance had weakened that connection. Half a stack of Thin Mints later, I picked up the phone.

First I inquired about Sam's health. I always did even though it irritated him. If he was ever anything less than fine, he didn't confess. We exchanged pleasantries for a few minutes.

"What's wrong?" he asked.

"Why does something have to be wrong?"

"Come on, I can tell. Spit it out."

So I told him how Woodson had backed his truck into the concrete block walls of the Save-More Butchers and dinged it up pretty good. How he had been arrested for DUI. How often he'd missed work. How his stomach pain was escalating. How I planned to call every morning now to make sure he got up for work.

"What do you want me to do about it?"

"I don't know. Maybe you could come home and we could talk to him together. Convince him to try AA."

"I don't think it would help."

"We won't know if we don't try."

"Feel free to talk to him if you think it'll do any good."

"You might live in Santa Fe but you still have a family."

"I avoid negative people. They're a drag on your immune system."

"What about Mom? Don't you think it hurt her when you never came back to visit?" That wasn't what I wanted to say.

"She could have left him. She made her choices."

"That's not fair. She always stood up for you, took your side."

Silence on the other end. Finally: "Yeah, after she let him run me down for not playing Neanderthal sports, she would tell him I had other interests and she would hand me a cookie as if that made everything okay. But the damage was done, Molly, it was already done and she just watched it happen over and over again."

That wasn't the whole story, and Sam knew it. When Woodson taunted Sam—"you little sissy"— for quitting Pop Warner football, Sam knew how to retaliate. One of the few ways my father had ever been able to show us love was teaching us to play the piano. So Sam refused to play. The lessons stopped. It was mostly my father's fault, but Sam wasn't completely innocent. The one person who was, I thought, was my mother.

"But she loved you."

"I loved her too."

"You don't know how she missed you. You could have come home."

"No, I couldn't. I don't belong in Alderson. I never did."

He wasn't coming—I knew that, but I took one more shot. "You wouldn't have to stay. Come in for the day, like you did for the funeral."

"Not going to happen. I wish you all the luck in the world, but I don't think there's a thing you can do to change him."

Maybe not, but I had to try.

Seven

I fumbled through my satchel for the graphic organizers I had finished at midnight. Headings across the top and sides of the paper helped students arrange information into learnable chunks. In an early faculty meeting, I suggested it might be better if we taught students to make their own study devices.

"That's the old way of thinking," our new principal said. "The kind that led to your not making Adequate Yearly Progress at Alderson. Students and parents today have different expectations, and we have to learn to meet them."

Heaven forbid students actually met our expectations instead.

Miraculously, no one stood in front of the copy machine, a sign, I hoped, of a good day. I slid in a fistful of the goldenrod paper I had purchased after my paper ration from Mrs. Alford ran out. While seventy-eight copies of the first organizer shot into the bin, I scooted across the lounge to the bathroom—my last chance until lunch.

I fretted to Betsy Mulharin, who entered the bathroom while I was washing my hands. "How's any school supposed to make Adequate Yearly Progress when your test scores have to improve every year?"

There were A-rated schools failing to make progress—because they didn't get better. Well, how good could you get? Alderson achieved above-average pass rates on all five state-mandated graduation exams, but staying the same wasn't good enough for Adequate Yearly Progress.

Betsy finger-combed her blonde hair as she passed by the mirror and disappeared into a stall. "I know. It's stupid that even special ed students have to show substantial improvement. It ought to be enough that scores don't go down."

Back at the copy machine, Miss Baker in her navy blue suit shifted her weight efficiently from one foot to the other as she removed my graphic organizer.

"Hope you were finished." Miss Baker held out the master to me and put her own master under the machine's lid and tapped in one hundred for the number of copies. Four more master sheets dangled from her left hand. Goldenrod copies slid into the bin. There went my paper.

Loud voices swelled from the cafeteria again. Miss Baker sighed. "You know, a lot of these blacks were better off when they lived on the plantations. At least they had food, clothes, and a job. So many are unemployed today. No wonder they don't have anything better to do with their time than file senseless lawsuits and spawn illegitimate children."

I was too stunned to speak. It was impossible to reconcile what I knew about her with what she'd said. Miss Baker had devoted her life to teaching in a school with mostly black children. This woman stayed after school most afternoons until five working with those who needed extra help. It was Miss Baker's push and letters of recommendation that sent my friend Liz and hundreds of black children like her to college.

But Tessa, who'd come into the lounge behind Miss Baker, wasn't operating under my constraints. Her New Jersey voice belted out. "Yeah, I bet bunches of them are itching to get back to the good old days when they had better things to do with their time than file lawsuits. Like getting lashed or lynched, being raped by the massa, and waving goodbye to their children when they got sold off to another estate."

Miss Baker drew back, her face as red as Hester Prynne's scarlet letter, her lips quivering. It was her turn to be speechless. Only for a moment. "Those things didn't happen. Not around here, they didn't."

Tessa had been out of line to jump into the conversation the way she did. What did she know of Alderson? But then again, what did Miss Baker know? Not much, if she believed those things never happened in Alderson. Once on a family shopping trip to Valdosta, my father had pointed at a grandfather oak along the highway. "Man was lynched over there," Woodson said. "How would you know?" my brother responded, with the edge of sarcasm he always deployed as a weapon against Woodson. "My daddy was there," Woodson said. "He saw it."

Probably helped knot the rope.

We ate hurriedly, mostly in silence. On the way out of the lounge, I tried to explain Miss Baker to Tessa.

"She's not really a racist, you know."

"I know she doesn't think she is," Tessa said.

"She's not," I said. "Look at how hard she works with these kids."

"I'm not saying she's a bad person. She's a product of her upbringing, a product of Alderson."

I stiffened. "I'm a product of Alderson too."

"I'm not saying it's a bad place. I was a little worried what we were getting into at first—you know, that ugly mess with Francis Brown, all the Confederate flag decals on the back windows of trucks. That's kind of like parading swastikas around in front of Jews, don't you think? Still, nobody I've met is intentionally racist. Just a little blind and insensitive sometimes."

A little insensitive. Like my father, who had one of those decals on his truck.

A little blind. Like me, I supposed. But Tessa hadn't seen all there was to see about Alderson either.

J.D. eased toward class, his motion slowed by Marissa Powell. She squeezed his arm with perfect rhinestone-studded fingernails. A simple white peasant blouse belted over skinny-leg jeans set off her toffee-colored skin. He looked at her as if she were his favorite dessert and he couldn't wait to dig in. Liz was going to have trouble swatting the boys away from that little beauty. Smart, too. Brian's main competition for valedictorian.

As J.D. followed Marissa through the door, I instituted my plan. "Nice shoes, they new?"

He smiled. "Yeah, thanks." He went to the third row, sixth seat, the one I'd assigned. It wasn't much, but it was a start. At least class wouldn't begin with a power struggle. Next time, I hoped to praise his ideas or skills. The kids were all too obsessed with brand name shoes and clothes as it was.

While students wrote in journals, I took roll. J.D. took my attendance report to the office and returned immediately. I expected the best from him—and so I would get it. That simple.

Next I checked homework questions on the play. At Shaniqua Garner's desk I paused to read each carefully crafted sentence. "Looking good," I told her. What puzzled me was her refusal to share her answers in class. Ever. She hadn't said two words yet this year.

When I got around to J.D.'s desk, he didn't have his homework. Things weren't going to be that simple after all.

"I hate to see you start off with a zero. Did you forget or what?"

"Football practice, so no time, you know what I mean?" Gold metal twinkled around the white star of his grill.

He was so wrong if he thought a smile or football practice would win him any concessions. I pointed out that several others in the class played football, and they had their homework.

He smiled winningly. "Won't happen again, promise. About that after-school detention—"

I wondered how often that smile and turned-on charm had worked for him. "You have two days to serve. You can still come."

"Yeah, well, it's like this, there's football practice. How about I just apologize for listening to tunes in class? See? I'm sorry."

"Nope."

"How about if I write a paper on nature versus nurture—that question up there." He pointed to the large sheet of newsprint taped above the chalkboard. "I have lots of experience with the females. I could write a frigging fantastic paper."

I bet he could. So far, I had no trouble steering students toward exploration of the social and psychological aspects of sexual identity instead of biological differences. I sensed J.D. could change all that. He might write a paper I wouldn't care to read. I decided to have some fun with him.

"No matter how you *entreat* me, nothing less than fifteen minutes of your precious time will *appease* me." I emphasized the words I wanted the class to notice. Shakespeare had used both in *Taming*.

J.D.'s brow furrowed. "Say what?"

Brian jerked a dictionary from under his desk. "You've been Culpeppered!"

Ceci bolted out of her seat to grab the magic marker dangling on a string beside the Beautiful Word Wall.

I offered J.D. an alternative to missing practice. "I allow students to come in the morning instead. See you fifteen minutes before class starts." I moved off and pretended not to hear his excuses.

Brian informed the class "entreat" was a verb meaning to beg or plead. Ceci added it to the Beautiful Word list along with the sentence I'd used it in. It took Orville a bit longer to find "appease."

"Hey, J.D., you made the list twice in one day." J.D.'s head swiveled toward me. "That's ten—when's the quiz?"

"Hold up—you want a quiz?" J.D. asked.

Brian's brown eyes shone with enthusiasm. "It's extra credit, man, ten easy points."

Even though Brian was such a little grade-grubber, I'd rather have a student like him than one that didn't give a flip any day.

"That's lame," J.D. said.

"No, it's easy points," Brian said. "See, 'loquacious,' Miz C. called me that 'cause I talk a lot. And 'reticent,' that's Shaniqua 'cause she's so quiet. And 'disport,' that word belongs to Orville because he's always playing around. 'Egalitarian'—I brought that one in because I think everyone should be treated the same, black and white, men and women, all the same. Most words are easy to remember because they're ours."

J.D. faked a yawn. "I'm about to have a boregasm."

I considered throttling him, despite a grudging admiration for the coined word.

As we discussed the psychology behind Petruchio's methods in *The Taming of the Shrew*, students offered examples of how their parents trained them. Everyone contributed except Shaniqua.

Moving to the front of her row, I smiled with what I hoped was encouragement. "Do you think Petruchio is going to be successful in taming Kate?"

Her brown eyes, already large, widened even more. Then she shrugged a little and shrank physically into her seat, as if trying to disappear.

"What do you think?" I prodded.

She mumbled something. I could only make out the words "he" and maybe "Kate."

"I couldn't hear you. Please tell me again. I'm really interested in your opinion."

Instead she stared at her desk. I directed my question to Brian, who always wanted to talk. As surreptitiously as I could, I slipped a note to Shaniqua, asking her to stay after class a minute.

After the dismissal bell, J.D. paused in my doorway to examine the poster taped in the center panel. He read it aloud: "If you expect respect, be the first to show it." His eyes slid up and down the poster. Then he nudged Orville, who was trying to squeeze past. "You know who I respect? All the guys who break their necks keeping their ho's in check—Tupac had that 'bout right, didn't he? You gotta make 'em know their place, know what I'm saying?"

Orville, a hulking freckle-faced farm boy, might be playful and immature, but his parents raised him to be respectful, especially toward women. His eyes darted over to me with a hint of apology and he made a hasty exit.

"J.D., your language is unacceptable. I don't want to hear you use that term for women again."

He snorted, his eyes wild. I was trying to like this new kid, I swear, but he made it hard, obsessed as he was by a dead rapper with questionable values.

When the room cleared out, I leaned across my desk to hear Shaniqua. It helped to watch her lips move.

"I'm so scared I'll say something wrong, my brain won't work right. It's like it won't connect with my tongue. I have nightmares, Miz, I really do. I answer a question and what I say is so stupid the whole class laughs at me, even the teacher."

I thanked God, not for the first time, I would never have to endure adolescence again. Whoever said high school was the happiest time of your life had either forgotten the brutality of peer pressure or had been abnormally well-adjusted.

"When I check your homework, your answers are usually right."

"I know that—after you've gone over them—but sometimes they're wrong. I don't want everyone to think I'm stupid."

"You're not stupid, and a wrong answer isn't the end of the world. Remember the class sometimes learns more from a wrong answer than a correct one. There's probably someone sitting beside you who hopped on the wrong train of thought too."

"I know, I know, you're always telling us that, but I can't make myself do it."

"Well, let's both think about it and see if we can't figure something out. For the time being, I want you to go home and visualize raising your hand and answering a question. Picture your classmates smiling as you give the right answer. This is going to work."

I could tell by her expression she didn't think it would, and to be honest, neither did I.

Eight

The next morning J.D. served his detention. During his fifteen minutes he watered my golden pothos planters and wiped away the chalk dust that had settled on my bookshelves. I sent Brian to the library to research material for his essay, so I could talk privately with J.D. I pulled a chair up and studied his face. Skin the color of dark chocolate, nose not too broad, lively eyes. More of a Jamie Foxx than a Denzel Washington.

"Like your shirt." I nodded toward the "Change we can believe in" slogan he sported.

He looked surprised. "You gonna vote for him?"

"Shoot, yes."

The story behind my family's Obama campaign sign established a connection that allowed us to share other parts of our lives. Our favorite places to go for barbeque (Tiny's), what he liked best about football (running), what subjects he liked best (social studies and math), and what he wanted to do when he graduated (play pro ball).

"From what I've heard, you're a terrific player, but don't go to college thinking of pro ball as your only option. One injury can ruin a career. You have tons of potential. Major in business or finance so you can manage all the money you'll make if you do go pro. And if you don't, you'll still have a great career. Or major in education and be a coach for the next generation of players." Geesh, I sounded like a preachy teacher. Couldn't help myself.

He looked sheepish. "Nah, I could never put up with what you all do. Kids are bad."

"Not so bad. I know you weren't here to read the play with us, but you heard the end of our discussion." Actually he might not have heard much with music plugged into his brain, but I babbled on anyway.

"Kate behaved horribly for a grown woman—throwing stuff at her sister, beating on her, sassing her father, being rude to suitors, and yet inside, she wanted someone to love and admire her. I think that's true of most people. Everyone wants others to see something good in them, don't you think?"

His eyes shifted around as he answered. I hadn't convinced him. "Maybe with some that's true, but lots of folks are just plain bad and I don't think nothing can change them."

I gently corrected his grammar. He might be right. David would have agreed. Once he had laughed at me for displaying unfettered optimism, called me a pathetic Pollyanna. Maybe nothing could change other people, but I chose not to believe that.

J.D.'s detention was over. Five minutes of socializing time in the hall remained before class. When he rose to leave, his pants fell down and bunched around his knees.

I stifled the urge to take the Lord's name in vain. If I unleashed, all my efforts to establish rapport would be wasted. I pulled a face of exaggerated horror and covered my eyes.

"Good grief, J.D., I'm trying to get to know you, but I don't want to know you that well. I like for my students to keep some secrets."

He chuckled as he pulled his pants up. "Sorry, Miz C."

Rummaging around in my desk drawer, I extracted a ball of string and snipped off about five inches. "Here—tie this between two belt loops so it doesn't happen again. Your tee-shirt will hide the string. No more loose pants, okay?"

In my last period class, journalism students were finishing the first issue of the *Eagle's Cry*. Eight staffers corrected stories or Photo-Shopped pictures on the computers. Another was designing pages on the computer nearest my desk. Leaning over her shoulder, I commandeered her mouse, going through the menus until I found the format she needed to import a graphic on AIDS for our center spread. She clicked the button and the chart appeared in our publication.

As I stood up, my eyes scanned the newspaper's bulletin board, full of staff photographs from the last twelve years. Editors in three photos held Best All Around Newspaper trophies from state competition. Beautiful young faces. Beautiful young minds. I felt so fortunate to have known them.

This issue would rank as one of the best ever. The main story on the front page examined Afghanistan from the view of students whose relatives were deployed there. The sidebar, which ran on a vertical gray screen, contained a first hand account from a former student posted to a mountain village. The design looked very professional.

I barely made it back to my desk, thinking those pleasant thoughts, when Tameka Coakley, the editor, returned from an interview with an expression terrifying as Cruella de Vil's when she contemplated skinning a puppy. I wondered who Tameka was ready to skin.

She threw her notebook onto the desk with such force it skidded off onto the floor. Her cornrow beads clicked against one another as she shook her head. "Guess what The Weasel's done now?"

"Calm down, and let's show some respect. It's *Mister* Van Teasel. What happened?" I had never seen Tameka this angry before. What had the Weasel done? Banned blue jeans? Canceled Homecoming?

Staff members clotted around Tameka's desk. She had asked the principal what he felt our country, our school, and each person needed to do to fight the AIDS epidemic. "He said we don't need to write about that kind of thing in the school newspaper, that it doesn't have anything to do with us. I showed him statistics from the county health agency about the high number of STDs here, and he told me parents don't want to read negative stuff in the school paper. This was the whole center spread, Miz C. His comment was all I needed to finish it."

A chorus of outrage swelled around her, comments directed at no one in particular: "Parents! Since when is the school paper for parents?" "I want to read about stuff like AIDS—doesn't my opinion count?" "Who does he think he is, anyway?"

"Now just a minute." I held my hands up like a traffic cop to calm everyone. "It doesn't do any good to get angry. Let's talk about this rationally." The moment I finished speaking, the buzz of voices resumed, each indistinguishable from the other: "I'm going to get my parents to call the school and say they want the article printed—he's a control freak—it's not like we're distributing condoms at school, we're distributing information—someone *should* be distributing condoms at school, if you ask me."

I turned the overhead fluorescents out. They hushed.

"Sit down," I said. When the scuttle of bodies stumbling into chairs ended, I turned the lights back on. "Now, we have plenty of other stories to work on. Each of you get busy on your assignments, and I'll stop in after school to talk to Mr. Van Teasel. I'm sure I can persuade—"

The intercom crackled, and all eyes shot to the ceiling as if the Almighty Himself was about to speak. Mr. Van Teasel's voice boomed into the room. "Miz Culpepper? Miz Culpepper, you there?" I answered several times, but he couldn't hear me. He continued calling, the pitch of his voice rising each time. "Where is she? Why doesn't she answer?" In the background I could hear Mrs. Alford instructing him to let up on the button. He told me to bring Tameka's story to him at once.

"But I'm in class. Do you mean you want me to leave students unattended?"

"Of course, they're a responsible group of kids."

For a moment, the irony rooted me to the ground. When I recovered, I took Tameka's notes and started down the hallway toward the office. This story had been her idea, but it meant more to me than she could imagine. The legal rights of students—that would be my best argument. The Supreme Court's Hazelwood decision said the principal could only censor out of educational concerns.

As I entered the office, the staff stared at me. Everyone there had heard Mr. Van Teasel commanding my presence over the intercom. I felt a blush creep up my neck as if I were a school girl sent up for an infraction. I slunk past Mrs. Alford and scrunched into the farthest corner of the wooden bench outside the principal's office. I felt as if I'd sassed a teacher. Cut class. Written graffiti on the bathroom wall. I sneaked an antacid out of my purse and chewed until the chalk taste overpowered the cherry flavoring. A buzzer sounded and Mrs. Alford picked up her telephone. "You can go in now, Mrs. Culpepper. Try not to take all day because he has an appointment at 2:40 and we wouldn't want to make him late, would we?"

He could go to his appointment right now and it would be okay with me. I cracked the door wide enough to peek inside and be noticed.

Mr. Van Teasel gestured me to a chair. He wore a gray suit with a white shirt and red striped tie. In the photo on the credenza behind his desk he wore jeans and a polo shirt, hugging his two sons, one under each arm. The principal before Mr. Van Teasel, Dr. Parker, wore polos to work and encouraged us to bring our concerns to his office.

No one came in Van Teasel's office by choice.

"You have the story?" Mr. Van Teasel held out his hand.

I deposited four typed pages on his outstretched palm.

He sighed, withdrew his glasses and rubbed the bridge of his nose, which had reddened slightly under pressure from the nose piece. "I should have had you in for a talk before this, so we could be on the same page." He repositioned his glasses, thin lenses encased in bronzed frames, on his narrow, pointed nose. "Mrs. Culpepper, this story is inappropriate for a student paper. Anything to do with sex is verboten, is that clear?"

"Er, the Supreme Court's Hazelwood decision says students have the right to—"

He cut in as if I hadn't spoken. "Look at the fuss parents made last month over the half-second shot of Romeo's backside in Zeffirelli's movie—and rightly so—you don't want a mixed group of fourteen year olds seeing something like that. I had to get the TV teacher to edit that shot out."

"I don't think that's legal, sir."

"If she hadn't, your English department couldn't show the movie anymore—would you have preferred that? A conservative group took over after the last school board elections; surely you've noticed the changes. The change of leadership." He meant himself. "The emphasis on accountability. The new student dress code."

I thought of the sea of baggy britches in the hallways, thongs showing above low rise jeans or mini-skirts barely covering the bottoms of those same thongs. On any given day I could tell you what color underwear half the student body had on. Mr. Van Teasel could too, if he opened his eyes.

"Yes, sir, but no one enforces the dress code." This wasn't going well. How had we drifted into a discussion of clothes?

"Well, teachers should, and I'm going to see that enforcement improves. Things will change around here, Mrs. Culpepper, rest assured of that."

"If you would just read her story, Mr. Van Teasel, you would see that it's full of good information students need to know. It could keep them healthy. Maybe even save their lives."

He read aloud the first paragraph of Tameka's story: "'By 2010, deaths from the AIDS pandemic will surpass the 93 million killed by the bubonic plague, according to the World Health Organization. Right here in Mason County, Georgia, the Health Department reports 63 known cases; five of these are high school students.'" He shook his head. "I suppose some of them are our kids. What kind of homes do they come from?" He touched his glasses again. "This article contains valuable information, but I'm afraid you can't print it. You have to remember innocent fourteen year olds read this paper."

Some weren't so innocent. At least four freshmen were pregnant, one with her second child, according to the lounge grapevine.

"Don't you think students need to know they're at risk?" I asked. "If you look closely at the local statistics, a couple of those teenagers are girls. Too many people still think of AIDS as a gay male disease that doesn't affect them, but it can. It's everybody's disease." The faces of Mr. Van Teasel's sons stared back at me from the credenza. The youngest one looked as if he might be in fourth grade. With the gap between his upper front teeth and the sprinkling of freckles across his nose, he resembled my brother Sam at that age, reminding me this fight represented more than mere words to fill space in a high school paper. "What if someone in your family contracted AIDS? How would you feel about this story then?"

"No one in *my* family has AIDS."

"But what if they did? Wouldn't you give anything to have prevented it?"

"You're kicking a dead horse, Mrs. Culpepper. No one in my family will *ever* get AIDS."

Yeah, well, I had assumed that once too. "What if one of your sons contracted AIDS—wouldn't you feel terrible you hadn't done everything you could to prevent it?"

He bristled. "My sons are good Christian boys and won't need to know—and whatever they do need to know, I'll tell them at home. The school board is looking for any excuse to save money by shutting you down. This story would hand them your head on a platter. A bunch of kids went to Mexico over the summer and built a church. Write about that instead."

"Already typed and laid out on one of the feature pages." Such a nice story. A heart-warming story. What parents wanted to hear about their kids. No one wanted to hear that their kids might contract deadly STDs. Mr. Van Teasel certainly didn't. I steered the discussion back to the legal angle. "The paper states in the masthead it's a forum for student opinion, and as such, students have legal rights to express—"

"They can express their opinions on something less controversial. Like who will win the regional championship this year in football." He held his hand out for Tameka's notes, and I relinquished those too.

I left his office, feeling as if I'd failed Sam all over again. The first time, I'd been a sophomore in high school, two years behind my brother. I had half a crush on Mr. Fresnel, this slender boy-man newly graduated from Auburn with long, pale fingers and shirts crafted from the finest fabrics. I wanted so much to caress those cottons and silks between my fingers and thumb the way we girls touched clothes on shopping trips to big city department stores. I could tell his clothing had what my mother called "a good hand." All the girls cherished Mr. Fresnel. He was an emissary from the world we hoped awaited us outside Alderson, a world where males were mature and refined, where their wit blossomed beyond the pull-my-finger jokes boys our age found so amusing.

One afternoon I walked into Mr. Fresnel's classroom and saw them together, Sam and my refined social studies teacher. They weren't touching, nothing overt like that, but I just knew. I don't know how. I should have told my mother as soon as I suspected. When Sam revealed his orientation to my parents two years later, my mother only loved him even more because that's what he needed from her. Had she known sooner, things might have turned out differently. I imagined her laying the groundwork so my father could accept the news of his son's homosexuality with grace. I imagined her steering Sam toward a gentler style of revelation. Instead, years of father-son struggles culminated in a final blow-up. I don't know who was more devastated, Sam hearing his own father shout, "I didn't raise my son to be no God damn queer," just before he punched him in the jaw, or my mother when she heard her only son saying it would be a cold day in hell before he set foot in their house again. If I hadn't known it before, that incident drilled into me how conditional my father's love was.

Rationally, I knew I over-estimated my mother's ability to change things. As Sam's mother, she had surely guessed his orientation. He had always been a bit different, more interested in reading novels and sketching landscapes than playing the sports that would have made my father proud. As for my father, well, he was who he was. Not even my mother had ever been able to change him.

The flame from the candle threw off such soft light I could barely make out the contents of the kitchen junk drawer. Somewhere in this mess, there lurked a flashlight. I knew it was there. I'd seen it last time I'd flung a pink rubber band from the broccoli inside the drawer. Finally my hand recognized the cylindrical shape. I pushed the power button. Nothing. Not even a flicker. I handed Quinn the candle and shook the flashlight. Smacked it good. Still nothing. I unscrewed the bottom. No wonder it felt top heavy.

"All right, where are the batteries?"

"I borrowed them, Mom." Quinn's voice whined with apology. "I needed them for my robot and forgot to put them back."

Aha. His Boy Scout project. "Well, go get them."

Quinn hesitated, and then admitted he'd left the robot at school. "Mrs. Henderson wants to show my robot to her science classes. She wants me to enter it in the regional science fair."

"That's wonderful, Quinn!" I ruffled his hair. Now what? The flashlight I carried in my purse for school emergencies. I dug past my billfold, several pens, a box of breath mints, and a lint roller. The candle was almost no help. I couldn't aim its light into the cavernous recesses of my bag.

Quinn answered the phone. "Yeah, the power's out here too . . . No, Mom found a flashlight, but I'm in trouble 'cause I took the batteries out . . . Okay."

"Who was that?" I asked when he hung up.

"Mr. Piscetelli. He's coming over with a flashlight."

"Now?" It was only eight o'clock, but I had on my jammies. I scurried to the bedroom and pulled on jeans and, using the little light I'd found in my purse, retrieved my tee-shirt from the laundry basket.

Lodge Piscetelli stood in the foyer holding Dusty in his arms when I returned to the living room, which now was illuminated by a large lantern.

"That the only flashlight you got?" He motioned with amusement toward my penlight, whose beam all but vanished in the lantern's glare.

"No, of course not. Just the only one I could find with batteries. Batteries have a way of disappearing around here." I threw Quinn a look. He shrunk like a strip of bacon in the frying pan. I shrunk a little too, from guilt. He was a good kid, really he was.

Lodge extended a twelve-pack of D cells. "You can never have too many batteries or flashlights in your house. I laid some extra flashlights on your kitchen counter. You should keep at least one in every room."

Four lights of various sizes rested on the countertop. C. Lodge must be some Boy Scout—always prepared. Over-prepared. People rarely gave things away for free. What did C. Lodge Piscetelli want?

"I couldn't possibly take all those. Don't you need them?"

"Got dozens more. I stock up when they're on sale. Consider them a gift."

"Well, thanks."

"This neighborhood go dark often?" he asked.

"Not really, but it always seems to happen at the worst time, when you're right in the middle of something." Like typing a test on the computer. I had lost everything because I hadn't saved my work. I knew better, but I'd just forgotten. I tried to hold back the sigh, but it escaped anyway. "I really need the test I was typing for tomorrow morning."

Lodge explained how I could retrieve it as soon as the power came back on. "My computer has battery back-up. You can finish typing at my house."

I left a note for Graham, who was at choir practice, and we followed Lodge across the street. I didn't get much of an impression of his living room as we hurried through with the flashlight. He led me to a computer in the den, which sat on a cheap hutch, the kind you can pick up at any home improvement store for a hundred bucks. I sat in front of it on a black vinyl swivel chair, one lantern on each side of the workspace.

"You go right ahead and finish up that test," he said. "Quinn and me'll just take a look-see at the computer I'm building in the next room."

"You build computers?" Quinn asked.

"Yeah. Keeps me out of trouble."

"Cool," I heard Quinn say as they withdrew to the other room.

Teak bookcases lined the walls. A brown leather easy chair angled next to the window. The room gave the overall impression of functionality rather than attention to décor. Which was okay by me.

At first I found it difficult to concentrate in strange surroundings. I yanked at the neckline of my tee-shirt. Somehow it didn't seem right to leave Mr. Piscetelli in charge of entertaining Quinn while I worked on a test. Every now and then Quinn's laugh would float through the air from the adjoining room. I began to relax and enjoy the good fortune of living in a small town where neighbors cared enough to check on each other when the lights went out.

What in the world was wrong with the neckband of my shirt? It was putting a choke hold on me.

The power came back on. I saved the nearly finished test to my flash drive. As I retrieved my textbook from Mr. Piscetelli's desk, a fat file folder underneath caught my eye. Its label read "Blacks For Progress vs. City of Alderson Board of Education." I stared. Hesitated. Knew I shouldn't. But finally I whipped the file open and scanned the top page written in legalese, most of which would have required a dictionary to interpret. What I could determine was the name of the attorney representing Blacks For Progress. C. Lodge Piscetelli. So this was the business that brought him to town. Some business. Dirty business. I closed the file and went to retrieve Quinn.

"Thanks for letting me use your computer," I said.

"Any time."

Why was he smiling in that smug way—and trying to hide it? I couldn't figure this guy out.

When Quinn and I walked inside the house, all the lights were on and the clocks on the microwave and stove were blinking. Everything would have to be reset. When I leaned close to the microwave's front panel, the glass door presented me with a hazy reflection. I looked all strange around the neck and shoulders. Hump-backed. I pulled my tee-shirt away from my body and realized it was on backwards. A few years ago David and the boys had bought it for me at the beach as a Mother's Day gift. I pulled my arms inside the shirt and turned it front to back, finding now with my fingers, the sticky heat-stamped front, "Teaching is a Class Act."

"Why didn't you tell me my shirt was on backwards?" I demanded of Quinn.

"Didn't notice, Mom."

Of course he hadn't. Mothers were invisible. Not to everyone, I thought, remembering Lodge's smile.

Nine

J.D. showed me his homework. I praised him loudly and made sure he saw the hundred entered in the grade book. Shaniqua displayed her homework, two immaculate pages. When we began to discuss the last scene of *The Taming of the Shrew*, I called on her first, thinking she wouldn't have time to work herself into a panic. Her hands clenched her textbook and tears welled in her eyes. What was I going to do with that girl? I called on Ja'Neice instead.

Next I asked the class if Petruchio really tamed Kate at the end of the play. J.D. was among those who raised their hands. After checking to be sure no wires ran into his ears, I called on him.

"Nah, Kate's learned to run the game," he said. "That dude's going to give her anything she wants so long as she treats him right. It's like Tupac says—"

I cut him off with a few words of praise, and he rewarded me with a flash of his gold grill. I didn't want to hear anymore about keeping ho's in line. His insight into Kate was keen, especially considering he had only been in class for the last few scenes. I felt sure J.D. and I would get along fine.

Wrong again. By the end of the period, he'd earned another fifteen-minute detention for making suggestive remarks to Marissa. He f-bombed me when I placed the detention slip on his desk. Another fifteen.

The extra at our lunch table occupied my seat. Since she'd been one of my favorite students a few years back, I suppressed the urge to ask her to scoot over one chair, but from time to time, my jaw twitched involuntarily.

Lauryl Moore was substituting for a semester to decide if she really wanted to be a teacher. In high school while other kids hung out at the swimming pool or went off to the beach, Lauryl had volunteered at a summer camp teaching horseback riding to kids with disabilities. Education needed to attract more young people of her quality. I couldn't help but feel a little bit flattered that my former student chose to follow in my footsteps.

Liz scrunched her lips up. "I don't care what he says, I'm going to wear what I want. He wants dresses? I'll plaster a mini-skirt over these big hips. See what he thinks of dresses then."

Ever since yesterday's faculty meeting, Liz couldn't get off the subject of Mr. Van Teasel's new teacher dress code. It disturbed me that we were talking about clothes in faculty meetings when we had failed to make Adequate Yearly Progress.

Tessa chuckled, a sound surprisingly more pleasant than her voice. "I think all of us at this table are past the mini-skirt stage, except for Lauryl and Betsy, of course."

Liz was so busy being angry she hadn't started to eat her lunch, and it was our special potluck day. "He makes me so mad. I bought a bunch of capri outfits before school started—the long kind that ride below the calf and they have nice matching tops and jackets, very professional—and now he decides we can't wear them anymore." She lowered her voice an octave and mimicked Mr. Van Teasel. "'Slacks must cover the ankles, if you must wear them, but I really like to see my *lay*-dees in *dress*-es.' His *lay*-dees. Like we're stuck in the '50s—" Behind her, Mr. Van Teasel appeared in the lounge door. I nudged her and coughed, but Liz powered ahead. "—His *lay*-dees, what are we—June Cleavers, for heaven's sake?"

I kicked her shin, lightly, then more urgently.

"What? What?" She turned her head and saw Mr. Van Teasel. He avoided eye contact. Liz stuffed her mouth with gumbo, nearly choking as she tried to swallow. I was afraid it was going to spew out.

"Nothing wrong with June Cleaver," Tessa whispered, as we watched Mr. Van Teasel's stiff progression to the Coke machine. He dropped two quarters in.

"I always liked her aprons," I whispered back. I could feel my face grow red with stifled laughter.

He pushed the button for Diet Coke and it rumbled down. He picked it up and strode by our table without looking right or left.

"Have a good day, *lay*-dees."

As soon as he shut the door, we burst out laughing.

"*Lay*-dees," Liz repeated.

Lauryl, a bit uncertainly, addressed Liz and me. "This is a side to you I never saw as a student."

"It's not always like this in here," I told her.

"Yeah, it is," Liz said. "Don't lie. She'll be crazy too if she sticks with teaching. Well, he can't fire me, can he? I have tenure."

"You do," I said. "You're fine." And she was black. No one black was going to be fired for any reason short of a felony. Not with the lawsuit pending. The scarcity of black teachers was one grievance mentioned in the suit, and it was a legitimate complaint, one we didn't know how to solve.

For the first time since arriving at work, I remembered the missing boa. "Found that nasty snake yet?"

She hadn't, though she and the Science Club had spent several hours after school searching.

"If that snake finds its way into my room, you're gonna wish you were fired." I half meant it, too, but not enough to stop me from slurping another spoonful of the gumbo she'd made. "This is great—where'd you get this recipe?"

"My cousin has a gumbo and sandwich shop in New Orleans. Her secret recipe, and it's a dandy, but dish out those brownie sundaes, Dessert Queen."

I assembled white chocolate chunk macadamia brownies topped with vanilla ice cream and two sauces: raspberry and hot fudge.

"I have died and gone to heaven," Tessa claimed, way too loud as usual.

"Umm. This is the best yet, even better than your Death By Chocolate cake," Liz said.

"I'd weigh a zillion pounds if I lived in your house, Mrs. Culpepper," Lauryl added.

I hoped she wasn't implying I already weighed that much. I changed the subject. "Seriously, I'm really worried about trying to enforce the student code."

"It's going to be a battle, that's for sure," Liz said.

"Especially since they didn't start enforcing it at the beginning of the year." I dreaded telling J.D. to wear his pants at the waist. That reminded me to let Tessa know he had finally served detention and I wouldn't have to write a referral.

"Good thing," Tessa said. "Mr. Van Teasel asked us to figure out how to cut down on referrals because of this lawsuit. I've been instructed to make up a new three-step procedure you have to go through before you can send any student to the office, and get this—if you have too many referrals, you'll have to attend remedial instruction in classroom management."

Others grumbled quietly. I said nothing. Until Liz commented on this lawsuit one way or the other, I wasn't going to either. I reached for my stash of antacids. Popped three into my mouth. Who decided what constituted "too many" referrals? Teachers with at-risk students who functioned below grade level often had discipline problems through no fault of their own. So did teachers who handled behavior-disordered kids.

I rarely wrote referrals since I taught honors courses. Occasionally a kid crossed the line between good-natured humor and outright disrespect, either for me or a classmate. Usually I handled it with a little after-school discussion during detention. Or someone got too rowdy and couldn't settle down—something I expected to encounter occasionally. They were teenagers, after all. But with this dress code crackdown and racial lawsuit mess and J.D. stirring trouble up, things could spin out of control. Sometimes administrators forgot how easily school became an us-versus-them situation instead of realizing we were all on the same side working toward the same goals. Seemed to me like some people in the community had forgotten it too.

Ten

After lunch I faced an uproar in my journalism class again. Not over the AIDS story as I'd expected.

"At a meeting last night Reverend Bolden spoke in support of the lawsuit," Tameka said. "I took notes, did interviews, and got the story half-written. Come on, Miz C., this is the biggest story of the year."

"No way," I said. It was the biggest story of the year. The lawsuit stuffed all the elements of news into one neat package—it was bursting with conflict, happening right here and now, had important people involved in it, and affected the whole community—but these kids lacked the finesse and experience to tackle such a sensitive issue. Without a doubt, any story they wrote on the subject would get me fired, sued, and drawn and quartered—not in any particular order.

"It's not the kind of story you can write quickly, for one thing." I grasped at the first excuse I could think of. "You would have to let the school's attorney read it first. We wouldn't want to write anything to cause the school more legal problems, would we? Every time they have to pay legal fees, it means less money to spend on textbooks, computers, and field trips."

"Don't forget football," Tameka said bitterly.

"Yeah, that too. And the newspaper." I thought I'd better remind her who really published this rag.

"Can we take our time and put it in the next issue?"

"We'll see." Maybe the topic would blow over by then. At least I might have a better excuse composed. "Right now we need to find a center spread."

"Let's do teen pregnancy," Tameka said.

Recalling Mr. Van Teasel's use of the word verboten regarding sex, I began to feel like the Wicked Witch for stifling every idea Tameka had. "I don't think so, honey."

"You're just afraid we'll tell the truth about what's going on around here."

She had it all wrong. I wasn't afraid. I was terrified. I needed this job. I had two boys to support.

"Jeez, what can we write about? I suppose Mr. Van Teasel'd like that junky stuff in other school papers, like how Halloween got started or the sweet little teacher of the month who enjoys gardening and reading. Booorrring. What about dress code enforcement?"

It sounded like a topic that could get us in trouble too, but at least it stayed away from race and sex. For a moment visions of University of Georgia boxers and silky tangerine thongs peeping out of low-cut jeans danced in my head. The topic wasn't overtly about sex, anyway. The dress code posed fewer problems than race, and the principal *had* been making announcements every morning that he would enforce the code strictly next week.

I relented with a warning: "Make it factual and try to cover all sides." I, for one, agreed with the code in spirit, but every time a previous administration instituted a stricter code, they hadn't backed up teachers in enforcing it. When teachers played dress police, it broke whatever rapport we had established. I had a bad feeling about the crackdown, but maybe I was being paranoid.

Eleven

From the field, cheerleaders chanted "A-H-S," three children screeched and chased each other beneath the bleachers, and a male voice boomed hype over the loudspeaker from the press box. Yet through all the din, I could hear buttery popcorn and grilled hotdogs calling my name. I ignored them, or tried to. They smelled so much more like real food than the grilled chicken salad we had eaten for dinner. Quinn, still at loose ends, tagged along with me. I enjoyed his company but knew he'd rather be sitting with kids his own age. We scooted by the Tarkingtons, the Davises, the Boldens, and the Barneses. I took a good look at that Reverend Bolden, the one spearheading the Blacks For Progress lawsuit. A white clerical collar stood out starkly against his black attire. He rubbed a handkerchief across the bald spot that began at his crown. A strip of charcoal fuzz extended around the back of his head from one ear to the other. He didn't look like such an evil man, but looks could be deceiving. What kind of person would sue the school and make life hard on the very teachers who were trying to help kids? I sent angry thoughts his way. When he caught me staring at him, he acknowledged me with such benevolence I was forced to look away. I was glad for the distraction when Bill and Vivian Barnes thanked me for tutoring Ceci on her SATs.

Friday night games ranked as the biggest social events on fall weekends in Alderson. Until Graham joined the team, I had never bothered attending, not even when David had worked security detail. "A bit uncivilized, isn't it, to go slamming into other people?" I asked David. Usually the boys had gone with him, leaving me a night to myself to grade papers, read a good book, or luxuriate in a hot bath fragrant with green tea and cucumber bubbles. By Friday I needed a decompression chamber, a chance to recover from combat fatigue. I would rather be in a hot bath now, except I wouldn't miss Graham's game for the world. My duty was obvious: to cheer him on loudly enough to make up for David's absence. After three home games, I understood the rules much better.

The cheerleaders formed two long lines by the field house. Two nymphets held a giant run-through sign depicting an Eagle snapping up a Bulldog by its neck. The band began a drum roll with the home crowd rumbling along. Quinn and I jumped up and stomped our feet on the metal bleachers along with everyone else. The team snapped through the banner, destroying hours of hard work in two seconds.

"There's Graham!" I pointed at Number Three.

Quinn pulled my arm down by the shirt sleeve. "Mom, do you always have to do that?"

"Do what?"

He wouldn't meet my eyes, his body twisting back and forth rhythmically, his voice emerging as a cross between a croak and a whisper. "Announce that it's Graham, like I'm stupid and won't recognize him or something."

I winced. "Sorry." Quinn had always been the easy-going child. I might not survive if he became as difficult as his brother.

"Hey, Grandpa!" Quinn waved to get Woodson's attention. I was relieved my father had shown up. He'd always attended some of the boys' sporting events, but since his accident I encouraged the boys to make a fuss over how much they wanted him there. The busier we could keep him, the less time he had to drink.

AHS won the toss and elected to play defense first. Graham's kick-off sailed fifty-eight yards down the field. During the scoreless first quarter, the announcer yammered about both teams trying to establish their running game. I wished they'd hurry up and connect a pass—that's what I liked to see, and if Bill and Vivian Barnes didn't hurry up and finish their popcorn, I might have to snatch the box away and wolf it down myself.

In the second quarter, I got my wish. The quarterback pumped his arm toward the left side of the field, changed directions, and threw a thirty-yard pass to his right. "Too high," Woodson said. "We need a new qua—"

Before he could finish his sentence, J.D., without losing a step as he crossed the field, looked over his shoulder. He turned at the precise moment the ball arrived, leapt into the air, brushed the leather with the fingertips of his left hand, drew it down to the right, and tucked it under his arm. Looked so easy. An orange jersey loomed in front of him. J.D. feinted right; the orange jersey followed. J.D. cut left, feet flying past the remaining orange jersey to score.

"Go Eagles. Go J.D.!" I screamed. "That's one of my students," I told Quinn.

Bill Barnes leaned closer to me. "That kid runs the 40 in 42."

The 40 what, I wondered. I didn't want to appear ignorant so I didn't ask. Besides, Graham was warming up on the sidelines.

Bill persisted. "He'll be playing college ball some day, you mark my words."

I hoped to get J.D. ready for college, whether he played ball there or not.

Graham trotted onto the field.

"That's my boy!" I told anyone who'd listen. "You go, Graham!" The place-holder received the ball, bobbled it. The ball bounced down the field away from Graham. He took off after it and hurled his body to the ground, trapping the ball under his chest. Five bruisers slammed on top of him.

"Foul!" I jumped to my feet. "You can't tackle the kicker! Come on, ref. Do something about it!"

Quinn pulled my shirt sleeve. "Mom, they can tackle him if he doesn't get the kick off."

"Graham didn't tell me that." In fact, he swore kicking was a safe position.

"Probably didn't want you to worry," Woodson said. "Look, he's all right, he's getting up now."

My baby wobbled toward the sidelines and flipped the ball sideways to the officials.

"It doesn't seem fair that five people can jump on top of him," I said. "Just no call for that."

"Lighten up," Woodson said. "You don't want to turn him into some kind of fairy."

"How many times have I asked you not to use that word?" Every time he said it, I visualized my brother Sam, his face hardening against the slur.

"What—you think the kids aren't going to hear it somewhere else?"

"I know they'll hear it, but I hope they won't use it. You're supposed to be a role model."

Woodson put his arm around Quinn. "Goober, do everything I say and don't do anything I do."

Quinn laughed. "Okay, Grandpa."

Woodson turned toward me. "How's that?"

I rolled my eyes heavenward as my answer. He pulled out a pack of cigarettes and lit one, in direct violation of the no-smoking policy in the stadium. "Wanna know who I was talking to at Fred's before I came here?" he asked.

No, I wanted to know why he was at Fred's when he was supposed to be here at the game watching his grandson.

"Francis Brown. I bought Francis Brown a beer."

"You would rather share a drink with a racist pig than watch your grandson play ball?"

"I got here when the game started, and Francis is okay."

"Okay? Okay? Not even you can think what he did was okay."

"What he did wasn't okay. He's okay. There's a difference."

"Please."

"Have a little sympathy, Molly. Brown's burned because NASA let him go while some incompetent black dude who worked under him kept his job. We can blame affirmative action for Brown's behavior. We can blame affirmative action for Brown's behavior."

"No, I blame Brown for what Brown did. Isn't it ironic—his calling someone else incompetent?"

"I'm not saying what he did was right. He made a mistake. A bad one. He screwed up, Molly, but who hasn't? He's had a hard time lately. Financial problems. Bank's foreclosing on his house. The man has his side of the story, and he needed to tell it to someone who would listen. That someone was me."

"Congratulations. I can tell you're very proud." Thank God Woodson dropped it before we got into an even worse argument in public. I didn't know why I kept the dialogue going. Why couldn't I just shut up? Maybe Brown did have a story—didn't everyone? It didn't excuse inflicting his venom on the very kids he was paid to nurture. If I saw Francis Brown, I wouldn't buy him a beer. I'd be tempted to throw it in his face. I blamed him for the lawsuit. I blamed him for the division in our community.

At halftime Woodson bought popcorn for Quinn and me. I practically inhaled it with a Diet Coke. I suspected Woodson had spiked his cola with something potent.

In the fourth quarter J.D. scored two more touchdowns and Graham nailed both extra points. He also booted a thirty-two yard field goal in the last minute of play to win the game, and I faked enthusiasm for his achievements. Inside I was tormented by visions of broken legs, head injuries, paralysis—my imagination wouldn't let go of all that could go wrong. What if something happened to Graham? He had told me the kicker was safe.

David had told me jogging in the mornings was safe too, and look what happened to him.

I woke up a little after 4 a.m., exhausted from a night of dreaming I was late to school and a vague feeling I couldn't find Graham. I had misplaced him somewhere. I couldn't get back to sleep. On nights like this I really missed having a warm body to snuggle against. I latched onto David's pillow, a sorry substitute. I needed someone to see me as a whole person again. Not Miz Culpepper or Mom, but me, Molly Trask Culpepper, a woman with dreams and nightmares of her own. I wanted someone to laugh with me at those nonsensical elongated corridors that kept me from getting to class on time. I might be forty years old, but I still wanted to catch my breath when a man I loved came into the room. I wanted someone to see me again—all of me—a woman with a body, mind and spirit. I wanted a relationship like I had with David—no secrets, complete openness, total commitment. I wished I could find someone to love me, cellulite, belly fat, and all.

The earnestness of my wish triggered a memory. When confronted by the circle of candles on my tenth birthday cake, I had agonized over my wish. The candles grew shorter and still I couldn't decide.

"Make a big wish," Mama urged. "Ask for the most wonderful thing you can think of. It never hurts to dream."

My father had grunted. "Wish in one hand and shit in the other and see which one fills up first." Like so many of his sayings, it was crude. And all too true.

Twelve

I caught J.D. on his way in and praised his performance against the Eagles. He accepted this acknowledgement as his due.

Following instructions on the board, students moved into small groups. Some would type papers about *Taming of the Shrew* on the computers. Others would read poems and complete basic grammar assignments. Later in the week, the groups would rotate until everyone took a turn on the computers.

Brian, Marissa, and J.D. formed a group assigned to Lewis Carroll's poem "Jabbberwocky." Together they were to figure out the part of speech of each invented word and then replace it with a real word. The assignment always met with some resistance at first, but once students understood what to do, they found it more fun than traditional study of grammar.

I wandered about the room to monitor their progress. Kneeling by Shaniqua's desk, I validated her idea to replace the word *Jabberwock* with *Vampire*. Wings fluttered overhead. She cringed and looked at the hole in the ceiling. We could hear excited chirps from the crawl space where the air conditioning and heating pipes sprawled like a silver-tentacled octopus.

"Not vampires, just birds," I said. "Stay on task."

"Ever since the janitors removed those ceiling tiles, those birds creep me out," Shaniqua said.

Those black holes in the ceiling were creepy. The janitors had removed the tiles because of complaints about the roof. In some places it leaked so severely, the ceiling tiles were not only water-stained, but buckled with the weight of accumulated water. One of mine had given way during class and poured down on Tameka. No wonder she wanted to write a story on the roof and ceiling! Unfortunately, custodians had run out of replacement tiles before they could complete the job. The assistant principal said the tiles were back-ordered at the discount store he used, so we would have to live with black holes a while longer and hope no birds decided to dive bomb us.

"This is a great poem!" Brian's voice carried across the room. It always raised an octave when he got excited—or when he talked to Marissa.

"It doesn't make any sense," she said.

"Sure it does."

"Whatever—I don't like it."

If Brian hated the poem, Marissa would have claimed she loved it. They squabbled like siblings. Or like two adolescents who really liked each other but were afraid to show it.

J.D. slouched in his seat. "It's stupid. What's 'brillig' supposed to mean anyway? If I wrote a poem like this, the Doughboy'd flunk me."

I knew he meant me, but selective hearing can be a virtue in a teacher.

"It's a poem about a monster, the Jabberwock," Brian said. "You can figure it out if you're smart enough."

"You trying to say I ain't smart, dickhead?"

On the other hand, some things can't be ignored. "J.D.—watch your mouth!"

He waved a hand my way to indicate he understood. As soon as he thought I wasn't looking, he scratched his chin with his middle finger and flicked his eyes toward me, grinning at Marissa. She grinned back, forgetting all the Girl Scout cookies and church raffle tickets I had bought from her over the years. It shouldn't have bothered me the way it did.

"I'm just saying you have to work to get at the meaning," Brian said.

J.D. studied the xeroxed copy, then leaned his shoulder across his desk and nudged Marissa, raising his eyebrows suggestively and appropriating words in the poem for his own purposes. "You want to 'gyre and gimble in the wabe' with me? I would be all 'mimsy' if you would."

She giggled. "You wish."

Brian threw his sheet down on his desk. "All right, fine. Either you two help with this assignment or I'm going to find another group."

"Okay, okay, don't get all wigged out," J.D. said. "We got you covered."

Overhead the intercom crackled. "Is it on?" Mr. Van Teasel spoke softly. I knew Mrs. Alford stood over him, coaching. "It's on? Okay." Then his voice boomed into the room. "Good morning, Eagles. I want to address a problem I have perceived since arriving here at AHS. Dress code violations have continued despite warnings all last week. Complaints have poured in from parents and community leaders about your visible undergarments."

Snickers rippled across the room.

"Since we began our Dress for Success campaign last week, I've seen little improvement. Gentlemen, your pants still ride too low, and young ladies, your skirts are still too short. Today the warnings end. Any student with visible undergarments and any girl whose skirt doesn't reach beyond her fingertips goes home. Also, bellies must be covered completely. I repeat, offenders—will—go—home."

Students grumbled—no surprise. "That's so not fair!" "He's nuts!" "What's more important, our clothes or our education?"

The principal continued. "These regulations are set forth in the student handbook every student received on the first day of school. It's the responsibility of first period teachers to ensure full compliance. All teachers must stop whatever they are doing immediately and check every student. Send all offenders to the office. And it is not okay if boys with baggy pants hike them up temporarily. Teachers, if a boy's pants don't ride at the natural waistline, I expect you to send them to the office. Now."

Administrators would be the first to tell you to protect class time. Right after they stole ten minutes here for homecoming elections, a half hour there because the Chamber of Commerce President wanted to recruit students to pick up litter. They arranged hour-long pep rallies and sales pitches from class ring salesmen.

I sighed and began with students at the computers, working my way around the room. Each kid stood in turn. Dalonega's dress only reached her knuckles. Office. Orville, Shalonda, and Nan passed inspection. Leon's pants sagged. Office. Shaniqua, Ceci, Brian, and Marissa passed.

Ja'Neice's thong was fuchsia.

"Office," I said.

"What? You can't see my—"

"Honey, I've seen dental floss thicker than the satin strung across your backyard."

Ja'Neice laughed. "Okay, okay, I'm outta here."

J.D.'s turn. His boxers were navy plaid. I would have given a lot not to have known. "Office."

"Come on, Miz . . . Miz . . ." He appeared to be at a loss for my name. "I'll pull them up." He hooked his thumbs into the waistband and hitched them an inch, not enough to cover up his butt anyway. "See? Chill, it'll be okay."

"Sorry, you heard Mr. Van Teasel."

"I'm new. I didn't know."

"You've heard the announcements, same as everyone else, and I have a paper in my filing cabinet that says you received, read, and understood the rules in the student handbook."

He stared at me a moment, eyes hard, muscles taut. "Why you always picking on me?"

I blinked. "I don't pick on you. I expect you to follow the rules, same as everyone else."

"I been here all of two weeks. Cut me some slack."

"Sorry."

Next he called me a word he hadn't learned in my classroom. In minutes, J.D. held a referral in his hands. When he tore it up and refused to leave, I did something I'd never done before. I pressed the panic button on my wall, then felt sick. A school resource officer wouldn't respond because we didn't have one anymore, thanks to our broken budget.

Instead Mr. Van Teasel and Coach Haswell arrived.

"Come on down to the office and we'll talk this out," Haswell said.

"I'm not leaving this room."

"Come on, J.D., you don't want to do this."

"Yes, I do. She got no right to send me home. I haven't done nothing."

Mr. Van Teasel stepped into the argument. "Son, she has every right. Mrs. Culpepper is just doing her job."

"I'm not your son."

Haswell laid his hand on J.D.'s arm, intending, I think, to steer him toward the door. It was the wrong thing to do. J.D. jammed an elbow into the coach's ribs, and when Mr. Van Teasel seized J.D.'s other arm, the boy landed a solid punch to the principal's jaw, knocking his glasses from his face. They flew across two aisles and landed somewhere on the floor.

As the two men struggled to restrain J.D., two desks overturned. My students retreated to the corners of the room, staying out of harm's way, their voices instantly swelling to pep rally levels. The thuds and J.D.'s language drew students from other classes to my door. Chants of "Fight! Fight!" traveled down the hall. Students ignored teachers' orders for them to get back to class. They shoved and elbowed their way to the front lines of battle. Exaltation shone in their faces. Bloodlust gleamed in their eyes.

Mr. Van Teasel and Coach Haswell held their own against J.D. The principal, though small in stature, was an ex-Marine. Haswell had played football for UGA in his day. Neither backed down in the face of J.D.'s uncontrolled fury. Finally, the principal pinned one of J.D.'s arms, the coach the other. The boy's body writhed, and for one moment, his eyes locked with mine, channeling hatred so intense I couldn't fathom its source. A lump of fear settled between my ribs.

"You kids get back to class! Now!" Haswell yelled. They scrambled to get out of his way but lingered in thick clots against the lockers. Haswell and Van Teasel half wrestled, half dragged J.D. down the hall. I stood in my doorway, arms spread to block students who wanted to follow the action. They pressed against me, standing on toes, leaning so far forward they kept losing their balance and pushing into me. The trio had nearly reached the entrance to the office when J.D. unleashed a howl like nothing human I'd ever heard before, a purely primal sound. An image of a wolf, leg bloodied in a steel trap, rose in my mind. From behind, a hand gripped my elbow. Ceci's face reflected the horror I felt inside. Patting her hand, I motioned everyone back into seats.

"It's over now. It'll be all right." I didn't believe it, not even then, not deep down where instinct writes the truth in our guts. I had seen plenty of fights before, but never one like this. I needed to restore order and a sense of normalcy as quickly as possible. As I stepped back into the classroom, the leather sole of one of my slides crunched on something. The principal's glasses lay on my floor, both lenses broken, an ear piece snapped off. The smell of sweat lingered in the air.

The intercom crackled with extended morning announcements on impending Homecoming elections. We lost almost the entire class period. Gone, and no getting those precious minutes back.

During class change Mr. Van Teasel came on the intercom again and insisted I write down everything J.D. had done and everything he'd said, as if the principal hadn't seen and heard enough himself. I wouldn't have minded nearly as much if he hadn't demanded the paper work immediately, which meant I had to ignore second period students.

To think of all the time I had wasted. My life was frittering away, one minute after another, and I wasn't accomplishing anything. If this were the last day of my life, is this how I wanted to spend it? It could happen. It had happened to my mother and to David.

During my planning period, I visited Tessa's claustrophobic office. Book shelves lined three walls of the closet-sized space. College and vocational school guides and advice books on everything from teen pregnancy to eating disorders stuffed the shelves. The fourth wall squeezed in three vertical filing cabinets, a chair and a doorway. Two chairs for guests were pushed almost on top of Tessa's desk with little room for legs. I squeezed into one of these.

She sucked on one of her ubiquitous mints and blew out her breath. "They have decided to suspend J.D. for three days."

"That's it?" Even ordinary fights got students ten days. No discussion permitted.

"Mr. Van Teasel consulted with J.D.'s mother and Coach Haswell. J.D. has to sign a behavior contract before he comes back." She handed me a sample. "You can customize this with your class rules, but it's a place to start. His mother said he only got so upset because the terms of his probation say he can't have any unexcused absences."

"Whoa, slow down—probation?"

"Yeah, he got into some trouble in Atlanta." She continued, but not with the part of the story I wanted to hear. "Haswell went to bat for J.D. Said as a new kid, he should have gotten a warning."

I was surprised Haswell had stood up for J.D., but then again, not too surprised. Coaches won games or they lost their jobs, and J.D. ran faster than any player who'd ever worn an AHS jersey.

"Tessa, I'm never going to be able to work with him after this.

We've really gotten off on the wrong foot." I remembered the way J.D. had looked at me while his arms were pinned behind his back and a shiver ran up my spine. "I think it would be best for everyone if you moved him to another class and let him start fresh."

"Miss Baker's the only other class he can be moved to."

So? Everyone obeyed Miss Baker. Maybe J.D. needed her brand of take-no-prisoners discipline. Or why couldn't he move into an easier level English class?

Tessa pushed gray-sprinkled bangs away from her forehead. "I found out more about him, things I think you should know before you make up your mind. The judge in Atlanta sentenced him to regular school attendance. If he gets in further trouble, he has to go to the alternative school. And that's the best case scenario. The worst is the judge'll remand him to the Youth Detention Center."

"Maybe juvie jail is where he belongs." I couldn't believe I'd said that. I had never believed that about any student of mine.

When I was a high school junior, Woodson had gone through a terrible drinking spell. My journal in English class overflowed with despair over my family, my low SAT scores in math, my inability to pay for college. Every time Mrs. Richards collected the journals to grade, she wrote encouraging notes in the margins. She wouldn't let me give up my dream of going to college. She arranged tutoring for me in math. She set up an appointment with the guidance counselor to discuss scholarships, loans, and grants. My senior year, she chose me as editor of the school newspaper, boosting my respectability in my own eyes and in the eyes of my classmates. She never gave up on me, even when I let her down and was late with an assignment.

I had vowed to be the same kind of teacher. Without the encouragement of my mother and Mrs. Richards, I don't know where I'd have ended up. I was ashamed for wanting to give up on J.D., but I couldn't erase that moment of pure hatred I'd seen in his eyes. I shuddered just thinking about it.

"There's something else you should know before you decide. His mother knifed his father—killed him—right in front of J.D. when he was only four. Apparently she got tired of the black eyes and broken ribs. Anyway, she went to prison and J.D. entered foster care. Social services separated him from his brother and sisters, and he bounced from one family to another. Finally ended up with an aunt in Atlanta. Even that wasn't as good as it sounds. The aunt's supposedly a drug addict or mentally ill or something, I don't know the whole story. God only knows what the kid has been through."

My brain began to connect stray pieces of information. "Wait—is that the Anita Scruggs case, the one where the governor pardoned the mother recently?" I'd read about it in the paper, thinking how pleased David would be if he'd known.

Tessa confirmed my suspicions. "She's gone back to using her maiden name, Marshall. Changed the kids' names too, even the older one not fathered by Scruggs. Not that it matters. As long as they stay here, everyone will figure out who they are. Anyway, to make a long story short, she has custody of J.D. and his brother and two sisters. She's trying to put her family back together again."

The phrase "all the king's horses and all the king's men" sprung to mind—but details kept coming back to me. David had worked this case. He had testified to this woman's injuries, swore it hadn't been the first time he'd been called to their house by neighbors convinced Ray Scruggs was killing his wife and children. J.D.'s sisters were twins, who must be in the eighth grade by now. The older boy would have graduated from high school—or dropped out.

The period leading up to the trial had been the worst of our marriage. It consumed David, and he put in obscene amounts of overtime. Hugely pregnant with Quinn, I had accused my husband of neglecting me and Graham, who was still a toddler. Neither my tantrums nor tears swayed David.

"This is something I have to do," he said. "Come on. It's only until the trial's over."

When I said I was tired of his waking me up whenever he finally decided to come home at night, he started sleeping in the guest bedroom. He stayed there through the last month of my pregnancy, my stubbornness keeping me from inviting him back; his, preventing him from backing down. It took Quinn's birth to heal our rift.

I remembered photographs of Anita Scruggs that had run daily in the city paper, a woman with close-cropped hair and beautifully defined cheekbones. She was tall, slender, sensual. All the things I wasn't, especially in my last trimester. I still had those photos in David's scrapbook. He had kept clippings of all his major cases, more from this particular one than any other.

When the trial finally arrived, months after Quinn's birth, Dr. Clevenger testified that Ray Scruggs had broken a child's arm. I remembered thinking that a woman would do anything to protect her child. Even kill a man if it came to that. I had approved when the governor finally pardoned her. If Anita Scruggs—Marshall—was trying to salvage her family, I wanted to help if I could. Raising boys without a father demanded all the strength a mother could summon under the best of circumstances. No one knew that better than I did.

I could hear Mrs. Richards in my mind, whispering, "Don't give up. Things will get better."

Then I visualized J.D.'s sneer, the bird he'd flipped me, the way he'd fought and howled like a cornered animal. I almost changed my mind.

Thirteen

Alderson is blessed with an excellent city sports complex that stays busy year-round. A dozen other parents shared the soccer field's metal bleachers, which felt mighty hard on the behind after a while, even one with superfluous padding like mine. Loblolly pines, live oaks, magnolias, dogwoods, birches, and ginkgoes forested the land beyond the chain link fence. On the field behind us, a tee-ball team kept the dust stirred up as preschoolers skittered around the bases like little chipmunks.

"No, you're running the wrong way!" one father yelled through laughter. "The other way."

Amused, I turned around to watch the little girl reverse direction, and I clapped along with her parents. It didn't seem that long ago when Quinn was playing tee-ball, with David, my parents, and me cheering him on.

I caught a sneeze in a tissue. Either the dust or ragweed was giving me fits. We needed a good rain to settle things down.

Quinn's team wasn't much to watch—the match looked like another shut out—but with that thick thatch of chestnut hair, the even teeth and square jaw, Coach Russ Freeman resembled a GQ model. How could his wife have left him? Without explanation to anyone. Not even to the grocery store, where she was assistant manager. Russ seemed a decent sort. He wasn't one of those fools who cursed at players over every mistake, as if that would make them play any better. And he didn't have a mouthful of disgusting chew dribbling from the corner of his mouth either, like Sonny Haswell.

Our opponents scored another point. This late in the game, what would it hurt to put in the sixth graders?

"Why the hell don't the coach put Quinn in?"

I knew that gravelly voice and its cussing all too well. "I don't know. Guess he has his reasons."

"Scoot over." Woodson nudged me down the bleachers. "Sorry I'm late. Had to repair a major break in a line. Some fool road construction crew chewed through the cable, and half the ladies in Alderson was calling in and complaining because they couldn't watch their soaps." Still in his work uniform, he unscrewed the cap on his thermos and took a long swig.

Claymore's whiz kid stole the ball, feinted left, and caught our goalie standing flat-footed. The ball flew by him into the net.

Woodson megaphoned his hands around his mouth. "Hey, Freeman, put Quinn in!"

"Shush, Dad! You'll embarrass Quinn."

"Shoot, that's not gonna embarrass Quinn. What's embarrassing is sitting on the bench. That Freeman kid never did have no sense."

"He's hardly a kid. He's older than I am." He had graduated in David's class, he and Sonny Haswell both.

"He's a kid to me." Woodson screwed up his face and jumped to his feet as the other team stole the ball again. "Freeman, you panty-waist, give Quinn a chance!"

Parents in the bleachers turned to frown at him.

"Dad, now you're embarrassing me." Why did he always have to use those words—fairy, panty-waist, queer? Sometimes I thought he did it just to remind everyone in town he wasn't gay, even if his son was. "The coach doesn't play any sixth graders. Russ is good with the boys. You should see how kind and encouraging he is at practice."

He gave me a long look of disgust and took another drink from his thermos. "Nothing wrong with a man standing up for his grand-kids." He scratched at the dark stubble on his cheek, studying Freeman again. "But there is something wrong with a man that don't sweat. Ain't natural. Look at him—every hair in place, those girly-boy pants still creased. He don't act like a coach."

"What—because he doesn't grab his private parts and swear like a sailor?"

He took another swig from the thermos. "Sorry panty-waist if you ask me."

"Well, no one did." My eyes slid over Russ Freeman's muscular arms and came to rest on his firm butt. I grinned wickedly. Not only had I found an occasion to use a word I just learned, but I knew it would irritate Woodson. "I myself would describe him as callipygian."

"Why can't you speak plain English? I hope you don't talk like that in the classroom. Cow-lee-pig-whatever, Miss School Marm. Whoever heard tell of such a thing?"

Ignoring his tirade, I sniffed the air and whispered, "What's in that thermos?"

He feigned innocence. "Coffee, whadya think?"

Betty Louise Thompson was the closest person to us, and she seemed to be looking our way with her nose in the air, but then her nose usually rode high, so it might not mean anything. "I can't believe you brought that in here," I said. "There are signs all over the place—no alcoholic beverages."

"I can't believe you put so much store in signs. Besides, it's just coffee."

I didn't believe him for a minute.

He lit a cigarette, inhaling deeply. "That kid behaving in your class now that he's back?"

"Yeah, seems to be." I don't know why I had shared my worries about J.D. with Woodson. I think the little girl who still lived inside me wanted my daddy to take up for me and set the world aright even though I'd given up the illusion that he could work such miracles. J.D. had been back a week, and though I'd held my breath, things eased into a routine. He avoided eye contact, and I avoided calling on him anymore than necessary. His behavior wasn't perfect, but his infractions would sound petty on a three-step discipline plan.

J.D.'s mother met with all his teachers before he returned. She had aged since the newspaper photos I'd seen of her during the trial, but despite hollowed eyes, her face was still compelling. Thinner now, she tended toward bony rather than sinuously slender. She wore a white blouse of slippery fabric under a fuchsia jacket with a matching skirt. Church-going clothes. She seemed to study me in particular of all those gathered around the oblong table. Her eyes would flit briefly at J.D.'s other teachers as they spoke and then settle back on me. I wondered if he'd complained to her specifically about me.

We worked out a system where each teacher would fill out progress reports on J.D., which she'd collect from the guidance office after sixth period. If his reports were good, he earned privileges like using the phone and watching his favorite TV shows. Coach Haswell got copies of the reports too. If they were bad, J.D. would run the bleachers until he dropped.

"Guess I got into a fight or two back in my school days," Woodson said, drawing me back to the here and now. "I could understand that. What I can't understand is anyone calling a teacher the names he called you. Someone should teach that boy a lesson."

I hoped he'd already learned one.

"Why don't you get him transferred to another class?" Woodson asked.

"What? Dump my problems on someone else? I think I can handle him."

"Molly, there's something you should understand. There's bad blood—"

Bad blood. Code words to justify antiquated racial discrimination. "I don't believe in 'bad blood.' There's plenty of good inside J.D. I can feel it."

Woodson shook his head. "Suit yourself. Saw the *Eagle's Cry* today. Looked good. Don't know why you let those kids complain about the dress code, though. They need to keep their butts covered up."

"No kidding."

"If you think so, why'd you let them run the dress code down?"

"It's called freedom of expression, Dad. The First Amendment, you heard of that?"

"No need to get mad. I said it was a good paper. Just seems like kids are a little too free sometimes."

I didn't bother to respond. He had no idea how hard I tried to balance their constitutional rights with enough good sense that I wouldn't lose my job. He had no idea what it was like when the computer crashed the day we were supposed to go to press. We rebuilt the center spread layout from scratch and pleaded with the publisher to extend the deadline. Then the computer crashed again and we lost the same pages. I pleaded for another extension. Finally I stomped into the school's computer center and asked if someone had been fiddling with the network server.

"We just got it serviced," Evie Barclay, the librarian, told me. "Why, you having trouble?"

I explained what had been happening with the paper.

"You know," the librarian said, "the technician mentioned something about shifting around partitions to change the available storage space. You think that could have anything to do with your problems?"

You think? Duh! My father had no clue how angry Mr. Van Teasel was about the dress code story, despite the fact that Tameka had quoted more people who supported it than those who didn't. Advising the school paper was a pain, but I believed in giving kids a voice and in teaching them the importance of a free press in a democracy. And nothing else taught them to write like having a real audience, so I served as adviser even though I knew I would swallow half a dozen antacids with my dinner and would lay awake half the night thinking of clever comebacks, all those things I could have said to Mr. Van Teasel.

The crowd groaned as the other team stole the ball from us yet again.

"You notice Graham acting a little different these days?" Woodson asked.

His question tickled a vague uneasiness. Nothing specific. Nothing I could name. "Why, have you?"

"I don't know. Seems a little distant or something. Probably just normal growing up."

"Yeah, he's changing, that's for sure." The freshman year could be a hard adjustment for kids, but since Graham's grades were stellar, I figured he must be on the right track. Now that Woodson mentioned his concern, I wasn't so certain. Maybe we were both feeling old ourselves as we watched Graham grow so much taller than either of us. It didn't help that it had become hard to have a conversation with him. Graham navigated a world unfamiliar to us. He knew how to text message. How to download music to an iPod and watch videos on YouTube. Knew which candidates led the competition on *American Idol*.

Claymore took a penalty kick and missed. Mercifully, the game ended, 0-4.

"I think I'll stick around and have a talk with that Freeman kid," Woodson said.

I could imagine Quinn's humiliation. "You'll do no such thing."

"Then you should. Someone needs to straighten him out about candy league ball, what it's for." He grinned. "Candy league coach.

That suits Freeman. He's definitely a candy."

For once Woodson and I sort of agreed. Freeman was candy, all right: eye candy.

As I led Quinn to our SUV, Russ Freeman waved and flashed perfect teeth, a friendly smile. I wished I had the courage to ask him to have a cup of coffee, and we could talk about Quinn getting some playing time and maybe I'd find out why his wife left him. Not that I'm nosy, but it's important to know the people your kids spend time with, right? As if I had time for coffee! I had two mountains to move this evening. A giant pile of ungraded papers and huge clumps of dog hair that were accumulating behind doors, under barstools, and beneath the kitchen cabinets.

Fourteen

I hadn't been able to reach Woodson by phone for several days, so we made the ten-minute drive outside the city limits to the house where I'd grown up. We left behind the neatly manicured yards, sidewalks, street lamps, and fire hydrants of Alderson and passed into expanses of wiregrass and longleaf pine broken by occasional turkey oaks, nutalls, dogwoods, and hickories. As we drove up the sparsely graveled road to my father's, I frowned as I spotted delicate sprays of chickweed and purple plumes of rattlesnake weed twining through the azaleas my mother had been so proud of. Several bags of garbage were stacked one on top of the other in the backyard, the bottom ones torn into by stray dogs or raccoons.

In the kitchen, food-crusted dishes and dirty glasses sat on the counter. The worst surprise of all was all the cookware piled high in the kitchen sink, pans with food blackened on the bottom, skillets scorched beyond salvation. My mind constructed my father's past few days. Drunk comes home needing to eat. Slops food into a pan. Turns electric burner on. Passes out. Food cooks all night, maybe well into the next day, until charcoal residue is all that remains. Woodson was lucky he hadn't turned himself into charcoal too.

"Holy cow!" Quinn said. "You'd whip our butts if we left the kitchen looking like this!"

He was right.

"Grandpa?" Graham called out. He turned to me. "Didn't you tell him we were coming this afternoon?"

I had tried. He hadn't answered the phone or returned my messages.

Graham went to the foot of the stairs. "Grandpa?" he yelled up.

Boards creaked. Something dropped. A book? A shoe? Finally he answered. "Hang on. Be right down."

When he appeared, unshaven and bleary-eyed, he asked what time it was and seemed surprised to learn it was quarter after one. "Why aren't you in school? You playing hooky?"

Graham laughed uneasily. "It's Sunday, Grandpa."

"We brought you some sausage from the General Store," Quinn said.

"And eggs," Graham added.

"I'm going to make us all breakfast for lunch," I said. First there were all those dishes to wash up. "Why don't you boys help Grandpa pull weeds and carry that trash out to the dumpster while I work in the kitchen?"

Quinn banged out the screen door and then thoughtfully turned around to hold it open for Woodson. "You okay, Grandpa? You don't look so good."

"Stomach's been bothering me," he said. "Antacids don't seem to help."

Neither did the alcohol. "You seen Dr. Roberts yet?" I asked.

"No. Maybe I should."

Lord, he must be feeling bad. "I'll make an appointment for you."

"I can make my own appointment." He shambled down the steps. The screen door slammed.

"Better do it right away," I called out. I didn't care if I sounded like a nag who wanted the last word.

With steel wool, I tackled the pans. I chucked three into the trash—too far gone to save.

Fifteen

S tanding in the parking lot, my son's dark eyes traveled along the road fronting the Sports Complex, flicked to his Harry Potter watch, and returned to Donnie Marcinek's robot. I wanted to warn him: Don't get your hopes up, Quinn. Don't count on your grandpa for anything and you won't be disappointed. As a child, I learned the hard way when he didn't show up for swim meets or my National Honor Society induction. Even worse, on my wedding day he arrived straight from Big Fred's Bar and Grill and I wanted to die on the spot. I had grown calluses all over as far as Woodson Trask was concerned. Thought he couldn't hurt me anymore. Wasn't true. Watching my son worry that his grandpa would break his promise hurt more than anything else Woodson had ever done to me.

Donnie's plastic sphere approached a rock on the asphalt and navigated around it. The scout troop had laid out an obstacle course on the basketball court, one the robot was managing with ease. Parents applauded, myself included, though my emotions bounced so fast between empathy for my son and anger at my father I felt dizzy. For months, Quinn had soldered and wired and tested and tinkered with his robot to earn his merit badge in electronics. Since he and Donnie were the only boys in their scout troop to attempt such complicated projects, they were rivals of a sort, each hoping to outperform the other today. Part of the reason Quinn pursued robotics so enthusiastically was that his grandfather had never met a circuit board or relay switch he didn't like. I knew Quinn was setting himself up for disappointment but I didn't know how to stop it. He'd already withstood more in the last two years than any eleven year old should have to: the deaths of his father and grandmother and his best friend moving across the country to Colorado. I wanted to build a cocoon around him and deliver him intact to adulthood.

The robot wound its way around a branch, a Matchbox car, a deck of playing cards—all part of the obstacle course. For a finale, Donnie stepped in front of the robot, causing it to turn away each time he moved.

We applauded again. Graham left the cluster of teens—three older brothers and sisters who'd come to watch—and sidled up to me.

"Where's Grandpa?" he asked, his voice low, perhaps hoping the mothers I was standing with wouldn't hear. "Wasn't he supposed to be here?"

"Said he would be." I did my best not to bad-mouth Woodson to the boys. Controlling my tone was not as easy.

Quinn took one last look around, a slight drawing together of the eyebrows and a tugging on the right ear, the only outward signs anything was wrong. He lifted his robotic car out of its protective case. The clear plastic vehicle glinted in the sun, its fenders split by lightning-shaped decals. He had decided not to paint it so you could observe the internal mechanics. A black solar panel jutted above the roof, detracting from the sleek lines of the body. The solar-power option had been my idea. I convinced him to study renewable energy sources that might steer us away from total planet destruction. Graham wouldn't have listened to me, being embarrassed and annoyed by my existence, but Quinn hadn't pushed me away—yet.

Quinn made the car roll forward on its tractor treads. After he executed a series of commands, he removed the solar panel. Woodson arrived just in time to watch Quinn stow it away.

"Hey, Grandpa!" Graham said.

"Hey, yourself." He punched Graham's shoulder. "How'd an ugly old cuss like me get such a good-looking grandson?"

Graham punched him back. "I must have lucked out and gotten Dad's genes."

A joke, but it was true. He replicated his father from blonde hair to eyes the color of rain, sometimes blue, sometimes gray. At five foot ten, Graham was well on the way to duplicating his father's athletic build too. Mary Wade Marcinek, Donnie's sister, wiggled her index finger and Graham jumped back to his friends.

"Sorry I'm late," Woodson said. "Got called out on a job."

His breath and even his skin gave off that sour-sweet smell produced by fermented grain. I wanted to rip out his scraggly whiskers, one by one. "Job at Big Fred's?" I asked.

"Nah." He tried to sound offended. "Had to repair a break over on Symonton Street. Ladies got to have their Oprah, you know."

"Um, hum." Big Fred's Bar and Grill was on Symonton, and Mr. Kelso should have known better than to send Woodson anywhere near the cable lines over there. Ever since I was a kid, I'd heard the story of how my father had won a bet over who knew all the words to "Danny Boy" and got to name the bar. Woodson must have been drunk when he thought it up because Fred Novak weighed 135 pounds dripping wet and he didn't even own a grill. The only decision you needed to make after you ordered your drink was how you wanted your peanuts: boiled or roasted. Or you could buy one of the pickled eggs Fred kept in a glass jar on the counter. The Lord only knew how old they were.

"Really, Miz School Marm, that's only Astring-o-sol you smell."

My lips clamped together, barely holding back a growl. "Does anyone ever buy that story?"

"It kills germs. Really, I poured it on a cut—want to see?" He pushed up his sleeve to reveal a scraped elbow. Looked like road rash.

"Did you fall down in Big Fred's parking lot?"

"I'm here now, aren't I?"

"Yeah, just in time to watch him pack it up."

To be fair, it wasn't quite over yet. The solar panel safely tucked away, Quinn demonstrated how his car also ran on battery back-up. He maneuvered the vehicle 360 degrees around the deck of cards. We all clapped. All but Woodson, who stuck two fingers in his mouth and nearly blew out our ears with his whistle. When Quinn saw his grandpa, his face broke into a smile.

Woodson grinned back, exposing the gap between his left cuspid and front tooth. In a fight at Big Fred's earlier this week, he'd lost an incisor. He was starting to look like one of those homeless guys who panhandle at the highway junctions in big cities like Tallahassee and Valdosta. The violence was something new, and I hoped it didn't become a habit. Until now, I'd only known him to throw a punch that once, years ago, at my brother.

Both Donnie and Quinn maintained solemn faces throughout the badge presentation, their excitement betrayed by subtle squirming and slight shifting of weight from one leg to the other. As soon as the handshakes ended, Quinn flung himself at his grandfather, who tussled my son's dark hair with tobacco-stained fingers.

Woodson gloated over top of the hug. I read his message loud and clear: *See, Miz School Marm, everything's okay.*

I turned my back on him.

Sixteen

I zipped home to let Dusty outside. My new diet—no lunch at all. By going home midday, I hoped I could prevent the puppy from messing all over the laundry room.

As soon as I opened the front door, the odor weakened my knees. I hesitated, not sure I wanted to see the damage. Ecstatic at the prospect of having company, Dusty launched himself repeatedly at the baby gate, yapping and wagging his entire body. Inside the laundry room, he had been having a party. Shreds of urine-soaked newspaper dotted the floor like confetti from the gate all the way to the door that led to the garage. He had pooped at least twice and left tiny brown paw prints all over the almond linoleum. The blanket left as a nest now was minus its binding, which dangled like satin kite strings along two sides. Nearby, a rawhide chewie drowned in a puddle. Dusty stood up, front paws propped against the gate. I reached down to pet him and he smiled with mouth and eyes and tail.

"You little stinker. It's a good thing you're so cute or you'd be out on the streets again. Whoever got rid of you knew what they were doing." I held him away from my good clothes and carried him outside. As soon as I set him down, I realized the front gate was ajar. Dusty scampered right to the sidewalk.

"Stop! Stay! Sit! Dusty, come back here!" If he ran into the street and a car hit him, I would never forgive myself.

At the curb he collided with C. Lodge Piscetelli.

"Whoa! You little scamp!" He scooped up the puppy and let him lick his nose.

"Look out. He's filthy. You should see what he did to the house."

He commiserated but tucked Dusty against his chest. "You're not usually home this time of day."

"No, I thought I might prevent a mess if I came home at lunch. No such luck. The laundry room is a disaster."

"Have you tried crate-training?" Lodge asked.

I had never heard of it. He offered to loan me a crate and a video on its use. "You sure it isn't cruel?"

"Not at all. To a dog, a crate is like having his own little cave. He feels safe there."

I trusted Lodge on canine matters. His ninety-pound Lab rode around in his van and behaved better than most kids. Even without a leash, the dog stayed right beside him.

"Don't you need it for your dog?"

"One leg of his wouldn't fit in it now. He has a bigger one these days. Nine o'clock sharp every night, Baxter heads for his crate. Loves it. The thing is, with a puppy you can only shut them in for their age in months plus two hours."

I sighed. "I'll still have to come home at lunch. We only have twenty-five minutes."

"Look," he said, "I could come over and let him out at noon. I mean, I work out of my house anyway, so it's no trouble. That is, if you wouldn't mind having me inside your home."

I hesitated only a second before he went on.

"Oh forget it, that's stupid of me. Of course you don't want some-one you don't know in your house, forget it, I don't know what I was thinking."

I laughed. "Only one way to resolve the problem. Get to know each other."

He set Dusty down.

"Come on in and I'll fix you a glass of tea and show you where he stays, but you'll have to excuse the mess."

"Just a minute." He commanded Dusty in a no-nonsense voice: "Potty, hurry up."

Darned if the dog didn't squat right then and there. Lodge and Jolene Baker shared "the voice" in common.

After work, I accompanied Dusty into the front yard. For the first time I came home to a clean house—no dog mess to deal with. The crate was a blessing. Eileen O'Halloran got out of her big Lincoln, her heels clicking across the sidewalk toward me, a plastic sack of grocer-ies dangling off each arm. I wondered if she'd be offended if I offered her some of my canvas grocery bags.

She leaned over the fence. "Couldn't help but notice you talking to our new neighbor at lunch today."

At first I wondered why Eileen would have been home at lunch—she taught school too—and then I remembered she now worked in administration at the Mason County Board of Education, so she got an hour off for lunch every day and could do what she pleased—which must include peering through her curtains at the neighbors.

She sniffed. "He hasn't been very friendly. I took him a batch of my Ranger cookies when he moved here, but he didn't invite me inside."

He hadn't invited me in either, but who said he had to? He'd certainly been helpful with Dusty and the flashlights. "He's friendly enough, but maybe a little shy."

"Piscetelli," she said. "What kind of name is that?"

"Italian, I guess."

She hung the grocery bags on my pickets as though she planned to stay and chat a while. "Not many Italians in Alderson. Wonder why he moved here. Did he say?"

I didn't like the criticism implied in her questions even though I'd wondered the same thing myself. The denizens of our street were educators, lawyers, and accountants. Family folks. Men with short haircuts who drove SUVs and women who carried small leather purses and kept potted geraniums on the porches. It was an odd location for a long-haired hippie with a van. What had made him move here?

"I didn't ask."

"What do you suppose the 'C' stands for?"

I wondered that, too. "I have no idea. Why don't you ask him next time you see him?"

Dusty hitched up to do his business beside the chrysanthemums lining the fence. I grabbed the pooper scooper and stood ready to snatch up the mess. He had a nasty habit of sniffing and tasting if I didn't act fast enough.

"Oh, it doesn't matter," she said. "I thought you might know since you're getting to know him so well. I mean, he gave you the puppy and all."

I corrected her misperception, explaining we found the dog in our yard. Eileen maintained she saw Mr. Piscetelli getting out of the van with the puppy. Honestly, she must be blind as a mole to confuse big old Baxter with teensy little Dusty. Obviously, Eileen was not a dog person. She withdrew quickly when I approached the fence with Dusty's mess to deposit it in the garbage can devoted to Dusty's business. Another $6.99 dog purchase. Leash and harness: $34.88. Poop scooper: $24.99. Toys: $15.99. Treats: $6.99. Vet bills: $169 and mounting. And that didn't count all the time I spent in the kitchen making him turkey-loaf dinners. He turned up his nose at kibble. No such thing as a free dog.

I laughed as he leapt after a small yellow butterfly—a sulfur—which danced out of his reach. When I picked him up, he kissed my nose.

Some things were priceless.

Graham and Quinn stood stiff as little soldiers, one on each side of me, surrounded by the smell of antiseptics and cleansers meant to chase away death. Hooked to a web of monitors and IVs, Woodson lay in a bed at Alderson Memorial Hospital. We could watch him through a pane of glass. The last time I'd been here, I stood in the very same place, and Dr. Roberts had told us there was nothing they could do for my mother, so the smells, powerful as they might be, weren't always enough.

The bleeding had stopped. That was the good news Dr. Roberts brought out of Woodson's room in ICU.

"An ulcer might not sound all that serious, but sooner or later we won't be able to stop the bleeding," he said. "It could happen the next time. It might not be until the time after, but this much we know— if your father continues to drink like this, he's going to kill himself."

Although I couldn't see their faces, I could feel the boys blanch. I squeezed their shoulders. Why hadn't I talked with them about their grandfather's alcoholism, prepared them better for this day?

I was the grown-up in charge here, but without my mother I didn't know what to do. Her wisdom had guided me through Graham's roseola and Quinn's stitches and David's sudden death. The only one available for advice was Dr. Roberts.

"What can we do? I encouraged my father to sign up for AA, but he refused."

"You can't do anything," he said. "It's not up to you."

That sounded like defeatism. "We can't just watch him die."

"That might be exactly what you have to do. He'll get out tomorrow, but after that—"

He trailed off, leaving the dire consequences to our imaginations.

"Maybe he doesn't care if he dies," Quinn said. "Maybe he misses Grandma so much he wants to be with her in heaven. We need to ask God to make him want to stay with us instead."

I hugged the little wise man to my side. This child was such a blessing, how could anyone want to leave him? I stared through the window at Woodson's pale shoulders and prayed. How could he not want to know what kind of men Quinn and Graham would become? *Life, Daddy, life. We cling to it because it is so wonderful—and so awful—and all we know.*

Seventeen

My stomach knotted up as soon as I got out of bed. By the time I had unlocked my classroom door and smelled chalk dust, I was nauseated. It had been the same every morning since the fight. I hated feeling this way about my job. I hated J.D. for making me feel this way, though I tried to push away that thought every time it threatened to surface. But it was a fact. I hated J.D.

During the next week, he stopped tapping on his desk when I asked him to. He was reading Ernest Gaines's *A Lesson Before Dying* with the rest of the class. I considered skipping the novel since the plot centered around a black school teacher visiting a relative on death row. Since J.D.'s mother murdered a man, I thought it might hit too close to home, but eliminating the only novel by a black author in the sophomore curriculum didn't seem like a good move. J.D.'s behavior improved to the point I began to hope the worst was behind us. One thing left me uncertain. His eyes filled with fun when he looked at his classmates, especially Marissa. When his eyes shifted to me, they hardened to black ice.

Miss Baker dashed to my doorway and called out a hello. "You see the headline this morning?"

I nodded. Superintendent Rice had to produce evidence that he had made an effort to find black teachers, that their scarcity wasn't due to biased hiring practices.

Miss Baker leaned closer until her nose was about two inches from mine. I took a step backward, enough to breathe again, though not so much, I hoped, to give offense. Her voice rumbled as she bore down on me. "It's worse than what the paper says. We have to submit curriculum guides and sample lesson plans to the court. I think they're looking to replace some white teachers with blacks."

My throat caught. I couldn't be fired—how would I support my boys? Just because I was white did they think I couldn't teach black children? Even as I was thinking of myself, part of my brain processed that blacks had been judged by skin rather than ability for years. Yet surely it wasn't true anymore. We had a multi-racial presidential candidate, for heaven's sake. Yet that didn't really change anything. Right across the hall, Francis Brown had written the word *picaninny* on the board. Hate still lurked under a veneer of politeness. Sometimes it seeped out. Even Jolene Baker herself had suggested life on the plantation had been a fine thing. Maybe that comment wasn't hate-inspired, but it indicated a stubborn blindness.

"Anyway," she continued, "you need to get one unit plan and ten daily plans to me by Friday. Make them your best."

When I finished laying out the materials I needed for the day and writing starter directions on the board, I fingered through my binder of lesson plans. I skimmed one, then another, finding something imperfect in each. I flipped and scanned and bit my lip, wondering what to choose, what would impress, what would keep me employed, what would make me less white. When the bell rang, I gave up and opened with a question about *A Lesson Before Dying*'s hero.

"I'm confoozled," J.D. said, earning laughs with his word choice. That J.D. could be a card, a real charmer. "Would you please explain why you think this teacher dude is the hero?"

"Grant qualifies as the protagonist because he loses faith in himself and in society, and in the end he changes into someone who accepts responsibility," I said. "He stops running away."

"Well, to me, Jefferson is the hero. He's the one falsely accused and put on death row."

"Jefferson is a hero of sorts. As I've mentioned before, Jefferson is a Christ figure in the novel. His life is sacrificed—"

The façade of charm shattered. "Sacrificed, shit—he's murdered and he ain't done nothing. Nothing. You don't like Jefferson 'cause he stupid. You like Grant 'cause he a school teacher who act all white."

The cursing, the belligerence, the grammar—none of these was going to make me lose my temper. "One of Grant's problems—"

Brian raised his hand but didn't wait for me. "Could I comment, Miz Culpepper? See, Grant restores some dignity to Jefferson, makes him realize he's not a hog like his lawyer says. Grant will live on after Jefferson is dead, remembering the lessons he learned from him. He will help change the black community in the future."

J.D. whispered something to Marissa and they giggled.

"What's so funny?" Brian asked.

"Nothing," J.D. said.

"No, what?"

"It's just—you and Grant, you alike." The whites of J.D.'s eyes grew enormous and he leered at Brian as he emphasized every syllable: "Or-e-o's."

My eyes flicked from one boy to the other, taking in J.D.'s sneer that dared Brian to do something, and Brian's clenched fists, those muscles taut, primed to respond.

"J.D.!" If my voice had been a hammer it would have nailed him to the wall. "Respect for others is our first classroom rule."

Ja'Neice chimed in, her chin thrust out, her head shaking. "Uh-unh, you don't have to take that, Brian baby, uh-unh, no way."

The situation was sliding out of control, until quiet little Shaniqua reached in front of her and gently laid a hand on Brian's arm.

"He's an asshole, Brian," she said, her voice barely a whisper. "He's not worth it. Don't let him provoke you into doing something that'll get you suspended."

J.D. laughed, wild-eyed. "Take a chill pill, everybody. I was just joking. Can't nobody take a joke?"

Brian turned his face away from J.D., his body still rigid with anger.

"Fifteen," I said to J.D.

J.D. slammed his fist on the desktop. "None a you can take a frigging joke."

"Thirty."

"Okay, okay, no problem. In the morning."

Gradually tension seeped from the room. I made a mental note right then to move Brian and J.D. apart.

When J.D. came to serve his detention, our eyes locked in cold recognition of mutual dislike. I couldn't help it. I felt what I felt.

With effort, I suppressed my antagonism. "How are you doing in your other classes?"

"Okay, I guess." He shrugged. "Having some trouble in biology."

"You have to pass all your major subjects to stay eligible for football. How about I get you a tutor for biology?" I knew a junior who whizzed through science and I thought she would do it.

He shrugged again. "I guess, yeah, that would be all right."

"I'll have Shonda call you and set up a convenient schedule."

I handed him his detention assignment: to tell me his life story and to keep writing the whole half hour. I can't tell it any better than he did, so here it is, grammar and spelling errors intact.

My Story

By J.D. Marshall

I know you don't like me, and don't take it personel, but I don't like you neither. You teachers are too much like the social work ladies. I'd like to see any one of you live my life. Ha. You wouldn't last a day. The last fosters I stayed with was the Johnsons. I live there for most of a year. You wouldn't last a day in that house, I can tell you that. That old woman mean as a rattlesnake and she fat like a pig cause she eat all the food and be stingy hogging it all for herself. She only keeps foster kids so she can get free food. There were four of us fosters in that house, all piled up in one bedroom like a stack of dirty laundrey. When she got mad at us for playing too loud or breaking one of those little glass clowns she collected, she locked us up in the basement. The dirt floor was damp and stunk like wet sneekers and there was only a peephole window, so dirty it didn't let in hardly any light. She so busy eating all the food she forget she'd left somebody down there until one of the others reminded her and hoped they wouldn't get beat for talking to her. You couldn't make no noise down there or scream or cry or she'd never open the door. Every time you yell let me out, she adds another day on to your punishment—that was her rule.

Spider Sims come next. I muled for Spiderman from time I was seven till I was ten. That's why he want a foster kid—free laber. We got along okay for a while. I could run real fast and

I was real good at hiding from the po-po. None ever did catch me. Then one day I saw these tennis shoes I really wanted in the window at the Foot Locker. I started to pinch a little off from every delivery and stored it away in my own little baggie until I had enough to sell myself. I was determined to buy me them shoes. When I wore them back at Spider's, he beat the crap out me and said I was nothing but a worthless little nigger and he'd kill me if I ever pulled a stunt like that again. Then he got busted. Went to jail his own self. Like my Mama.

There was a preacher once, but that didn't last too long. I couldn't stand all the rules he made. Church on Wednesday nights and practically all day on Sunday. About had a stroke every time I cussed, just like you. I had to get out of there.

Last place I stayed was with my Auntie in Atlanta. She kind of messed up, not quite right in the head, but I liked staying with her the best. Hot-Lanta is one cool town. I miss hanging with my crew, you know what I mean? Alderson's boring, man. Dead.

My Mama, she good to me, but she don't make much money. Not enough to take care of four kids, so I do what I can to help, you catch my drift? She good to me, but she don't like to talk. I ask her questions, but she don't want to tell about my daddy or the trial or the Big House. I can't remember nothing from those days because I was too little. She don't want to listen when we want to tell her what happened to us after she went away. What good it do to dwell in the past? she says. All is sunshine and freedom now, she says, so put those bad days behind us and trust in the Lord to show us the way. I'm not putting my trust in nobody. The Lord ain't done so good by us so far. My Mama, she trying hard, but like Tupac says, "for a woman it ain't easy trying to raise a man." Tupac, he's the greatest artist of our times. I think he still be alive somewhere.

Anyway, you teachers are like the social workers who dumped my sisters in one house and my brother in another and me in with the Spiderman. All these nice white ladies think they gonna make things better for you and then they go home to their nice big white houses and there soft white beds and don't wonder what happens after they drop you off like a sack

~~of~~ load of garbage. Had to be blind not to know. If anyone of them social ladies had gone down in that basement, they'd have knowed. Sometimes you could smell the piss and ~~shi~~ (sorry Mrs. Culpeper, I know how you hate cussing, so excuse me, excuse me, no more fifteens) all the way up in the living room. We didn't have no where to go except in the corner on that dirt floor. That River Jordan the preachers always talking about couldn't wash the stink out of that house.

You white ladies think you're so much better than us niggers because you blind. You don't see your kids the ones buying the smoke that keep me in nice tennis shoes. So I guess I should say thanks cause your nice white salary buys my clothes. Thanks for being blind.

Let's see. What else? Football. I like football. I like to run. That's when I feel really free, like my feet be going so fast I might just take off and leave this sorry little town behind. I'm going to college, UGA I hope, and then I'm gonna turn pro soon as I can. Why wait until I graduate and take a chance on getting injured? My Mama, she want me to graduate though. She be begging me all the time to pay attention in school, she say education is the key, but hey, I want the bling-bling. Football, that's my ticket. Run, J.D., run. (Joke from Forrest Gump. I like that movie though I like Lawrence Martin the best, he one crazy fool.)

"It's Me against the World baby, Me against the World, I got nothin' ta lose, It's Me against the World." That's my man Tupac, and I guess he says it all. I really think he be alive somewhere. And my half hour better be up cause I'm about to click.

When I finished reading J.D.'s story, I folded it in half, overcome by a crushing pressure, like stones heaped upon my chest and throat. All children should be born into homes with two parents who love and nurture them, and who love and nurture each other. In an ideal world, that's how it would be.

Unfolding the paper, I re-read the beginning with shame. I wished I could say he was wrong about me, that I did like him. I should have loved him—I should have. I pitied him, yes, but I didn't feel the love

I felt for my other students. It was easy to love the Brians and Marissas and Shaniquas, kids who were trying. It was nearly impossible to love a kid whose outlook and values struck me as completely alien.

I didn't think much of the state's required Moment of Silence. Not that I would have objected if students would actually meditate or pray for a minute, or even sit quietly. I rarely used the minute to reflect on the day, as the voice on the intercom asked us to. Instead I comforted whoever chose that moment to run wild-eyed to my desk begging to call home because the American History paper he'd spent all weekend working on lay on the breakfast table. Or I shushed the girls who couldn't stop giggling or threatened bodily harm to the boys sending up a fleet of paper airplanes if they didn't quit. But right then I vowed to change. Every morning for the rest of the year during the required Moment of Silence I would repeat my desire to love this child. I would ask God to set this child and me on a better path. If I prayed long enough and hard enough, maybe the words would accumulate in God's ear like a wad of wax.

"I'm going to tell her if you don't." That was Tessa's New Jersey voice I heard all the way outside the lounge. "I think the boy suspects the truth."

Liz responded with her soft, Southern drawl as I opened the door. "No, you can't. Her father hasn't told her, and I've known all these years and haven't breathed a word."

Tessa persisted. "If she finds out from someone else, it'll be worse."

I deposited my lunch sack on the table. "What'll be worse?"

Liz and Tessa looked at each other. Liz picked up an apple. The skin of her palm was lighter than the skin on Tessa's arm. How odd, I thought, that whole cultures got built around those minute differences. The insanity of it!

Tessa took a bite of a sandwich. Mustard dripped from one side and I handed her a napkin. She didn't make eye contact. I got the creepy feeling they had been talking about me.

Eighteen

F riday's football game felt like Christmas morning, packed full of surprises. Brian Jones trotted over in his band uniform, trumpet clutched in his hand, to tell me he had asked Marissa Powell to the Homecoming dance and she said yes. The sophomore class chose Marissa as a princess, so Brian would escort her during halftime ceremonies in addition to taking her to the dance. He could barely stand up straight, he was that giddy.

The second surprise was when Quinn asked if it would be okay if he sat with Donnie Marcinek. I watched them go off together, Donnie juggling a box of sugared popcorn, an extra large cola, and a hot dog. After they finished building their robots, they decided to collaborate instead of compete, so Quinn found himself a new best friend. Donnie owned an upscale electronic keyboard and joined Graham's yet-unnamed band. A child prodigy, Donnie had begun piano lessons when he was four. Last Saturday when Donnie took a bathroom break, I zipped into the garage and ran through one piece with the band. Sure, it qualified as showing off, but so what? I could still play. My daddy had taught me well.

My eyes roamed the student section of the bleachers until I located Donnie's sister, Mary Wade, sitting with the most popular freshman girls. She had come by Saturday, too, and added her vocals to the Kenny Chesney piece they were working on. She hung on every word Graham said as if it were worthy of committing to memory. Her flirtation repertoire included raking fake fingernails through a thick mass of caramel curls, twisting her torso back and forth at the waist, and emitting an occasional high-pitched giggle with one hand poised coyly at her mouth. Since Graham let her hang around, I guess he didn't share my view that she was even more annoying than a Barbie doll. At least Barbie didn't squeal.

I didn't spot Tessa's son Noah in the football crowd. Noah added his guitar to the band's mix. Noah's hair hung a little bit too long and stringy for my taste, but he thanked me for letting him come over. I took an instant liking to him. Politeness goes a long way. Betsy Mulharin thought Noah discourteous because he didn't say "ma'am" when he addressed her, but I explained kids from up North didn't mean to be rude. Over the years, transfer students taught me that in Northern states a kid would be laughed out of class if he addressed adults as "ma'am." Betsy was a newbie, so she couldn't be expected to have known that.

Noah preferred alternative to country, and so the group tried out a few pieces he knew from his days with a band up in Ohio. As the group grew, it struggled to find its voice.

I watched Quinn and Donnie clamber up to a section of bleachers where a young crowd hung out, Quinn topping Donnie's height by two inches. He was growing so fast. Maybe he wouldn't end up being a shorty like me after all, though he'd clearly inherited my dark coloring.

In the first quarter, Graham kicked two field goals, a twenty-six yarder and a forty-yarder. Years of soccer made him very accurate. J.D. turned in an attention-getting performance, too, with three passes caught for sixty-five yards. He also collected two fifteen-yard penalties for personal fouls when he got into shoving and trash-talking competitions with his defender. Coach Haswell kept having to spit out his chew so he could chew on J.D. instead. Coach must have worried he'd run out of tobacco because in the second quarter he benched J.D. for a spell.

At halftime I stood up to search the crowd again for my father. He had promised Graham he would be here to watch the game. Since his stay in the hospital, he had remained sober. I hoped his absence didn't mean a relapse. No sign of my father, but I spotted Roosevelt Pitts, David's former partner, climbing the bleachers in my direction.

At that moment my third surprise of the evening occurred when the completely gorgeous Russ Freeman dropped into the seat vacated by Quinn. I could hardly suppress the thrill when he wanted to talk to me—until I learned what he wanted to talk about.

"Heard about the trouble you had with that Marshall kid."

Bill Barnes, sitting on my left, overheard the name Marshall and sensed an opportunity to display his boosterism. "Did you know that kid runs the 40 in 42? Mark my words, he'll play college ball."

Russ didn't smile. "He's fast because he has practice running from the law. Heard he assaulted a police officer up in Atlanta. Put him in the hospital."

My stomach heaved.

"You shouldn't believe every rumor you hear," Bill said. "That boy has some real talent."

I stood up to hug Roosevelt, who had just arrived. How he had managed to remain single at thirty was a mystery to me. Liz said plenty of young women at her church tried to land him, but he dodged commitment the way J.D. dodged defenders on the field.

Roosevelt verified what Russ had told me. "It's not a rumor, it's true. I wanted to make sure you knew. It would be best if you got him transferred out of your class."

The selfish part of me agreed, but the vain side insisted I could cope with J.D. as well as anyone else. Probably better.

"I'm not worried. He'll soon succumb to my personal charm and extraordinary teaching skills. No student is strong enough to resist." He'd succumb or I would beat the crap out of him.

"You have any more trouble, you call me, you hear? I'll take care of him." He spoke so softly with a slight rasp that if you didn't know him you might mistake those gentle ways for weakness. That would be a mistake.

Sunday morning before church I vacuumed, dusted, and cleaned the bathrooms while Quinn folded laundry. Defying my first predictions that Dusty might be helpful by licking up crumbs, the little beastie left a trail everywhere he went. Fur clumped behind doorways, under barstools, and in corners. It became commonplace to open the refrigerator and find a strand of dog hair clinging to the produce drawer or the side of a ketchup bottle. Despite my brushing enough from his coat every night to stuff a pillow, he continued to shed. By even my most conservative estimates, he should have been bald three times over by now.

Graham surprised me by volunteering to wash the Ford Escape. I ventured to guess he was envisioning his own hands on the wheel next year. He nagged Quinn and me while he disposed of used French fry bags and candy wrappers. "From now on, for crying out loud, shake off your shoes before you get in the car. Just look at these floor mats."

After church, I slid a pot roast in the oven and found my mother's recipe for egg noodles tucked inside the binder of my *Better Homes* cookbook. She had penciled it onto an envelope flap for me. I smiled when I came to the instruction to "fill an egg shell twice with water and add to flour." Only my mother! I rolled and cut the noodles and set them to dry on a cutting board. Woodson would be pleased—this meal was one of his favorites. He hadn't eaten half right since Mama died. Though I told him he was always welcome at our table, Sunday afternoons were about the only time he took me up on my offer of hot meals.

I curled up on the couch with vocabulary quizzes, leaving the front door open to enjoy the breeze through the screen. The boys finished their chores and took Dusty into the yard for training. The clever little dog already had mastered "sit," "come," "stay," and "give me five."

"Goober, stop giving him a treat every time he sits," Graham said.

"Why? You do it."

"Do not. The training book says he's only supposed to get a treat occasionally. Make him do two or three tricks before you reward him."

Quinn was trying to teach Dusty to fetch a little velour frog, but so far he would only flop down and chew it.

"Let me try, Goober." Graham snatched the frog away.

"Give it back!"

Graham dangled the frog over his head.

"It's my frog. I bought it for him." Quinn batted his hands at the toy. "Give it back, Boogerhead!"

"Oooo—the little dweeb has really insulted me now."

"Mom, make him give me the frog back."

"Oooo—the little baby's going to get his mommy to help him."

Without moving off the couch, I hollered, "Stop monkeying around, you two, or I'm going to send both of you to your rooms."

Graham threw the frog across the lawn. "I don't want it anyway."

Through the window I saw C. Lodge Piscetelli cross the street and wrap his hands around two pickets on our fence. The boys stopped quarreling. I let the screen door screech shut behind me as I went out to offer thanks for his help with Dusty.

"No problem," he said. "I enjoy playing with him. The reason I'm here is I have an old Bose amplifier and set of speakers I'm not using anymore—used to be in a band myself—and I thought your boys might like to have them, but I wanted to ask your permission."

First the crate, and now the music equipment—such a generous man. If only he weren't a lawyer for the other side, I could really like him. I supposed if the boys wanted his old stuff—and they seemed quite excited by the possibility—I didn't mind. He refused my offer to pay for his equipment.

Woodson's Chevy truck, a relic from the '80s, rumbled up in front of the house. Hadn't looked good for years, and looked even worse since he'd wrecked it.

"When you going to trade that rust bucket in and get a decent truck?" I asked.

"What for?" He tossed his cigarette butt onto the curb. "It's just getting broken in real good. Until a truck is nicked up a little, a man's afraid to use it for what it's made for."

Quinn jumped off the porch to hug his grandfather and relieve him of the customary sack of Sunday donuts. Graham, with the new-found reserve of a fourteen year old, shook Woodson's hand instead. When, I wondered, had this change occurred? Lately I hadn't been observant enough. Too many details slipped under my radar. After the handshake, Graham discarded the formality and scarfed down a donut.

"Where were you last night?" I asked.

"Sorry," Woodson said. "My stomach was acting up again. Took some medicine and went to bed."

I hoped it was true. The thought of becoming an orphan scared me more than I wanted to admit.

"Well, who's this?" Woodson eyed Mr. Piscetelli from his graying braid to well-worn jeans. Lodge introduced himself as our neighbor and said he was just leaving.

Woodson grinned. "What, with that great pot roast in the oven? No way. Molly, where's your manners—invite this fellow to stay to Sunday supper."

I stumbled through an invitation. Should have thought of it myself.

The men hauled over the amplifier and speakers and helped the boys set them up in the garage. It turned out to be a glorious fall day, a smattering of cirrus clouds floating on a sky as blue as Graham's eyes, the air crisp enough to need a long-sleeved shirt. Through the screen door I could hear Woodson and Lodge on the porch talking fiber optic cable, DSL, portals, and Linux. Woodson's knowledge of electronics meshed well with Lodge's hobby. I liked to think I was tech savvy, but their conversation showed me how little I knew. Graham stayed in the garage, fiddling with the new equipment. The computer talk drew Quinn outside. Since he built his robot, his interest in technology had intensified. Lodge and Woodson patiently answered all Quinn's questions about processors and motherboards. I boiled the noodles in beef broth and went outside to call them in.

"Look," Lodge said to Quinn, "if you really want to understand this stuff, you should come over to my house some afternoon and help me build a computer. It's the best way to learn."

Woodson expressed his approval. I worried Quinn would turn into a pest.

"No way, your kids have terrific manners," Lodge said.

Woodson beamed as if he were personally responsible for their merits. "They do, don't they? Not like some kids. Molly tell you what this boy in her class called her?"

My father would have recounted every nasty word J.D. whipped out if not for my suggestion that maybe they were words that he shouldn't repeat in front of the boys and maybe he shouldn't say them at all, let alone on a Sunday. I conveniently ignored that I had repeated them to him or he wouldn't have known about them.

"J.D.'s had a hard life," I said.

I leaned away from Woodson's snarly exposure of yellowed teeth, afraid spit might accompany his words.

"That's no excuse for what he called you or for assaulting a police officer. Crap happens to everybody. You either wipe it off and go on, or you wallow in it. Your choice."

So my father had heard about the assault. Probably everyone in town knew by now. With a chill, I remembered Roosevelt's warning "You have any more trouble with him, you call me, you hear? I'll take care of him."

I hoped I never had to make that call.

Nineteen

J.D. wasn't the one who caused trouble. At least, not right away. Vashawn and I had experienced a few minor skirmishes before, nothing serious. I would get a little aggravated because he chattered during a lecture and he would ignore the stern look I sent his way, so I would have to stop giving directions to the class in order to correct him. His mouth would curl with irritation when I interrupted his discussion, which he obviously held in higher esteem than learning poetry terminology or examining the layout of the Globe theater. Then on Tuesday during my demonstration of how they should structure a PowerPoint on novel characters, Vashawn got up from his seat. I asked him to sit back down.

"I'm fixing to." He walked over to J.D.'s desk, handed him a paper, and leaned over, whispering.

"Now!"

"Just chill. I need to take care of some business."

I speared him with a look. "Do you expect the whole class to stop and wait for you?"

"Sure, why not?" That bought him a few nervous giggles.

"Sit down."

He ignored me, continuing to whisper to J.D.

"Sit!"

This time he reared up to full height. "Now that's bootleg—you can't talk to me like that!"

"Yeah, she can," J.D. said. "She don't like black kids."

"You stay out of it, J.D." I turned my attention back to Vashawn. "Look, I'm asking you to do the simplest thing: sit down."

"And I said 'in a minute.' This is important, and you got no call to disrespect me."

"Do you want me to write an office discipline referral?"

"Do what you have to do."

Looking back, I could see there might have been better ways to handle him, but my temper got the best of me.

In the lounge, discipline dominated our lunchtime chatter, and my esophageal sphincter put the squeeze on me big time. I graduated from antacids to acid blockers. Proton pump inhibitors. My colleagues vented their troubles with a handful of black students, a direct result of the lawsuit. In their homes and churches these kids heard charges of black students singled out for behavior tolerated in white kids. Whether true or not, the statements took on a life of their own as people repeated them until they seemed like truth. What kid can't think of a time when a sibling got away with something that his parents had punished him for, no matter how fair they tried to be? As students searched through their inventories of grievances, of course they could think of someone who did the exact same thing and didn't get caught (though the teacher must have heard him or seen him). Resentment rose as these allegations circulated through the community.

Shaniqua and Brian came by my room after school together. "We know how hard you work for us," Brian said. "We just wanted you to know we appreciate it. Not all of us support this lawsuit."

"That's right." Shaniqua even said it loud enough for me to hear the first time.

Liz stopped coming to the lounge for lunch. When I stuck my head in her door to ask if she was all right, she said yes, that a backlog of papers kept her at her desk. I knew it was a lie. She felt uncomfortable with all the talk. The controversy placed her in the sticky middle, being both black and a teacher. But a lot of the laughter left our lunch table along with her. I imagined myself going into her room and bridging the chasm that divided us. I would ask her straight out if she thought the lawsuit had merit. She didn't really think I would treat a black child differently, did she? I didn't. I wouldn't ever. Not deliberately. But what if the differences were so subtle I didn't even realize I was doing it? Did I call on whites more often? Praise them more? Use a different tone of voice? I didn't think so, but I wasn't sure of anything anymore.

At least I should march in there and tell her she would always be my friend, that we had gone through new teacher orientation together, taken an interest in each other's kids, and baked pies and hams for each other when grief had laid us so low we weren't sure we'd rise back up again. She had been there for me when David and my mother died. I tried to do the same when the grandmother who'd raised her passed and when a car accident took her brother and his children. Those bonds cemented us together.

That's what I should have gone in there and said. I was a coward. In a few days I would put a miss-you card in her office mailbox and hope Hallmark could say what I couldn't.

Our young substitute Lauryl Moore came in at lunch with her blouse torn. She stood in front of us with a shattered expression I'd never seen on her face before. A black girl had grabbed her by the neck and tried to choke her.

Lauryl's voice wavered as she spoke. "All I did was ask her to sit down before the tardy bell rang." Two boys had to pull the girl off. "When I went to the office with the girl, she claimed I hit her. Mr. Van Teasel sent her home for the day, but he said he couldn't do anything else about it. He said he didn't believe her, but it was one person's word against another's. So I told him he could find someone else to cover Mrs. Yost's afternoon classes. I'm outta here."

I pushed my chair away from the table and went to her, putting my arm around her shoulders to show support and affection. "Honey, don't give up. It's this lawsuit. He's scared to do anything that might stir up more trouble."

She sniffled back tears. "No, I'm through with teaching. I'm going into human relations. It will only take me one extra semester to finish up my degree. But I didn't want to leave without saying good-bye to all of you."

I patted her shoulder and returned to my lunch table. I didn't blame her for giving up, but what would happen to our children if all the Lauryls in the world gave up?

Before Lauryl left, she stood in front of Miss Baker. "I wanted to be respected, the way everyone respects you, but I can see now teaching's not for me. Those kids didn't have any respect for me at all."

Her declaration stung a little. It was my room Lauryl had stopped by to visit every Christmas vacation since she'd left for college, but it was Miss Baker she chose as a role model.

Mrs. Baker wished her good luck. "I'm sure you'll be a great success in the human relations department of some corporation, and you'll make a lot more money than you could as a teacher."

When Lauryl closed the door behind her, Miss Baker lifted her chin. "I could have told you that girl wasn't cut out to be a teacher. Not enough backbone."

Though I disagreed, I didn't say anything. My colleagues and I needed some cheering up, so I told what I considered a funny story about Dusty. I had let him out after a bath and blow dry. Half an hour later he trotted back inside wearing a look of total satisfaction.

"What is that smell?" Quinn asked.

I checked the garbage can. Not the source. Not the bathroom. Not the kitchen sink. Not the sewer lines or drains or potato bin. Quinn sniffed out the problem. Dusty. "Yew. What's in his mane?"

I reached my fingers down and raked them through the still damp fur. Something slimy slid off on my fingers. I brought my hand closer to my face, then shook my fingers trying to release the mess. "Yuk! Dead worms!"

Dusty wagged his tail, delighted at all the attention. I had to plop him in the utility sink a second time for a dousing with oatmeal shampoo.

Tessa laughed at my story, and I thought again how infectious her laugh was, how real.

"And he smelled so sweet, like a baby after his bath, what'd he want to go and ruin it for?" A rhetorical question—I didn't expect a response.

Miss Baker didn't crack a smile. "There must be nothing worse in the world for a dog than to smell all perfumed. They probably consider it animal abuse."

My eyes filled with tears. I wanted to tell Miss Baker as long as a dog wanted to share my house and my couch, Eau de Dead Worm was unacceptable cologne. I wanted to tell her that sometimes she could be a pompous ass, but I held my tongue. June Trask raised me to be polite and respectful, especially to my teachers. Sometimes I wished I could be more like Woodson.

A vague sense of uneasiness tightened my throat. A panicked feeling that was occurring more frequently at unpredictable moments. The year was slipping away and my classes hadn't achieved enough. One thing after another chipped away precious minutes of class time, particularly in first period. Voting for Homecoming princesses, random dress code checks, a disaster preparedness drill, morning announcements. On top of all that, every Friday Mr. Van Teasel required students to take a ten-question quiz on whatever state graduation test objectives the week's lessons focused on. I could understand Mr. Van Teasel's goal of improving test scores and getting AHS off the list of failed schools, but even these quizzes snipped away at instruction time. I shook off my anxiety and scanned the room as I prepared to present one of my favorite lessons.

Ja'Neice looked sporty in a new turquoise dress. I pulled her out of her chair and into the hallway. On top of her dress, I layered on an old cardigan and overcoat and had her pull on a pair of Graham's hunting boots. I wrapped a black plastic garbage bag around her head, handed her some old newspapers, and made sure she knew her cues.

"We're going to dramatize Lucille Clifton's poem, 'Miss Rosie.' When I recite the lines 'Used to be the best looking gal in Georgia/ used to be called the Georgia Rose,' you fling aside the bag woman get-up and vamp a little." I planted my left hand on my hip, wiggled, and made a foolish attempt to look sexy. "Got it?"

Back in the classroom, we pulled two desks together as a makeshift bed. Ja'Neice lay down and pulled the newspapers over her body. I sat beside her in a chair. When her classmates hooted at her, she stuck her tongue out. I quieted them and began to recite Clifton's beautiful words. They told the story of someone who descended into mental illness to become a "wet brown bag of a woman." All eyes were on Ja'Neice and me, spellbound. When I read the last lines—"I stand up through your destruction, I stand up!"—I sprang out of my seat with my fist raised overhead to demonstrate the poet's defiance against homelessness. My eyes followed my fist and came to rest on the black hole over Ja'Neice's head. The custodians still hadn't replaced the ceiling tile.

In that dark space something moved. At first I convinced myself it must be an illusion. Then two eyes gleamed and dipped out of the hole. I screeched and pushed Ja'Neice out of the way. The boa eased his head from the ceiling, then slithered until his spotted body dangled half in, half out. By the time the snake dropped to the floor, I had high-tailed it to the hallway, hands cradled over my head. I plunged through a dozen like-minded girls, all trying to get to the hallway first. Drawn by the shrieks, students poured into the hall from other classes.

Brian and Orville laughed at us. Orville picked up the snake.

"Gosh, Miz Culpepper," Brian called out, "it's only Hairy."

"We'll take him back to Miz Powell," Orville said. "She's been worried sick about him."

The girls and I backed farther out of the way as they came through the door. I shivered. Deep breaths, deep breaths, I told myself.

"We're all fine," I assured Miss Baker, who emerged from the quiet of her room to find the cause of the commotion. She never would have run screaming from Hairy. Hairy would have run screaming from her.

"You need to straighten your hair, dear," she said. "It's come loose from your ponytail."

Strictly speaking, it wasn't a ponytail. Ever since David died, I'd worn my hair pulled back at the nape of my neck. The simple style saved time and money. I trimmed my own bangs and skipped the beauty parlor. I re-fastened my hair and tried to regain some semblance of dignity, of being in charge.

"Wash your hands afterwards," I called to Brian and Orville. "Snakes carry diseases."

Orville denied it, but I insisted I had read it somewhere. "Salmonella or something like that." I urged everyone back into their seats. Enough was enough. The assistant principal had to put in replacement tiles, even if he had to pay full price. If he refused, I would buy them myself after school. Hairy must have been the reason we hadn't heard birds overhead for the past week.

"Now back to 'Miss Rosie.'"

"Miz Culpepper, you got to be kidding," Ja'Neice said. Her turquoise dress hung askew at the neckline.

"Class time is precious. We've spent enough time off task already," I said. "Now, where were we?"

"I was standing right beside you when you shoved me so you could run out the door first," she said.

"I pushed you so the snake wouldn't fall on you."

"Yeah, right!" Ceci said.

I didn't like her tone.

"Come on, give us a break," Ja'Neice said. "No one can talk about 'Miss Rosie' right now. We can't think about nothing but that snake."

"Anything but that snake."

"Whatever. I know I'm going to have nightmares."

Shaniqua nodded. "I'm saying!"

Me too. Miz Liz and I were going to have a little talk about snake security measures.

That panicky feeling gripped me again. I couldn't let this poem fade away without discussion. They could learn so much from it—understanding and awareness far beyond how to answer standardized test questions. I heard J.D. snicker to Orville did he see Miz Culpepper's face when she ran out of the room. J.D. laughed so hard he couldn't sit up straight.

"All right, that's enough. Class time is precious. We're going to answer the questions on the board about the poem together and you will turn in the responses at the end of the period. An easy hundred."

After a few grumbles, the class settled down and we discussed the first two questions. When we came to the next question, I shared a story about a college friend.

"I knew her as a normal girl, beautiful, a classy dresser, who got A's in her classes. She went to dances and ball games."

J.D. tapped out a rhythm on his desk. I kept talking about my friend, how something in her mind broke. "She dropped out of school and became a street person."

J.D.'s tapping became louder and he muttered something unintelligible.

"Two years later I saw my friend walking down the shoulder of a highway on a hot summer day, talking to herself, shaking her head. She wore a long wool coat." J.D. continued to tap. I walked by his desk and checked his paper. Blank.

"J.D., you need to answer the questions."

He ignored me and kept on tapping.

"Please stop that." No response. My jaw tightened. "Please step into the hallway so the rest of us can finish these questions before the bell rings."

His fingers stilled on the desktop. His eyes narrowed. "How'd you like to come in some morning and find a snake in your desk drawer?

Would that make you crazy?"

"That isn't funny."

"You see me laughing? You think you know everything, but what do you know about crazy anyway?" He left the room.

We finished my list of questions, but my heart wasn't in it. While I listened to student responses and nudged them in the right direction, I filled out a detention slip giving J.D. another fifteen minutes. What had set him off this time? Something Tessa had told me buzzed in my brain. Something J.D. had written about. The aunt J.D. stayed with who might have been mentally ill. Was that it? How was I supposed to avoid all the subjects that might trigger his explosions?

After that, J.D. began to ask questions. He took great care to appear interested in learning. I distributed a detailed example of how to organize the paragraphs for the graduation writing test. After hearing a five-minute explanation of the process, J.D. raised his hand, wanting to know why the first paragraph needed to state a thesis.

"Writers need to state the main idea early for readers."

"Why? It ruins suspense."

I paraphrased my explanation.

"I don't see why it needs to be in the first paragraph," he said.

I paraphrased a page from the June Trask Child-Rearing Manual. "Because the State Department of Education says so."

Other days questions arose over why I made them double space papers, what I meant by supporting details, why he couldn't use a semi-colon to introduce a list in a sentence if he felt like it. He didn't want answers. He wanted argument.

Then came the day I introduced the concept of hubris.

"I still don't understand what you mean by hubris," J.D. said after my lecture. "Isn't pride a good thing? My mama's always telling me to be proud of myself, not to let nobody put me down."

"You shouldn't let anybody put you down, but hubris has more to do with your own opinion of yourself than what others think of you. It's when your opinion is over-inflated. Let me tell you a story about a party I went to over at the Y when I was a junior in high school."

He chuckled to Marissa sitting beside him. "This happen before or after Abe Lincoln freed the slaves?"

I ignored him. "The swim team was having a party to celebrate our taking first place in the state meet."

"*You* were on the swim team?" J.D. asked.

"Yeah," Orville said. "She was. Her name is still posted over in the gym—butterfly record, wasn't it?"

I nodded, grateful for Orville's support. "Yeah, anyway, we were having a victory celebration, and I was wearing my sexiest little yellow bikini and I thought I was really hot. We were lying on beach towels, playing cards. I propped myself up on one elbow like this—" I stopped to demonstrate the angle of my head, the way my chin had rested on curled fingers— "and I batted my eyes at this boy I had a crush on."

Ceci interrupted. "What was his name?"

"Jerry Griffin, but everyone called him Griff. Anyway, we finished the card game and Griff dove back in the water. I stayed out of the pool because I wanted to keep my hairstyle fresh a while longer. I took the opportunity to get out my make-up mirror and lipstick. I wanted to make sure I looked perfect, aaannnd, guess what?" I paused for effect. "This big old booger was hanging out of my nose!"

The class erupted in laughter.

When they quieted, I continued. "I was guilty of hubris—thinking I was 'all that'—instead of an ordinary flawed person."

"I still don't get it," J.D. said.

"Pride should be something you earn for achievement and it should be tempered by the knowledge that you aren't perfect and there's always someone out there better than you."

"Unless your name is J.D., then there's no one who can touch you," he said, laughing a little. His tone changed, and his eyes frosted me. "I still don't get your point."

I stared right back. "I'm afraid I can't explain it any better." This kid was going to have to learn about hubris the hard way.

"But that's your job, to explain it."

The last of my patience evaporated. "You can come in before school and we'll go over the concept together."

He f-bombed that idea.

My hands clenched the sides of the podium. "On second thought, meet me in the guidance office after school. I'm going to invite Mr. Van

Teasel too. We're *all* going to discuss hubris. Maybe you'll get it then."

He walked out. I let him go. The door slammed into the silence of the room. Twenty-nine pairs of unfriendly eyes stared at me.

"Your paragraphs are due tomorrow," I said. "Complete directions are on the board. You may have the rest of the class to work on them."

I scribbled out a note to Tessa explaining all that had happened and asked her to set up an after-school conference. I was losing the whole class. Losing something in myself, too.

During my planning period Mrs. Alford sent a note to the library telling me to come to Tessa's office. J.D. and Mr. Van Teasel already occupied the chairs in front of her desk. I pulled a chair from the reception area into her office though the tiny office really didn't have room for another chair.

"Now, what's this about your walking out of class?" Mr. Van Teasel asked J.D.

"She acts like my questions are dumb. She won't answer them."

"There's no such thing as a dumb question." The principal intoned this as if it were a Bible verse while looking at me. Clearly he had not been in a classroom for years. There were plenty of dumb questions. Not the kind where kids were trying to learn. The kind where they weren't listening. The kind that were smart-alec. The kind they asked to prove you couldn't teach—and you couldn't if they didn't want to learn.

"Did you refuse to answer his questions, Mrs. Culpepper?" Mr. Van Teasel asked.

"No, sir. I answered them, and when he still didn't understand after a lengthy discussion, I suggested he come in before school to get further help."

"Sounds reasonable." He looked at J.D. "Son, why didn't you take her up on the offer for more help?"

J.D. f-bombed the principal. "I'm not your son, and why should I have to come in before school because she can't teach? That's bullshit!"

Mr. Van Teasel leaned away from J.D. as if he'd been gut-punched.

"There's no call for that kind of language. We're trying to have a civilized conversation here. We're trying to help you."

J.D. f-bombed him again. "No one's trying to help me. No one's on my side."

I felt malicious glee when Mr. Van Teasel assigned J.D. to Saturday detention, which meant cleaning up school grounds. I harbored fleeting thoughts of peppering the lawn with confetti Friday afternoon. Or I could sprinkle the contents of Dusty's waste can over the grounds. You could safely say it wasn't love I felt for J.D. at that moment.

"J.D.'s questioning is classic passive-aggressive behavior," Tessa said to me afterward, "but you can see how quickly he loses control if he doesn't get his way."

Exactly. It was his loss of control that worried me.

Twenty

Saturday morning I drove Quinn over to the Radio Shack in the strip mall to pick up a relay switch he needed. Another electronics project. After he made his purchase, I suggested he might like an ice cream. The leaves on the Bradford pear trees along Jefferson Street were decked out in candy corn colors and lent a festive air to downtown. I pulled into one of the angled parking spaces in front of Franchi's, which to my knowledge was the one remaining mom-and-pop soda fountain in the whole state. I ordered a diet soda while Quinn got what I really wanted: a root beer float made with hand-packed vanilla bean ice cream. While we strolled through town with our drinks, a light breeze lifted my bangs and stray strands of hair from my face. We crossed the brick-paved street to check out a new cheese shop that had recently opened.

Every once in a while we could hear a swell of voices, an ebb and flow that piqued our curiosity. We walked toward the noise, past the music store, the Mexican restaurant, and the hotel that was converted into an assisted living home. A mass of people had gathered at the courthouse. At some point, I became aware that the entire crowd was black except for a few police officers on the periphery.

I put my hand on Quinn's arm. Didn't have to say anything. He stopped too.

The Reverend Bolden stood on the courthouse steps, elevated above the crowd. "Can we improve our children's education?" he shouted.

A chorus answered him: "Yes we can."

"Can we stop discrimination in our schools?"

Again: "Yes we can."

I remembered chanting "Yes we can" for Obama, but now the words seemed co-opted by a group that didn't understand the message. Their use of the slogan troubled me. As a white I didn't feel part of the "we." I felt excluded. Accused of being the problem rather than part of the solution, and I didn't want to feel that way.

I wasn't alone. A woman in a blue jacket passed by and spoke to me—I guess me since I was white and standing there—"If this country elects that man there will be trouble, mark my words."

"Don't be ridiculous." I couldn't let Quinn think I approved of that kind of divisive talk, but the damage inflicted by Francis Brown's words was a festering wound. Instead of healing, the cut was growing more inflamed and pus-filled by the day. We were lining up, taking sides, pulling farther and farther apart.

Twenty-One

The red and blue decorations adorning every hallway marked the approach of Homecoming. Sophomores had chosen me as class sponsor, which meant arriving at work even earlier and staying late to supervise the decorating crew. Sprawled across my floor, Shaniqua was coloring in the last of the stars and stripes in the background of a five-foot wide cardboard eagle Ceci had sketched at home the night before. Beady-eyed and sharp-beaked, the eagle looked mean enough to snatch up children and puppies. As soon as Shaniqua finished, Brian and Ceci suspended it in the hallway with fishing line tied to paperclips that hooked around the ceiling tile grid. From my doorway I could see the eagle flying behind twisted strands of red and blue crepe paper that criss-crossed the hallway ceiling like spokes of a giant wheel.

Ceci stood back to survey the result. "Sophomores rule! We're going to win the class competition this year."

"For sure," Shaniqua said. The girls began work on a poster designed to look like the Declaration of Independence.

When the bell rang, I made Ceci and Shaniqua put away the magic markers and poster board. I paced up and down the aisles, dictating the weekly vocabulary quiz. I began with "nadir." The center fluorescent fixture buzzed intermittently, the noise accompanied by a flicker, bright, then dim, bright, dim, bright, dim. I'd asked the custodian the day before to replace it. He'd either forgotten, or lights were something else I was going to have to buy myself. I squinted and tried to ignore the aggravation. I prowled past Ceci, Shaniqua, and Orville. I paused to search my list for the next word. I don't know why I glanced over at Brian's desk, perhaps something furtive in the way he slid his fingertips beneath his paper that registered at some subconscious level. With shock, I realized the edge of a cheat sheet protruded from his quiz. Without a word, I collected both quiz and cheat sheet. For one moment, Brian's anguished eyes met mine. Then he collapsed onto his desk, arms folded into a protective screen. I sailed up the aisle to my desk, deposited both papers to deal with later, and went on as if nothing had happened. Although I couldn't show any sign of softness, part of me wanted to go over and squeeze his shoulder. It wasn't the end of the world.

As I patrolled the room, dictating the rest of the words, I tried to unearth some reason to explain his cheating. He'd been volunteering such long hours in Obama's last minute push to get-out-the-vote he didn't have time to study. The excitement of Homecoming week made him forget about this quiz. He'd been overwhelmed by daydreams and an adolescent hormone surge because of his upcoming date with Marissa. He was preoccupied with the essay contest for Leadership America. It must be something like that because cheating was way out of character for him.

The light fixture's humming and flickering increased a notch. My head ached; my teeth were on edge.

I dictated the next word, "liberal," and moved between the aisles until I stood behind J.D. To my amazement, he pulled his sweatshirt jacket open slightly with his left hand, his neck canting downward until it touched his chest, eyes slanted toward the inside. From where I stood, I could clearly discern a two-inch wide, three-inch tall piece of paper adhered to the jacket with masking tape. I couldn't believe it. Since I'd just caught Brian not five minutes before, I would have bet money everyone else would be too nervous to try anything. Like the way you drive slower for at least a few minutes after seeing an officer issuing a speeding ticket. J.D. let loose of the jacket and began to write. All the while the light buzzed bright, then dim.

Without asking, I picked up his quiz, causing his pen to skid across the page.

He snatched the paper back. "Hey, what do you think you're doing?"

I whispered to keep the transaction low-key. "Taking up your quiz. I saw the cheat sheet inside your jacket."

"What you talking about?"

There was no point in my whispering if he was going to yell. "Game's over, J.D., I saw it."

"That's messed up. I only used it on one word."

"Too bad. My policy is students get a zero for cheating."

"But I knew all the words except that one."

"You should have taken a 90 then. Please hand over both papers."

His eyes narrowed. "You got it in for me, don't you? Why you never catch white kids cheating?"

"Doesn't matter who cheats, I treat them the same." Ridiculous, the way this kid made me feel guilty. Why did I let him affect me this way?

"Yeah, sure." He ripped the cheat sheet out of his jacket and handed it to me, but he held onto his quiz. "I want to finish."

I walked away with the cheat sheet, folding the masking tape so it wouldn't stick to other papers, and put it under the desk calendar with Brian's. "Feel free—you already know what the grade is."

He mumbled something I couldn't quite make out, but I could guess the general nature.

"What did you say?"

"Nothing."

"That's what I thought." I sounded like such a jerk. My skin tingled from the tension in the room as I dictated the tenth and last word. Antipathy rolled off J.D. in waves each time his body rocked forward and back in his desk. The muscles around his mouth and eyes tightened until I thought they might snap like over-extended rubber bands. This boy had assaulted a police officer; he had watched his mother kill his father. I had no idea what he might be capable of.

The center light fixture buzzed on, buzzed off, buzzed on, buzzed off.

Twenty-Two

First thing the next morning I had Graham help me replace the buzzing light. I decided I'd rather buy the bulb with my own money than put up with the aggravation another day. The morning passed without incident until my planning period.

Hunched over my usual table in the back corner of the library, I had graded a quiz or two when I became aware of a presence. In his trademark black suit and clerical collar, the Reverend Bolden loomed in front of me. The lawsuit had landed on my doorstep, so to speak. I felt like throwing up. Was I in trouble because I'd caught two blacks kids cheating?

"I'm here on behalf of Brian Jones." His voice resonated with concern. Lowering himself into the chair across from me, he rested his elbows on the table and interlaced his fingers. "Brian told his mother about cheating and she e-mailed his father in Iraq."

That made me even sicker. His father, a colonel in the National Guard, had other things to worry about, like staying away from IEDs and suicide bombers.

"Brian's father is taking what his son did very seriously," he said. "He wanted me to tell you Brian can't go to Homecoming."

The knots in my stomach relaxed as I realized no one was going to blame me. Every year, at least once, some parent came charging in, angry because their child had gotten in trouble. Most parents were like Brian's and supported his teachers. Most, but not all.

Empathy quickly replaced my relief. "I didn't expect any additional punishment. He got a zero on the quiz. Punishment enough."

"His parents feel it's important for him to learn a lesson about honesty. The reason I'm here is to find out if this incident will go on Brian's permanent record. I would hate to see the boy kept out of college for his mistake."

The only record resided in my own file. "As far as I'm concerned, it's over with. The zero won't hurt his average. I give tons of grades and his are all A's."

"That's all I wanted to know. He's a good boy, and I don't want to see a blemish on his record. He's really embarrassed, especially because he thinks a lot of you. He told me how good you've been to him."

Even though I was glad to hear it, I waved off the praise. "Nothing special, just doing my job."

"You and I both know it's more than that. You proofread his essay for the Leadership America competition and wrote recommendations for him. On behalf of the community, I want to thank you for your service to our youth."

The Reverend Bolden was not at all the rabble rouser I had expected him to be. "It's my pleasure to work with young people like Brian. I hope to vote for him for mayor or even president some day."

"Me too, me too, and the day has come when a black man can be elected president, praise God."

I felt such a strong rapport with the man, I dared to raise the question on every teacher's mind these days. At least every white teacher. I still didn't know where Liz stood. "Reverend, there's something I just don't understand. You seem like such a reasonable person, why are you involved with this lawsuit? You know, I have been campaigning for Obama, but when I heard you all chanting "yes we can" at the courthouse Saturday, I felt betrayed. That slogan was meant to include everybody, not exclude on the basis of skin color."

He frowned. "We weren't trying to exclude."

"Sure felt like it. The crowd was all black and the things you were saying were all about black kids. It's a mostly black school, so mostly blacks are going to be disciplined. Racism doesn't have a thing to do with it."

"Nobody's calling it racism. Did you know that in proportion to their numbers in the student body, blacks are four times more likely than whites to receive discipline referrals and five times more likely to be assigned to the alternative school?"

"No." I considered what the numbers might mean. Surely not what he was reading into them. "I know the teachers on this staff. There's not a single one who would punish a child because of his race." At least none I could think of. Then again, who would have thought Francis

Brown would call Obama a picaninny?

"Now, I'm not saying it's racism," he said. "I don't think that. But a lack of cultural sensitivity might account for the disparity."

Sounded like a bogus way to shift the blame onto the teacher. "What do you mean by 'cultural sensitivity'?"

"Maybe there are traits—for example, the way kids dress or a tendency in black children to talk louder than whites—that teachers respond negatively to. Also many black children tend to not meet your eyes when you're scolding them. You ever notice that? I've heard teachers say, 'Look at me when I'm talking to you,' but many black children have been taught to look away when an authority figure corrects them. Let me ask you this. Have you ever seen a person and felt negatively about him without even knowing him? Maybe you don't even know why; it's happening at a level you aren't aware of."

A movie of J.D. pimping through my door in his baggy pants and calling me "dawg" rose in my mind as clearly as if it were happening at that moment. I shook my head. Even if I didn't like a kid's attitude, I would never assign detention for anything but clear infractions. "Seems to me you're putting all the blame on teachers. What about holding students accountable for their own behavior? Sometimes they just need better manners and a little respect for authority."

He nodded. "Couldn't agree more. We're trying to use the Big Brother, Big Sister program and Upward Bound to mentor children and show them better ways to negotiate in the world. We know part of the problem lies with the students. We just believe that part of the solution lies in greater understanding and sensitivity to differences from our teachers. Don't be too quick to dismiss the idea. Think about it. Pray on it. How bad could participating in a sensitivity training day be?"

Sounded like a waste of time, but it wouldn't be the first time I'd felt that way about in-service training. If that's all it took to make the lawsuit go away, I'd be the first to sign up.

"For a lot of these kids, problems start way before high school." Thinking of J.D., I added, "Even before grade school."

"We know. We're looking at that, too. A task force is looking into starting a nurse-family partnership program that tries to foster secure family relationships right from birth. The idea is to send a nurse into at-risk homes and bolster parenting skills and deal with nutrition and health issues. Families who've been involved with these programs have experienced 59 percent fewer arrests at age 15. Imagine if every child lived in a home that provided a secure environment for emotional development."

I remembered J.D.'s autobiography. He had found one good home and run away from it. What a difference it might have made if he had been placed in the minister's home first before exposure to street life.

"Sounds like a wonderful idea," I said. "In light of today's deficit issues, I doubt if it will attract the funding it would require."

"You're probably right, but we're going to try." The Reverend produced a letter from the inside pocket of his suit jacket. "Brian asked me to give you this."

I didn't need to open it to know it contained an apology. The Reverend left me to what remained of my planning period, but I couldn't concentrate on the quizzes. I kept seeing Brian's head down on his desk and knew how hard it would be for him to stay home Friday night while Marissa walked across the field with someone else. Once, when I was thirteen, I sassed my mother in front of her friends. She refused to let me go on a ski trip to West Virginia with my church group. I remembered the pain of being left behind, imagining my life was ruined. I never sassed her again. Brian, I knew, would never cheat again. This incident would be carved on his character for all time. Maybe his parents were right to inflict this punishment. Who knew how many temptations he'd walk away from because of this lesson? Still, I wished they could have found something that would hurt him less.

I wondered what would happen to J.D., if his mother would follow through with consequences when she read the daily progress reports we teachers had been filling out since his fight with Mr. Van Teasel and Coach Haswell.

I almost didn't answer the phone because I thought it would be a telemarketer or a charity begging for a contribution. I didn't have time to waste on them. In half an hour, an emergency meeting of the school board would convene.

"What do you mean I have to come back in?" I asked Vivian Barnes.

"Dr. Roberts wants to discuss your blood work."

"Why? What's wrong?" The doctor had ordered the tests as part of a routine annual exam.

"I'm not supposed to discuss it with you."

"Why not?" After swearing us to secrecy, Dr. Roberts' secretary discussed every other illness that came into that office with the entire First Baptist Sunday school class. "Come on, I'll worry all night and think I'm dying if you don't tell me—I'm not dying, am I?" I had two boys depending on me.

"Well, okay. I don't think it would be Christian to let you worry. Your blood sugar is running a little high and the doctor wants more lab work to see if you're diabetic. He wants to talk to you about diet. Says you need to lose about forty pounds. Maybe put you on some pills. Nothing to worry about, so don't lose any sleep."

Don't worry? You could lose a lot more than sleep with diabetes. My grandfather had diabetes and lost toes on both feet. I was extremely fond of my toes. And even more so, my sons. My diet suddenly assumed cosmic importance. The weight had to come off. Forty pounds? Was I really that fat?

Next time I missed church, I supposed Vivian would be blabbing my weight and blood sugar around the way she'd gossiped about Miss Baker's problems all over Alderson. Jolene suffered from swollen ankles and had to sit with her feet up at night.

"Say, Molly, did you hear that some men threw a brick through Reverend Bolden's window last night?" Vivian asked. "At least three men screamed ugly nonsense outside his house. I wish this whole nasty mess would just go away, don't you?"

For a second I stopped breathing. Woodson couldn't be involved, could he? He threw the "n" word around easily enough, but he wouldn't throw bricks, would he? He was friendly with the blacks he worked with.

"Me too, Vivian. Me too."

Custodians scrambled to find extra folding chairs. This many people had never attended a board meeting before. Citizens segregated themselves to one side or the other of the room as if someone had posted signs: blacks to the left, whites on the right. Liz and I sat next to each other, each on our own side of the divide. Students, I had noticed, nearly always sat by racial groups, too, if left to their own devices. The low hum of voices and chair scrapes accelerated as the meeting room filled. Anita Marshall entered and sat on the black side.

"There's J.D.'s mom," I said. "My blood boils every time I think about how she didn't do a thing to punish him for cheating except take away TV privileges for a week."

Liz slid her purse under the folding chair. "Let it go, Molly."

"Can't Marissa find someone else to escort her? It really doesn't seem fair that, of all people, J.D. gets to replace Brian."

Liz listened politely to my concerns and put her hand on my arm. "Honey, you get too involved in all their personal stuff. This job will wring you dry if you let it. Just teach your subject and go home at night and relax with your kids."

That was a little easier for her than it was for me. "In English, we can't give all objective question tests. We have to grade essays and writing, which takes hours and hours out of my nights and weekends."

"So throw a few sets of papers out without reading them once in a while," Liz said. "The kids will thank you for it. Besides, that's not what I'm talking about. You need to stop getting all worked up about things that are outside your control, like whether this boy gets to go to a dance. You two obviously have a personality clash."

Her words went down like day-old coffee. I couldn't tell if she was implying race caused the clash.

Since I'd snooped into Mr. Piscetelli's file the night the lights went out, I wasn't surprised when he came in and sat on the black side by Reverend Bolden. They shook hands and leaned toward each other in earnest conversation. Not only was Lodge the only white on the left side of the room, he was the only man on either side with a ponytail. He was an odd one, but not bad looking in a suit and dress shoes. Sort of cute, in a bad-boy way. I wondered what made him tick. He caught me staring and nodded. I half raised my hand in acknowledgment.

It soon became apparent Superintendent Rice wasn't going to run this show. He wasn't in attendance. Rumor had it he was going to be fired for the way he had handled the Francis Brown episode. Mr. Van Teasel stood behind the podium and recognized C. Lodge Piscetelli.

Lodge looked relaxed at the podium. "Mr. Van Teasel, members of the Board, as you know I am the attorney of record for Blacks For Progress and will represent the organization in the pending lawsuit. We understand you are going to take up the matter of Francis Brown's employment this evening. Blacks For Progress would like to go on record stating that the termination of Francis Brown's employment would serve as a good first step in showing the Board's willingness to work with us on the issues raised in the lawsuit. Any possible resolution of the suit out of court must begin with this act of good faith."

Mr. Van Teasel remained in his metal seat, facing the audience. He removed his glasses, rubbed the rim, and slid them back onto his skinny nose. "Neither I nor members of the Board can comment on personnel matters publicly. We will discuss Mr. Brown behind closed doors at the end of the public portion of our meeting."

"I understand that. Blacks For Progress still wants to go on record with a request that you immediately terminate Mr. Brown's employment. He should not be retained in any position, whether in or out of the classroom, because of the blatant act of racism he committed on September 17 of this year. His actions demonstrated willful disregard for the sensibilities of the young people he was supposed to be educating."

"So noted, Mr. Piscetelli."

Lodge sat down, having done an excellent job, I thought. Articulate, smooth. Mr. Van Teasel recognized Reverend Bolden, who stood and turned to address the gathering. Chairs scraped against the floor as those present turned to get a better view of the Reverend.

"First, let me reiterate Mr. Piscetelli's statement regarding the dismissal of Francis Brown. Until that happens, it will be difficult to proceed with our other concerns. Blatant racism must have consequences. Serious consequences."

Mr. Van Teasel spoke for the board. "I believe we understand your position, Reverend."

"Good, good." For the first time, the Reverend smiled. "We'll assume you're going to do the right thing tonight and we'll proceed with this meeting. I want to thank the guidance department for the effort it is undertaking to ensure discipline is equitable. I have great hope the new three-step referral system will address many of our problems.

"But people, this problem is faarrrr bigger—" He rose up on his toes and opened his arms as if the enormity was too great to contain any longer, then rocked back on his heels to continue. "—faarrrrr bigger than Mr. Brown. Even when he goes away, our problems won't. Our issues are bigger than one act of racism. They are much bigger than discipline discrepancies. This problem isn't one thing or the other. It's a veritable mountain—" He was back on his toes. "—a mountain of problems, good people, layered one on top of the other. We're talking about dismantling a whole system of institutionalized discrimination. A whole set of practices as evil and troublesome as that snake in the Garden of Eden. It is time to cast out that snake. Let's cast him out right now. Let's begin by casting out the rigged elections."

Blacks applauded. Some shouted amen. Whites, including me, sat in rigid silence.

At the podium, Mr. Van Teasel squirmed. "I don't think it's fair to call the elections 'rigged.'"

"Why then, why then, pray tell me, in a school that's seventy-five percent black, is there a black Homecoming princess and a white Homecoming princess for every grade level? And why are class officers always two blacks and two whites? There's no way those results are legitimate." The blacks shouted amen again and the Reverend Bolden stepped back and waited for a response.

Voices rumbled and swelled and echoed off the high ceiling. I heard outrage on both sides of the room.

"Are the elections rigged?" I whispered to Liz.

"What do you think?" Her voice implied I was stupid for asking.

I hadn't given it much thought when year after year each class elected a black class president and white vice president. I hadn't wondered how Mary Wade Marcinek and my son earned the right to walk on the field along with Marissa Powell and J.D. Marshall. The race of the Homecoming court might seem trivial in the face of world problems. But when you considered what these kids were learning about democracy from rigged elections, these matters took on greater importance.

Maybe Reverend Bolden was right. The problem ran deeper than Francis Brown. Maybe it snaked through every decision we made in Alderson. Maybe I had been as blind as Miss Baker in my own way.

Mr. Van Teasel squinted through his wire rims. "The school has to allow for minority representation. White flight will almost certainly increase if we can't ensure some honors will go to white children. The school board is trying to prevent court-ordered busing."

What he wasn't saying, but we all knew to be true, was if the school became all black, our funding would dry up even further. White students not only had moved to the mostly white county high school, they had also abandoned us in alarming numbers to enroll in private and charter schools. When they left, they took state dollars with them.

I sympathized with Mr. Van Teasel. He had the difficult job of keeping the many factions of parents, teachers and the school board happy. As the fourth principal in the past six years, he knew how precarious, how political his job was. For varied reasons, his predecessors now worked in administrative posts at the Board Office—the equivalent to being fired. One lost his job when the rival county school reported better graduation exit exam scores than AHS; another, when he proved too wishy-washy on discipline; and they fired the third, a man we teachers dearly loved—and I swear to God I'm not making this up—when it began to rain during graduation. The ceremony had to be moved inside. Not everyone in attendance would fit inside the gym, so irate parents demanded his removal. He now administered testing for the city school system. Mr. Van Teasel knew he had to tread carefully on the issue of white flight.

Reverend Bolden countered that we should consider other solutions to stop the exodus of white students, that rigged elections sent the wrong message to all students.

I agreed. Tension in the room mounted, and I felt the two camps, black and white, pulling even further apart. Someone had to offer an alternative.

I stood up. "What about making Alderson a magnet school for the arts?"

Vashawn Diggs's father stood up. "That woman"—he pointed at me—"is one of the worst with black kids. She talked to my son like a dog, like a dog."

Immediately I flopped back into my chair. Any response I might have made dried up on my tongue. If only I could shrink physically the way I was shrinking inside. I was acutely aware of the eyes of my colleagues, my boss, and my neighbors, especially C. Lodge Piscetelli, all turned toward me.

Rev. Bolden spoke up. "Now, I know Mrs. Culpepper and I find that hard to believe."

Mr. Diggs shook his finger at me. "'Sit,' she told him, 'sit,' like he was a dog."

I wanted to say I didn't have to repeat the command for my dog, who behaved much better than his son had that day, but looking around at the angry crowd I thought better of it.

Reverend Bolden smiled pleasantly. "Well, Mr. Diggs, I'm sure you'll agree that a school is not like a church where you can stand up whenever you please and shout 'Amen.'" A wave of laughter rippled through the room. "A teacher has to keep order or no learning can take place."

I was beginning to love this man. I admired the minister's skill at working a crowd. The Reverend went up another notch in my esteem when he responded warmly to the concept of a magnet school.

Mr. Diggs objected. "But a school for the arts. That's not what our kids need. Artsy fartsy crap isn't going to get them jobs. That's what wrong with Alderson now—too much Shakespeare and elitist crap and not enough real world relevance."

I couldn't have agreed more. Every student didn't need to read four Shakespeare plays, the number we presently decreed necessary. But the state required Shakespeare in the curriculum, so every student must be—and should be, I thought—exposed to the Bard, but perhaps not on such a grand scale.

"We could offer business-oriented English to upperclassmen instead, but that won't stop white flight. A magnet school doesn't have to be artsy—" I caught myself before I repeated Mr. Diggs's language— "impractical."

"That's right," Liz said. "It can be a magnet for math and science or an IB—that stands for International Baccalaureate—program to prepare students for college."

"And even the arts can be practical," I said. "Several years ago, I developed a curriculum for at-risk students. It combined hands-on graphic arts with English."

"How did that work?" Rev. Bolden said.

"Students would produce and sell a different product every nine weeks. One quarter they'd design and screen print tee-shirts and market them. On the English side, they'd learn to write a marketing plan and read technical manuals. Another quarter they would create a magazine. They would come up with the concept for it, write the stories, take photos, use computer software to design it, and market it to students and the community. And one quarter they would make an instructional video for every department in the school. Half the proceeds would be distributed to students in the class. The rest would go toward replenishing supplies for the course."

"Why, if you spent the time to develop an interesting curriculum, aren't you using it instead of making Vashawn write all those pointless essays?" Mr. Diggs asked. "Money is one of the only things that motivates my boy."

The room became quiet and everyone stared at me, waiting for an answer.

"We couldn't afford it. The principal—not Mr. Van Teasel, Dr. Parker was principal then—said the program would take too much money to start up and the schedule didn't have room for it anyway. The class would require a two-hour block."

"Let's find the money and the time," Rev. Bolden said. "Miz Culpepper, why don't you generate some possibilities for fundraisers before our next meeting? And let's figure out what kind of magnet school we could turn AHS into. Miz Powell, can we count on you to work with the community on that idea?"

I knew Liz thought her pastor walked on water right beside Jesus and wouldn't deny this request anymore than she denied him the secret ingredient in her sweet potato pie that she refused to share with our lunch table.

He continued. "And maybe the guidance department can line up a cultural sensitivity workshop and also generate ideas to enrich the rest of the curriculum for learners not inclined toward college-style classes."

The Reverend looked at his watch and remarked on the lateness of the hour. "Here's what I propose. We'll hold off filing any further motions in this lawsuit while we try to sort out our differences outside of court. Mr. Van Teasel, Mr. Piscetelli, and I will sit down and discuss the elections process, the golf team, the school play and report back at the next meeting. I ask y'all to go home and pray on these matters. Our goal isn't to divide the community. We want to find a way to make our school challenging and exciting for all our kids, black and white, because kids who are interested in learning don't get into trouble."

Several amens went up in the audience, including a silent one I offered myself. Mr. Van Teasel, who had all but surrendered control of the meeting until now, reasserted himself and said committees should report to him in a week.

The temporary hold on the lawsuit Rev. Bolden proposed was a relief, but how could we come up with funds to start the graphic arts class? I didn't want to be in charge of fundraising. Didn't want to be in charge of anything. I had enough to do already. Should have kept my mouth shut.

Mr. Diggs's accusation ricocheted through my head on the drive home: *One of the worst with black kids.* I checked on the boys, and then called Liz.

"Tell me the truth. Am I really one of the worst teachers with black kids? Is that the reputation I have?"

"Honey, don't you let that mean old man get on your nerves." Her rich voice flowed into my ear like a balm. "If someone hands him a cup of black coffee, he thinks it has something to do with race. You're a little blind sometimes, a little naïve, but you're a good teacher, you know you are. Your heart's in the right place."

I hoped it was. I wanted it to be.

"Did you hear?" Liz sounded excited. "They fired Brown and Superintendent Rice has been moved to the district office. I think he's going to be in charge of vocational education or something like that. Harlan Montgomery will step up from assistant super to the real deal."

A black man as superintendent! Looked like change was coming, whether Alderson was ready for it or not.

At 2:10 a.m. the phone rang and Dusty began barking. I answered on the first ring, my heart pounding, my breath frozen, mind racing. What now? Almost a year ago my father had called in the middle of the night to say my mother had gotten up from bed with a headache and collapsed on the floor. A massive stroke. She never regained consciousness. Who was sick? Hurt? Who was in trouble?

On the other end of the line I heard someone breathing. I said hello again. More breathing met my greeting, so it wasn't a wrong number. I hung-up. I went to check on the boys, both asleep in their beds—and why shouldn't they be?—but some instincts are hard to fight even when your children are far past babyhood. When the phone rang half an hour later, I lifted the receiver. Again, my hellos elicited heavy breathing.

"Listen, you pervert, get some Listerine. Your breath stinks." I punched my pillow and tried to let go of my anger. Ten minutes later, it rang again. I picked up the receiver, hung up, and turned the ring volume down. Should have unplugged the phone. But what if my father's ulcer bled again? What if he had another accident, a serious one this time? What if it was Sam, miles away in Santa Fe? What if someone tried to break in and I couldn't dial 911? I lay awake for some time, waiting for the next ring, but it didn't come.

At 3:30, sleep still out of reach, I figured I might as well grade papers. I managed thirty essays before time to get ready for school. By the light of day, I felt foolish. It had been a stupid prankster. Don't know why I let it bother me.

Twenty-Three

The day after the country elected Obama president by wide margins, black students displayed unprecedented joy. Obama shirts filled every classroom. Students exchanged fist bumps and grins in the hall. Social studies classes tuned into newscasts analyzing the victory and what it meant to our country. Victory dances broke out spontaneously in the halls. Maybe it was my imagination, but for the rest of the week, black students seemed to walk a little taller and smile a little more joyfully. I even thought they completed their homework with an extra measure of devotion.

By Friday, the focus returned to school and our local problems. Namely the lawsuit and how to make it go away. Eight students parked their posteriors on top of a cluster of desks in my room before the sun came up.

"How about a car wash?" Shaniqua suggested.

"Nah, everyone does car washes," Ceci said, "and they don't raise much money. We need an idea no one else has tried."

"What about a walkathon?" Vashawn said. "You get people to sponsor you and give money for each mile you walk." I was surprised when Vashawn volunteered for the committee, but he radiated enthusiasm I'd never seen in him before. He offered to do whatever he could to make the graphic arts/English class a reality as long as I promised him a spot in it next year.

"I'd poop out before I made a mile," Shaniqua said, and it might be true. She looked as wispy as a leaf. "I'm the least athletic person alive."

"You!" Ceci said. "I fall over my own shoelaces."

"At least you ride horses," Shaniqua said. "I don't even do that."

"Oh, I don't either," Mary Wade said. "I'm scared of their teeth." She giggled, a sound capable of rattling windows, but Graham smiled at her as if she were the cutest thing since the Teletubby he used to take to bed with him. I couldn't see it myself.

"You were a swimmer, right, Miz C.?" Brian asked.

He used the past tense, as though I couldn't possibly still be athletic—which I wasn't because I didn't have time, what with teaching school and raising two boys on my own.

"Second place in butterfly," I said. "State high school swimming competition, 1981."

Vashawn snickered. "I'd have paid money to see that."

I wheeled toward him, my face hot, ready to tear into him. I wasn't that out of shape. Then what he'd said sunk in. "How much?" I asked.

"How much what?"

"How much would you pay to see me—I mean some other teacher—swim in a race?" My face heated up again, this time at the thought of putting on a bathing suit. Surely I could find someone else to volunteer for the job. I'd bought my last swimsuit before Quinn's birth. The last time I tried to purchase a new one, my thighs looked so dimply under those glaring lights, I'd run in horror from the dressing room. You'd think the department stores would install more flattering lights.

Vashawn was taken aback. "I was just joking."

"I'm serious. Would people pay to see teachers and students compete against each other?"

They looked at each other. Finally Vashawn spoke. "Yeah, I think they might."

"An athletic student could coach the teachers and Coach Haswell's staff could work with students," Marissa said.

Graham suggested a triathlon: swimming, bicycling, and a mile-run. They shaped up rules for the contest. Anyone who played a team sport was out. There weren't enough non-coaching men teachers to field a guys' team, so it would be girls only. Every participant had to complete each event or our sponsors didn't have to pay up their pledges.

"Hey, why don't you swap the bicycles for tennis rackets?" Brian said.

Vashawn high-fived him. "Yeah, then Brian and I can coach the teachers. The tennis team has plenty of old rackets stashed away in our garages, so you won't have to buy anything except new balls."

Ceci and Shaniqua volunteered to be on the student team. Marissa and Mary Wade said they would cheerlead the event. Tameka

Coakley, my editor, took charge of publicity.

"And how about a concert?" Mary Wade said. "Graham, our band could perform."

"Mary Wade, I don't think we're ready to—" my son began.

"Oh, sure we are—or at least we can be. This isn't right away?" She looked at me for confirmation. I nodded. We were looking at a date six weeks off, just before the Christmas holidays. Mary Wade nudged a blue-jeaned knee against Graham's thigh, smiled prettily, wiggled a little, and got her way.

"All right, let's go for it," Noah agreed.

"You need to ask Quinn and Donnie if they think the band is ready," I said.

"The Goober'll do whatever I tell him to or I'll bust his head open," Graham said, eliciting a giggle from Mary Wade.

"Graham!" I said.

"What? He'll do it."

Mary Wade said Donnie would too.

Shaniqua and Marissa thought they could line up some black entertainers as well, and we decided to conduct a bake sale throughout the day.

I would type up official sponsor forms and get Mr. Van Teasel's approval.

"Miz C., will you emcee?" Noah asked.

"Surely you can find someone else." I know this sounds strange, coming from a teacher, but while I felt comfortable getting up in front of students, adults made my hands sweat.

"I'll do it," Brian said.

"Perfect!" I agreed. Everyone slid off their desks and gathered up their belongings.

"Ha! Mom, I can't wait to see you trying to swim. That's gonna be a hoot! I bet you've forgotten how." The kids snickered.

I sent him one of those brow-knitted, thin-lipped, slant-eyed looks I'd perfected. It didn't work on him as well as it did on others. The committee's plan might raise oodles of money, but no way was I putting on a bathing suit in front of these kids. Someone else would have to do it.

After school Ceci and Ja'Neice slumped like rag dolls, eyes down-cast, in two chairs pulled up by my desk. For ten minutes I let them stew without looking at them while I proofread copy for the school paper. Ja'Neice pressed her lips together, trying to look tough. Ceci worried her cuticles until I feared they might bleed.

I put down my emerald felt-tip pen—I never graded in red—too brutal—and stood in front of them, my right hand firmly grasping the confiscated list. "This is what you do instead of completing a graphic organizer to summarize the main characters' traits in the novel?" I willed my face to look grim. I could do grim when forced to. "How do you expect to pass the class with this kind of nonsense going on?"

They didn't answer or look up.

"What would your mothers say if they knew?"

Ceci shivered.

"Do you think my test is going to be a piece of cake?"

"No, ma'am," Ceci said. Shaniqua shook her head, unable to talk.

"Then get out of here and don't let me ever catch you doing anything like this in class again."

Shaniqua was so relieved she found her voice. A squeak. "We won't."

They practically ran to the door, but Ceci turned back. "Are you going to dock our grades?"

"Not this time."

"Oh, thank you, Miz Culpepper, thank you," Shaniqua squealed.

As soon as they left, I bounced down to Liz's lab. She dangled a live white mouse over her boa. I cringed and backed out to the hallway to wait until she finished. How could an animal lover like Liz stand to watch that mouse suffer? What a horrible death. I couldn't watch and I wasn't even that fond of mice.

"How can you stand that thing?" I asked.

"What, Hairy? He's harmless."

"He's gross." But I hadn't come to argue over her snake collection. I handed her the list. "Check this out."

As her eyes trailed down the paper, she giggled. "Walter Anderson—yeah I can see that, but Orville Chidester? No way." We giggled hysterically, drawing Betsy from her room.

Liz handed her the list.

She read the heading aloud: "Top Ten Booties in the Class of '08."

We giggled some more, trading stories about confiscated notes.

"Oh, to be fifteen again!" Betsy said.

Betsy was barely past the I'll-Die-If-He-Doesn't-Ask-Me-To-Prom stage herself. Not for a minute would I want to be fifteen again, but being a teenager had some benefits. When you were fifteen so many eligible behinds surrounded you that you could find ten you thought were cute. Offhand I could only think of one. A certain soccer coach's.

Twenty-Four

First thing in the morning, I called Mrs. Marshall, but it was J.D. who asnwered the phone. "I need to speak to your mother, please."

"What you calling here for?" J.D. said.

I repeated myself.

"She ain't home."

I didn't believe that for a minute. I knew for a fact she worked at the zipper factory and their morning shift didn't start until 8:30. "When do you expect her?"

"Who knows? She didn't say."

"Why didn't you come to detention this morning?"

"Didn't get up in time. Listen, I gotta go or I'm gonna be late to first period, and you know how you are when people are tardy."

I did know how I was: irate. June Trask raised me to show up at least ten minutes early for everything, said only rude people expected others to wait on them, and I wholeheartedly agreed. I hung up, not the least bit happy with the outcome of the call. On J.D.'s daily progress sheet, I wrote that he failed to serve detention. Mrs. Marshall hadn't picked up the last three, so I had little confidence she would see this one either. It was time for other recourses.

The next morning J.D. showed up for detention, bad attitude written all over his otherwise handsome face. Coach Haswell benched him for one game for not serving his detention. I knew it hurt Sonny to do it, because J.D. was his star, but Sonny slipped a note into my mailbox, saying building character was more important than winning games. I respected him for that. When I mentioned the benching to Mrs. Alford in the office, she reminded me the team we were playing hadn't beaten us in ten years, no big sacrifice, but I still appreciated Haswell's support.

J.D. sagged into a desk, head down, eyes closed. I stood beside

THE COLOR OF LIES

him and said his name. When his eyes remained shut, I touched his shoulder gently and repeated his name.

He flinched and jerked away. "What?"

I handed him a half sheet of paper.

"What's this?"

"An assignment you missed."

"I ain't missed no days."

"No, you haven't missed any days, not officially, but when you were out for Homecoming escort practice, you missed this one. Marissa has already made it up."

His eyes flicked over the sheet: describe an object that's really important and beautiful to you.

"What'd Marissa write on?"

"A rose."

"Figures. Girl shi—stuff."

"Right. Well, it's only a paragraph. You should be able to finish it easily in your fifteen minutes."

To my surprise, his pencil skated across the page, the words flowing with apparent ease. Now and then, he would pause and re-read what he'd written with this mirthless half-smile that gave me the willies. When the bell rang to begin classes, he handed the paper in and I stuffed it into the bin for first period. I didn't give that paper or J.D.'s smile another thought until I got home and emptied my satchel that night.

This time, when the phone rang at 2 a.m., my mouth went dry.

Mr. Van Teasel's face knit into a frown as he lowered J.D.'s paragraph onto his desk. "What was the assignment?"

I handed him the half sheet of paper containing the directions.

He studied them carefully. "The young man followed the directions, didn't he?"

"Well, yes, but that doesn't make the paragraph any less scary." When a .45 Glock was the most important and beautiful object a kid could think of, it was time to worry. J.D. had described the heft of the gun in his hand, the way the bullets felt as he loaded them, how he preferred the stopping power of a .45 to a .22. The poetic language J.D. used—"a bead of silver that could split a cop's heart open, the only way to kill those vampires that sucked the blood of society" — made it even more chilling. He called the Glock "a man's gun, all angles, no curves."

Off came Mr. Van Teasel's glasses, his fingers massaging the bridge of his nose, before he repositioned the wire rims. "Of course this paper is disturbing. J.D.'s obviously very troubled. But what can we really do about it? That's my point: he did exactly what you assigned, and he did it well."

I think he mumbled "too well" after that, but I couldn't be sure.

"He wrote this to get a rise out of you. You know what I'd do? Put an A in the grade book and throw the paper out. No, on second thought, let's put it in his file in the guidance office. It might be useful later, but I don't think we can do anything about it at this point. I'm sorry, Mrs. Culpepper. Try not to let it worry you. I'm sure it's just a childish stunt."

That night when the phone woke me up at 2:30, I didn't even try to go back to sleep. I pulled a bottle of wine out of the pantry. Tried to open the screw cap. I torqued. I twisted. I plowed my whole weight and will into it. It wouldn't budge. I gave up and slumped onto the couch. I let the tears wet my face. David had always been the one to open bottles and jars. Why wasn't he here?

At the end of the period, I handed back a few stray papers.

"Look, she wrote 'scintillating' at the top of my description." Marissa held up her paragraph so Brian could see. He scrambled to get the dictionary out and Vashawn beat Ceci to the Beautiful Word Wall.

"That's lame," J.D. said. "A rose. I wrote a great paper, didn't I, Miz?" He watched me closely for a reaction I refused to deliver. "You gonna hand back my paper today?"

"Haven't graded it yet. What was it about?"

He shrugged, eyes shifting away from me.

Brian located the word in the dictionary. "Here it is, 'brilliantly clever.'" Shaniqua wrote the definition beside the word.

"We need more words so we can have another extra credit quiz," Brian said. I knew he wanted to make up the points lost from cheating.

"I got one for you," J.D. said. "Chub rub."

Marissa laughed. "What's it mean?"

Although he directed his remarks to Marissa, his eyes angled toward me. "It's when a fat person's legs rub together when they walk," he said. "Here, I'll use it in a sentence: A certain teacher has a bad case of chub rub."

Orville snickered.

J.D. walked up to the Word Wall and snatched the marker from Shaniqua. "Let me add it to our list."

The class fell silent, holding its collective breath, waiting.

"I don't think so, J.D."

"Why not?"

"It's not a respectful term."

His eyes narrowed. "What about 'loquacious'? You dissed Brian with that word."

My brain froze for a moment with guilt, until I realized he was manipulating me again. "That's different. The word describes a quality of his, like 'reticent' describes Shaniqua. I didn't intend to hurt anyone's feelings."

"I'm not trying to pick on anyone either," he said, all innocence. "Why, you don't like my word?"

My answer flew out of my mouth before my brain found time to register what I was saying. "I'd describe your language as 'nugatory.'"

Brian couldn't wait to find that one in the dictionary, his fingers leafing through the pages. With almost supernatural vision I thought I could see the section headings pass by: nas, ne, nub, nug. My throat squeezed shut. Inwardly I was flinging one abusive word after another at myself. How could I have said that? I was older than J.D., trained to handle discipline problems. I was supposed to know better. I wasn't like Francis Brown. I wasn't.

"'Nugatory: Of no real value. Worthless.' Snap! She Culpeppered you!"

"Oh, I gotcha," J.D. said. "I see where you're coming from now. I'm just another worthless nigger to you, ain't that right?" The bell to dismiss rang.

"No, I was talking about your language, not you." My words, hollow even to my own ears, fell on his back.

Twenty-Five

Now that Blacks For Progress had delayed the lawsuit, Liz returned to the lunchroom. We acted as if she'd never left. I wondered, not for the first time, if she ever felt awkward being the only black who ate in the lounge. Two black female teachers ate in the cafeteria at a table with the office staff, and the other two ate in their own rooms. I assumed the lone black male ate with his fellow coaches. Principals at AHS had tried to recruit more black teachers, but so few minority kids were majoring in education. Too little pay, our seniors said. Too little respect from the kids.

No men ate with us. They were scared, I think, the conversation might center on husband-bashing, PMS remedies, and vaginal fungus.

"My committee," Liz said, "decided on an IB program. We think it would create the strongest magnet school."

The International Baccalaureate program challenged students with honors level work to prepare them for highly competitive colleges. Other schools had already developed the curriculum—a definite plus. To gain access to the program, students must commit to pursuing the strenuous work.

"I like the idea," I said. "My only concern is that we won't be able to recruit enough kids from both races, especially boys. It'll only make our problems worse if mostly white kids sign up. I only have two or three black males in any of my college bound classes."

"Reverend Bolden and other pastors are going to promote the program from their pulpits," she said. "High time our young men stop equating good grades with acting white. The Reverend's going to set up after-school tutoring for kids in the IB program, and he's going to solicit rewards of some sort from the business community for students who enroll."

The lounge buzzed with approval.

Liz raised her voice to silence the chatter. "We have even bigger plans for the future. We hope to start a KIPP—that stands for 'Knowledge Is Power Program.' We hope to develop the program at the elementary schools next year and phase into middle school the year after and eventually start it in the high school. KIPP has a track record of improving the performance of kids from all sorts of backgrounds and ethnic groups."

Miss Baker frowned. "I've seen those programs on the news. Don't the teachers have to jump through all sorts of hoops? Work longer days? And a longer school year?"

Grumbling erupted at every table. I wanted to support Liz, but a longer school year would be hard to take. I was exhausted by December. Totally drained by May. One last straw away from committing either suicide or murder by June.

"KIPP does require us to change," Liz said, "but it requires kids and parents to change too, and the results are astounding. Over 85 percent of graduates go on to college."

Those results were impressive, but I was leery of anything that asked for extra work. I was just about to say so when Miss Baker sniffed and beat me to it.

"My students already go on to college. I'm not fixing to change a single thing about my methods. They've worked well for going on forty years. No way I'm working longer days or teaching all summer."

Liz's face burned. Humiliation? Anger? I wasn't sure. She changed the subject. "How about the fundraiser? Marissa said something about a triathlon?"

I had been thinking about how to pitch this to the staff, but since nothing I'd thought up had worked out in my mind, I plunged ahead with no idea what I wanted to say. "I think we can make a ton of money. Teachers pitted against students in athletic events. A triathlon."

Liz said it sounded like a great idea. "The coaches will all volunteer. They can whip the pants off those kids, too, don't think they can't. I've seen them play pick-up ball on the weekend, and those guys still got what it takes."

I winced. This wasn't going so well. "Yeah, see, only it isn't the coaches we need to volunteer. We're looking for the least athletic teachers and the least athletic students. Being on a team disqualifies you."

Tessa exhaled mint breath. "You mean people like us?" She thought about it a moment. "I could do it, I guess. I walk a couple of miles every once in a while. What are the three events?"

"A three-mile run and a game of tennis," I said. "Brian Jones and Vashawn Diggs have volunteered to coach us."

Liz slapped a palm lightly on the lunch table. "All right! Now that's what I'm talking about, girlfriend. Free lessons. Brian and Vashawn are fantastic—have you seen those two scoot around out there on the courts? I've wanted to learn how to play ever since I started watching Venus and Serena on ESPN. I'm fixing to sign up."

I handed her the clipboard. She positioned a pen over the sign-up sheet and I saw it wasn't open. I reached over and clicked it.

"Me too," Tessa said. "I'd love some tennis lessons. It's a great sport for the South. You guys can play year round. What's the third event?"

"The third? Well, let's see. There's the five mile walk/run, tennis, and—" I wanted to get their names on the sheet before telling them, but Liz's brown hand was waiting—"the third is actually swimming."

The clipboard smacked onto the table. "Unh-uh, no way," Liz said.

"How'd you let them talk you into that?" Betsy asked.

She didn't have anything to worry about—she was young and slim and would look fantastic in a bathing suit.

"Crazy," Tessa said.

My colleagues crunched apples, chewed ham sandwiches, and crackled cheese puffs. The whole thing was falling apart. Maybe we'd have to come up with a different third event, though the kids seemed determined to have those three.

Miss Baker, the department chair, broke the silence. "You say the kids will get two credits for this class, English and fine arts?" It was Tuesday, her gray suit day.

"That's right," I said, enthusiasm returning to my voice. "Two-hour course. They read technical materials, and they write articles for the magazine and scripts for the instructional videos. The class meets all the state English standards, and at the same time, the kids do hands-on projects to earn money. It could motivate those reluctant learners."

"I hate to give in to them because maintaining our standards is important, but kids have changed since you were a student, Molly," Miss Baker said.

I had noticed, but until now I wouldn't have guessed that she had.

The inimitable Miss Baker continued. "It's hard to teach Moby Dick to a bunch who couldn't appreciate Melville unless he produced a music video. Maybe it's time to let some of them write about LL Cool J instead."

Frankly, I was surprised, not only that Miss Baker knew who LL Cool J was, but that she supported the idea for this new course.

"I'll do it," Miss Baker said. "It's my duty to support your project since you decided to follow in my footsteps and become an English teacher."

I did my best to keep my eyes from widening over her misconception. Sandwiches and junk food stopped midway to mouths. Had Miss Baker missed the part about swimming? None of us had ever seen her in anything but her gray and blue suits for as long as we could remember, except for Sundays when she traded them for a royal blue dress worn under a choir robe. She scooted her chair back, jumped up, and charged over to my table in her low-heeled black pumps.

She reached for the clipboard and signed her name. "I'll do it and y'all will too."

Liz signed first, though how she was going to swim when water terrified her, I didn't know. Miss Baker willed things into being, her ninety pounds exuding an inexplicable power. She walked the sign-up sheet around the two lunch tables, handing the clipboard back to me with seven signatures: Jolene Baker, Liz Powell, Tessa Kauffman, Betsy Mulharin, Darla Higgins, Martha Mae Beckwith, and Fran Snodgrass. Bessie Haynes received a pass because of recent knee-replacement surgery, and Colleen Yost because of her heart condition. Otherwise, the whole lunch room signed up.

"Now the success of this project rests with you." Miss Baker scrutinized me as if she were St. Peter about to open or close the gates. Finally, she added, "You always were one of my favorite students, Molly. Lots of potential."

I beamed and felt like an eleventh grader again when she'd moved me ahead of Jerry Griffin.

She tapped a gnarled finger on the sign-up sheet. "Where's your name? It should have been the first one on there."

I scrawled my name as she watched. She frowned. "Good handwriting is a sign of clear thinking and good breeding."

I felt as if she'd banished me to the last seat. With great effort, I resisted the urge to turn the clipboard over to hide my signature.

Miss Baker sat back down. "If your program succeeds, Molly, maybe the school system won't feel obligated to turn Alderson into a KIPP school. We can count on GAE and NEA to fight against programs like KIPP, so I don't think it will happen, but if it did, I might have to retire."

Liz and I looked at each other, and I knew she was thinking the same thing: Miss Baker would never retire. They would carry her out of AHS feet first and she'd be wearing either her navy or gray suit. After lunch, Tessa and I accompanied Liz on her way toward the lab.

Tessa ran her fingers through her graying hair while we dodged our way through the crowd. "The School Board is looking into grants to fund field trips. You could take the kids to the Okefenokee Swamp, get a biologist to lead them on a hike on the Appalachian Trail, maybe take them to the Marine Lab down at the coast or the Magnet Lab at FSU."

"Uh huh. Me and who else?" Liz said. "A busload of kids would drive me crazy, girlfriend."

Tessa volunteered to go with her.

"Sounds good," Liz said, "as long as there are plenty of chaperones. Maybe we can improve things enough without turning AHS into a KIPP school. Reverend Bolden sure likes the idea, though. I hate to abandon KIPP, but with Miss Baker dead set against it, it probably won't fly. I've also been toying with the idea to use the science and math on TV shows like *Numb3rs* and *CSI* to make classes more fun. You ever watch them?" Liz asked me.

"TV? Who has time? But Graham and Quinn like those shows."

"Here's an article idea for your newspaper," Tessa said. "Reverend Bolden's church and the guidance office are looking for more mentors for the Big Brother/Big Sister program. We think we can reduce drop-out rates, low school achievement, and violence. The program has a proven track record."

"About violence." I pulled the paragraph J.D. wrote about the gun from my purse and showed it to Liz and Tessa. "Do you think J.D. could be dangerous?"

Students shuffled around them as they huddled over the paper.

When they finished, Tessa exhaled loudly. "Sometimes a messed up kid turns out to be a Columbine-style killer. Sometimes he's just a messed up kid. If only we knew how to tell the difference!"

Liz wrinkled her broad nose. "He's probably fooling with your head."

"If it makes you feel any better, most incidents of school violence have been committed by white kids," Tessa said.

Most. Not all. The crowds in the hallway were thinner now as we approached the lab. J.D. stood with his back to us, holding court with a group of guys. His voice carried clearly.

"I'm telling you, that Marissa, she be one eminently pokeable bitch, purely bootylicious."

"I hear that," one of his crew said.

"She be so—" J.D. didn't have a chance to finish before Liz got in his face. The other boys saw her coming and took off.

"Don't you ever, ever come near my daughter again, you hear me?"

"Liz—" I put my hand on her arm, fearing she would attack him. Rigid with rage, she shook me off.

"Chill, ok?" J.D. said. "I didn't mean nothing by it."

"You take your trash mouth and get on out of here. Go on, git!"

Tessa intervened, taking J.D. to the guidance office.

"That boy has no respect, none at all." Liz's face was still purple. "I don't know what Marissa sees in him."

I knew exactly what her daughter saw in him. J.D. had a sensuality that drew a girl in. He had a way of looking at her that made her feel as if she were the only girl in the world he would ever want to touch. I had watched him work the girls in the hallway with his dark eyes, had seen the irresistible lure of the bad boy. He can't be all that bad, the girls think. Each one believes she is destined to tame that wild streak. Only she can save him from himself. I knew what Marissa saw in him because I had a mad crush on a bad boy my senior year in high school. How lucky I'd been that he preferred girls tall and slim as a slash pine instead of shrubby little gals like me—though I didn't think so at the time.

I offered to take the first fifteen minutes of my planning period and cover Liz's class—she looked as if she could use some time to cool off.

"No, I'll be fine," she told me. "He just better never come near my baby ever again, I can tell you that, he better never. Pokeable, my big fat behind. I'll poke him a good one, right in the jaw."

After school Shaniqua came in to discuss her participation grade.

"You don't have to talk a lot in class," I said, "only a little, and I'll triple the points I usually award for participating so you can catch up."

"I can't."

"Sure you can. You have to stop thinking you can't. That's the problem." I remembered an old trick a speech teacher had once told the class in college when some of us expressed nervousness over getting up to talk. "Everyone in the room is an ordinary person like you. Even the President of the United States is just an ordinary guy. Everyone puts his socks on one foot at a time. Everyone sits on a commode in the morning. Everyone wears underwear." She giggled—a good sign. "Imagine the people in the class doing one of these things and you'll get over your fear."

"I'll try."

"That's all I ask—try."

I should have stopped with the socks. If there was any chance I'd encouraged her to imagine me in my underwear, I'd be the one who couldn't talk.

We trained every other night, no excuses. Vashawn led us in stretching and warm-ups. He and Brian moved around the court teaching us how to serve. My muscles ached so much from a week of tennis and running, I actually felt grateful for the night we began swim practice instead.

The school's swim season didn't start until January, so the YMCA indoor pool was nearly deserted. Rain forest humidity and the pinch of spandex made it hard to breathe. When I emerged from the locker room, all I could think about was how fat—and naked—I looked in my bathing suit. It was black, because fashion mags claimed the color made you look smaller. Killer whales were black and they didn't look small. Neither did I.

Jolene Baker showed up late. Instead of dressing out in a swimsuit, she wore knee-length spandex exercise shorts with a modest exercise tank top. I felt a lightening inside. I could wear a similar outfit.

Wouldn't hide every bulge, but it would be an improvement over my too-tight suit. I thanked heaven, once again, we didn't need the boys as swim coaches. I remembered enough from my swim team days to do the job. First I had to teach Liz to float. "Relax," I said, but she floundered like a beetle flipped on its back.

"Can't relax. Black folk don't swim."

"No way you're going to get by with that sorry excuse."

Tessa tucked her short hair into a swim cap. "Imagine this. Lem's been gone for months. When he gets back, he takes you to a swanky resort and he says, 'Honey, you just lie on your back and I'm gonna treat you the way a good woman should be treated.' You just relax and let him have his way with you."

After we all stopped laughing, Liz arched her back, my hands underneath for support, and it worked. By the time I moved away, Liz actually smiled as if she enjoyed floating. Occasionally a deep-throated giggle bubbled up from her that made me wonder what kind of fantasy she was having. Teaching her to swim proved more difficult because she didn't want water in her face. Breast stroke was the best option, so I gave her a foam board and she practiced frog-kicking her way down the pool while I swam with the others.

At first I clumped down the lane, my arms and legs out of sync, but as the hour passed, the rhythms came back to me. Of all three sports, once we stopped obsessing about our lumpy shapes, we enjoyed swimming most. The buoyancy of our bodies in water. The joy of stretching arms and legs to full length. The power of self-propulsion. At some point while aching and moaning about how sore we were, we began to have fun.

Twenty-Six

O n the sidelines, Russ Freeman stood with his arm over Bobby Tidwell's shoulders, watching as the team's best kicker, Connor Morse, sent the ball into the net. The coach said something to Bobby and swatted the seventh grader's butt as he scrambled onto the field to give Connor a breathing spell. Connor, red-faced, bent over gasping for air. He had played an amazing match so far, scoring twice and putting the team ahead by one with only a little time left to go. I had missed Quinn's last game because of triathlon practice, so I yelled twice as loud this time.

"Put Quinn in!" Woodson called out. With only one game left in the season, Quinn had yet to play. He had improved tremendously in practices, both in blocking and kicking. I wasn't just saying that because I was his mother either.

Woodson grunted. "Freeman's a sorry excuse for a coach."

I took a swig from the thermos of water I carried with me everywhere now. Dust rising from the hard-packed path that bordered the field and the sweet scent of soft drinks filled the bleachers. Wished I had one. I screwed the cap off the thermos again and chugged.

Woodson squinted at me as if something puzzled him, an expression I noticed at once because my father generally believed he already knew everything. "You look different. You losing weight?"

I was. Eight pounds in two weeks. Dr. Roberts would be proud. I would beat this pre-diabetes thing before it could beat me. Brian and Vashawn insisted all the teacher triathletes adhere to a training diet. Sweets and junk food were out. Protein and complex carbohydrates were in.

It tickled me that Woodson noticed my weight loss. "Yeah, I've been exercising for a school competition."

"Wondered when you were going to tell me about that. Why haven't you asked me for money?"

I wasn't surprised he'd heard about it. Two radio stations were promoting the triathlon, and Channel Eight taped a story on us that hadn't aired yet.

"You want to sponsor me?" I asked.

"Sure. Fifty bucks for each event you complete."

He must have been very confident I would flop. "I'm going to finish all three events."

"Don't doubt it. You've always finished everything you started."

Yes, I did but my father didn't. I wondered if he would pay up after the triathlon, or if this would be one more time he would let me down.

He stopped to yell at the coach again, and then turned back to me. "Seen that Lodge fellow lately?"

"Not really. He lets Dusty out at lunchtime. Quinn's been over at his house some. Says he's building a computer for Mr. Piscetelli. There's some big deadline before Christmas. The whole thing makes me nervous. What if Quinn messes up? I mean he's only eleven."

"I wouldn't worry. Lodge knows what he's doing. He's a real solid guy. You should get to know him."

Like I needed that kind of advice from my father. Hippie lawyers weren't my type. On the other hand, my eyes shot to the field where Russ Freeman looked especially fine in a lime green golf shirt. He called Quinn's name and motioned him over. Without taking his eyes off the action, Russ leaned down and said something to my boy. Quinn went in on the next substitution.

Woodson was elated. "I think the little fairy heard me and decided to give Quinn a chance."

I snorted. "More likely he's noticed Quinn's improvement."

"I think he heard me yelling."

"You yell the same thing every game and it never made a difference before."

"So? He finally listened."

"Mr. Big Shot, everyone listens to you."

Quinn effectively blocked a kick and prevented the other team from scoring. I wished Graham was with us to see it, but he had gone off somewhere with Noah Kaufmann this afternoon.

"You go, Quinn!" Woodson yelled. He turned to me. "See? Freeman should have listened a long time ago."

No one ever won arguments with my father. His stubbornness was as legendary as his ability to consume large quantities of alcohol. The combination kept him from apologizing to my brother Sam.

Woodson criticized Freeman's hair and clothes again, but I didn't follow the specifics. Standing by my car at the edge of the lot, J.D. nodded to acknowledge me. He pointed to my son on the field and drew his finger across his throat. Our eyes held a moment, but at this distance I couldn't see the emotions reflected in their depths.

Instinctively I reached for my father's arm. I couldn't say a word, but he followed my eyes to where J.D. stood, scratching the side of his head.

"Who's that kid?" Woodson asked.

I couldn't answer. Was J.D. trying to get at me by threatening Quinn?

"He the one been giving you trouble?"

I nodded.

My father jumped to his feet and stalked off to the parking lot, but by the time he got there, J.D. had disappeared. Thank the Lord— what could Woodson have done anyway? A skinny old man two years from retirement, his body wasted from years of abuse? I winced at the thought of this unlikely Don Quixote.

Woodson returned, his work boots kicking up little clouds of dust behind him. He sat down. "What'd he do anyway?"

Already I doubted what I'd seen. I must have misunderstood J.D.'s gesture. Maybe an insect had skittered against his neck and he'd brushed it away. With relief, I accepted that explanation. If only David were here. He remained rational in situations that sent me into hysterics.

"The kid might be trying to intimidate me," I said. "I think he's been calling the house all hours of the night."

"That little n—"

"Don't you dare!" I already regretted involving Woodson. The last thing I needed was for anyone to hear my father shouting racial epithets.

"Why don't you ask Roosevelt for help?" he said.

Funny, how my father could put down a whole race in one breath, and tell me to seek the help of an individual of that race the next. Apparently he saw no contradiction. "J.D. hasn't done anything exactly, nothing I could prove."

"Let Roosevelt be the judge of that." His voice crescendoed in anger now. "Why can't you ever ask for help? You've always been this way. Remember in Scouts when you were trying to make a bird house and you sawed halfway through your finger and didn't even tell anybody?"

Of course I remembered. My left index finger still bore the scar. I made the bird house myself because my father had passed out on the couch, and my mother, God rest her soul, was too busy picking up the slack for Woodson by mowing the lawn and repairing leaky faucets for me to bother her with it.

"Why do you always have to bring up that tired old story?"

"I'm just saying, self reliance can be a good thing, but maybe you got too big a dose."

"This kid is worth saving. There has to be something I can do to connect with him." Yet everything I said and did seemed to be wrong.

"Not everybody wants to be saved."

Woodson was the perfect example.

Twenty-Seven

I went to the library. I re-read *Bringing Out the Best in People.* I checked out a book on anger management, thinking I could work with J.D.—and myself—on controlling our tempers. I knew I could do more. When he talked during my lecture, I assigned detention by placing a slip of paper on his desk instead of saying "fifteen." He still cursed. When he came to serve his time, I talked about breathing techniques and relaxing facial muscles when he felt anger coming on.

"Repeat to yourself, 'I can control my anger,'" I told him. "Say it in your mind, or say it out loud if you need to. Verbalizing can make it happen." While I talked, he wore this smug expression, arms crossed, feet sprawled out into the aisle, his head turned away to underscore how ridiculous he found my advice—and I wanted to slap him.

My father called or came over often to check on me, to ask if I'd made any progress with J.D., to see if I had called Roosevelt yet.

I hadn't. I was still trying. I researched Tupac on line, hoping to find lyrics I could use in an upcoming poetry unit. A strong voice cried out in those songs, a voice I admired. It captured the despair of racism and poverty and street life, but I couldn't bring the foul language or the hatred toward police and women into my classroom. His violence was poison.

J.D. kept asking about his paper on the Glock, so I returned it after making a copy for my files. I attached a note: I hope you don't own this gun. As I'm sure you know, possession of a weapon when you are on probation is a felony. The mark of a great receiver isn't that he never drops the ball. It's that he practices relentlessly and tries to hold on to the ball the next time. This is your next time.

When J.D. half-finished a paper on Ernest Gaines's *A Lesson Before Dying,* I complimented the ideas he did express. When he missed four of ten vocabulary sentences, I found his best one and penned "excellent use of word" beside it in green ink. Nothing softened his attitude toward me, and consequently, nothing eased my guilt over calling his language worthless.

I wasn't the only teacher having trouble with him. He cussed out Mrs. Yost and got into a scuffle with an assistant coach. His latest progress reports showed him failing four out of six subjects, but knowing of other failures did nothing to mitigate my own.

During the morning moment of silence, I continued to pray, asking God to help me love J.D., but if He heard me He wasn't talking back.

A mother knows how to reach a child sometimes when no one else does. I called J.D's for another visit. She arrived at 4:30, still in her work clothes. Jean skirt. Ruffly, flowered blouse. Sensible soft-soled shoes. Dark quarter moons under her eyes that revealed a lot about her life.

"You looking good, Miz Culpepper." She fiddled with the sleeves of her blouse. It wasn't my imagination—she was definitely uncomfortable around me.

"New haircut?" she asked.

Everyone noticed the change in my appearance. I had splurged on a new stylist Betsy Mulharin had recommended. Thirty dollars for the feathered long layers, but worth every penny. A real confidence booster. Also I hauled out the sewing machine to alter my clothes. Fifteen pounds sweated off. Who'd have thought exercise would do what countless diets alone failed to accomplish?

"We were off to such a good start with the daily behavior reports," I said. "J.D. was doing so well, and I wondered why you'd stopped picking them up."

"J.D. disrespects me," Mrs. Marshall said. "I can tell him he can't go out, but if he want to go, he's gonna go, no matter what I say. He's hanging with a bunch of no-goods down on Fulton Road. I've talked until I've run out of words. I don't know how to put a stop to his nonsense. You know, he be so bad one minute back-talking me, and the next he be bringing me home red velvet cake—that's my favorite. Or he be helping Jamilla and Rayleena with their homework and telling them how they needs to do good in school and says when he plays pro ball, he gonna send them to college so they can be nurses like they want. I don't know what to make of him."

"I imagine this year is a hard transition for him," I said. "That's why it's so important to stick with our plan."

"Things been worse ever since Homecoming. Guess you was right about having them consequences because now he don't do nothing I say. He tunes me out like I'm not there."

"Consequences are important, but I don't think that's all that's going on. You might be right about the peer group. Friends are a huge influence. Can you think of anything else that could account for his behavior?"

"No, ma'am." She gathered up her purse as if to leave, but then settled back into the chair. "You know, there is something else that might be bothering my boy. Someone told him things about your husband." Her eyes flickered over my face and flicked away. "About how he arrested me and all. J.D. wanted to know why I hadn't told him. I just want to let go of the past. Maybe I was wrong-headed."

My mind spun. I hadn't realized she had made the connection between my late husband and me. After all, we weren't the only Culpeppers in town. J.D.'s hurt and shame and anger suddenly came into focus. He was four years old again and I was the wife of the man who took his Mama away from him, separated him from his brothers and sisters, gave him to strangers to raise up. I didn't know how to overcome that kind of hurt.

"I should have told him David was nothing but kindness. He never forgot me," she said, "Even brought me red velvet cake over to the state prison."

"What?" I was missing something here.

"Uh huh, your husband said I did the right thing. If I hadn't killed Ray, he would've killed me or the kids sooner or later. I tried leaving that man and he beat me so bad he dislocated my jaw. I can't hardly hear in my left ear from where he walloped me. I didn't mean to hurt J.D. none. When my boy grabbed my arm like he did, I was so mad at Ray, so mad over finding that woman's panties in my bed—my bed—I paid for it—I couldn't see straight, no, ma'am, that's what happened. When I flung my boy away, to go after Ray, poor little guy fell against the bureau drawer. I didn't mean to hurt him. Your husband told me to say it was Ray broke J.D.'s arm. Said it would make me more sympathetic to a jury. No sense in leaving four kids with no parents at all, he said. Miz Culpepper, your husband was a good man."

I had always thought so. I thought he was the most honorable man I'd ever met. Now this woman was telling me he helped her lie to get away with murder. She called him by his first name. He knew her favorite cake. What was Anita Marshall to David? Even after a decade in prison, she was attractive by anyone's standards. Back then, she was downright beautiful, more beautiful than I had ever been on my best days, on my skinniest days, certainly more beautiful than I felt when I carried eight months of pregnancy clumsily around my middle and when my wrecked hormones had me crying one minute and angry the next and exhausted all the time. I wondered again: who was this woman to David?

With effort I managed to form a few words. "He told you to lie in court?"

She licked her lips, and her eyes darted toward the closed door. I could tell she wished she hadn't started this conversation. "It wasn't exactly a lie. Ray beat me and the kids, lots of times, that's the honest-to-God truth. Your husband said the kids would be better off if they had their own mama raising them. I know that's true. Those foster homes messed up J.D. real bad. Worse than my other kids, I think."

I tried to apply my mother's moral code to the situation. White lies were the little ones you told with good intentions, such as sparing someone's feelings. Covering up your own sins was a black lie. *You blister in Hell for black lies, so you better not tell any,* my mother said. I told plenty of fibs but tried to tell the truth about anything important. I dreaded those blisters and, even more, I dreaded my mother's disapproval.

David's lie corrupted the justice system he said he believed in. I remembered the hours he spent reviewing testimony, his exhaustion in the months before and after the trial. Who was Anita Marshall that he'd lie for her under oath?

I wasn't sure I wanted to know.

No, that was a lie. I needed desperately to know.

The morning after the conference, I avoided interacting with J.D. until I could reassess my strategies. We needed to have a frank discussion of my husband's role in the arrest and trial, yet dread overwhelmed me when I thought of bringing it up. Any reference to his mother's incarceration would arouse emotions that could spiral out of control. He was so loosely bound by civility anyway.

I called on Shaniqua, but she whispered something unintelligible and her brown eyes turned liquid. She must have been imagining me in my underwear. Sometimes it brought tears to my eyes too. To divert attention from her, I quickly called on Orville. He never feared sharing his opinion even if he hadn't read the material.

Nothing I'd learned in college education classes or in-service training prepared me to deal with real students and the problems they faced. After class, I whispered to Shaniqua to stop by after school. I had one more idea I wanted to try.

At lunchtime Tessa and I entered the lounge together.

"I had another conference with Mrs. Marshall," I said.

"Really? What did she tell you?"

The counselor's tone and expression held way too much concern for an ordinary parent conference. I could hear voices in my mind, Tessa warning Liz: *It'll be worse if she finds out from someone else.* Everyone else knew about David and this woman, was that it? Everyone had known but me. Had he loved her? I couldn't believe it, not of David. It had to be something else—but what?

"Molly? You okay?"

"Yeah, sorry, what did you ask?"

"What did Mrs. Marshall have to say?"

The lounge was filling with people. There was only so much I could put out there in public view. "J.D. knows that my husband arrested his mother and testified at her trial."

Tessa unwrapped a peppermint. "So you think he's grown especially hostile toward you since he found out about your husband? That makes sense. I can't think of anything else that could account for his anger, can you?"

"No, not a thing." Nothing. Nada. Nugatory. Just a word game that back-fired and a husband who was entangled in some way with J.D.'s mother. Again, I felt like I was playing The Accused Witch in Early America game, and the judges were testing me by piling stones on my chest and esophagus to force me to confess. I couldn't. Instead, I dug in my purse for the acid blockers.

"His mother says she can't control him anymore," I said.

"She shouldn't give up. Parents have more leverage than they think." Tessa pronounced it lee-ver-ij, with a long "e."

Miss Baker, sitting at the next table, overheard. "It's lev-er-ij." She pronounced a soft "e."

Tessa scooted her chair from the table and stalked out of the lounge. Liz and I looked at each other briefly and then back at our food. The lounge grew uncomfortably quiet. A minute later Tessa returned with a dictionary. I sucked in my breath.

Tessa thrust it in front of Miss Baker, her index finger tapping the word, her nasal Jersey voice loud enough for people two counties away to hear. "Lee-ver-ij. The first pronunciation listed. I believe that means it's preferred."

Miss Baker's lips twitched as she read the entry. "Well, no one pronounces it that way."

"Well, I do, and so does Webster." She slammed the dictionary shut, turned on her heel, and left the lounge.

I followed her into the hall, careful to avoid Miss Baker's eyes. "Why did you do that?"

Tessa spoke loudly, not at all concerned who might hear. "You all treat her like she's some kind of goddess, and I'm tired of it, that's all. She doesn't know everything."

I guess she didn't. Just almost. Sure, some students clamored to get out of her classes, but many clamored to get in. It was a badge of honor to survive Miss Baker. Her mythology extended beyond the classroom. Tessa didn't understand. Miss Baker's maternal grand-mother had been an Alderson. One of *the* Aldersons. At seventeen, Miss Baker sang for the governor of the State of Georgia. That was about the closest you could get to being a goddess in Mason County. My mother had seen her perform "Somewhere Over the Rainbow" in a rehearsal before she left for the capital. Her voice, my mother said, filled the auditorium with almost unbearable presence. Besides, she had taught here for thirty-eight years without missing a single day. Not one—unheard of! That degree of devotion deserved some respect.

"Something else you should know about Miss Baker," Tessa said. "She's called in the big dogs."

"What do you mean?" I asked.

"NEA lawyers to fight the ideas Liz and her committee have come up with for improving our education system. So who are you going to back? The National Education Association or your students?"

She delivered the question like an accusation. As if she knew I didn't want a longer school day. Or a longer school year. If a heart could cry, mine was sobbing great wrenching tears at the hint of more work. Miss Baker and the teachers union would likely win. They were powerful and moneyed, and it was difficult to change the status quo.

"Liz, of course." What else could I do?

Twenty-Eight

Bleary-eyed and edgy, Shaniqua looked as if she'd over-dosed on caffeine. Other students responded to the first two questions I tossed out about Anne Sexton's poem "Oysters." Then I came to the one Shaniqua and I had chosen after school. "What do you think Sexton means by 'father foods'?" Several hands shot up before the last words left my mouth, and I hoped no one would shout out the answer. Quickly I called on Shaniqua.

Her hands gripped her textbook.

I sent waves of good thoughts across the space between us: *Come on, girl, you can do it, don't whisper, let it out.*

She practically yelled her answer. "Foods you are afraid to eat!"

Ceci and Brian swiveled in their desks to stare.

In a more modulated tone with a smug grin, she continued. "They are the foods you have to develop a taste for, the ones you hate as a kid."

Peas, tomatoes, squash, liver, broccoli, snails—oh, I loved listening to my students rattle off their own father foods. Endorphins surged through my body.

Orville revealed he had shucked oysters at a restaurant for a while. "Sexton calls them eyes because of their gooey texture and the shell looks like an eye socket."

"Gross!" Marissa said. "How can anyone eat them?"

"How many of you have eaten raw oysters?" I asked. Only three raised their hands.

"How many have never seen one before?" A dozen innocents. From a tiny cooler behind my desk, I withdrew a Styrofoam carton with an oyster on the half-shell and handed it to J.D. to pass around the room. He hadn't raised his hand, but from the way he studied the contents of the carton I suspected he was meeting an oyster eye-to-eye for the first time.

"Why does Sexton say the speaker ate 'one o'clock' and 'two

o'clock'?" I looked around the room as if considering who to call on. I ignored the raised hands and called on Shaniqua again, a risk I thought worth taking so her success wouldn't be a one-time thing.

Her eyes widened and her arms went rigid. Everyone turned to watch her. I nodded encouragingly.

She hesitated so long I readied myself to accept this setback and move on. Then she sat up taller in her seat. "The dozen are served up in a circle like the hours on the face of a clock."

"Exactly right. Fantastic answer!" I directed my next question to the whole class. "For the speaker, the end of childhood arrived when she overcame her fear of eating oysters for the first time. What are other fears people might have to overcome in order to grow up?"

Responses varied from asking out a girl you really liked, to facing rejection, going off to summer camp for the first time, and moving away to college. While the class blurted out ideas, Shaniqua's lips lifted like a new moon. I remembered the answer she gave to this question before she left my room yesterday afternoon. I winked at her. Yes, there had been the death of childhood in Mrs. Culpepper's room this morning. Shaniqua had won.

Life was good and soon would be even better. Only four more classes until the Thanksgiving holiday.

Twenty-Nine

November 30 was a date burned in my memory. It had been a school day like any other. A Wednesday. I remembered Dr. Parker, our principal then, making a point to tell me the newspaper that had come out that day was the best we'd ever done. Quinn had walked over from the elementary school for a ride home. We picked up Graham from soccer practice. Ate beanie weenie for dinner. So stupid, the things you remember. Later I had graded paragraphs comparing Creon and Antigone as tragic heroes and fallen asleep during Letterman. The phone call had come at 1:30 a.m.

One other person would be remembering. I hadn't seen my father for a few days, not since Thanksgiving supper, but I had called every morning and he'd made it to work. After playing two sets of tennis with Liz, I swung home to pick up a vase of camellias I'd cut that morning and took them to the cemetery. To my surprise, someone had placed a spray of gardenias on her grave. It must have been my father, but why? They were out of season. Must have cost a fortune.

As I drove out to his house, it crossed my mind more than once that I might be wasting my time. He could be sitting on a barstool at Big Fred's, but no, the old truck sat on the graveled driveway. I poked my head in the door. Soft chords rose like penitent prayers from the piano in the living room. I hadn't heard him play for years. When I was a little girl, Woodson had played carols while I snuggled beside him on the bench, singing "O Come All Ye Faithful" and "Joy to the World," my hair French braided in a long plait and tied with red ribbon—my mother's touch. She and Sam stood behind us, her hand resting on my shoulder. On weekends when Sam and I were young, my father and mother would invite other couples over and they would dance or sing while my father pounded out everybody's favorites. He could make the keys jump and jive like Jerry Lee Lewis. When his drinking worsened, the parties stopped.

I drifted through the kitchen and dining room, drawn by "Claire de Lune." The melody poured from the keys like liquid sorrow. Still in the navy uniform he wore to work, his long, thin fingers stroked the ivory, his body swaying slightly, back and forth, back and forth. The shape of his hands looked too refined for the manual labor that had stained his cuticles and chipped his nails. A glass of bourbon sat on the back of the upright. Between a pair of candlesticks surrounded by framed family photographs stood a nearly full bottle. He finished the piece, his hands still resting on the keys.

Without turning around, he said, "This was your mother's favorite song. Did you know that?"

I quietly absorbed this unexpected glimpse into my mother's life. There was so much I didn't know about her. She had always been busy—cooking, cleaning, working in alterations at a local department store. After I'd grown up, I was busy, too, raising kids and grading papers. I'd never stopped to ask her questions about herself. Thought there would be more time. Had always thought it would be my father who went first. My mother took care of herself—and us. My father worked so hard at abusing his body—and us. Yet he lived and she died. I'd spent the last year thinking it wasn't fair, resenting my father a little for not dying in her place. What if he joined her instead?

Ice cubes clinked as Woodson upended the highball, spilling a sickly sweet scent into the air and a few dribbles down his shirt. A water ring was forming on the piano's mahogany finish where the drink had rested. While he refilled his glass, I tissued up the condensation and slipped a coaster into place.

"Dad, you don't want to end up back in the hospital."

"Give it a rest, huh? Today of all days, I need to take the edge off."

Sighing, I studied their wedding photo on the back of the piano: two young people who smiled as though every day of their lives would be as magical as that one. "What was she like back when you were dating?"

"Very opinionated. When we got married, she insisted on gardenias for her bouquet even though they were out of season and cost a fortune."

"I thought she liked camellias best." Had I just assumed that because she was once the Camellia Queen?

"She liked them too. Said they would have been perfect if only they had fragrance. Haven't you noticed she chose most of the flowers in her garden for their scent?"

I hadn't. Now I understood the white blooms on her grave. He must have special-ordered them.

"I don't blame her for loving gardenias," I said. "They do smell like heaven. Do you remember how she'd hum when she was fixing dinner, how she'd do little dance steps in front of the stove, and she'd lick the wooden spoon and put it right back into the saucepot? When I'd catch her, she'd say not to worry—the heat would kill the germs."

He laughed. "She never served anything she didn't taste first. Several times. She was always trying to get me to test stuff for her, but I never could tell whether a dish needed more oregano or parsley. Everything she made tasted good to me." He picked up a framed photograph of Sam and me. I looked about four and had just begun to lose my baby fat. "She dressed you like a little prince and princess. Sewed all your clothes, matching outfits."

"She made those?" The brother-sister ensembles were navy with vee-shaped white insets at the neck with tiny pin-tucks like tuxedo shirts. They looked perfect. Store-bought.

"Oh yeah, that's how she ended up doing alterations and pageant and wedding gowns later on when I couldn't work after the accident. Everyone in town knew she could sew because they'd seen you kids."

"Accident? I thought she went to work when you went to live with Gran and Grandpa in Atlanta for a while." I remembered a seven-year-old girl, betrayed by a daddy who disappeared for what seemed like forever. We saw less of Mama, too, since she was working.

"Went to live with them?" He snorted. "I was laid up in the hospital for a couple months after the accident and couldn't work. Don't you remember your Aunt Helen keeping you so your mother could visit me several nights a week?"

"No." How strange to have such a big chunk of personal history rewritten. "Do you think Mama might have lied to protect us?"

His voice emerged sharp, edged with anger. "Your mama never lied. She was the most honest person I ever knew."

He continued his story, how he'd lost control of the car on a curve, the painful physical therapy that followed, but my mind raced in another direction. My mother *had* lied. All the time. *Sorry, Mr. Kelso, my husband has a cold and can't come in today.* Or she'd tell me, *Maybe you'd better not invite Carolyn over this afternoon. Your father needs some rest.* My father would have busted a gut if he'd heard her telling Mrs. Alford how proud they both were of Sam. He hated having an interior decorator for a son, no matter how successful he was. My mother and David lied to cover up other people's sins. What color of lies were those?

The only one in my family who always told the truth, no matter what, was my father. He didn't care who he offended or pissed off or hurt. He said what was on his mind. Always had.

"Mom and Pop didn't really love each other, far as I could tell," he was saying now. "Stayed together to take care of us kids. Later on out of habit or because it was expected, I don't know. They were regular churchgoers. Pentecostal. Teetotalers. Hard on us kids. Took good care of us, though. Food on the table. Shoes on our feet. Nursed me back to health after that accident. I stayed with them a couple of months after the hospital threw me out."

I could only imagine what a terrible patient he'd been. "I'm sure you deserved it." Not wanting the connection between us to end, I rested my hand on his shoulder. "You told me what Mama liked. What did you like back then?"

He laughed, but the sound was hard and bitter. "Your mother. I liked your mother. Even in high school there was no one else." He drank the bourbon down in one gulp and refilled the glass. "Have one with me?" He held out the bottle.

I hesitated, didn't want to spoil the closeness of the moment. "No, I detest the smell."

"Glass of wine instead?"

It sounded good and I deserved one after such a rough day. But there were so many rough days. Was that how it started? I wanted to ask him. I needed to hear him say the drinking hadn't started because he didn't love us or because we weren't enough to make him happy. But I couldn't ask, no matter now much I wanted to know the answer.

"No, I'd better not. I have to pick up Quinn at Donnie's. I just wanted to see if you were okay. Why don't you come over for dinner tonight?"

His fingers raked across the keyboard. He lifted his hand and pounded a fist in a cacophonic explosion "Ah, go on then. Be that way, for chrissakes, prissy little school marm."

Tears stung my eyes. Why did I let him get to me? He'd always been sociable one minute, angry the next. Caused by the alcohol, sure, but I wanted to love my father, really love him, and he made it so hard.

His voice emerged ragged and bereft. "She was so proud of you, you know, for becoming a teacher. She always said teachers changed the world, one child at a time."

And what about him? Was he proud of me? No, I was just a prissy little school marm.

"I can't believe she's gone," he said.

She wasn't—gone. I carried her with me everywhere I went, maybe even more strongly than when she'd been alive. Hers was the voice I heard inside my head. Right now she was adamant: I couldn't let him sit there and drink himself to death tonight. I picked up his glass and the bottle.

"Dinner's in half an hour. Chicken and biscuits. You'd better drag your sorry butt off that piano stool and be there on time. If you aren't, the boys and I are coming back for you."

His fingers caressed the keys again. The notes of "Claire de Lune" rained down as I left the bourbon in the kitchen and went to get my son.

Thirty

The following weekend when I opened the front door, Dusty shot between my legs, down the porch steps, barking furiously. He hurled himself at the base of the live oak. Bits of bark showered down on him, knocked loose by the squirrel that scampered out of reach and mocked him. I was beginning to think I existed only to open and close the door for a little dictator and to toss biscuits on demand. He liked to stand beneath the treat canister and tilt his head from me to the biscuits repeatedly until I got the idea. He sniffed at dry kibble and turned his tail on it. So I gave him canned or home-cooked dinners. No one in the family dreamed of arguing with Dusty. The tone of his bark was as peremptory as Miss Baker's. Delayed gratification was not a philosophy he tolerated.

I'd let him out three times already since Saturday night supper and yet was afraid not to let him out again in case he actually needed to potty. When he ran back to me, I intended to scold him, but he smiled so joyfully, rump wagging, that I scratched behind his ears instead.

Quinn had gone camping with the Scouts, and Graham had walked over to Mary Wade's for pizza and a rented movie. On the sly, I called her parents to make sure they would be home. So it was Saturday night, just me and Dusty and two sets of five-paragraph essays to grade, but me and the essays weren't talking to each other. I couldn't get in the mood. I hated the defeat written on students' faces over low mechanics grades. To balance the negatives, I wrote at least three positive comments on every paper. On the weakest papers, it took a long time to come up with compliments. I'd spent the afternoon grading one class-set and I was thoroughly sick of locating thesis statements and supporting details.

The house was quiet except for the periodic thrum of the heater. Too quiet without my boys. I sat down on the piano bench and patted the empty space on the cushion beside me. Dusty hopped into

my arms and promptly curled up, a warm little wooly worm against
my thigh. I folded back the key cover, leafed through a collection of
songs I hadn't played for ages, and selected the Beatles' "Sgt. Pep-
per's Lonely Hearts Club Band." I followed it with "Do You Wanna
Dance" by Johnny Rivers and The Blues Brothers' "Flip, Flop and Fly."
I banged the keys with enthusiasm as joyful rhythms flowed through
me. Finally I gave in to the wistfulness I truly felt and played "Moon
River." The music made the yearning inside inflate like a bubble until
it filled me up, and the ache poured through my fingers and made my
ears cry. After I touched the last chord, I sat lost in silence, absently
stroking Dusty's thick fur.

Bolting from the cushion, the dog speed-raced to the front door,
barking frantically. He clawed three times at the strike plate. "Okay,
okay, I'll let you out."

Before I could get there, the woodpecker knocker clacked. The
handmade creation had been a gift from my husband's partner, Roosevelt Pitts. With my eye pressed to the peephole, I got a fish-eye's view
of C. Lodge Piscetelli, his wire-rimmed glasses and nose distorted to
House of Mirror proportions. I opened the door.

He stood there awkwardly, in flip flops and jeans, his hands behind his back, hiding something. "Hey, I heard you playing and—"

"How'd you know it was me?"

"Quinn said you played. He confessed you were disappointed neither of your sons took to the piano."

"Guess I was, a little. You want to come in?"

He did. So did Baxter, who stood quietly behind him while Dusty
yapped and circled this interloper at a safe distance. Mr. Piscetelli's
arm came around revealing the gleaming brass of a saxophone. He
smelled wonderful, like freshly laundered cotton just retrieved from
a clothesline. "Up for a jam?"

"I'm not good enough. I don't—"

"All you have to do is keep playing like you were and I'll join in.
Didn't I hear 'Moon River'? Let's start with it."

"What about the dogs?" Dusty was throwing a fit, all stiff-legged,
barking and lunging as if he thought he could mount a serious challenge to Baxter. If the Lab had a mind to, he could dispense with
Dusty with one swipe of his club-sized paw.

"Leave them alone," Lodge said. "They'll work it out. Be friends before you know it."

While we played "Moon River," the Lab stood still and let the little Pom approach and sniff his butt. After several more lunges and quick back-tracks, Dusty determined the Lab meant no harm.

Next we played some classic B.B. King and Duke Ellington. As I relaxed, I sometimes sang along even though my voice tended to stray off pitch and my limited range forced me to change octaves frequently. Lodge's saxophone poured out slow golden honey, moaned like a broken heart, jived like a jitterbug. I have always loved a saxophone. It ranks right up there with the piano in my book.

Then I took a risk. From the collection of music stored inside the piano bench, I hauled out a book of Manilow songs my sons and David always made fun of. Sappy, David called them. Dorky, Graham said. My fingers sought out the notes to "Mandy." Lodge didn't lose a beat. His saxophone cried right beside my piano. It came to me that I felt happy. More like the real me, not just the teacher or the mom, than I had for a long time.

"I'm fixing to play one just for you, now," he said. "Sit on the couch and close your eyes. I think you will really feel this one."

I thought he was exaggerating until the song began to slide through the air, a melody I'd never heard before and yet I felt as if I'd always known it, as if it had replayed in my heart many times. My bones dissolved, melted into each note. The longing, the love—Lodge captured everything that ached, everything I lived for, in his song.

For several seconds after he finished, I remained under the song's spell. When I opened my eyes, Lodge was staring at me with the deepest green eyes I'd ever seen. Haunted eyes. I could smell his good clean scent, as if he'd just stepped out of the shower. I felt as if we'd seen each other naked. We didn't know each other well enough for that. I hustled into the kitchen. To cover my confusion, I opened a cabinet and searched for something I could put out for him to eat.

"What was that song?"

"A piece written by Carlos Santana called 'Europa.' One of my favorites."

"I can see why. Want something to drink?" For the first time in years my refrigerator wasn't stocked with sweet tea—a result of training and diabetes prevention. I still had a liter of soda for the boys. "I don't have much to offer. No chips. Veggie sticks—how about that?"

"Water's fine," he said.

When he aimed his backside at one of the stools along the breakfast bar, I warned him it wobbled. "I've been meaning to fix it, but those funny little silver things underneath are hard to tighten."

He upended the stool and examined the assembly. "I'd be happy to do it. Where's your socket wrenches?"

"What kind of wrenches?"

He disappeared across the street and returned with a plastic case arrayed with shiny tools in different sizes. He selected the right one on the first try. I guessed he'd done this sort of thing before. He righted the stool, shook it to test its stability, and sat down.

While Lodge talked, I cut up red bell peppers, cauliflower, and celery. With the kitchen counter between us I was able to relax. Using his foot, he swiveled the stool back and forth slightly the way my boys did, which was probably what loosened the assembly in the first place.

"Quinn's a great kid," Lodge said, "a quick learner and a whiz with computers."

I wondered if that's why he had come over, to talk about Quinn.

"He seems happier lately," Lodge said.

"Happier than what?"

"Than when I first moved in. He'd come over in my yard and ask if he could play with Baxter. He seemed mopey, like he was missing his dad. He talks about him a lot. I think it helps."

"To you? He talks about David?" Why would he talk to a stranger? And then the answer came to me. Because he couldn't talk to me. When one of us accidentally let the word "Dad" slip, we tensed, watching each other from the corners of our eyes to see if we had drawn blood, aware we had picked at a scab better left alone. And yet it was hard not to talk about David; his shadow remained in every corner of our lives. In the living room recliner, which everyone avoided as if David had nodded off to sleep there. In the everyday tasks he used to do—igniting the grill, winterizing the lawn mower, washing the pots and pans after I cooked—tasks someone else had to take over in his absence. In Graham's hair and eyes, in Quinn's sweet concern for others, in every pore of my skin that remembered his touch. I shook off the memories. They felt false somehow, tainted by secrets he'd kept with Anita Marshall. Yet they were the truest things I'd ever known. I was thoroughly confused.

"He talks about a lot of stuff," Lodge said. "How hard you try to be both mom and dad, how you never miss a game."

But I had missed a game or two lately. "Oh, no, is he upset that I missed—"

"No, no, he is glad you are doing the triathlon. Said you needed the exercise, and his grandpa comes to most games anyway."

I was relieved. It seemed he knew a lot about us while I knew next to nothing about him. "What about you? Ever been married? Got kids stashed away somewhere?"

The smile went out of his eyes. "Married once, no kids."

"What happened?"

"Ancient history, best forgotten." After an awkward silence, he asked me how I'd met my husband.

I had been a first-year teacher. When the school resource officer went on maternity leave, David filled in for her. He was tall and blonde and All-American in the looks department. I remembered him from high school though he'd been two years older and we didn't run with the same crowd. He hung out so often by my doorway during class changes, one of my students finally told him to ask me out and get it over with. So David did, right then, to the wild applause of those who happened to be standing nearby.

"How'd you know he was the one?" Lodge asked.

I closed my eyes. I didn't know how to put it into words. Finally I thought of this: "You know how you feel inside when you play a song on your saxophone and it matches your mood exactly? That's how I knew. He made me feel that kind of joy." I wanted to ask him if his ex-wife ever made his insides feel like a song, but he obviously didn't want to talk about her.

"Lodge is an interesting name. Were you named for someone in your family?"

"Grandpa."

"What's the C. stand for, anyway?"

He grinned. "Anyone ever tell you that you're nosy? By the way, I read in the paper you're looking for sponsors for the triathlon, and I hoped you'd sign me up."

So that's why he'd come over. He wrote "Lodge Piscetelli" on line 47, right under Woodson Trask and most members of my Sunday school class. Ka-ching. I could hear the money piling up.

Lodge pulled a deck of cards from the back pocket of his jeans. "You know how to play gin?"

I wasn't Woodson's daughter for nothing. Piano wasn't the only thing he'd taught me.

Thirty-One

M rs. Alford had been out with a sick grandchild again, and I was more than willing to pray for the kid's rapid recovery if it meant I wouldn't have to sit through another of Mr. Van Teasel's Sunday lectures. Served me right for turning Mrs. Alford down as a substitute Sunday school leader. I could get in front of kids and talk all day, but put me in front of a group of adults and I stumbled over my words. I truly empathized with kids like Shaniqua.

Mrs. Alford conducted class in such a pleasing manner. We began with a short prayer and song, followed by illuminating discussions. The Weasel preached, in the worst, most sanctimonious sense of the word. This morning he had lectured on why women should stay at home and defer to their husbands in all matters. What did his wife, a hospital administrator, think, sitting in the chair in front of me? I knew what Jolene Baker thought. She'd stopped me on the way in to the 10:45 service and pointed out the silly fool hadn't stopped to think about what he said. If the women in the class half listened to him, the high school would be short five teachers come Monday morning. Not to mention the bank would toss him onto the street at the end of the month when he couldn't make the mortgage payment without his wife's salary.

Having to stare at Mr. Van Teasel for an hour this morning had been especially unnerving. When I had walked out with Lodge onto the front porch near midnight, the Van Teasels were getting out of their Lexus. I didn't know why I felt so guilty standing there under the porch light, but even a glimpse of Mr. Van Teasel always made me search my conscience for what I had done wrong. Surely something. Playing cards. Being unchaperoned with a man I wasn't married to. Having holes in my granny pants.

"I have half a mind to start calling the church to find out if Mrs. Alford is going to be there or not before I go next time," I fumed to

Woodson while I sautéed chicken breasts, turning them with tongs.

"Why don't you change churches?" Woodson said.

I wiped my hands on a dish towel and flung it on the faux-wood countertop. "I was baptized and married at First Baptist. Why should I be the one to leave?"

"I don't see why you go at all. Won't catch me wasting a good Sunday morning."

True. My mother had seen to it that Sam and I went. "Heaven forbid you try to edify yourself in any way. I go because it's good for the boys. Besides, I like the people. I feel like I miss something when I'm not there."

He laughed. "Gossip, you mean."

"That too."

"Talk about missing something, I miss your fried chicken. When you gonna fix some?"

"It's not on the training menu—too greasy." No need to tell Woodson about the borderline diabetes and my doctor's command to change my eating habits. "Besides, you'll like this Chicken Piccata."

"I'm too old to care if fried chicken's bad for you. If you gotta go anyway, you might as well go having fun. How's the training coming along?"

Quite well, actually, as we rolled into the final two weeks. The possible proceeds from sponsors totaled $7,000. We didn't know how much the entertainment would bring in. Graham and his band were up first, followed by a step contest Marissa had arranged. We set admission at $5 and how many would attend was anybody's guess. Step teams paid $30 to enter. So far five groups had signed up, for a total of $150. Awards 4 You donated trophies, so all the money would go toward new classes.

We were also holding a bake sale throughout the day. School clubs and the PTA would contribute items and, of course, the bunch in the lounge would donate their best cakes and pies. I bought ingredients for two versions of The Next Best Thing to Sex, one with sugar and regular cream cheese, the other fat and sugar free for my family. No way I was making it and not getting at least a taste. Quinn said he had a surprise planned for me on the day of the event, but he wouldn't give me a hint no matter how much I tried to pry it from his lips.

Woodson wandered into the garage with the boys. He only half shut the door behind him. I could hear my mother now, asking him if he was born in a barn and him saying a little fresh air never hurt anybody. If she complained about cost of the heat or air conditioning going right out the door, he would tell her to turn them off and save even more.

Metal clanged and tinkled against the concrete floor of the garage. "Jezuss H. Kee-rist! What moron put those there?"

I suspected I was the moron and he had tripped over the paint tray and spilled the brushes on the floor. Good thing they were dry. Storage space, always at a premium in the garage, was nonexistent in the year since the boys had moved their band in there.

In a loud voice I could hear from the kitchen, my father tried to convince the boys to include old time country songs in their repertoire, but Graham flat-out said no. They were having enough trouble defining their sound as it was. I was glad Woodson was here. Graham refused to speak to me because he'd found out I called Mary Wade's parents to make sure they would be home as chaperones.

Somehow the guy talk shifted to sex and whether the boys knew about it. They laughed at him.

"What do you want to know, Grandpa?" Graham said. "Don't be afraid to ask."

"You know so much, Mr. Smarty Pants," Woodson said, "then you'll understand why you boys might need to spend the night over at my place sometimes, give your mother a little breathing room."

What in heaven's name was he talking about?

"Mom!" Graham's voice moved an octave higher than usual. "You gotta be kidding!"

"Yeah, your mom. She's a good looking woman, and she's young—too young to spend the rest of her life alone. It's about time she started going out again, don't you think?"

He was nuts—I didn't have time. When would I go out? At midnight when I finished grading papers?

"You mean on a *date?*" Quinn sounded incredulous. Mothers didn't have dates or sex or bodies anymore than teachers did.

I scooped six half teaspoons of capers out of a tiny glass jar and sprinkled them over the chicken breasts. They looked like rabbit poop.

I hoped they tasted better than they looked. I didn't want my father to know it was a new recipe because he didn't like me to experiment on him. I hated to admit he had a valid point about my situation. I didn't want to spend the rest of my life alone, but I didn't know what to do about it. I hadn't been on a date for over sixteen years. There weren't any single men my age at church and I sure wasn't going to hang out in bars with Woodson. It was nice to know he would keep the boys at his house if I ever did have the opportunity to date again. Not that I could see it happening in this lifetime.

"Dad!" I yelled. "I need your help in here."

He came out of the garage, leaving the door ajar again. "You know I'm no good in a kitchen."

I handed him a lemon and a knife. "Thin slices, please."

The clean scent of citrus rose from the cutting board. "You invite Lodge over for Sunday supper with us?" he said.

I flipped the chicken to brown on the other side. "Why would I?"

"Why not? Didn't you have fun last night?"

"How'd you know about that?"

"I told him the coast was clear. No kids."

Oh, Lord, the last thing I needed was my father playing matchmaker.

"So, why didn't you ask him over today?" he said.

I didn't know. I could easily have invited him after gin. We tied in number of hands won, and it had been fun, but there was something about him. His secretiveness about his former marriage. The skinny braid that squiggied down the back of his head—what was up with that? I'd never known a man with a braid before. And those green eyes— they were so intense. I was a little afraid of how they made me feel. Like I could lose myself in them. Or find out something about myself I hadn't known before. Besides, he was the lawyer for the other side.

"I hardly know him."

"What's to know? He owns his own computer business, he's down-to-earth, he's nice to my grandsons—he's coming over later to teach them to fine tune an equalizer, by the way. What else you want to know?"

It wasn't enough. "Why he's divorced, for starters."

"Wife left him for his best friend and ex-law partner. Satisfied now?"

When I'd asked Lodge why he'd come to town, all I'd gotten was a lie. Business decision, my foot. Guess it was understandable, a man not wanting to talk about a mess like that. Explained that sad puppy look he had too.

"How do you find out these things?"

"We shared a six-pack. Loosens the tongue right up."

I shook my head. My father seemed hell-bent on killing himself, one drink at a time.

Woodson dumped the lemons into the skillet and frowned. "You sure this tastes good? Those little green things look like rabbit poop."

After we ate, Woodson and Quinn drove to the Quik-mart for milk so we'd have some for breakfast. I cracked the door to the garage to ask if Graham had done his homework. I stopped when I heard Lodge's voice. Helping Graham learn to use the equalizer, I thought.

"What's with this green goddess stuff on your notebook?" Lodge asked.

I felt awkward around Lodge now because of my father's match-matching attempts and started to shut the door, but curiosity stopped me. What was green goddess besides a salad dressing and why did Lodge sound so disturbed?

"Just a girl I know. I tried to draw her—pretty cool, huh?"

"I'm not stupid, Graham. I know what the 4:20 beside it means too."

"So?"

Graham often used that defiant tone on me, but I'd never heard him turn it on anyone else.

"Bet you've tried it," he said.

Tried what? It dawned on me he was talking about some drug. Green. Marijuana. My kid? Alcohol experimentation I half expected at some point in high school, but not this. I had seen his notebook a hundred times and hadn't read anything evil into the fantasy-girl drawn on the cover—he often doodled, and 4:20?—why surely a reminder of some meeting with Mary Wade, the time a movie started, or when Noah planned to come over to rehearse. Lodge seemed to think some sinister meaning lurked behind that penned-in time.

"I have—" Lodge began.

Oh Lord, he could at least lie about it. No way was he going to encourage Graham. I shifted my weight forward, ready to march in there and give them both a piece of my mind.

"—but I was much older than you, and even then it was a bad idea." I waited.

"All the bands do it," Graham said. "You know they do."

"Yeah, I did it with a band, but I was in college and being stoned made me less of a musician than I could have been. You probably don't care what I think, but I'm going to tell you anyway. It's dangerous when kids your age dope up. It makes you lazy and unmotivated at a time in your life when you need all the energy you can drum up. You understand what I'm saying? The next eight years will make or break your life. Another reason you should stay away from that stuff is that teenagers' brains aren't hard-wired yet. Drinking and doping can change you permanently."

"Yeah? And how do you know about brains—you a brain surgeon?"

"I read while I listen to music at night. *Newsweek, Popular Science, Rolling Stone*—read it in one of those. Anyway, my advice to you is to wait at least until you're out of high school."

I admired Lodge for ignoring the snotty tone of Graham's question. Don't know if I could have.

"I thought you'd be different, but you're not." Graham sounded like a pouty brat. I could just imagine his expression. "You lecture 'don't do this' and 'don't do that' while you party your ass off."

I'd never heard him swear before. All those years of church youth groups and Boy Scouts—they didn't amount to anything. Did he talk that way all the time when I wasn't around? How long had this been going on right under my nose? Where did he smoke it? In the garage? At Mary Wade's? A thousand questions pestered me and I wished David was here—I didn't know how to raise a boy. If Graham smoked dope, did it mean Quinn did too?

"I played better once I went straight," Lodge said. "All you gotta do is look around and you'll see a boatload of musicians who messed themselves up on drugs. Elvis, Kurt Cobain, Jim Morrison, Charlie Parker, Keith Richardson, the list goes on and on. Okay, no more lecture—we have work to do on this equalizer and you're gonna do what you want to do anyway, but I'll leave you with this thought: what would your dad think—he was a police officer, right? What would he say to you if he stood here right now?"

Actually he'd have said pretty much the same things. And then I felt as if Lodge had read my mind. "Hey, Quinn isn't—"

"I'm not that stupid. I'd break the little goober's arm if he tried. He's just a kid."

Thank you, God, for that huge blessing!

"So how much you been doing?"

"I only tried it a few times. It's not like I'm a stoner or anything. You gonna tell my mom?"

"I think you should."

"No way—she'll go ballistic—throw me out of the house."

"She'll be mad, but not that mad. You're her whole world. You ought to talk to her. She might surprise you."

They began talking about the equalizer and I backed out, leaving the door cracked, since a squeak would alert Graham to my presence. I felt dizzy like the world stopped spinning but my body was still turning circles. I leaned against the wall, having no idea where to go from here.

What were you thinking, David, leaving me alone to raise these boys? I can't do it. I don't know how. I realized tomorrow it would be two years since he abandoned us. Maybe it was even longer than that. I didn't know what to think anymore.

Noah Kaufmann shuffled in on untied sneakers, followed a few minutes later by Mary Wade Marcinek. She prissed by on rhinestone-studded flip flops, her little brother Donnie trailing in the wake of her Herbal-Essenced hair. Quinn had come back from the store and was already tapping out a rhythm on his drums.

Lodge shook hands with my father. "Hey, Woody, thanks for the tip about the pool hall hot dogs. Best I ever had."

"Knew you'd like 'em." He lit a cigarette.

Woodson and I shared the front porch swing while Lodge sat on the wicker chair catty-corner to us. A fog of unreality swamped me. Winter sunlight, pale and harsh, streamed onto the porch. I couldn't focus on the music drifting in from the garage or on the conversation. My mind vaguely registered the pink blossoms on my Debutante camellia. They looked like those tissue-paper carnations we used to make as dance decorations. Fragments of conversation filtered in, Woodson saying that for a girl with such an annoying laugh, Mary Wade possessed a pitch-perfect soprano, Lodge commenting on the mix of modern country and alternative. The band only performed seven songs, but they were all good ones, and their renditions improved with every rehearsal. Lodge thought Noah brought energy to the band, a harder edge. My legs grew rigid, stopped the swing. Noah—was energy all he'd brought to the band? Hadn't Tessa said something about Noah's being mixed up with kids in Ohio—or maybe it was New Jersey—who were a bad influence? Noah might *be* the bad influence.

Something J.D. had written in detention came back to me: *You don't see your kids the ones buying the smoke that keep me in nice tennis shoes. So I guess I should say thanks cause your nice white salary buys my clothes.* He tried to tell me. Me personally. My nice white salary. J.D. sold pot to my son.

Woodson looked at me strangely. My face must have revealed I was angry enough to beat the crap out of someone. J.D., Graham—both of them. Over the years I had seen other parents faced with this dilemma—had been sympathetic but also a little sanctimonious, a little removed from their pain. Never thought it could happen to my family. Part of me wanted to rush into the garage, yank my son into the house, and demand an explanation. I wanted to ask him if he'd forgotten who his father was. I wanted to slap him silly. But these were not solutions. I had to steer his course in another direction, preferably letting him think it was his idea. I closed my eyes and for a second I drifted back fourteen years. I was lying in a maternity ward bed and felt Graham's tiny fingers curl around my pinkie for the first time, and I was overcome by such terrifying love. I couldn't afford to make a mistake. Not now.

My mother always said when life looked bleak and you had no where else to turn, it was time to turn to God. Like most of her advice, it was sound.

Thirty-Two

A coffee mug stuffed with red carnations and yellow daisies sat on my desk when I arrived Tuesday morning. The janitor must have let someone in. A card leaned against the arrangement. The signature made me smile: Shaniqua. "My dream is to become a minister when I graduate," the note said, "but I didn't think my dream was possible because I got so tongue-tied. You are always talking to us about free will versus fate. Well, maybe fate led me to Room 104 B this year, but I'd like to think it was God. Because you wouldn't give up on me, I am talking now in all my classes. Not a lot and I'm still scared, but it's a start. Thanks, Mrs. C."

I was so happy for her. Now if only something or someone would help Graham. I still couldn't decide how to approach him, but I didn't have time to dwell on personal problems. I ran off handouts, tutored Ceci, took attendance, signed a tardy slip for Ja'Neice, gave Orville a wad of toilet tissue for his runny nose, handed Brian a stack of quizzes to distribute, and collected homework. All this by 8:10. Then we got down to work.

Groups of students were researching the death penalty on the Internet to prepare for a debate. All except J.D. He came in late and immediately put his head down on his desk as if to sleep, against class rules. I walked over and said his name. He didn't respond. When I touched his shoulder and asked if he was all right, he flinched. I left him alone the rest of the period. Maybe he didn't feel good. Maybe I just didn't want more trouble. Maybe I'd stopped caring.

I assisted the rest of the class with their research, though they didn't need much help. I eased onto a desktop, tugging my skirt hem down over my knees. The room filled with noisy chatter as Marissa discovered a site listing innocent people who'd been executed. Then Shaniqua found statistics comparing the relative costs of life imprisonment versus execution.

"I never really thought that much about capital punishment before we read this book," Shaniqua said. "I figured the ones they executed had it coming, but I think I'm changing my mind. I thought they'd be more careful to make sure they got the right guys arrested."

"Hey, look at these two cases I found," Brian said. "Both had eyewitnesses who identified men who were executed on the basis of that testimony. Later DNA evidence proved they hadn't committed the murders. I don't get it. Why would people lie like that?"

J.D. sat up in his seat and seemed to be listening intently.

"They probably weren't lying, not intentionally," I said. "Eyewitness testimony is the least reliable of all. If you ask ten people what they saw happen, every single one will have a different version."

"But murder isn't something you see every day," J.D. said. "You'd think anyone but a total retard would remember every detail."

Of all people, he should know that wasn't true. He remembered nothing about the one he'd witnessed. I wondered if it was worth antagonizing him further by pointing out he shouldn't use a slur like "retard." Decided I could only deal with one issue at a time. "Memory's a funny thing," I said. "How many times have you struggled over the answer on a test, and hours or even minutes after it was over, knocked yourself in the head when the right answer suddenly came to you? You knew the answer all the time, but it wouldn't surface."

"Yeah, I've done that," Ja'Neice said. "And then I wonder, why couldn't I have remembered that while I was taking the test?"

"Story of my life," Ceci said.

Eventually J.D. went to the computer by the window. I left him alone. Near the end of the period, he asked for the bathroom pass. I handed it to him, then helped Ja'Neice determine which organization had posted the legal opinions she'd found. When the bell rang, I felt pleased with the progress the class had made. I walked past my desk on the way to the door—hall duty was required during class change. I didn't mind. I liked to greet students as they came in. I smiled as I touched the velvety petals of the daisies from Shaniqua.

Then I found the note lying on my desk. It erased my smile.

"Mrs. Culpepper, there's no way to prove J.D. wrote this." Mr. Van Teasel held the plain white typing paper in his hand.

"He was the only one who passed by my desk first period."

"You say you were working with students at the computers. Couldn't someone have slipped in your door while you weren't looking?"

I supposed they could have, but J.D. was the only kid I was having trouble with. Oh, there were the usual small irritations: Sophie had been angry when she failed her last test, Lenny when I wouldn't excuse him from making up an assignment he'd missed when he was absent, and Monterius when I told him he needed to set his alarm ten minutes earlier after he was tardy for the fourth time last week. None of these students had the anger or temperament required to type out a rhyme referring to me as a female dog. The rhyme claimed the speaker wasn't scared of no cop and talked about popping a cap. I couldn't claim to be up on street slang, but I knew "pop a cap" meant to shoot someone. It sounded like a threat to me. And it sounded suspiciously like Tupac lyrics I'd seen on the Internet.

"If you falsely accuse him, what with this lawsuit hanging over us—I'm sure you see my point."

I saw. He was too scared to do his job. Fine. I'd handle it my own way.

Thirty-Three

Tessa pulled J.D. out of class for counseling with a promise to keep him all period. "I don't know if I'll get anywhere with him, but at least you'll have a break from all this tension."

I held in my smile, but there was no stopping every pore in my skin from turning into a happy face. J.D. and I needed a vacation from each other, and maybe Tessa could get him to confess he'd left the nasty note, one I knew he had written even if I couldn't prove it.

Tessa's eyes skimmed over my blue plaid jumper. "You really look great. How much have you lost?"

Now I had double reason to glow. I had lost so much weight I had to pin the waistband of my slip so it would stay up. I should have bought a new one, but Graham needed new shoes and Quinn wanted some part for a robot that cost $22. My paycheck would only go so far. "Eighteen pounds. How about you?"

"Twelve, and I feel ten years younger. Wish I'd started exercising like this years ago."

Not even Mr. Van Teasel scurrying in to perform my second evaluation could ruin my mood. A blessing, really, his choosing this morning when my worst student sat in the counselor's office instead of polluting my room with all that negative energy.

I distributed a handout, explaining how each group of four would perform and interpret a different poem for their classmates. They would create some type of visual aid: a diorama, a poster, costumes and dramatization, or a PowerPoint presentation. From the metal supply closet in front of the room, I brought out a student-made diorama. The shoebox, painted gray on the outside, contained a small sailboat fashioned from corrugated cardboard. Part of a pick-up stick served as a mast with a bit of handkerchief wrapped around it as a sail. Crayoned ocean waves lapped in the background. In the foreground, a tiny figure of a man gazed out at the sea. Holding the box over my head so all could see, I tilted it toward the class and began to traverse the room.

"This diorama was made by last year's sophomores for a poem we've already read." I almost asked who knew which one, which would have made half the class shout out "George Gray." Thank goodness I caught myself before Mr. Van Teasel could write "Teacher should control noise levels in classroom" on this evaluation too.

"Raise your hand if you know which one." To my surprise, the reticent Shaniqua was among those who raised her hand. If only Mr. Van Teasel realized what a milestone this was. She answered, and I resumed my walk across the room, aware of Mr. Van Teasel's eyes following each step. He nodded as if he approved and bent his head to take notes on his legal pad. After spewing out example after example of ways they could construct dioramas, I paused to inhale. When I exhaled, a rush of nylon flowed down my legs and puddled around my navy Mary Janes. I lowered the sailing scene to chest height.

"If you'll turn now to the second page of your handout, we'll go over the grading rubric."

Papers rustled. I used the distraction to blink downward. My slip lay in waves about my feet. Gray waves because I often failed to separate whites from coloreds. It was a serviceable garment, a thin band of lace at the hem its only concession to fashion. I always figured, who cared? No one would ever see it.

It was not the first time in my life I was wrong.

Balancing on my right foot, I lifted my left shoe, kicking it out of the elastic band. I could see now where the pin had sprung open.

"Ten points will be awarded for elocution, for speaking loud enough that every person in the room can hear." The students were used to my using words like elocution that they might not know. I trained them to listen for the definition that would follow. I hoped Mr. Van Teasel appreciated my technique. "You earn twenty points for dramatizing or acting out the poem."

Like a crane, I shifted all my weight to my left foot. I flopped my right foot around, but the nylon clung and wouldn't let go.

"Thirty points for thoroughly interpreting the poem. Every significant word choice, every image, the title—all must be explained to the best of your ability." I risked another downward glance and saw the problem. My shoe anchored the waistband. Moving slightly to the left, I wriggled my ankle again. This time I broke free from the elastic mooring.

"Now, look at the next item," I said. "Thirty points for the quality of visual aids." With one smooth movement, I dipped down and retrieved the slip, balled it up, and stuffed it into the shoebox. In my haste, I broke the little sail, but this was no time to mourn the loss. I slid the box into the supply closet and clanged the door shut.

A bubble of hope rose in my breast. Quite possibly no one had noticed the little drama played out before them. Keenly focused, Mr. Van Teasel scratched notes across the page. Students in the front two rows still had eyes trained on their handouts, reading over the requirements, except for Orville, who was doodling "Alicia, Alicia, Alicia" in the margins. Ja'Neice looked sleepy, but then it was only 8:20. Studies claimed teenagers couldn't be alert before 10 a.m. Maybe their brains were all cob-webbed, not quite focused on the here and now. Brian was smiling, but that wasn't unusual. I dared to hope my reputation was intact. (If a slip fell in the classroom and no one saw it, did it really fall?)

Orville raised his hand.

See, Mr. Van Teasel—I do control the noise levels in my classroom.

"How can we use a PowerPoint to teach a poem?" Orville asked.

"Good question." In my embarrassment, I had overlooked showing them an example. I glided toward the computers and, passing Shaniqua's desk, spied her head down between her arms. Normally, I would correct a student for inattention, but her shoulders convulsed violently, as though she were heartbroken or raging with chills and fever. She rolled her head up, our eyes connecting for the briefest moment before she buried her face again, and I knew with certainty neither sorrow nor illness caused the tears coursing down her cheeks.

My reputation doomed, I stretched my spine an extra half inch taller and continued to demonstrate the PowerPoint poem, which projected onto a big screen television.

At this point, Mr. Van Teasel nodded in my direction and left. Perhaps all was not lost. He showed no sign of anything amiss.

When I finished the demonstration, Shaniqua raised her hand. What happened to the quiet little girl who never volunteered to say anything until today?

"Miz, it's too bad J.D. isn't in class." She paused to brush thin fingers over her glistening cheeks. "I think he might have gotten the hang of hubris after your demonstration today. You could turn this into a great story for next year. This would be way better than the booger story."

"Yeah, great performance, Miz Culpepper," Brian said, his eyes twinkling. "You deserve an Emmy."

The class hurled questions at them. "When did this happen?" "All the way to the floor?" "She put it *where*?" "It's in that closet?" "Did she get that goofy expression on her face she always gets when—"

"Yes, that expression I get when I slip up," I said. No sense in taking myself too seriously.

"No, it slipped down," Brian said.

Ah. An opportunity to review our Shakespeare unit. "What do you call word play like this?"

"Puns," Orville said. He didn't raise his hand. In fact, no one had for some time and noise levels swelled considerably. Once again, I was grateful the principal had left when he did.

"That's right. Now, enough. Class time is precious. Let's get back to your poetry presentations. Any questions?"

Shaniqua waved her hand in the air again but didn't wait for me to call on her. "Just so you'll know, that little plaid jumper looks real cute on you, with or without your slip. You can still be proud."

To think I'd encouraged her to talk.

"Lawd, let's start class over—I can't believe I missed it," Vashawn said.

Mercifully, the dismissal bell rang.

Shaniqua continued to tease as she danced down the hallway. "The show must go on, class time is precious!" She and Vashawn fell into each other, cracking up, arms wrapped around each other's waists for support. "I thought I'd die laughing" drifted over her shoulder as they disappeared into the science wing.

I looked down at my legs, hoping no one could see through my jumper. I felt positively naked. Our venerable department chair, I was certain, had never lost her slip. For the hundredth time, I wished I could be more like her.

Kevin Fresnel arrived for second period. "Hey, Miz, I can't wait to see your diorama!"

A long day loomed ahead.

In the lounge over lunch, Tessa, whose position in the guidance office meant she found out everything before the rest of us, announced Blacks For Progress couldn't reach an agreement with Mr. Van Teasel and the Board of Education. The Board refused to budge on Honor Camp criteria, and they insisted on retaining the vice president and treasurer positions in each class for the highest white vote-getters. Same for homecoming and prom courts. Minority representation, they said. I could see both points of view, but the current method added up to over-representation of whites. Now a judge would decide.

Bless Jolene Baker's heart—she tried to raise our spirits. "We can't let this lawsuit stop our efforts to improve the school. The triathlon is a week from Saturday and we have made such progress together."

No one answered.

She persisted. "Haven't we all had fun? I know I have. I'm going to ask the Board members to fund a Wellness Program for in-service credit next semester so we can keep working out together."

Good news, everyone agreed. The Board would fund the program, too. No one said no to Miss Baker.

Gloom still hung over my colleagues. Finally I couldn't stand it any longer. Sometimes you have to make a sacrifice for the greater good. It meant giving up any hope of becoming a school legend like Miss Baker. "Not everything about our exercise program is so terrific. Guess what happened to me this morning in first period?"

It wasn't too big of a sacrifice. At that moment, the story of my slip was probably spreading through the cafeteria faster than the smell of the over-cooked broccoli the ladies were dishing out for lunch. Perhaps I would become a legend in my own way. Just not quite as I'd imagined.

At the end of the day, my evaluation was in my mailbox. Everything "exceeded expectations." Looking good. Then I read the last comment: "The strong rapport you have built with your students was evidenced by the way they withheld comments on certain slips until your evaluator left the room. I listened from the hallway and I must say the teacher exhibited courage and seized on the teachable moment. Your students will surely not forget what a pun is. You didn't let the opportunity 'slip' by."

I supposed he thought that was funny.

I reckon it was.

Thirty-Four

The next day almost a hundred black students stayed home from school to protest the school board's decision. They vowed to stage a protest one day every week until the issues were resolved. The Black and Blue Day protest drew mostly middle and lower level students. The kids who could least afford to miss. Only two from my morning honors classes were missing. Vashawn and J.D.

"This is ridiculous," Liz said over lunch. Considerable numbers of her mid-level science classes missed a lab on blood-typing. "If these parents were really concerned about their kids' educations, they'd have their behinds in school every single day. They would wait for the court to decide the remaining issues."

I was relieved to hear her weigh in on the school's side. "I heard they're holding a rally at the courthouse at one o'clock."

"That's only half of it. They plan to march to the school and circle the building."

Great. I supposed the protesters would yell and scream and we wouldn't be able to teach a thing all afternoon.

At the end of our lunch break, the intercom crackled and Mr. Van Teasel's voice boomed out. "School will be dismissed immediately following lunch for safety reasons. Students are to go straight home. Your parents have been notified by our automatic calling system."

I suspected the heart of the decision was the school board's desire to deny the protesters an audience.

"We have the afternoon off," Liz said. "Let's go shopping."

We dropped Graham, Marissa and some of their friends off at the mall, but I wanted to know what was going on at the school. Liz and I drove back and watched from across the street.

Maybe seventy people, a mixture of students and parents, some carrying signs, stood in the school parking lot. Newspaper and TV camera crews jockeyed for position. Vashawn's father stood on the hood of a truck leading the protests.

Liz hunched over the steering wheel, frowning. "Crowd's about what I expected. Most of those kids just skipped."

I searched for Rev. Bolden but didn't see his rotund form. Besides, if he'd been there, surely he would have been the leader. I did spot J.D. and Vashawn, fists raised over their heads. No signs. "You think the protest will do any good?"

"If having a lawsuit filed against them didn't change the board's mind, I don't know why this would." She pointed at a red pick-up. "Look in the back of that truck."

I craned my neck but couldn't see from my side of the car. "What?"

"Cases of beer. Truck belongs to one of my students, Joey Fortson, you heard me talk about him. Little guy with that big mean girlfriend."

Now that she mentioned the beer, I could see some of the boys in the back of the group, the ones closest to us. They held cans in their left hands, right fists pumping the air. It was a chilly day. Surely their hands would get cold. No good came of teenagers getting drunk.

"I've seen enough," I said.

Liz and I went to the garden center and bought poinsettias to place on our porches. Then there was one more place I wanted to visit. I talked Liz into driving me there.

Liz turned down Saint Joseph Street. I had never ventured into this part of town before. From several of Alderson's main boulevards—Jefferson Street and Baker Avenue, especially—you could see the red clay roads of the All Saints neighborhood, roads my mother had warned me away from. The dirt might rub off. Most of the time, I drove by and didn't even notice them, but when I did, I couldn't prevent a miniscule surge of fear. A vague feeling of distress from being so near the crack houses and assaults and alleged gang activity I read about occasionally in the newspaper. Did we really have gangs in Alderson? I couldn't believe it, but David had sworn it was true. He said Crips and Bloods had affiliates in every town in the country. He had shown me confiscated knives with their insignias carved into the hafts.

Now I saw the unpaved roads as if for the first time. Blacks in All Saints were citizens of Alderson like everyone else. Why weren't these roads which bordered downtown paved?

"This is a mistake," Liz said. "You don't want to visit J.D.'s home. Especially unannounced."

"No one's home. I just want to see where he lives." I was obsessed with Anita Marshall, wondered how she fed four kids on her factory salary, what her house looked like. Something personal had shaped her relationship with David and I needed to know what it was.

The homes we passed looked like dollhouses, too small to hold real families, worn out by years of careless play. Faded blue and green paint peeled like birch bark from wood siding that looked as if it would shiver and groan every time it stormed. The small yards were lined with chain-link fences, I supposed to keep strangers out and children in. Hopefully they also kept the pair of slavering pit bulls we saw in one yard contained. Their growling and lunging made me nervous enough to raise my window.

Yet even the ugliest yards littered with trash had some form of relief: planters of pansies sitting on the front porch post, chest-high azaleas that would be glorious in spring, a cluster of camellias planted decades ago. The residents might be poor, but someone in those houses was still trying.

We parked across the street from 3436. Once, the Marshalls' house had been white. The paint had flaked away, displaying the weathered boards underneath with such uniformity that the eye first perceived the house as gray, an effect similar to that of a Monet painting though he never painted such a depressing scene. The porch sagged under the weight of a rusted washer and dryer and an exhausted couch. Thick torn plastic covered the front window, flapping in the breeze where duct tape had loosened in one corner. There couldn't be more than four rooms in that house, including the bathroom and kitchen. Despite all the evidence of poverty, Anita Marshall was making an effort. Two poinsettias, like the ones Liz and I had purchased and stashed on the floor behind our seats, stood proudly on either side of the front steps. We sat there for what seemed a long time, the weight of that house laying on us.

Finally I heaved a breath. "Let's go." We rode in silence to the YMCA for swim practice. While I tugged the elastic leg of my bathing suit into place, the chlorine burned my nostrils. Did the smell of despair that hung over All Saints frighten Liz the way it did me?

"I can't believe five people live in that house," I said.

"Six," Liz said. "You can bet there are six. An 'uncle' always finds his way to a pretty woman like that."

Had David been an "uncle"? No, of course not, I chided myself. I dove in, letting the water wash over me. I welcomed the chemical burn in my eyes. I swam eight laps hard and fast, two of each stroke, ending with my specialty, the butterfly. Liz was sitting on the edge of the pool when I finished and hauled myself up beside her. I felt an urge to break down the barrier our skin placed between us. Full of ignorance, I only knew one remedy.

"Liz, has it ever bothered you—being the only black teacher in the lounge?"

Her lips twisted into a sour expression I'd never seen on her face before. A brief flicker before her features rearranged themselves into their usual pleasantness. "Honey, if I let little things like that bother me I'd never get through the day."

"No, really. Does it bother you? Deep down?"

"You really want to know? Yeah. Yeah, it bothers me that they don't hire more black teachers to teach black kids. And when they do hire a black teacher, she always gets the low level classes. Never honors. It bothers me those kids might grow up thinking blacks aren't good enough to be honors teachers. Or principals. Or doctors or the CEO's. But at least now they can see a fine black man stand in front of them as Superintendent of Schools and as President of the United States. And a fine black woman as First Lady. That's something. Not the same as a decent number of black teachers in their high school, but it's a start."

The vehemence of Liz's words seemed to shock her as they settled in the air between us. I'd noticed before no black teacher in our school taught honors courses, but I'd pushed it out of my mind the way I'd refused to see those unpaved roads in All Saints. If I admitted our teaching assignments were based on race, the right thing to do would be to offer to share my honors classes with the one black English teacher, Mrs. Wilson. With shame, I realized I didn't want to. I didn't know Mrs. Wilson well—the way I knew Liz—so that made my choice easier. I didn't think I could cope if I had to teach a whole class full of J.D.'s, and I was afraid that's what those low levels contained.

Liz and I were silent a moment; then she nudged me with her elbow. "But the lounge is all right because I have my good buddy, the Dessert Queen."

"Yeah, you do. Always. AHS wouldn't be the same for me without you." The laying bare of emotions embarrassed both of us and we rose to our feet together.

An hour later, one of Joey Fortson's passengers was killed in a car accident. Joey lay in the hospital and would probably be arrested—DUI—when he was released. The Black and Blue protests ended.

The next day as students returned to class Orville and Vashawn playfully shoved at each other on the way in.

"Settle down," I said.

Before the tardy bell, Brian and Marissa argued in a friendly way over who was the best R&B artist. Down the hallway J.D. flirted with some girl I didn't know. He would be late if he didn't hurry up.

Everything back to normal. A relief after yesterday's tension.

Orville knocked Vashawn's books to the floor. Big grin on his face. "Cut it out," I said.

Giggling foolishly, Vashawn kicked the books out of the bin under Orville's desk.

Enough was enough. "I mean it! All of y'all stop monkeying around."

J.D., coming through the door, froze, eyes nailed on me. "Who you calling a monkey?" His eyes were downright crazy looking as he played to his classmates. "Vashawn, you got any balls, now's the time to show it." He turned toward the rest of the class. "Next thing you know she'll be telling us to go back to Africa where we came from and you niggers will sit there and take it."

The door slammed behind him. Even so, I could have sworn I heard him stomp all the way to the office.

Silence enveloped my classroom. Not even Brian met my eyes.

Thirty-Five

Eileen O'Halloran, head full of curlers and a fuzzy pink bathrobe belted around her middle, padded down the sidewalk toward our house. My heart seized, remembering another morning she had approached in her robe with news of David's accident. She waved and held up a finger to indicate she wanted to speak to me. Leaning across the picket fence, she balanced a cup of coffee in one hand and a copy of the *Herald* in the other. Was there a story in the paper about what I was calling in my mind "the monkey incident"? Normally, such a thing wouldn't make the papers, but that was before Francis Brown and this lawsuit. Mr. Van Teasel planned to schedule a meeting after school as soon as he could get all the parties involved together. I fretted all night long about it.

But no, Eileen didn't know about the monkey incident. In the county school system where she worked, a job had opened up in public relations.

"Right away I told myself, 'Molly Culpepper would be perfect,'" she said. "You do such a great job with the school newspaper. I bet you'd like to get out of the classroom. Those kids get worse every year. I have never regretted moving over to the board office, I can tell you that."

Someone actually thought I did a good job. Pathetic, how good that felt. "Thanks for thinking of me. I'll certainly consider it."

"Such a shame about the Widener boy." Eileen shook her head. "It's on page four—arrested for possession. Lost his scholarship, a boy with so much promise, too. Don't you know Sally Widener is fit to be tied?"

I was shocked. Brad Widener seemed like such a good kid. "I'm sure she's heartbroken. Any mother would be." The Widener boy was a product of the city schools. Our shame. That accounted for the undertones of gloating I detected beneath Eileen's façade of concern.

I didn't really want to leave the classroom. I liked interacting with the Shaniquas and the Brians and the Cecis every year. Yet I couldn't overlook the benefits: the job with the county would remove me from involvement with the racial lawsuit, it would take me out of J.D.'s path, and most important, I might not have a choice. I could be fired if J.D.'s interpretation of the monkey incident stuck.

"Here's another tidbit from the paper this morning. Francis Brown shot himself in the wee hours of the morning. Breaks my heart. Man was a patriot, just like John McCain. Served his country in the space program all those years. It's just so sad."

I admired John McCain's and Brown's service to our country too, but in my opinion, no amount of service could atone for Brown's blatant racism. I wished I had the nerve to tell her it was time to take the McCain/Palin sign out of her yard. The boys and I had dug up our Obama sign the week after the election because I wanted to be gracious in victory. Didn't want to rub it in my neighbors' faces.

My hands shook as I held my copy of the paper. I had been angry at Brown, sure, but I didn't want him dead. I thought about how my father had bought him a drink. Probably the only act of kindness the man had known since he'd scrawled the nasty words on the blackboard. My father had said *He's screwed up, Molly, but aren't we all?* I had blamed Brown for all the town's troubles. But our troubles stemmed from every field plowed, every dish washed, every floor polished with the unpaid labor of slaves. Every lynching and unfair arrest. Every "whites only" establishment and every unpaved road in town. Troubles it would take generations to erase because we whites built our fortunes and security on the fruits of that labor performed for our ancestors. Yes, Obama gave us hope for change. But change wasn't going to come easy.

Back in the kitchen over a cup of rooibos tea, I turned to page four to read about the Widener boy, our shame. When my sons came in for bowls of Cheerios, I read aloud some parts of the story.

Graham's eyes widened. "How can they take away Brad's scholarship? It's based on grades, right?"

I seized the opportunity. "Sure, but other conditions have to be met. No drugs, for one thing, and no trouble with the law. I sure hope neither of you boys experiment with drugs. There can be so many consequences you don't even think about." I tried to read Graham's expression. Guilt? Anxiety? "I'm sure Brad never dreamed this could happen to him. And now for years to come, this arrest is all anyone will think about when they hear his name. Not how good he was in baseball, not how smart he was. They'll hear his name and say, 'Isn't that the kid who got busted?' It'll be an obstacle he has to overcome to get a good job in this town."

When I finished with page four, Graham pulled it from my hands and read over it himself, slowly spooning cereal into his mouth. Milk dribbled onto his jeans, but I didn't say anything to distract him. I wanted those words to sink into his brain. Quinn scuttled back to his room to get ready for school.

"Man, Widener's toast," Graham said.

"Well, I wouldn't say that." I never wanted to overstate the case against drug use. "I'm sure his parents will stand by him even though he's made a mistake. I'd still love you. By the way, I wanted to talk to you about that 4:20 on your notebook cover. In a teacher's meeting last week the counselors mentioned it as a signal for marijuana use." I had googled it, but I didn't want him to think Lodge had ratted him out. "Have you been using pot?"

His eyes held mine only for a second, long enough for me to see fear. "Course not."

"So you just want all your teachers to think you're a pothead?"

"No! I'm not a pothead."

"Graham, you're forgetting I changed your diapers. I know when you're lying to me." I wasn't sure I could tell, not anymore. With his straight A's, we counted on his getting a Hope scholarship. I didn't have the money to send him to a top tier university on my salary alone. Not unless I sold the house. *If* I could sell the house, unlikely, the way the housing market sucked these days.

"I love you dearly—and because I do, you'll be an old man before I let you off restrictions if there's even a hint you're messing around with drugs again." We were running late. "We'll talk about your punishment later." I called Quinn and slapped lunch sacks into hands. I almost forgot Dusty. I pinged the crate door shut behind him. Keys clinked, doors slammed, the Escape engine rumbled. Quinn chattered about how Dusty knew how to roll over and play dead and bark on command, how Dusty could be in the movies—he was that smart. All his chatter disguised Graham's reticence on the drive to school. After

I dropped off Quinn, we pulled into the AHS parking lot. Instead of jumping out, Graham waited, his eyes directed at the windshield.

"You don't have anything to worry about. I don't want to wind up in the papers like Brad. And I'll bust Goober in the head if he even thinks about it." He opened the car door, swung his back pack off the floor mat, and left without a backward glance. I wasn't naïve enough to think the danger had disappeared, but I felt a little better, and would feel better still after I told Tessa my suspicions about where the drugs came from. This Widener story made a good springboard to open a dialogue with our kids. Page four waited inside my briefcase, ready for Tessa.

Right after lunch, I followed her back to her tiny office and closed the door, even though the crowded space always made me claustrophobic. I whipped the story out, laid it on her desk, and began to detail my discovery.

She blew out a noisy sigh of relief tinged with peppermint. "Thank God you know now. Noah told me last week."

"Oh." Her words jerked my story to a halt.

"Years ago we'd role-played all these ways of turning down drugs, but when Graham asked him if he wanted to smoke some pot, he caved immediately."

I swallowed hard. There went my theory that Noah, the Northern transplant, must be the instigator. Mentally, I had created a division, Yankees versus Southerners. Assumed we were better somehow.

"Starting all over in a new school and new town is hard at any age, but especially the early teens. Having Graham as a friend means a lot to Noah. I guess I chickened out of telling you about the pot for the same reason. I'm usually very outspoken, but you're the one real friend I've made here, and I didn't want to ruin it. I planned to tell you soon, I just hadn't figured out how."

I touched her sleeve. "You don't ever need to be afraid to tell me the truth."

She looked relieved. "I think the boys thought they should smoke pot because all the cool bands did. Noah promised me he wouldn't do it again."

"Graham, too, and I'm sorry he led Noah into doing something he shouldn't have." I was pathetic. One more parent who thought it couldn't possibly be my child—oh, no, not my child.

"You don't need to be sorry. You can't control what other people do, not even your own children once they reach a certain age. You know that."

"Yeah, it's just that everything's falling apart. Between J.D. and now Graham, you know what I mean. And my dad's been having health issues."

"About J.D. and what happened yesterday."

So she knew. I supposed everyone did. I wanted to crawl in a hole and hide.

"Mr. Van Teasel asked me to sit in on the meeting with Mrs. Marshall and Mr. and Mrs. Diggs. It's set for tomorrow. I'm sorry now I encouraged you to work with this kid. He's been nothing but trouble."

If I said anything, I would start crying, so I stared into my lap.

Tessa continued. "Most teachers would have given up on him by now. Have you thought about why you haven't?"

"Why? Because I'm his teacher."

"Maybe it's more than that. Do you think you might need to save your students because you really want to save your dad? You can't, Molly. Your father has to want to save himself."

The blood drained from my head. She had crossed a line where even my best friends weren't allowed to go. "Now wait a minute—"

"Everyone knows about his problem, Molly, even me and I'm new here. Your wishing he'd get better isn't going to change things. He's sick."

My father's saying ran through my mind: *wish in one hand...*

"His problem is not your problem unless you let it be." Tessa reached behind her to a shelf of books, ran her fingers across the spines until she located what she wanted, and pulled out a slim volume. She tossed it on her desk. It skidded to a stop in front of me. Its cover was white with red letters: *Adult Children of Alcoholics*. She slid another one my way: *How Al-Anon Works*. I willed the tears to stay inside.

"You should read these. And you should go to an Al-Anon meeting, talk to other people who are dealing with the issues you are." She touched my hand, a touch so gentle compared to the brassy sound of her Jersey voice. "Look, it's not such a bad thing, wanting to save everyone. You can't do it, but you're right to try. We all need help getting through adolescence, and I say, thank God for teachers who don't give up. But quit beating yourself up when you have to let one go. Everything's going to turn out okay with the monkey incident. The meeting will be tomorrow after school. Don't waste time worrying about it."

Easy for her to say.

The class change bell rang out in the distance. Benumbed, I didn't jump to my feet like the trained animal I was. Tessa hurtled along. "You aren't perfect—no one can be—but the kids know you care about them. That's what they'll remember. Not whether you succeeded in drilling Word Wall lists and Essential Questions and five paragraph essays into their heads." She stood up and clapped her hands in dismissal. "Alrighty then, you'd better hustle or you'll be late."

I grabbed the books and sprinted back to my room where my sixth period students were already assembling. Every minute of class time was precious—and who knew what those kids would get up to if I wasn't there watching. I hid the books she'd given me in my top desk drawer and pasted on a phony smile. I complimented Jackson on having the highest score on the principles of design test. Told Thomas to keep his hands off Angela. Accepted an absence excuse from Tameka, and noting a death in the family, offered condolences. Made a mental note to send a card to the house.

"Zacharia," I said, "in about ten seconds the tardy bell's going to ring and your bottom better be in your seat by then." Energy bounced off the walls after most of them had consumed a high carb lunch of pizza and corn with a box of raisins for dessert. Why would a meal planner combine those items on one tray? I held out my hand for Thomas's box of raisins, one of which had already landed on Angela's neck. He started to protest, but I arched an eyebrow. He deposited the box in my palm. I looked meaningfully at the floor by Angela and then back at him. He retrieved the offending raisin and deposited it in the trashcan.

I loved being in the classroom. They could take it away from me.

That evening Lodge rapped my woodpecker doorknocker loudly. He held out his arms, extending a gray plastic case toward me, his expression smug, in a sweet way.

"What's this?" I asked.

"For you. Open it and see."

I couldn't imagine what would be inside the box. Not chocolates, that's for sure. I would have killed for chocolate. Anything Russell Stovers. Hershey's dark with dried cranberries and blueberries. An Almond Joy.

I popped the lid.

"Oh, those wrench thingies. Very nice. Thank you, Lodge."

His face fell.

"Really, very nice," I added.

"Every household needs a good set of socket wrenches. Never know when you're going to need one." He pulled another wrench from his pocket. It looked like the one in the garage on David's workbench, only this one was adjustable. "You should have one of these around, too. Never know when it will come in handy."

I tried to sound appreciative, but beyond your basic screwdriver and hammer, I knew as much about tools as he seemed to know about women. If the bar stool ever broke again, I guess I'd have a tool to fix it, but what else was that conglomeration of silver thingies good for? I could string them together into a beaded necklace, but they were too heavy for that. Lodge stood at the door. I should invite him in. The polite thing to do, but I was too depressed over the "monkey meeting" to be decent company. I even skipped training after school. Pled off with a stomachache. Only partly a lie. I was nauseated. I wished I could confide my worries in Lodge. I could use an attorney's advice. If only he weren't representing Blacks For Progress.

Also pungent odors of chicken bones and onions rose embarrassingly from the kitchen trash can. That Graham. How many times had I reminded him to take out the garbage? He'd run off to choir practice and forgotten again.

"I'd invite you in, but I've got a ton of papers to grade tonight." Not that I could concentrate enough to do a decent job.

"I couldn't come in. Not this time. Conflict of interest. I'll be at the meeting tomorrow afternoon with the Marshall boy at Reverend Bolden's request. I wanted you to know." There was a significant pause while he searched my face. "And I wanted you to have the wrenches in case you needed them. You can never have too many socket wrenches."

He would be at the meeting as a lawyer. This could be serious, his expression told me. I needed my own lawyer. If it was a conflict of interest for Lodge to come in, it was, no doubt, a conflict to warn me. I was touched by his concern. He was a better friend than I had realized.

Lodge started to leave, but turned around on the bottom step. "By the way, did you read in the newspaper about the Widener kid? Such a shame. I know it's none of my business, but you should have a talk with your boys. It's never too soon to let them know how you feel about drugs."

"Thanks, I will." I admired the way he tipped me off to the problem without betraying Graham. That Graham. What was I going to do with him? I had already told him the next time I had to take out the trash, he would spend one weekend night restricted to his room. I didn't have time for this. It wasn't like I asked that much from the boys. Just a little cooperation. A few simple chores. I tugged and tugged at the white plastic trash can liner until it popped free. Onion skins spilled onto the floor. Mumbling my disgust, I retrieved the papery skins and began to tighten the red drawstrings when something inside the bag caught my eye. Graham's notebook, decorated with a green goddess and sprinkled with chicken bones and a clump of dog hair, winked up at me. My knees felt weak. I looked at the catch-all table next to the door to the garage where the boys piled up what they needed to take to school the next morning. Graham's book bag slouched in its usual spot. After a few seconds of mental debate over whether I was invading his privacy, I opened his bag and rifled through the contents. Homework papers were folded neatly in half and tucked between pages of his algebra book. There were notes from Mary Wade. Innocent, syrupy missives. No mention of drugs, no indications that their relationship was anything more than it should be.

But what made me quiver with relief was the new notebook, a harmless Ibanez guitar inked onto the cover. Beside it, in Mary Wade's handwriting, was her name and his in a heart. Maybe I wasn't doing everything wrong.

I called Mr. Van Teasel and he said the school's attorney would be present. "Just a precaution because of the lawsuit," he said. "Don't lose any sleep over this."

Right. At bedtime, I tried to open that bottle of wine again. I thought half a glass might help me sleep. Again, I twisted and torqued and couldn't budge that cap. Then I saw Lodge's gift sitting on the counter. Not the socket wrenches. I still didn't know what I'd do with them. I grabbed the adjustable wrench and settled it around the top of the wine bottle. It slipped the first time, so I clenched harder. This time I heard the metal breaking free and the cap twisted right off. I cheered. His gift wasn't a total bust after all.

The next day I gave a great imitation of one of those slacker teachers I despise. I wrote an assignment on the board and told the kids to do it. Stress tied me in knots. I didn't feel capable of interaction with my classes.

Finally at three o'clock, I locked my door, grabbed my satchel of papers, and dragged myself down to the conference room. A long polished table sat in the center. Graduation exit exam scores were taped to the walls. Mr. Van Teasel sat next to the school's lawyer, Katrina Cromartie, who had a legal pad in front of her. Mr. Diggs and Vashawn; Mrs. Chidester and Orville; and Mrs. Marshall and J.D. sat along the sides. Dressed in a lawyery suit with a laptop open in front of him was Lodge. He sat next to Mrs. Marshall. Tessa patted the arm of the empty chair beside her. Ready to vomit, I closed the door and moved to the empty chair, glad for a friend's presence.

Mr. Van Teasel spoke first. "Mrs. Cromartie and Mr. Piscetelli are present in case legal issues arise. All right. J.D., why don't you tell us what happened yesterday in Mrs. Culpepper's class."

J.D. rolled his shoulders as if they were stiff. "See, Miz Culpepper was standing in front of the class, when Vashawn—" J.D. flicked his chin at his classmate—"was retaliating for something that big white dude over there did." He flicked his head toward Orville as if he didn't know his name, hadn't played football with him the past two months. Miz Culpepper called out Vashawn. Called him a monkey."

Were Vashawn and Orville going to let J.D. get by with this lie? Did it all come down to teachers versus students?

Mr. Van Teasel looked at me. "Mrs. Culpepper, is this true?"

"No, sir."

J.D. curled his upper lip. "Admit it—that's all black men are to you, a bunch of frigging monkeys." Only he didn't use the word frigging.

"J.D.!" Anita Marshall covered her face with her hands. "I'm sorry."

Lodge leaned over and whispered something to J.D. Whatever it was, J.D. wasn't impressed, judging by the way his eyes aimed up at the ceiling, away from all of us.

"One more outburst like that and I'll suspend you right now," Mr. Van Teasel said. "At this time I would like to hear from Vashawn and Orville."

Tessa stood and strode to the door. I wondered if even she intended to desert me. "Just a minute, Mr. Van Teasel. Several other witnesses asked to attend this meeting and I told them it would be all right."

In walked Brian, Marissa, Shaniqua, Ceci—and maybe half a dozen others from my first period. Why? Then it dawned on me that where one or two kids might lie, the whole class wouldn't. They lined up along one wall in front of the test score charts.

Vashawn stood. "Mr. Van Teasel, I kicked Orville's book out from under his desk. I'd like to apologize to him, to Miz Culpepper, and to my classmates for wasting valuable class time. As Miz Culpepper is always reminding us, every second of class time is precious."

I was aware of Tessa's hand rising to cover her mouth, and I would have liked to join her but knew my laugh would have had a hysterical edge.

Mr. Van Teasel's beady eyes twinkled, something I'd never seen before. "Yes, I've heard she is fond of that expression."

Orville stood. "I'd like to apologize for shoving Vashawn's books and yeah, all the rest of the stuff he said. And I promise I'll try not to monkey around in Miz Culpepper's class again."

Brian stepped forward. "I want everyone to know that's all she said, to stop monkeying around."

Was that really Shaniqua stepping forward now? "She didn't call anyone a monkey. Miz Culpepper would never do that."

J.D.'s eyebrows drew together and he shoved away from the table and jumped to his feet. "She called Vashawn a monkey. That's what I heard."

Maybe he did hear that. We all are guilty of seeing what we want to see and hearing what we want to hear sometimes. It's what I had tried to explain to him about eyewitness accounts. J.D. flung open the door. In the front office he turned, one arm flung out, his face contorted by anger and tears. "Y'all just a bunch of frigging oreos." Only he didn't use frigging, and Mr. Van Teasel hissed like a pressure cooker ready to pop a gasket.

J.D.'s mother, Lodge, and Tessa went after him and tried to persuade him to stay and talk about his future. A lost cause. His classmates' united stand would only further alienate J.D.

I hugged all my kids as they left the conference room. We adult oreos stayed and talked for a while. For the next half hour, there was no black and white, just a community worried about that angry young man, all of us wondering how to reach him, wondering if anything could prevent the train wreck we could see coming.

Mr. Van Teasel assigned J.D. to In-School Suspension for three days. "A cooling off period." Anita Marshall agreed he needed one.

"I think we should ask Reverend Bolden to have a talk with him," Lodge said.

I remembered from J.D.'s autobiography the part about the minister who fostered him. J.D. had run away. I wasn't very hopeful, but anything was worth a try. I thought of Roosevelt Pitts, too. Another strong role model. But would J.D. listen to a policeman anymore than he would a minister?

As we left, I thanked Tessa for arranging for my first period students to stand up for me.

"Can't take credit," she said. "Brian and Marissa's idea. You'll appreciate this: they spent quite a few minutes in my office arguing over whose idea it was first."

After dinner, Mr. Kelso called and said Woodson hadn't worked in two days. I'd been too preoccupied with my own problems to check on him. I left Graham and Quinn in charge of the dishes and drove out to his house. The kitchen smelled like charcoal. Burnt pans and filthy dishes towered haphazardly in the sink. Mechanically I climbed the steps, using the railing for support. My father lay across the bed, a towel stained with bloody spittle beside him. I touched his cheek. Warm. Alive. His fingers and toes, though, had turned blue with cold. I tugged a blanket off the floor and covered him. I tiptoed down the stairs.

My mother's voice sang in my head: *My goodness, clean this mess up!* I turned on the tap and grabbed a piece of steel wool. The sink filled with sudsy water. Grabbing the top pan, I began to scrub, but other voices began to drown out Mama.

Enabler! the author of a book accused me.

He has to want to save himself, Tessa said.

You can't do anything. It's not up to you, Dr. Roberts said.

We can't just watch him die. My own voice.

That might be exactly what you have to do. Dr. Roberts again.

Some people just don't want to be saved. My father's voice. He knew all along what I refused to see.

I set down the scrub pad, wiped my fingers on my jeans, leaving streaks of pink foam behind.

Thirty-Six

The week before regional playoffs, Graham hurt his ankle. He skipped practice on Monday and Tuesday, and we applied heat and ice to ease the pain. I wanted him to stay off his ankle the rest of the week, but on Wednesday he insisted he felt well enough to practice.

I relented. "But you have to stop right away if the pain gets worse."

When he got home, I was adding brown sugar substitute to an apple and pork casserole. "How was your ankle during practice?"

"Fine."

"Want me to fix you an ice pack?"

"I'm not a baby, Mom."

"Didn't say you were."

"If I need ice, I'll get it myself, okay?"

"Okay."

Like so many other nights, he didn't have much to say during dinner and disappeared into his room soon after. I loaded up the dishwasher and sat down in front of the computer to make out a test. I had only completed two questions when someone knocked on my front door. Not Lodge again, surely. Maybe Eileen O'Halloran wanting to know why I hadn't applied for the P.R. job.

To my surprise, Sonny Haswell stood on my porch. Haswell had been a friend of David's in high school and was Graham's coach, but we'd never seen each other socially.

"Hey, Molly, sorry to show up unannounced, but something's happened you should know about." He sounded so serious, but then he cracked a half-smile. "Don't worry—I won't bring my Skoal into your house."

I winced, remembering the note I'd stuffed in his mailbox. He sat down at the breakfast bar and I fixed him a glass of unsweetened tea and slid the sugar bowl toward him.

"J.D. and Graham got into it tonight," he said. "Things got real ugly."

My muscles tensed. I'd been half expecting something like this.

"They've been running neck and neck as the team's top scorers, you know that. Well, J.D. doesn't like sharing the spotlight and he started trash talking about how field goal kickers were pussies—I apologize for the language, but I don't know how else to make you understand what happened."

"It's okay. I need to hear this. I imagine that made Graham pretty mad."

"Yeah, I'm sure it did. He told J.D. to shut up. He didn't, of course. He went on about how kickers weren't really part of the team, said they were faggots because they didn't take hits like everyone else. Graham said about what you'd expect—'You want a piece of me, come on.' So I got between them and told J.D. to lay off, save it for the other side on Friday night, but the fool wouldn't let it go. He made a bunch of comments about white boys and got the whole team stirred up. You know how tense things are anyway with this lawsuit."

"Heavens, Sonny, what did you do?"

"Sent J.D. to the showers, but on the way off the field he made an extremely tasteless remark about Mary Wade's titties, and Orville and Coach Underwood had to hold Graham back or there would have been a vicious fight."

"Thank God you stopped it!" But I knew how these things worked. Just because it didn't happen on the field didn't mean it wouldn't happen later.

"That's not the worst of it," Sonny said. "In the locker room, J.D. urinated in Graham's gym bag. I didn't know about it until Mrs. Chidester made Orville call and tell me."

"He *what?* You've got to be kidding." The grim set of Sonny's mouth told me he wasn't. "That boy's nothing but an animal, an absolutely—" I couldn't let myself go any further, but I could hear J.D. accusing me of calling him a worthless nigger. The word grew so large in my mind it pushed every other thought out. I berated myself for allowing it space, but it dominated, exploded, refused to be banished.

The muscles in my jaw twitched as violent images flamed through my mind. I smashed J.D.'s gold grill. Gut-punched him until he doubled over. Kneed him so hard he would never have children. But in the real world, I could only release my anger and frustration through words. "It's a good thing J.D.'s not standing in front of me right now. I'd throttle the little bastard." Yeah, I cussed. I wasn't proud of it.

"Don't blame you a bit. If Dave was still here, I know he would."

The faint thrum of the dryer came from the laundry room, something I hadn't noticed until now. Graham must have laundered the bag himself without saying a word to me.

"I can't believe he didn't tell me."

"I wouldn't have told my mother either," Haswell said. "At Graham's age, you don't go running to your mommy or your coach with your problems. J.D.'s off the team for the rest of the season. He's gone too far."

What with all the pressure Sonny was sure to get from boosters and parents, I worried he might change his mind. Without J.D. the team didn't have much chance at winning even the first round of regional playoffs.

"You sure about this, Sonny?"

"Never more sure of anything in my life. You know, I thought I could help him get his feet on solid ground after all his family's been through. He worked hard, I'll give him that. He would stay late after practice watching tapes. Studied the plays of pro games over and over. Ran all over town after dark so he'd have more endurance. But I've bent over backwards to work with this kid. Brought in college scouts. Even took him and his family out to eat a couple of times. I don't know if there's anything I can do to repair the damage he did today. There was dang near a race riot in the locker room tonight. It's only going to get worse when everyone finds out I benched J.D. I'm sorry I let this get so far out of control."

"Not your fault. I think J.D.'s anger toward my family goes beyond football." I hesitated, not sure if Sonny would think I was cracked for dredging up something so far in the past. "My husband is the one who arrested J.D.'s mother."

Turned out I didn't need to tell Sonny Haswell. He remembered, said everyone did. Alderson was a small town. "There's more to it than that. I imagine you know the history better than anyone."

I felt faint, not sure I was ready to hear this story. "What do you mean?"

"Your family's history with Anita Marshall. Surely your father or David told you."

I closed my eyes. Even my father knew. "No, I don't think they did."

"Time you knew, then. Woody had just come back from Korea," Sonny said. "He had a habit of stopping by the General Store to shoot the breeze with my grandfather—you remember Ely. Everything was quiet, a normal day at the store, when a black fellow toting a gun pulled a ski mask over his face and charged through the door. It was the second time in a month the same guy tried to rob the store. Your father chopped his arm real hard and the gun skittered away. They fought and Woody held his own until the black fellow kicked him where it hurts the most. The robber scrambled across the floor for his gun. Granddad kicked it away. By then, your dad caught his breath again, and he was pissed off now. He pushed a row of shelves over and knocked the robber down. Woody started to kick him in the head with those heavy combat boots he always wears. Granddad tried to pull Woody off him. Couldn't. Woody only quit when Granddad collapsed. Heart attack. He survived that one because your dad called an ambulance and did mouth-to-mouth resuscitation he'd learned in the military. Guess who the thief was, Molly?"

I didn't know, but I suspected it had something to do with J.D.

"J.D. Marshall's grandpa, that's who. Came out later he needed the money because his son had sickle cell and he couldn't manage all the medical bills. Guy was just trying to take care of his kid. Don't make what he did right, but it's kind of sad. If he'd have just told people why he needed money, folks around here would have seen to it that his boy was taken care of."

They would have, too. We organized pancake suppers for people having trouble. Jars collecting quarters for someone's surgery always sat on check-out counters at the grocery store. Then I stopped to wonder: had any of the faces on those jars been black? Surely they had, but as I searched my memory I couldn't be sure.

Thirty-Seven

Feeling somewhat foolish, I went to check the doors. All locked. Part of me still thought of J.D. as only a kid, but I needed to leave that kind of thinking behind. Ten minutes ago, I had been willing to keep trying with J.D., despite everything. From now on when my former teacher Mrs. Richards whispered in my mind that there were no throwaways, I would tell her to hush.

Everything had changed. If J.D. wanted to ruin his own life, fine, but he wasn't going to ruin Graham's. J.D. wasn't the only kid who'd lost a parent, who'd taken some hard knocks. Those things might excuse mistakes, but they didn't give him to right to be mean. They didn't give him the right to be cruel. I was finished with J.D. He could rot in hell for all I cared.

I almost stepped on Dusty when I turned around too quickly. He followed me into Graham's room. I had tried to respect my son's privacy. Tried to give him some space, but that space had turned into a yawning gap where he had tried pot and endured appalling abuse without telling me, his mother, the person who loved him more than anyone else in the world. The secrecy had to end.

A poster of Lindsay Lohan hung behind Graham's bed. I knew her name only because it was written across the bottom in fancy script. Who was Lindsay Lohan, anyway? That I didn't know seemed another sign I'd lost touch with my son. His back toward me, Graham hunched over his desk working on a Spanish translation. Wires from his iPod earbuds spiraled down to his desk.

Gently I touched his shoulder, and he pulled a bud free. "Get your things."

"What for?"

"We're going to your grandfather's."

"Now? I have homework to do."

"You'll have to do it there," I said.

"Why?"

"Don't pretend you don't know. It's about what happened at football practice."

His jaw squared, his blue eyes hardened like glass—a stubborn look he surely got from his grandfather. "I can handle it."

"This isn't only about you. J.D.'s a disturbed young man."

"Tell me about it. But I can handle it—I'm not a baby anymore, Mom."

"I know." But he was a baby, *my* baby, and I didn't want him to get hurt. "I know that, but families have to stick together. It's not a crime to ask for help."

"Huh! That's great coming from you. Hasn't Grandpa been trying to get you to call Sgt. Pitts for weeks now? You said you could handle it. I heard you tell him J.D.'s just another messed up kid. If you can handle it, so can I."

The surprise must have shown on my face. "Did you think we couldn't hear him to talking to you?" he said. "Grandpa's voice carries, you know."

"Look, we'll discuss this after we get to Grandpa's. Pack what you need for tonight and for school tomorrow."

After I asked Quinn to get ready, I called Roosevelt. I made sure my voice carried loud and clear down the hall to Graham's room.

Woodson wasn't home, but I let myself and the boys in and waited for Roosevelt. I felt safe here in the house I grew up in, despite the mess my father left behind. My mother's presence remained in the cross-stitched apple tree hanging on the kitchen wall, her ceramic rooster collection, and the knitted afghan on the living room couch. Her goodness still formed the bones of this house.

Graham rummaged around in the pantry and found a liter of cola. "Guess Grandpa isn't any better."

I sat down at the kitchen table. "No, he isn't. He's sick. He's an alcoholic."

"You gonna leave the kitchen like this?" Quinn asked with wide eyes.

"Yes. Grandpa knows how to do dishes."

"I don't mind helping him." Quinn picked up a dirty glass and carried it to the sink.

Graham shook his head. "Goober, I think what Mom is saying is that this is something Grandpa is going to have to work out for himself. We can't be running over here and doing his dishes every night."

Sometimes Graham sounded so grown-up I could forget he was only fourteen.

When Roosevelt arrived, I filled him in: J.D.'s paragraph describing the gun, nocturnal phone calls, threatening note, and finally, the argument with Graham and defiled gym bag. With every detail I laid on, he chastised me again, wanting to know why I'd waited so long to call.

"I wouldn't be surprised if J.D. found out the whole story about his grandpa," he said.

"Did everyone in town know except me?"

Roosevelt assured me everyone—except maybe J.D.—thought my father was a hero. He had stopped a robbery and maybe saved Ely Haswell's life. "Your father-in-law and husband are heroes in my book, too. After the robbery, the Culpeppers started taking groceries over to the Marshalls' house. They paid medical bills for Anita's older brother. When old Franklin died, David continued to help the Marshall family. David never talked about it, but white folks toting groceries into the black community drew attention. Everyone in All Saints knew."

That was the David I loved. It explained why he felt compelled to help Anita and why she called him by his first name. They must have known each other even as children. I still couldn't believe he hadn't told me. Yet he had shared with me once a book his father made him read as a teenager. *Magnificent Obsession*. Apparently, the Culpeppers had tried to live the principle laid out in the novel: doing good and keeping it a secret.

"Your David was the best—you know that, don't you?" Roosevelt asked.

I did, and this story reinforced that opinion.

No wonder all this violence—first his grandfather and then his mother—had warped J.D. Was there any way to pull him out of that world?

"You'll be okay here. I'll go round up Woody," he said.

"Big Fred's—that's where I'd look first." I hoped I was wrong.

He shouldn't be drinking, not if that bloody towel I'd seen was any indication of what it was doing to him. No doubt he would wind up back in the hospital.

Roosevelt planned to come back in the morning and follow us into school. "I'll be on J.D. like white on rice until we can get this resolved. Talk about your classic example of why we need a school resource officer. Don't you worry; I'll be with you tomorrow even if I have to take a day's leave to do it."

At first I thought his baby-sitting J.D. sounded like a great plan. Then I had second thoughts. It would take care of tomorrow. But what about the next day—and the day after that?

After a little talking, I convinced Roosevelt to accept a slight alteration to his scheme.

When he left, I tried to finish my test on Woodson's computer. I half-heartedly completed a few questions. My first excuse for not completing the test was the smell of popcorn an only-slightly-drunk Woodson was making for the boys. Microwave popcorn didn't require a pan—good thing, because there weren't any that could be used. I gave up trying to work when Woodson ripped out a fart so loud I could hear it in the den. My sons gagged far longer than necessary.

I kept thinking of Eileen O'Halloran's invitation to apply for the job with the county. Maybe I owed it to Graham and Quinn to get out of the classroom. Get away from kids like J.D. Owed it to myself. Get away from the lawsuit. And now there was all this talk about accountability. Tying teacher pay to student performance on tests. Would Miss Baker's students perform better than mine because she only had 15 kids to my 30 and could give them twice as much time? What would happen to teachers of remedial classes? Would teachers be penalized for kids who didn't come to school regularly or who came late every day or who refused to complete assignments? All this uncertainty piled on more stress. I swallowed an acid blocker and went online to the county's website. I printed a job application, filled it out and tucked it into my satchel. Didn't have to mail it in. Didn't have to decide now.

I joined the boys in front of the tube. "What a trashy show *CSI* is. Everything on TV is formula writing these days—you've seen one, you've seen them all." My sons ignored me.

"Best show on TV," Woodson said. Every few minutes he massaged the outside of his ear. Finally I asked what was wrong. "Had an ear ache earlier, but I put some Astring-o-sol in there and I b'lieve it's working."

"It's mouthwash, for crying out loud. You shouldn't use it for ear aches."

"Why not if it works?"

I don't know why I bothered to argue. On the show, one technician took a casting of a tire tread and ran it through a computer data base. Another one analyzed minute threads snagged in a victim's necklace and traced them to a designer dress shirt as a third ran special spectrum lights over a crime scene to find blood spatter. For an hour I didn't think about J.D. even once.

Then Grissom, the lead CSI, quoted Shakespeare. Maybe this show wasn't such a cultural black hole after all. Not one hundred percent, anyway. I could see why Liz thought maybe she could use it in the science classroom. She could stage crime scenes and have kids gather and analyze evidence. Turn her students into CSIs!

When Dusty started barking at 10:30 for one last potty run, it was such a relief not to have to worry about J.D. lurking outside. And if he called my house, he'd be the one losing sleep, not me. After the boys went to bed, I sipped a cup of tea at the kitchen table. My father's hands shook as he poured coffee into a mug. It made me see what I didn't want to see, how strong a grip the alcohol had on him. I wanted to cry. The last few days had been too much.

"I tried to tell you there was bad blood between our families, but you wouldn't listen," he said.

He had tried to tell me, but I had misunderstood. Thought he was making some kind of racial crack. Did all fathers and daughters talk over and under each other's radar, or was it just us?

"I should have listened. Maybe someone else could have helped him."

"You coulda called Lodge tonight, you know. He's kinda sweet on you. He'd have run over there in a heartbeat and been happy to do it."

"How would you know?" I wasn't entirely disinterested in Woodson's answer. When I remembered the way "Europa" oozed from Lodge's saxophone, I still felt all gooey.

"He gave you that set of socket wrenches, didn't he?"

I groaned. "Yeah, and some flashlights. Really romantic."

"I'd think at your age you'd appreciate when a fellow tries to be considerate and practical. Socket wrenches are a cut above your typical gifts."

"How about chocolate?"

"You're dieting."

"What's wrong with flowers?"

"They die and you throw them out."

Just like Woodson to miss the whole point. "I think you're reading too much into it. He's trying to be neighborly." He'd never asked me out, like on a date or anything.

"Have it your way, but I know what I know. I run into him sometimes. We talk. He's sweet on you."

Thirty-Eight

Iinterlaced my fingers and paced across the classroom, making eye contact with Orville and another football player in my first period. They had spent ten minutes before class started alternating between grousing about J.D.'s benching and grumbling about the way J.D. had behaved at practice.

"You need to focus on your work," I said. Eventually they settled into the normal routine.

We were forty minutes into class, working in small groups, when J.D. slouched in. I could barely stand to look at him.

"That girl's in my seat." J.D. flicked his head in her direction. He couldn't bother with Ceci's name, even though they'd been in the same class for two months and collaborated in small groups before.

"As you can see, we're doing group work. You're with Orville, Ja'Neice and Shalonda this time." I gave him the assignment and accompanying grading rubric. I also wrote out a detention slip for his tardiness. If he hadn't been late, I would have goaded him into behaving badly, but he made it so easy. The handbook said students must make up the missed time when they were tardy. I knew it would tick him off.

After I handed him the detention, I gave him plenty of space. When he sat where he wanted to and ignored his group, I didn't complain. With my back to him, I worked with the rest of my class, the students I loved. Through sidelong eyes, I watched J.D. until he deposited a paper on my desk. When he returned to a computer, I strode over and glanced at his note. With a grim smile, I switched off the video camera discreetly positioned on top of my computer. I called Roosevelt on the cellphone Graham had loaned me. Roosevelt didn't have far to come. Just down the hall.

Francis Brown had never been my favorite person, but he was a human being and a colleague. After school, I stood behind my father and our ex-superintendent of schools as Reverend Brinkwater intoned words to honor Brown's life and comfort his family. The ex-wife didn't attend, but the current Mrs. Brown stood with the superintendent's extended family. Half a dozen men from the American Legion and maybe a dozen teachers from AHS also came to show respect.

Pallbearers included a banker, the owner of a dry cleaning business, and a druggist, all of whom I suspected of being one step above clan membership. Maybe one step above. Their comments in various news articles over the past year had formed my low opinion. They spoke in code. Obama was "elitist," code for "uppity." He couldn't have gotten into Harvard were it not for affirmative action, code for he couldn't possibly be smart enough to compete with white guys. He couldn't represent hard-working Americans, code for he's just a lazy "n" word. Yet I wasn't entirely different from these men. I couldn't forget how the room at the Board of Education meeting had divided into a black side and a white side. Only Lodge had crossed that line. God help the new president trying to bring us together. He had so much anger, so much frustration, and so much guilt he had to push past to help us heal.

A movement at the rear of the gathering caught my eye. Reverend Bolden, in his trademark dark suit and white preacher's collar, had joined us. I eased my way to the back to stand beside him. We nodded acknowledgement, each of the other, and then lifted our heads as the Rev. Brinkwater repeated Jesus's words: *I am the way and I am the light.*

I lost the rest of the eulogy, distracted by a breeze that carried a hint of freshly turned dirt and perhaps of rain to come. I became acutely aware of the blood red Yuletide camellias blooming near my mother's and David's graves to our far right, the longleaf pines reaching toward the clouds behind them, and the eerie yellow-green quality of late afternoon light.

I am the way and I am the light, I repeated to myself. I wasn't always sure about the literal details of the biblical story. Only six days for creation and all that. But one thing I did believe in with all my heart was that Jesus lived the life we all should aim for. A life of caring for our fellow man and forgiving others and ourselves for all our shortcomings. That's where Reverend Brinkwater was now, the trespasses part of the Lord's Prayer. I came back fully into the moment as we finished. Pallbearers lowered Brown's casket into a grave badly disguised by a sheet of Astroturf.

On impulse, I linked my arm around Reverend Bolden's elbow. He smiled down with his usual benevolence and patted my hand. It was foolish, I suppose, but I felt an unreasonable surge of hope.

Thirty-Nine

I wished I could take my boys and Dusty and leave town for the weekend, but with Graham's regional playoff set for seven and the triathlon the next morning, I knew we couldn't. Roosevelt promised me J.D. was under control. Everyone in school knew the police had hauled him out of first period the day before. By afternoon, the school board assigned him to the alternative school and he was under house arrest at night. A GPS ankle bracelet ensured police monitoring of his movements. Sonny Haswell stopped by my room to let me know Coach Underwood would take charge of J.D. at the alternative school.

"A strong black man in his life is exactly what this boy needs," Sonny said. "He'll get lots of one-on-one from Tommy Underwood."

I had gotten what I wanted. J.D. was out of my life. I should have felt better about it than I did. Every now and then I watched the classroom door, which I had closed and locked, in direct violation of school policy. I wondered where J.D. was, if he was sitting in Coach Underwood's class at the alternative school.

Training had transformed our Friday pot luck in the lounge. The muffalettas of two months ago were replaced by baby spinach tossed with raspberries, mangoes, green onions, grilled chicken, and a splash of balsamic vinaigrette. Whole wheat crackers replaced French bread. We still indulged in decadent chocolate for dessert, but instead of calorie-laden cake, we ate one ultra-rich sugar-free truffle apiece. The changes were welcome because they helped me comply with my doctor's orders.

I fidgeted over lunch, jumping at every noise, on edge about J.D. blowing us all away Columbine-style. Liz finally got up and locked the lounge door.

"Anyone wants in, they better know the secret password," she said in that soft Southern voice I loved.

"What is it?" Tessa asked.

"Anything having to do with peeing yourself," Liz said, which sounded about right since the only way to access the teachers' restrooms was through the lounge.

At least the newspaper had gone to press. That hassle was over with, and it was the best issue we'd ever done. We were in line to win another state newspaper championship, for sure. Everyone was going to love this issue. Even Mr. Van Teasel.

Forty

Mr. Van Teasel tilted his chin down and peered over the top of his wire rims. "Really, Mrs. Culpepper, what were you thinking, letting that article go on the front page?"

"I don't know, sir." Maybe that the school's roof would be repaired? That parents would read the article and see the need to pass the school bond? I sank deeper into the black club chair in front of his desk. Kitsi's photo of two garbage cans in the center of one classroom particularly disturbed him. The cans caught drips when it rained. Another photo showed a teacher arranging a tarp over her computer before she left for the day in case of inclement weather overnight. I had replaced the missing ceiling tiles in my room with my own money, but already they were leak-stained. In her article Tameka presented a case for passing the local school bond in December to make repairs to the aging building.

"Parents read stuff like this and they're ready to pull their kids out of AHS and send them over to the county school or enroll them in one of the private schools. Already today I've been chewed out by two board members. They said I don't exercise enough control over what goes on in this school. Well, no more. From now on, all articles need to be turned in for approval before publication."

"Yes, sir."

"And get that article off the Internet edition immediately."

"Yes, sir." I eyed the door.

Mr. Van Teasel handed me a survey. "I want you to run this schoolwide with the results published in the next newspaper. Students rank the amendments to the Constitution in order of importance. We hope to stimulate a discussion of the Bill of Rights around their signing date on December 15. Students choose five to eliminate. Which one do you think students will rank first?"

"Probably the same as the founders—the First Amendment."

He gloated, or at least it seemed that way to me. "That's always the first to go. No one likes the media anymore."

Maybe he wasn't trying to insult me, but I took it personally. A free press was essential to a democracy—I believed that with all my heart. "The Founders put it first for a reason."

"I suspect you're not really a Baptist at all, Mrs. Culpepper. I think you might be one of those bleeding heart liberals."

Liberal? I didn't like labels though I thought of myself as moderate. Not that there was anything wrong with being liberal. The term had been on my Word Wall this month, and I saw my chance to wipe the smirk off his face.

"The word *liberal* means giving generously, it means being tolerant and broad-minded, it means favoring progress and reform and democracy and personal freedom. I believe in all those things, and I bet most of my Sunday school class does, too, even though they think of themselves as conservatives. And I bet they believe in freedom of religion, which the First Amendment also protects."

Why was he still smiling?

"Oh, Mrs. Culpepper, I think this school is going to have some stimulating conversations about the amendments this month, I really do. A teacher like you lights a fire under any topic, and I can see this will not be an exception."

Had he just praised me or insulted me?

"Just try not to burn the school down while you're at it," he said. "By the way, J.D. reported to the alternative school like he was supposed to today. In looking over his discipline record, I noticed you and Mrs. Kaufmann met with J.D. and his mother twice to try to straighten out his attitude. Saw where you'd enlisted Coach Haswell's support too and sent home daily progress reports. I think you did everything you could. You can't save them all."

Maybe not, but we should. Somehow we should.

We lost the game. Graham hit one field goal and missed two, his ankle still sore. Our quarterback threw some solid passes, but Harrison Simmons couldn't hold onto them like J.D. could. Roosevelt worked security for the game. He climbed the bleachers to chat with me at the end of the first quarter.

"What's going to become of J.D. now?" I asked. "Think he'll drop out? Wind up in jail?"

"He could be back on the team by next year, and he still has a chance at playing college ball. All depends on how well he behaves at the alternative school. Don't you worry. I had a long talk with the kid and I think he's turned a corner."

I hoped he was right, but I couldn't help worrying. What if he found his way to the game? I wondered how closely that ankle bracelet was monitored.

Roosevelt also dropped a bomb, destroying one of my favorite fantasies. "Guess who's sitting in a cell tonight?"

Unless it was J.D., I didn't have a clue.

"Russ Freeman," he said. "Undercover guy caught him in an Internet chat room trying to pick up young boys. When we confiscated his computer, we found hundreds of illegal photographs. Don't think he's going to be coaching soccer again any time soon."

My stomach lurched and I thought I might lose my dinner. Weren't you supposed to have some kind of radar that told you when someone was a weirdo? Thank heavens I'd never asked him out for coffee. Even though my first thought had been about myself, I wasn't entirely self-centered. I latched onto Roosevelt's arms and shook him. "Quinn? The boys on the team? He didn't—"

Roosevelt calmed me down. "As far as we know, Freeman didn't bother any local boys."

"Told you so," Woodson said from his seat beside me.

I appreciated that he was sober and trying to be there for me, but it really galled me that he had been the better judge of character. "Yes, you did."

My father practically bounced in his seat. "Whoo-hoo! No wonder his wife left him."

I refused to look at him. "Nobody likes to listen to old gasconades, but your exegesis apparently was correct."

He whumped my arm. "There you go again, Miss School Marm—whacha want to use them big old words for? Nobody knows what the heck you're talking about."

I grinned. If I ever lost my job teaching, I figured I could go to work writing speeches for politicians. Roosevelt examined both of us, shook his head, and resumed his duties. I saw him chasing Trey Beckwith out from under the bleachers where he was untying his classmates' sneakers and retying them to the person sitting beside them. I imagined the rest of Roosevelt's evening, how he would snag two middle schoolers trying to climb over the fence to avoid paying admission and after that, how he would whistle as he approached the Mansfield boy's truck in case the young Romeo managed to get further than the first two buttons of Delphinium Williams's blouse. A little heads up warning. I knew Roosevelt's drill by heart. It had been David's job once. Oh, the stories David would tell. Only the kids' names changed from year to year.

Forty-One

By the time a haze of pale gold light filtered through my kitchen curtains, the boys and I had already been up for several hours. I wore the blue "Alderson's Angels" tee-shirt Ceci designed for the teacher team. She turned the "o" in Alderson into a smiling face with a halo over it. For the student team she designed a red shirt that read "Daredevils" in big print and "Wouldn't you really rather be a devil?" in smaller type. The "l's" spoked into pitchforks. Woodson parked himself on a bar stool, reading advance coverage of the triathlon. I made a special pot of coffee. None of my hazelnut for him. "That's a girly drink," he said, "something that homo Russ Freeman would like."

It figured that my father would confuse pedophiles and homosexuals, but I wasn't going to carry on a fruitless philosophical argument this morning.

On the front page in a sidebar labeled "If You Go," the triathlon logo Ceci designed appeared. It ran with a credit line that should earn her all sorts of parental approval. Also above the fold in a large color photo, Liz and I were jogging around the track. I didn't cringe when Woodson showed me the picture, the way I had last year when my photo was in the city paper for teaching a summer photography course. This time I didn't look fat. I looked healthy. I would never be tall and wispy like a fashion model—but I could find my waistline again. My muscles were more toned now than they had been for years.

We went outside to load equipment into Woodson's truck. Quinn pulled out a royal blue plastic tarp from the bottom of the truck bed. "Hey, Grandpa, what are all these Obama signs doing in your truck? Thought you didn't like him much."

Sure enough, a dozen "Change We Can Believe In" signs were scattered beneath the area that had been covered with the tarp. I nailed Woodson with a look that said if I had a baseball bat handy and if I didn't have so many other things to do, I'd bust him one for stealing my First Amendment rights. He had the decency to look a mite hang-dog in the second he dared to meet my eyes.

Suddenly I felt defeated in the wake of our victory. Many more like my father lived in Alderson and all over the country. We might have elected a black man president, but the divisions in our country were so wide we couldn't even allow each other the right to express our views civilly. McCain/Palin signs still dotted lawns all over Alderson—blustery announcements that the owners wouldn't accept the election results. I'd lived here all my life and felt as if I didn't know my neighbors anymore. Maybe I'd never known them.

The boys loaded all their equipment into the truck. Woodson covered their gear with the tarp and anchored everything with a weave of bungee cords resembling a primary-colored spider's web. Forecasters weren't predicting rain, but you never could tell. Woodson drove the boys to the school gymnasium to set up before events started. I headed to the tennis courts. Brian and Vashawn led us through some calisthenics and stretches, and we volleyed a few shots and executed a few practice serves.

By the time competition began at eight, the bleachers were already nearly full. The morning air felt cool, and dew still clung to the grass. In red and blue cheerleading outfits, Marissa Powell and Mary Wade Marcinek stirred up the crowd for both sides. The PTA manned the ticket booth and refreshment stand. Coffee, juice, doughnuts, and muffins sold best at this time of day, but I noticed quite a few kids with soft drinks. I didn't approve—I never let my boys have them until after dinner and preferred they didn't have them, period—but the PTA moms said we'd lose business if we didn't sell them.

Our committee had established special rules for our contest to allow us to complete all three events in one day. After every player had served once, the team in the lead won. If no one was ahead, we entered sudden death playoffs. On one court Tessa and the youthful Betsy faced the student team of Ceci Barnes and Angela Martin. The guidance counselor served first and was soundly defeated. Ceci's long legs galloped across the court and her arms extended to return balls anyone else would have missed. The little colt turned out to be a thoroughbred, and I bet the tennis coach would recruit her for spring season. Angela served first, a powerhouse that slammed into the backcourt. Betsy returned a short little chop that caught Ceci off guard. Tessa and Betsy fought hard to break her serve, but in the end, the students won their match.

Miss Baker lunged too aggressively after a shot that slammed down the line and hurt her ankle, but she wouldn't hear of sitting out the rest of the day. "I finish what I start," she said. "Besides, it's not hurt that bad."

My turn came to team up with Liz. I could hear Woodson whooping over the rest of the crowd and cringed.

"Get over it," Liz said. "At least he's still around. My dad went out the front door when I was eight and never came back again."

She had a point. I visored my hands against the morning sun and located Graham sitting in the bleachers in front of Mary Wade. She twisted and jumped and shook her pom poms around while Graham all but knelt at her feet. Quinn and Donnie climbed to the top row and began lobbing popcorn—this early in the day?—at two classmates sitting on a lower bench. Donnie carried a huge, half-eaten candy apple in one hand. Not my idea of breakfast. On the other end of the bleachers, Lodge Piscetelli scrambled up to sit next to Woodson, who was supposed to keep an eye on the boys while I competed. I didn't think Graham would sneak off to smoke pot before his performance today, but I planned to keep him on a short leash for a long time to come.

"Did you hear about Coach Freeman?" Liz asked.

"Crazy, huh? Quinn says he never saw him do anything more than slap a few butts on the way onto the field."

"That seems to be a coach requirement. Such a waste—Freeman was one of the few eligible hunks in Alderson."

"He's not that cute."

"Shoot girlfriend, I'm a married woman and I still appreciate those ripped pecs and glutes. A definite hunk. Don't tell me you weren't drooling over him."

"His nose is a little crooked."

Liz studied me critically. "Wow—you were drooling bad, weren't you? Slobbering, panting—"

"All right, all right. A little. I'm sooo over it."

She laughed. "Yeah, knowing he wants to play hide the weenie with little boys does have that certain 'yuk' factor."

We walked out onto the court to face Shaniqua and Ja'Neice. It felt strange competing against my students. No one was more surprised than I was when we won.

Vashawn came over to fist-bump us.

"Good match." I shook hands with Shaniqua and Ja'Neice.

Shaniqua pouted. "I'm no good at sports."

"Doesn't matter," Liz said. "As long as we finish each event, we win for the school."

Brian, always happy to be at the center of things, jaunted to the microphone and announced the tie, two points for the teachers, two for students at the end of the first round of competition. "And here's a bit of news to lift everyone's spirits." He paused for effect. "A last-minute donor has made an offer to double whatever amount we raise today through the triathlon if every participant completes all three events." When the applause died down, he encouraged the crowd to adjourn to the YMCA for the swim competition. Then he searched the dispersing crowd—I knew exactly who he was looking for—and he dashed off in the direction of Marissa.

Holding hands, Graham and Mary Wade started down Jefferson Street toward the Y. Quinn and Donnie showed their affection for their gang by nudging, punching, shoving, tripping, slugging, and giggling their way off campus. One boy reached over and shoved Donnie's face deep into his aqua cotton candy. I made a mental note to warn Quinn to stay out of the junk food. If Donnie didn't watch out he was going to be as porky as I used to be.

I drifted over to Woodson and Lodge, who were waiting by the bottom of the bleachers. Woodson flicked his cigarette ash onto the cement, right beneath a sign designating the school grounds as a smoke-free environment.

He motioned toward me. "This little girl is a butterfly champion."

I blushed, not sure what was worse: Woodson's bragging or his calling me a little girl. Lodge looked amused by my discomfort.

"That was a long time ago." Deep down, I was tickled that my father remembered.

"Like riding a bike. Once you learn—" he trailed off.

When he picked up a thermos from the bleachers, I groaned in-wardly, suspecting the coffee was spiked, but I wasn't going to say a word. It was his life and if he wanted to spend the rest of it sick, that was his choice.

And maybe it was just coffee.

I followed the flow of people down Jefferson Street, the duffel bag containing my bathing suit clutched in my left hand, Lodge setting the pace on my right, and Woodson on the outside next to the curb. Walking to the outside of ladies was the one etiquette rule he always followed. Almost the only one.

My new black knee-length leotard made me look ten pounds slimmer, but couldn't totally disguise the fat rolls remaining on my waist and thighs. I looked around the dressing room. We all looked healthier now than when we'd started. The students already had sauntered out in their swimsuits, unabashed. We teachers zipped and tugged on various cover-ups. No one moved to go outside.

I thought of the movie *Calendar Girls*. We had all laughed about it in the lounge. "Look, if a group of ladies in Great Britain could pose nude for a calendar to raise money, we can do this. It's not nearly as hard."

Liz held open the door for us.

Tessa went out first. "Sweetheart, I'm from New Jersey. I'm not scared of anything."

Liz stood like a brown boulder in the doorway. "Those women raised a lot, didn't they? Maybe if we don't raise enough today—"

"Hush your mouth, girl!" I shoved her in the back. "I wasn't trying to give you any ideas, only courage."

Tessa giggled. "You would actually raise more money if you took the pictures and then let us pay to keep the calendar off the shelves."

Miss Baker sniffed. "Ladies, let's remember who we are."

She didn't mean to be funny, but it sounded snooty, and I started laughing and couldn't stop. Soon we all were, even Miss Baker. Woodson later said he thought it must have been the influence of Tessa, being a regular at First Methodist. He'd never known any women from First Baptist to carry on and have as much fun as we seemed to be having.

Swimming events went much as anticipated. Shaniqua bested Liz in breaststroke, redeeming herself in her own eyes for her loss in tennis; Ceci easily defeated the injured Miss Baker in freestyle; Ja'Neice won backstroke. I won the butterfly, my broad shoulders proving they were good for something. I loved the slippery feel of water on my skin, the thrust of my arms, the rhythmic thuds of the dolphin kick as I powered down the lane. Miss Baker was right. We needed to keep doing this. It felt too good to stop.

No one dropped out, and no one drowned. The teachers were down by one point as the three-mile walk/run began. We probably wouldn't catch up, but I didn't think anyone would drop out either, so the money was almost as good as in the bank.

The only one who might not be able to make it was Miss Baker, and again I urged her to drop out. At her age, her injury might not heal that quickly. "No sponsor is going to bow out because you got injured."

"I will finish what I started," she said. "Even if I have to crawl over that finish line."

"Don't take off your shoes, no matter what," Vashawn said, "because your feet will only feel worse when you have to put them back on—if you can even get them back on. Your feet will probably swell."

With great enthusiasm we set out. During the third mile, I half-jogged, half-walked beside Tessa, whose breath still managed to smell like mint though I hadn't seen her pop one all day. Trailing somewhere behind us were Miss Baker and Liz. The students and Betsy Mulharin, her blonde ponytail bouncing, had long since passed us by. This section of the course wound through a linear park that stretched behind us through downtown Alderson and ahead of us past what I guess you'd call our suburbs—several middle class neighborhoods, composed of cookie-cutter style homes. They were newer, but would never muster the same kind of class as our old homes near downtown, with their high ceilings and fancy crown moldings—and monstrous heating and repair bills. We would run the length of the park and then circle back on Jefferson Street to finish at the school where refreshments and entertainment awaited us. The park ran between two streets, so thin in some places you could see and hear cars traversing the other side, so thick and wooded in others you wouldn't realize a downtown with its two- and three-story buildings and asphalt roads sprawled anywhere nearby. At several points along the trail, fans assembled, mostly students who cheered and jeered us on.

Tessa and I slowed down as we entered the fourth mile and were

back on the pavement of Jefferson Street. "Hey, wait up!" I heard Liz
call behind us.

Gladly, we slowed even more. Two months of training hadn't been
enough to transform our atrophied bodies into muscled machines ready
to power through a day as full of exertion as this one. My calves were
killing me and a blister tormented my left foot.

Liz caught up. Then I scoped the area behind her.

"Where's Miss Baker?" I asked.

"She shooed me on a while back, said not to dare slow down because of her, and you know how Miss Baker is—you can't argue with
her. You think she'll be all right?"

I didn't know, but I was going to find out. I sent them on ahead and
headed back toward the woods, my blister protesting with every step.

I retraced at least a half mile with no sign of Miss Baker. Under a
slash pine I squatted to rest on the sharp needles blanketing the dirt.
In a branch overhead, a Cooper's hawk perched patiently, its black eyes
following the unsuspecting squirrels skittering up a nearby oak. If I
listened very carefully, I could make out the hum of cars in the distance. Otherwise, this spot felt as peaceful and isolated as any in Mason County. I bent over my shoe and loosened the laces a bit. Vashawn
was right—my feet had swollen. Finally Miss Baker waddled up the
path toward me, her tennis shoes laced together across one arm. Her
socks were filthy.

I brushed the dirt and crumbled pine needles off my butt. "Why
did you take your shoes off?"

She made a face and huffed out fragments while she leaned over,
resting her hands on her knees. "I know Vashawn said not to. Got
a pebble stuck—in there. Poked—like a knife. My shoe—too tight
anyway. That tennis. My ankle. Just a little swollen. Not too bad."
She took another deep breath and straightened up. "Glad I got here
when I did."

"Why?"

"Somebody was coming up behind you. Thought it might have
been that Marshall boy. Course, I was too far away to tell for sure.
Anyway—" she paused to suck in air, "—whoever it was, veered off
into the woods. Probably a jogger. If it had been that boy, I was going
to run over here and beat him away with my shoes."

The unlikely picture made me laugh. "Probably a jogger, like you said." A little doubt hung in the back of my mind, but I brushed it away. If it had been J.D. intent on revenge, he wouldn't have let a tiny woman like Miss Baker stand in his way. "Well, let's get moving—we have a mile to go and everyone will start to wonder what happened to us." From the corner of my eye, I saw how she hobbled, pain evident in her eyes. I recalled Vivian's reporting to our Sunday school that Jolene suffered from swollen ankles. In a surge of pity and affection, I offered to carry her shoes, but regretted it almost right away. A dead mouse would have smelled better. She wouldn't have had to beat J.D. with them. If she waved those stink bombs under his nose, he'd have run for his life.

Forty-Two

In the school gym, a microphone clasped in his hands, Brian Jones announced the student team had won. His face took on a purple sheen under the fluorescent lights. Brian worked the crowd like a natural politician, smooth talking with an ear for strong sound bites, and an instinct for timing laughs and milking sentiment.

During the next hour a series of camera flashes followed speeches. My photographer knelt, stood on a chair, worked from the right, and then the left in her quest for the best angles. Kitsi jockeyed for position with the *Herald* photographer and Channel Eight News videographer. Her training showed, and she made me proud.

First she took candids: a wide shot of the crowd in the bleachers, a medium shot of Miss Baker massaging her foot, a close-up of Quinn and Donnie biting into hot dogs dripping with catsup and mustard. Then there were the formal shots.

Flash: The manager of Hennesey's Department Store distributes $20 gift certificates to each girl on the student team.

Flash: Quinn pulls a cloth cover off a state-of-the-art graphics and video-capable computer he made himself with parts donated by a smiling C. Lodge Piscetelli, standing to his right. (I am so surprised and touched I don't realize I am crying until Liz hands me a tissue.)

Flash: Me, blowing my nose. (Kitsi is the only one to capture this. Must find way to delete photo.)

Flash: Mr. Kelso, Woodson's boss at the cable company, shakes hands with Mr. Van Teasel, both smiling like fools for the camera. Kelso announces his company will donate installation of high speed Internet connections to every classroom in the school. (Astonished, I nudge Woodson. He shrugs as if it is nothing, winks.)

Flash: Brian announces pledges from sponsors total $8,255, which the anonymous donor will double for a total of $16,510. (I still haven't been able to find out who Anonymous is. Mr. Van Teasel isn't saying, and my Sunday school class has failed to ferret out the donor, but we will continue to work our sources. The truth is sure to come out.)

Finally it was time for the entertainment. Graham's voice trembled as he announced the members of his band, Graham's Quackers. Each member nodded as he acknowledged them, but when he came to Quinn, my youngest did an amazing drum roll and clash on the cymbals that brought on loud cheers from the sixth graders in the audience.

Graham turned and faced his band and launched into Carrie Underwood's "All-American Girl," with Mary Wade and him on vocals. As they moved into the second verse, Graham still showed us his backside. When they began the third verse, I realized he was pulling a Jim Morrison: he couldn't face the audience. I didn't see how he could have stage fright, considering he'd been in the church choir since he was five years old, but I could think of no other explanation.

Right behind me a gravelly voice I'd recognize anywhere called out: "Hey, Graham, lemme see your purty face!"

Red as Ronald McDonald's nose, Graham turned around and stopped singing. Noah's guitar whipped out a last riff; the keyboard and drum trailed away as Graham stepped up to the microphone.

"Hey everybody, that's my grandpa!"

Laughter rippled through the room and Graham's blush receded. "And in front of him is my Mom, who helped put this party together today. Let's hear it for our teachers!"

Another round of applause rose and died down and the Quackers started all over again with "Drive." It didn't bother me any. I'd heard them start songs over time after time after time. Whistles and rousing applause met the end of the number, mostly from the whites in the audience although blacks politely applauded too. I liked to concentrate on the ways the races are alike, but cultural differences do exist. My black students, overall, were not big fans of country and alternative.

Everything went smoothly until the band ended their fourth song. Donnie jerked to his feet and leapt off the stage, losing a flip flop in the process. He barreled through the crowd between him and the bathroom. His mother followed him to the restroom door. If only she'd been around earlier in the day to stop him from eating so much junk. I had seen him with popcorn, cotton candy, a candied apple, and hot dogs, and who knows what else he ate when I wasn't looking. He was in that bathroom puking up his guts. I'd have bet money on it.

Graham and Noah fidgeted on stage. Finally, Donnie's mother came over and whispered something into Mary Wade's ear. The band conferred in a huddle. At last Graham leaned into the microphone. "Folks, I'm sorry, but it appears we've lost a member of our band. If our short performance upset anyone, they can get refunds at the door. Brian?" Graham searched the crowd. "Isn't there another group ready—"

Refunds? I pushed my way to the stage. "Hold up. Wait just a minute now."

I planted myself in front of the keyboards, my fingers trembling as I looked out at Miss Baker, Mr. Van Teasel, Lodge, Woodson—half the town. I wasn't good enough for this. Hadn't played in public since college. Quinn gave me a drum roll and shouted, "The show must go on!" He was right. Graham and Noah coaxed the first chords of Dave Matthews' "Typical Situation" from their guitars. I could do this: I'd listened to them play their seven songs repeatedly until I heard them in my dreams. We finished off with Creed's "Human Clay" and Radiohead's "OK Computer." Not to brag, but we did okay.

Marissa took the stage next as part of the first team in the step competition: The A-Team Ladies. Those eight girls stomped white tennis shoes, wiggled butts wrapped in black shorts, and twisted torsos topped with matching red tee-shirts. The black kids in the crowd went wild. Those girls could dance. I thought they would be hard to beat, but then a group of fifteen guys with white head bands and red and white striped shirts nearly stomped the boards off. Although four other teams entered, none could top those first two for finesse and synchronicity. A panel of judges led by Vashawn declared the event a tie. Winners got gift certificates to a local pizza joint, a trophy, and bragging rights.

Meanwhile, the soft drinks, sweet tea, cupcakes and cookies flew off the bake sale tables set up in the back of the cafeteria across from the gym. As the day wound down, Woodson played sing-alongs on the piano. He started with "This Land is Your Land" and "Sing." Then the crowd shouted out requests. We were supposed to be out of the school by 4:30.

"Never mind," Mr. Van Teasel said. "Everyone is having fun." He patted me on the shoulder and whispered, "Good going, Miss Molly," and then shouted out to Woodson, "Play 'Only You!'"

Mr. Van Teasel's praise meant a lot to me. I was proud of the way the day's events had gone. Proud of Woodson, too. I had no idea he knew so many songs by heart.

The fundraiser was over, and there were only three more school days until Christmas vacation. Life was good.

After Woodson finished the principal's request, he invited everyone to a barbecue in his backyard. "Bring whatever y'all want to drink, and come on." Must have been more than forty, fifty folks told him they were coming. It was a great idea. Nothing like a big food bash to bring a community together. A final bit of healing.

I corralled my father. "Is this a good idea? The kitchen—"

"All cleaned up."

"All those burnt pans?"

"Threw them out. Bought new."

Forty-Three

After I showered, changed into jeans, and fed Dusty, I drove to Woodson's. Cars and trucks already lined the driveway and lawn. Two fires blazed in the backyard, one, I assumed, for cooking and the other, warmth. The cooking fire seemed to sit quite high off the ground. Woodson enlisted Graham's and Quinn's help in flattening ground chuck into patties. In the kitchen I found Mr. Kelso stirring a huge kettle of Five Beans Bake.

"Thanks for your pledge today," I told him as I pulled one of my mother's aprons off a hook in the pantry and tied it on over my jacket. I turned the fire down under some collards boiling on the back burner and opened the oven door to see what might be inside. The earthy smell of cornbread made me salivate.

"Just good sense," he said. "My grandkids and most of my future workers attend that school. Besides, your dad twisted my arm pretty hard."

From the kitchen window, I could see a good size crowd assembling. One Christmas, must have been a decade ago, my father had strung twinkly lights all over our pergola and back porch. He'd either forgotten or never bothered to take them down and now the scuppernong vines had hardened around them. Underneath the lights' friendly glow, Lodge played a fiddle and Liz strummed a banjo, laughing wickedly, while Roosevelt Pitts ran his lips over a harmonica. I stepped outside to hear better. They didn't sound half bad. For several minutes, I stood there on the back porch watching Lodge work that fiddle, his braid swinging back and forth with the music, and he looked so good, and that skimpy braid seemed so natural and right I couldn't imagine him any other way.

My father and Lem Powell rigged up an outdoor buffet by laying plywood sheets over several sawhorses. Behind the buffet, Mrs. Alford—who had a long-ingrained habit of taking over—assumed charge of food contributions. Many were dishes people had planned to serve their own families for dinner; others brought chips or paper plates or deli slaw they'd picked up on the way over. I handed Mrs. Alford the oblong dish filled with the Next Best Thing to Sex I'd saved for my family. Liz brought her special sweet potato pie. My dessert was sugar-free and I knew the pie wasn't, but Woodson's philosophy ran in my mind: you have to go some way, and you might as well go having fun. I had worked off enough calories that I not only deserved a piece of Liz's pie, I probably needed the sugar. Just this once. I started with dessert first.

Mrs. Alford and I debated what Liz's secret ingredient could be. "Coconut extract," I suggested.

Mrs. Alford disagreed. "I believe it's lemon rind."

Right behind me Reverend Bolden arrived with a huge container of potato salad he'd been planning to take to a church luncheon Sunday. "Guess I'll just have to make another batch early in the morning." He poured himself a glass of ice tea and took a long sip. "It was a fine thing you teachers did for our kids today, Miz Culpepper."

"We didn't do it alone."

"No, but I know how these things work. It wouldn't have happened without you teachers getting the job done."

"Does this mean you'll drop the lawsuit?"

He shook his head and sipped ice tea. "That's a different matter, I'm afraid. We still have unresolved issues."

"Even if this lawsuit hanging over our heads makes our jobs as teachers that much harder?"

His jowls sagged. "I'm truly sorry about that. I know your job is hard enough, but I can't stop fighting for what I believe is right for our kids."

I could respect that. We had so much in common, blacks and whites. We loved our children, our relatives, and our neighbors, even though they behaved badly sometimes. We loved Alderson High with all its rituals and traditions. And we all loved Liz's sweet potato pie. Maybe I could pry the recipe out of Reverend Bolden, since I'd never persuaded Liz to share it.

"We've come a long way, but we still have a ways to go," he added.

My father always said slavery wasn't his fault. People over a hundred years ago were responsible and they were all gone now. Time to move on. My mother used to counter that the inequities and injustices lasted long beyond slavery. They were both right. It was time to move on, but how did a country even out a century of advantages given to whites? A few decades of affirmative action weren't enough. Even the election of a black president couldn't erase every residue of racism—and it even caused renewed resentment in some Americans.

Rev. Bolden held out his hand. "Partners anyway?"

We shook. "Definitely." As an afterthought I tossed an idea his way. "You know, there are other ways to get what you want—like changing the make-up of the school board."

"I'll think on that, I truly will, but I'm afraid we might not have the power to make that happen. But who knows? With the Lord behind us—just maybe…"

I believed in the Lord, but as my Mama always said, the Lord helps those who help themselves. Very little of what you wanted in life came without hard work. There really weren't enough blacks on the school board.

"Why don't you run?" I said. He would be the perfect candidate: well-known, well-liked, a born leader.

He chuckled and refilled his tea. "Last thing I need is something more on my plate."

"I remember thinking the same thing when you appointed me as fundraising chair."

We both laughed, but a slightly unfocused look came over his eyes as if he were looking into the future.

Quinn formed the last hamburger patty. I walked beside him as he carried the first platter to his grandfather. Lifting each one with a spatula, Woodson arranged them in the bottom of a grocery shopping cart. One by one the crowd fell silent as people nudged each other to watch. Graham helped him remove the last burgers from the platter. Then Woodson rolled the cart over the fire. Now I understood why he had banked the fire up so high.

I stood in amazed silence as laughter bubbled up from the crowd. I didn't really want to know, but I had to ask. "Where'd your grandpa find the shopping cart?"

"SaveMore Butchers." Quinn's expression captured the wonder of it all. I could picture Woodson buying all the ground chuck they had, rolling the buggy out to his truck, and lifting the whole shebang into the back end.

"I tried to stop him, Mom, but Graham knocked me up the side of the head and whispered, 'When's the last time you've seen him this happy?'"

Woodson did look quite pleased with the world. And the rest of the crowd was too, judging by the tears rolling down people's faces as they inspected Woodson's grill. Even Sgt. Roosevelt Pitts doubled over, slapping his thighs. Then Roosevelt asked about the parking meter by the hot tub, and Woodson launched into one of his favorite stories. I held my breath, waiting for Roosevelt to ask where he'd gotten it, but he didn't. Since Woodson didn't face imminent arrest, I relaxed.

Betsy Mulharin cornered me and slipped a paper out of her pocketbook. "Now, don't tell Graham I gave this to you, but I thought you should read it."

What now? Was he smoking dope again? Had he written an obscene proposal to her? It wouldn't have surprised me—I saw the way he ogled her long legs in her bathing suit and in her track shorts today. Half afraid to read it, I unfolded the paper and skimmed his first paragraph: "Two years ago if you'd asked me who my hero was, I would have answered my dad. He was the best dad in the whole world, but since he died, my mom has more than filled his shoes, so she is my hero now." I folded the paper up and fished under my apron to find my jacket pocket.

"Thanks, Betsy. I can't read the rest right now, or I might start crying. Sometimes it seems as if Graham doesn't even like me anymore."

"He does—but he's fourteen and can't show it. You've done a great job with him. He's always prepared and unfailingly polite."

I was glad he was polite at school. That was more than I could claim about his home behavior. Betsy still looked fourteen herself. What was she—twenty-five? She could still remember what fourteen felt like. I bet she knew who Lindsay Lohan was. Not that it mattered anymore. Last night before the game Graham had removed Lindsay's poster from his wall and replaced it with a blonde beauty named Taylor Swift. I knew who she was. I liked her songs myself.

But thinking about the game made me remember why J.D. didn't get to play in it. I visualized him urinating into Grahams' gym bag and could almost smell the ammonia stench. My stomach knotted. What was J.D. doing tonight? What did a street kid do when he was forced by an ankle bracelet to stay home? Watch BET? Plug in his earbuds and listen to Tupac? It wasn't enough. I wanted him punished.

Mr. Kelso touched my arm. "Lost in thought?"

"Just thinking what a great idea this party was."

"Isn't it?" He smiled then looked startled. "Oh dear, I've been out here yakking and forgot about the beans."

"No worries. I'll check them." The screen door whined open and slammed behind me on the way into the kitchen. The beans were already stuck to the pot and burning. I opened the kitchen window to let the scorched odor out. Men! Five Beans Bake was supposed to be baked, not cooked on the stovetop. I didn't know if I should stir the burned beans off the bottom and risk ruining the whole batch. Instead I transferred them into a new pan and scraped the burnt beans into the disposal and ran water in the pan to soak. As I turned off the faucet, I couldn't help but overhear Mrs. Alford through the kitchen window. Maybe I did stand there and listen longer than I should have, but I swear I didn't intend to eavesdrop. I couldn't help it if Vivian Barnes and Mrs. Alford stood right outside the window.

"My Ceci designed the logo and program for the triathlon," Vivian said.

"Yes, she's quite talented," Mrs. Alford said. "I thought the way she abstracted the human forms was very like Matisse."

Vivian glowed under the twinkly lights. "She wants to go to design school. I think she'll do quite well, don't you? Just between you and me, I thought she wasn't going to be able to get into any college—such terrible test scores. Just terrible. Some kids don't do well on standardized tests. It's a common problem, Molly Culpepper says. But I gave Ceci a practice SAT last weekend and she's come up 160 points. Molly's been tutoring her. That's what made the difference. Ceci just loves her. She's going to be the school newspaper's artist next year. I'm really proud of her."

I was tickled that Ceci had earned her mother's approval. Her scores still weren't going to get her into an Ivy League college, but Ceci proved the point that every child was blessed with different strengths and it was worth the effort to figure out what they were.

"You know everything that goes on in that school, I know you do," Vivian said to Mrs. Alford. A blatant piece of flattery if I ever heard one. Also true. "So I bet you know who the anonymous donor is."

"Yes, ma'am, I do. I have the check locked away in the vault. If you promise not to repeat this, I'll tell you whose name is on it."

I pushed my palms against the countertop and raised my body off the floor until my nose pressed against the window screen. I held my breath so I wouldn't miss a word.

"Lem Powell," she whispered. Her voice returned to normal, and I dropped back to the ground, completely flabbergasted. How could Liz have kept this from me?

"His Marissa is sure to be one of the first students to sign up for that new IB program," Mrs. Alford said. "Mr. Powell said whatever he ended up donating, it'd be a whole lot cheaper than sending her to private school. Imagine that. He'd doesn't want a soul to know about the donation, so keep this quiet."

I went looking for Tessa and Betsy. I couldn't wait to tell them who anonymous was.

Guess I didn't have to tell Liz.

I wandered into the house, thinking to use the bathroom, but found it occupied. A privilege of once having lived there was knowing the location of the upstairs bathroom and feeling free to use it. When I finished, I passed by Mama's sewing room. Woodson had asked me to clean it out, but I hadn't been able to face the task. Her wicker basket of pastel yarns sat on the floor, a half-finished blanket sprawling over the edge. Knitting blankets for preemies at the hospital had been one of my mother's many good deeds. Claimed it kept her fingers busy while she watched TV at night. I opened the bi-fold doors on her closet. On the floor inside, three boxes were stacked on top of one another. In the first were letters from Sam—letters instead of the visits she really wanted. He could have put up with Woodson occasionally to make Mama happy. I didn't read the letters. Another time, perhaps. The second box contained old Mother's Day and Valentine's cards. I sifted through recent ones, some I remembered sending.

At the bottom of the box were cards from way back when Sam and I could only print our names in awkward letters. She had saved them all.

The third box contained more letters. I started to put them away, thinking they were more from Sam, when the handwriting snagged my attention—Woodson's sloppy cursive. A pale blue ribbon tied together most of the stack, but one sat loose on top. The letter was written on plain white stationery with a Camp Breckinridge logo at the top.

August 23, 1953

"Dearest June Bug,

I know you asked me not to press you for commitment before I left for Korea, but the war is over now, so they say. I have almost forgotten what my mother's pecan pie tastes like, but I haven't forgotten you. If anything, I love you even more through your letters. They have traveled with me from camp to camp, and have been all that gave me hope that I might live a normal life again after I left this horrible war-torn country. I have waited so long for this homecoming I can't believe it's finally here.

I know I should ask you this face to face, but I'm a coward. My question, one I ask with all my heart, is this: will you marry me? I know you think I'm somewhat of a scallywag, and you're probably right, but if your answer is yes, I will be the happiest guy on the planet. Maybe you think this question is premature, but I've been in love with you since I was in eleventh grade, and you know it better than anyone else.

Besides, I kind of need to have an answer right away. Juilliard has offered me a scholarship to study piano, and though I have always loved music, going off to live in the big city isn't my idea of a good time. What I want more than anything is to come home to Alderson and marry you as soon as possible. If you have no interest in me or if someone else has laid claim to you while I've been gone, then I don't want to live in Georgia. I think you can understand that. So if you say no, I guess I'll go off to New York and become the world's next famous pianist, but I'd a hundred times rather be your husband.

I will be visiting my parents Sunday afternoon a week from
now and hope you will be waiting at their house. If not, I will
know you've moved on with your life, and my wish for you,
then, is that you find the happiness you deserve. You will always be my sweet little June Bug."

He signed the letter, "Truly yours, Woodson." And he had been.
Truly hers. I realized that now more than ever. He never breathed one
hint about Juilliard to us. If he loved her so much, why couldn't he
have patched things up with Sam to make her happy? I would never
understand my father.

I reached under my apron and put the letter in my jacket pocket
before re-joining the party. Woodson and Roosevelt were still entertaining each other with stories. I sidled up to them and we chatted,
heaven knows about what—my mind still mulling over the letter.
When Roosevelt made a trip to the cooler, I brought it up.

"I never knew you could have studied at Juilliard."

He shrugged. "So?"

"But Juilliard. Haven't you ever regretted that you didn't go?"

"Hell, no!" Woodson's voice could've stopped a train, but everyone
was stomping and clapping while Lodge fiddled and they didn't notice. My father peered at me suspiciously. "How'd you find out about
that?" He looked at me as if I was unbelievably stupid. "Do you think I
would've missed one minute of my life with your mother or you kids?"

I didn't know what to say. Strange, how little you knew about
other people, even the people you lived with, the ones you loved the
most. He'd even said "kids," plural, meaning he valued time spent with
Sam. A month ago, if you'd have asked me about David, I'd have told
you he never told a lie in his life. If you'd asked me if my son smoked
pot, I'd have laughed in your face. If you'd asked me yesterday, I'd
have said I knew everything about Woodson. Too much. I thought I
knew everything about him except the one thing I'd wanted to know
for years: what made him drink so much. The books Tessa had loaned
me were helping me understand there wasn't anything in particular
that made him drink.

He pulled another beer from the ice chest—at least it was beer
instead of scotch—and asked me if I needed anything, but I still held

half a glass of tea. We walked back over to the fire. I thanked him for persuading Mr. Kelso to wire the school for high-speed Internet.

"No problem." He chugged his beer and flicked his head to our right. "Looky there—Lodge finally stopped fiddling and got himself a beer."

Lodge stood with his hand on Quinn's shoulder laughing at the parking meter by the hot tub. Baxter, dark as ink, was barely visible sitting quietly at Lodge's knee.

"You'd better get on over there and thank the two of them. That's who you need to thank," Woodson said.

His attempts at match-making weren't subtle, but they reassured me that my father loved me even if I never knew when the alcohol might make him mean again.

I walked over to Quinn. "I can't believe you really built a whole computer by yourself."

He shifted his weight to his heels, tilted his head away, and shrugged as if his accomplishment were nothing, but his eyes told me how proud he was. He began dancing around from foot to foot. "Lodge says he'll pay me if I want to help him build some more. He sells them on eBay and around town. Can I, please, Mom, please?"

How could I say no? Quinn sprinted off to brag to Graham that he had a job. Woodson and Roosevelt, singing a mostly off-key version of "Cheeseburger in Paradise," re-loaded the grocery cart with meat and shoved it over the fire. The heat was ruining the wheels. I suspected both men were well on their way to being drunk. I guess like Tessa said, I couldn't control my dad. I could only be responsible for myself.

Woodson let loose a huge belch. "Not bad manners, just good food."

I felt I should apologize for him. "My dad gets a little obnoxious sometimes."

Lodge waved my apology off. "Great party. This is the first time I've really felt like part of the community since I moved here."

"Why did you—move here?"

"I knew Pete O'Neal—"

"Oh, that's Ceci Barnes's grandfather—you know the really tall girl who won the three-mile run today?" I pointed her out. "And that's his daughter Vivian standing over there with Mrs. Alford. I motioned toward the buffet. "Vivian is Dr. Roberts's receptionist—though they're rich enough she wouldn't have to work a day of her life if she didn't want to. Sorry, didn't mean to interrupt."

"S'okay. You remind me of my mother. She's gotta lay out all the family connections too. Pete was a friend of my dad's from way back. I think my cousins are related to their cousins or something like that. I wanted a change of scenery; Pete said Alderson was a great place to live, so here I am."

That was the most he'd ever told me about himself.

"Why were you so anxious for a change of scenery?" I knew about the ex-wife, but I thought it peculiar a person his age would pick up and move away from all the rest of his friends and family.

"Anyone ever tell you you're nosy?" A grin saved his comment from being mean, but he drew inward, so quiet I thought I'd ruined whatever friendship had been developing. Finally he answered. "I wanted to put several countries between me and my ex-wife, but I settled for several counties instead."

I laughed. There were times I felt the same way about my father.

"Needed a career change, too, so I'm only doing a little pro bono work these days while I build up my computer business." Lodge tugged on my apron strings. "Whatcha wearing this for?" He pulled his hand away and wiped it on his pants. "Did you know those strings are all wet?"

"They are?" My surprise turned to horror as I realized why. I untied the apron and asked Lodge to come inside with me. No way was I going to confess I had the apron on when I used the bathroom. The strings must have dangled into the commode.

"I have something I want to show you, but you have to wash your hands first."

"Yes, Miss School Marm, anything you say."

I hated to be called that. I wondered if he'd picked it up from my father. Lodge went to the kitchen sink, Baxter following right on his heels. I dumped the apron into the washing machine behind bi-fold doors off the kitchen and washed my own hands. Now all I needed was something to show him. We went into the living room and I turned on the light by the sofa and sat down near him. I breathed in his clean cotton scent, and my skin tingled with awareness of how close he was. I stuck my hand into my jacket pocket and pulled out a piece of paper. I didn't know which one I'd handed over, Graham's or Woodson's. If I'd given him Graham's, he'd think I was bragging. If I'd given him Woodson's, he might think I was coming on to him.

"Wow, Juilliard!" he said, while still reading. "He must have really loved your mom."

"He did," I said. "I found the letter this evening in an old box of my mother's. Shows a whole other side of my dad, doesn't it?" I wondered how I could change the subject. All I could think of was Dusty, so I thanked him again for helping out. "I just love that little dog. I would have brought him tonight but I was afraid someone would step on him. He has the best personality of any dog I've ever seen." I was rambling but I couldn't quit. "I swear he smiles at us, and if he gets distressed about anything, his tail uncurls and droops and he just looks so funny. We can't stop laughing at him."

"I know. Poms are hysterical. My mother raises them."

I was struck by the coincidence. A memory tugged at me, something Eileen O'Halloran said about Lodge having Dusty in his van. I thought she'd been confused. Now I wasn't so sure.

"She raises them," I repeated.

"Has for years, says they're her babies."

"Did one of those babies find his way into our yard?"

He shifted his weight on the couch and touched his glasses. "You're not mad, are you?"

I shook my head, but I was, a little. He had some nerve.

"Quinn seemed depressed," he said. "I didn't know about his father dying then, but he looked like a boy who needed a dog. He kept coming over to play with Baxter, and Mom had a dog she hadn't sold that was already four months old, and he was gonna be too big to be a show dog, anyway, so—"

"Too big!" Dusty was perfect exactly as he was. "So you deposited him in our yard!"

"I wouldn't have let you take him to the shelter. I watched the whole time to make sure he was okay."

I remembered now how Lodge had come over to talk to us for the first time that night. "I would hope you were watching him."

I felt the warmth of his smile ripple through the core of my body and land in my thighs. I forced myself to concentrate and follow his words. "I'd watched you with your boys. I could tell you would spoil a puppy the way my mom does."

"Oh, you could?" I accepted the flattery gracefully. The bad things that happen to us are easy to count because we usually are aware of them when they're happening, but sometimes we don't recognize the good things that enter our lives right away. Take Dusty. To think I considered taking that dog to the pound. And then there was Lodge, whose eyes were lake green with golden flecks behind his wire-rims. My face felt flushed; my leg, warm and amazingly alive where it touched his through our jeans. I could barely breathe. I couldn't think of anything to say. He leaned close to me and I felt this intense connection flowing between us. I inhaled his cotton scent again, and somewhere deep inside where feeling runs deeper than words, I heard his saxophone moaning "Europa." My lips parted.

The screen door slammed and Quinn thudded into the living room, with Graham in hot pursuit.

"Mom!" Graham yelled. "Goober took something of mine. Make the little butthead give it back!"

Had it only been two days ago that I was thinking how grown up he was getting to be?

"Make me!" Quinn circled through the first floor, squealing, and locked himself in the bathroom.

I jumped up off the couch. "What'd he take?" I asked Graham.

In a silly falsetto Quinn called out from behind the locked door, "It's a love letter from Mary Wade, his lover. Oh, little Lovey-boy!"

"You little snotface, I'm going to kill you!" Graham rattled the bathroom door.

"No one's going to kill anyone," I said. "Quinn, come out here right now."

"Oh, Lovey-boy!"

I made my voice very quiet. "Quinn, if you don't come out now, I'm going to think you aren't old enough to hold down a job."

The door cracked open enough to slide the letter out. Reaching around me, Graham snatched it away. Quinn pulled his hand back into the bathroom and re-locked it.

"You little punk." Graham gave the door a punch.

"You got your letter back," I said. "Go on outside and cool off."

Lodge was so close behind me I could feel little sparks go up my spine from his body heat.

"Sorry about that," I said.

He shrugged as if he were used to it. "I have four brothers."

That was something else I hadn't known about him, and I guess that's okay. Getting to know someone takes time. Lodge seemed to be worth the effort, even if he did have that funny little braid. Maybe I was even starting to like it. A little.

It was already quite dark when Mr. Van Teasel showed up with his wife and he wasn't wearing a suit. Judging by the way people stiffened and tried to hide their drinks from him, he was about as welcome as a seven-foot gator in a backyard pool. Although he was smiling when he arrived, as he wandered about the party, he began to look like he'd swallowed a mouthful of dryer lint. He crossed the lawn toward me.

Woodson flipped his head in the direction of the principal. "Don't look now, but here comes your favorite Sunday school teacher, and he don't look none too friendly."

Mr. Van Teasel smiled stiffly at me. "Mrs. Culpepper, I know you raised a lot of money for the school today and we're all surely grateful, but you must know the amount of alcohol flowing around here in front of our students is unconscionable."

"Unconscionable." He repeated himself in case I hadn't heard him the first time. "Teachers have no business giving parties and serving alcohol when their students are in attendance."

Technically I wasn't giving the party, but that wasn't the point. Ceci, Mary Wade, Marissa, and Graham and a few others had clustered together around the back porch swing, behaving admirably as far as I could tell.

"No one is serving alcohol to the kids," I said. "I'd never allow that. Their parents brought them here and are drinking in front of them. They even brought the alcohol. I can't control everything other people do."

"Still, as the host, you're responsible," he said. "Teachers have to be held to higher standards."

I couldn't believe Woodson stood so quietly beside me. What was

wrong with him? I'd never known him not to voice his opinion—
usually in a voice as booming as the rap music that rattled cars in the
student parking lot.

Then Mr. Van Teasel noticed the grill Woodson tended. "What in
the Sam Hill is that?" Even in the dark I could see his face blazed as red
as the fire. "What kind of example are you setting for our children?"

My voice grew soft. "One I'm very proud of, thank you for asking.
I worked all day for these kids. We all did." I finished the last of my
tea. "Now, I'm going to get something to drink and I'd be happy to
get you something. What will you have? Tea? Cola? Beer?" He didn't
answer, so I marched across the lawn to the buffet. The nerve of the
man—he was following me. Woodson trailed behind, probably being
nosy. Ah, no, he was pulling another beer from a small cooler behind
Mrs. Alford. Odd, the small cooler, when there were two larger ones
filled with beer. Vaguely I remembered him reaching into them earlier, but I had other things on my mind now.

"Just a minute!" Mr. Van Teasel said. "You can't walk away from
me!"

That didn't deserve an answer. I could. I did.

He sputtered, "No teacher on my faculty is going to drink alcohol
in front of students."

"Well—I am." I snatched the beer bottle my father had just opened
out of his hands without asking. I took a big chug and almost spit it
out. Truly awful stuff—what was in that bottle? "Now, if you'll excuse me, I'm going to slip over there and thank Mrs. Kaufmann for
that marvelous Greek salad."

Before I could make my getaway, Graham and Quinn barreled
up to me, their faces glowing.

Graham grabbed my arm. "Guess what, Mom? We got a gig. Ceci's dad asked us to play at The Down Under next Friday night. He'll
pay us fifty bucks."

Besides being an attorney, Bill Barnes had part ownership of a
restaurant and a real estate license. "Well, I think—"

"Surely you wouldn't let them play there," Mr. Van Teasel cut in.
"It's a bar!"

I had line-danced at The Down Under with David several times.
The crowds were cheerful, but not rowdy. They served good food, and

before nine o'clock families filled the place.

I forced my voice to remain low-key. "Oh, you have nothing to worry about. They'll be well chaperoned. I plan to play with them on a song or two, if they'll let me." I accepted the quick half-hug Quinn bestowed on me and the "Thanks-Mom-you're-the-coolest" from Graham with a Madonna-like smile. They ran off to tell Mr. Barnes.

Mr. Van Teasel lowered his voice to a whisper. "Mrs. Culpepper, performing in a bar would be an affront to the First Baptist Church. I know Reverend Brinkwater won't approve."

He probably wouldn't. Ever since he'd taken to the pulpit a year ago and the Weasel had begun to mess with the Sunday school, church had gotten as tight and uncomfortable as my pre-pregnancy bathing suit.

I winked at my father, who had opened another beer. "You know, I've been thinking about joining the First Methodist. I heard they know how to disport themselves with considerably more esprit than Baptists."

Woodson busted out laughing, spewing beer all over his shirt and mine and my principal's too. I doubted if he knew what "disport" meant, but he'd caught the gist. He was seriously choking. Mrs. Alford was making noises like a strangled pig, but I was too busy tending to my father to find out what was wrong with her. I slapped his back while he pinched his nostrils trying to clear them. No one ever accused my father of having class.

I wasn't done yet. Someone in Alderson had to make Mr. Van Teasel understand. "You know, my Mama always said if you go around sticking your nose in other people's business, you can expect it to get dirty. You should take her advice to heart."

After that, he dissipated like a foul fart and we were all grateful he was gone. I wondered if it would be a sin to pray for rain at graduation. It might be, but I'm hardly an angel, no matter what my teeshirt today had proclaimed. It was worth a try.

As I slapped my father on the back once again, I noticed a burn on his hand.

"Good grief, what happened to you?"

He curled the red welt away so I couldn't see. "It's nothing. I poured some Astring-o-sol on it. Be right as rain in the morning."

He was impossible. A nutcase. "By the way, what's the deal with the nasty stuff in this bottle? Tastes like skunk water."

"Guy can't have any secrets around here, can he? I filled a few mostly empty bottles with water. Thought it might slow me down some if I drank water in between beers. My stomach ain't been feeling so hot lately."

Maybe there was hope for him yet. "You could have rinsed them out first." I thrust the bottle back into his other hand. I had something to do that couldn't wait. Sometimes you needed to defend your principles, no matter the consequences. I needed to act now while I still had the courage. I slipped into the house, turned on my father's computer, and entered the password to the school newspaper's website. With a few quick clicks, I opened the file of November stories and repositioned the one on the school's failing roof along with its photographs as the lead story on our Internet edition. If Mr. Van Teasel didn't like it, he could talk to my lawyer, Mr. Barnes. He didn't need to know Bill Barnes specialized in real estate law. Just the threat of another lawyer in his life should do the trick.

When I went back outside, Liz, Tessa, and Betsy clustered around me.

Liz laid a coffee-colored arm across my shoulders and leaned in close. "Mrs. Alford said you really Culpeppered him. What happened?"

I related every detail of my little set-to with the principal.

"Mmm, about time someone drew some boundaries for him," Tessa said in her too-loud, nasal Jersey voice. "He gets into our personal business way too much. Now if only you'd stand up to Miss Baker."

"I have half a mind to call and ask where she is," I said. Miss Baker was the only one of Alderson's Angels who hadn't come to the party. It was really too bad.

"No need—here she comes," Liz said.

Without thinking, I whirled around and blurted out, "Well, hey, Jolene. Glad you could make it."

I couldn't believe I'd called her by her first name. I studied her face to see if I had offended her, but she hadn't appeared to notice. So I began to feel right pleased with myself. It wasn't exactly standing up to her, but it was a start.

"Hey yourself!" She wore her purple windsuit. "I couldn't miss this big shee-bang. After all, we're a team, right?" She hurried on to explain her late arrival—when she'd gotten home the washer, which she'd left running in the morning, had burst a valve and flooded the floor, and she'd had to mop up that mess and wait on a plumber before she could even start to heat the squash casserole, and oh it wasn't any trouble to fix, an old family recipe, she could make it in her sleep.

She rambled on and on, but one of the first things she'd said caught and held me: we're a team. I looked around at Woodson, my sons, Lodge, the Powells, the Kaufmanns, Mrs. Alford, Roosevelt, Betsy, Miss Baker, Reverend Bolden, the Barneses—the whole community of Alderson High School. I guess we were. Quite a team.

At eleven, I was exhausted and ready to go home. The crowd had thinned out. Woodson asked Graham and Quinn to spend the night at his place so they could help clean up the mess in the morning. I thought it was a good idea. He wouldn't do anything too scandalous in front of his grandsons like go on an armadillo hunt with his shotgun or invite Miss Baker to jump naked into the hot tub with him. When I went through the kitchen, I snatched his truck keys off the hook by the kitchen door. I didn't think he'd try driving anywhere, but it was best to be safe. Especially where my boys were concerned.

I went into the living room to retrieve my purse from the floor by the couch. When I turned around, Lodge stood a nose-width away. My breath caught. He tucked a camellia blossom behind my ear, one I recognized as a Yuletide from my mother's garden. An improvement over socket wrenches. I wondered if Woodson had been giving him courtship pointers.

"Is it too late—I know you've had a long day—for us to share a glass of wine? I have chardonnay or merlot at my house, whichever you like, or maybe we could just have a cup of coffee together and talk some more?"

"It's not too late." My exhaustion slipped away as if it had never been. Then I blushed, wondering what everyone would think if we drove off at the same time. "Why don't you play one more song before you leave? That way—" I trailed off.

He seemed to understand. "I'll call you when I get home."

"No need. I'll see your car and come over."

A full complement of stars shimmered in the sky. In my yard, I opened my arms wide, my face tilted upward, to absorb the wonder of them. Was David's spirit up there dancing among the tiny flickering lights? If so, I thought he wouldn't mind about Lodge. You know, if something started to happen between us. It felt right, that it could. Possibly. I didn't want to presume anything, but it could, and that thought propelled me toward the front door. I needed to brush my teeth, comb my hair, make sure no big old boogers hung out of my nose. Just in case.

I danced three quick pirouettes toward my house, humming "Europa." A dark shape rose from my front steps. The motion-activated porch light turned on. I froze.

"Hey, Miz C."

I couldn't help myself. I screamed.

Forty-Four

From inside the house, Dusty yapped his head off and scratched at the door.

"Don't go freaking out. I didn't mean to scare you," J.D. said.

"Aren't you supposed to be home at night?" I looked at his leg. "Where's the ankle bracelet?"

"Took it off."

"Are you out of your mind? They'll lock you up and throw away the key. Jeez, J.D., you've really blown it this time."

"I gotta to talk to you."

He hitched up his pants. That's when I noticed the bulge at the back of his waist. A gun? The Glock he'd written about? I could hardly breathe. Couldn't take my eyes off that protrusion. My brain buzzed. I knew I should make a plan to protect myself, but I couldn't think of anything but my boys, my precious boys—who would raise them if J.D. decided to kill me?

I tried to sound tough but my voice came out shaky. "Not a chance. We've said all we have to say to each other."

I strode toward my car, assessing the possibility of help arriving. Someone was supposed to be monitoring that GPS bracelet. They'd know the instant he took it off, according to Roosevelt. Or would someone else come to my rescue? The Van Teasels' lights had been off when I drove up, and they couldn't see through the viburnums even if they were home. How long would it be before Lodge arrived? Or nosy Eileen O'Halloran might look out her window and call the police.

"Wait!" J.D. said. "Please."

If he had said "stop," if his tone had been rough, I would have taken off running. Instead, the yearning in his voice surprised me into turning around.

His arms hung at his sides. "After tonight I won't ever bother you again, promise, but please, someone has to tell me about my mother."

I said the first snotty thing that popped into my head. "Why would I know anything about your mother?"

I regretted it even before the words were out of my mouth. Our eyes met and understanding channeled between us.

"Your husband the cop that busted her. Pitts said I got the wrong idea about how things went down. He said your Old Man all right. He said I should find out the truth. So here I am."

For a moment, I wondered why Roosevelt hadn't told J.D. about the arrest and trial. Then I realized Roosevelt might not know all that much. He was still in high school in Albany when it happened. Still, not my problem.

"Ask someone else. After the way you've treated me and my family, I can't think of one good reason why I should help you."

"I know. You're right. But you're my teacher."

"So? I'm a mother, too, and a human being." Even as I spoke, I felt the pull of that word teacher. He was my student. Not part of some nebulous "them" I could hate or distance myself from. There was that bulge to consider. But he could have shot me already if that's why he'd come here, and he could shoot me in the back if I walked away.

"Please. I don't know anyone else who will tell me what really happened to my daddy. No one will talk about it. I just want to know the truth."

The truth. What truth did he want to hear? The one that I had believed in for so many years? Or the one where J.D.'s mother admitted to a crime of passion, that discovering another woman's panties in her bed drove her over the edge? I sucked in my breath, remembering the autobiography he'd written. As a four-year-old he had seen the murder take place but obviously had no clear memories of it. He wanted answers. No wonder his mother didn't want to talk about the past. Families never wanted to talk truth about the husband hooked on Internet pedophilia or the abusive mother or the alcoholic father. Close your eyes and it won't hurt—even as a child you knew the doctor was lying before he plunged the needle into your backside.

He reached for his waistband. My legs felt as if they might melt right down to my porch into a big puddle.

I forced myself to talk, wincing inwardly at the way my voice squeaked. "Why'd you bring the gun?"

"Huh?" His eyes flicked to the bump. "Habit, I guess."

I shook my head in disbelief. Was he really that foolish?

"It's a felony, remember?" I held up my palm. "Don't answer that. Let's sit down." Before I fall down, I thought. I gestured to the porch steps, trying to ignore Dusty's barking. The motion light glared down harshly on the steps. J.D. scooted out of its direct glare into the shadows.

I had to feel my way into this carefully. "Do you remember how your arm got broken?"

"No, not really. I don't remember nothing about that night. Only it sort of seems as if Mama hollered something like, 'My babies, my babies' as the cops—your Old Man—took her away. And I remember hurting real bad. That's all."

He slumped in the shadows with his head hanging down into his hands, the bulge at his waistline much more prominent as his tee-shirt pulled tighter across his back and shoulders.

I couldn't think while looking at it, so I stared across the street at Lodge's house. I closed my eyes briefly, swallowed, and told J.D. what I could remember. Everything David had told me, and everything I had read in the papers. I think it was the first time J.D. had ever really listened to me. I tried to gauge the effect of the story, but the few times he lifted his head, it was difficult to read his expression in the dark. The barking was getting on my nerves. "Dusty, hush up, for heaven's sake!"

I turned my head back to J.D. "My husband said there were hospital records from various times your father had beaten your mother. Once he blacked your older brother's eye and when your mother tried to stop the beating, your father turned his fists on her. She had a broken collarbone and two cracked ribs that time, I think."

J.D. jumped to his feet and rammed the toe of his sneaker into my front door as hard as he could. Must have hurt. The next time he leaned sideways and slammed the entire sole into the door like a kick boxer, then reached for his waistband.

My throat slammed shut. Do something, I commanded myself. Get up. Run. Use your triathlon training and sprint like your feet are on fire. Don't just sit there and let him shoot you. But the Wonder Woman genes must have bypassed me completely. I wasn't ready to save the day or even myself. Instead, I squeezed my legs together tight so I wouldn't wet my jeans.

A splendid wave of relief washed over me when I saw J.D. was only hitching his pants up so he could take aim at my door again with his sneaker. Dusty was going crazy inside, yapping and clawing. I'd had enough of J.D.'s temper tantrum.

"J.D, stop that! Do you want to hear the rest or not?"

"Why'd he do her that way? Why?"

"I don't know. Alcohol. Drugs. Not that they excuse bad behavior, but people unleash a lot of things when they're stoned that they would hold in if they were sober." Once again I warned the dog to hush.

J.D. collapsed onto the top step. I thought he was crying. Out of respect I didn't observe too closely. Finally Dusty relented. Maybe he'd worn himself out. Or gotten hoarse. I could hear insects scratching into the silence of the night. A breeze washed the tea olive's sweetness over me, and I hoped J.D. could smell it too. He needed some sweetness in his life.

"That night your mother was just trying to protect you kids."

"I knew it had to be something like that. I just knew it!"

Lodge's car pulled up in front of his house. His car door slammed, and his porch light winked on. If I didn't go over soon, he would wonder if I'd changed my mind, but I couldn't up and leave now. "I'm sorry for everything that happened to your family."

J.D. sniffled loud enough for me to hear. "Wasn't your fault. I know that. Just seemed like you Culpeppers was in the middle of everything. My Mama's right about one thing. I can see that. Time to move on and let the past be."

Before he moved on and out of my life, I had a question of my own. "Why me? Of all the people in this town who could have told you about the trial, why come to me?"

"'Cause I knew you'd tell me the truth."

I looked away. Hoped I'd done the right thing. What I told him might have been far too little, far too late to counter years of neglect and run-ins with the law. He might spend his life in and out jail. But believing in his mother, that she was only trying to protect him, was the best chance this kid had. Sometimes lies were necessary. Sometimes they were all that held a family together. What was left of it anyway.

He walked down the porch steps. At the bottom, he turned and kicked the last step, not so much in anger as in resignation. "Guess I've blown any chance of going to college."

"You dropped a big pass, that's for sure. Just remember what a great receiver does after he misses one."

J.D. flicked his chin up to the right, his version of a nod.

Roosevelt in his Thunderbird convertible and a police car arrived on my street simultaneously.

Moving faster than I would have thought possible, J.D. slipped the gun under the foilage of my poinsettia. He looked at me to see if I was going to tell. To be honest, I didn't know. I should tell—I knew I should—but if I did, J.D. would have done more than drop a pass. He would be out of the game. Probably for good.

Roosevelt reached me first. Those giant hands grabbed hold. "Molly, you okay?"

This was the moment. If I was going to tell, it had to be now. I swallowed. "Fine. We were just having a friendly conversation."

"You being straight with me?"

"Of course." I fought a powerful urge to inspect my poinsettia.

I didn't know what color the lies I'd told tonight were, but I was sure I'd crossed the line into a gray area. Then again, why did everything have to break down into black and white? Monochrome was too limiting when the world offered us a rainbow every day. My lies were crimson, I decided. Right or wrong, they stemmed from my heart, from the hope that J.D. would still find a path to college.

My heart was still pumping madly. I forced myself to take three deep breaths—one of my cop husband's tricks to counteract the adrenaline streaming through my system.

Roosevelt seemed amazingly sober for a man coming straight from the barbecue. He was like David: a man with a large frame who mastered the art of nursing a drink and laughing it up so that everyone else thought you were partying when you were secretly responsible.

Lodge, two bottles of wine in hand, jogged across the street.

The other officer, a new one I didn't know, slapped cuffs on J.D., despite my suggestion that I didn't think they'd be necessary. "Ma'am, he's got a history of violence and he's violated his house arrest agreement," he said. "He's in big trouble."

"What's going on?" Lodge lowered the wine bottles, one red, one white, beside his legs. Roosevelt got a good look at them anyway, raised his eyebrows, and shot me a knowing grin.

The new fellow said I'd need to come to the station and give a statement.

Roosevelt's voice held a note of laughter. "It's late, Kirbo. She can come down in the morning."

I ignored Roosevelt's gleaming teeth while Kirbo bundled J.D. into the cruiser. My brain still felt abuzz with flight-or-fight chemicals. I gave my head a little shake to clear it and puffed three more deep breaths.

Suddenly I remembered David's scrapbook and called after them. "J.D., I have some news articles and pictures from the trial. I'll bring them to you tomorrow." I'd have to censor them first to make sure nothing contradicted what I'd told him. I didn't think they would. Only his mother knew the real truth. And me.

Roosevelt leaned close, his voice nearly a whisper. "About time you found someone, Molly, and he seems like a nice guy. But here's a heads up. When I left the party, Woodson was looking for his truck keys, swore they weren't where he left them. I figure he'll either find his keys or find someone sober to drive him and the boys over here to rescue you. In a couple of minutes, all the folks still at the party will be knocking on your door." He winked and hopped into his convertible.

"Shhii—ugar," I whispered.

Lodge closed the gap between us. "You say something?"

"No, nothing." Guess it was destiny. I was never going be alone with Lodge.

"Why was the Marshall kid here at this hour?"

"He's just a messed up boy who needs counseling and a chance to straighten out his life." I hoped he got it. Wishing big, the way my mother always encouraged, I hoped to hear eight years from now that J.D. had graduated from college. But remembering my father's cynical view of wishes, I decided it would be enough to know J.D. was a productive citizen rather than another black male caught up in our prison system. The feeling I had for J.D. wasn't warm and fuzzy, but maybe it was a kind of love, or close enough.

"I could use some late night counseling myself—think you can help me?" Lodge asked.

That braid swung slightly to the left as he cocked his head, and I could hear my mother saying, *Be careful you don't get mixed up with the wrong sort of people.* (Guys with long hair were the wrong sort of people.) *If you lie down with dogs, you get up with fleas.* My father's voice countered, *He's down-to-earth, he's nice to my grandsons. What more do you want to know?*

Plenty, I decided. I wanted to know all about C. Lodge Piscetelli. All my life, the voices of my parents had banged around in my head. My mother warning about all the things that might hurt me. Drugs, fast cars, sex before marriage, sitting on public toilet seats. My father telling me I'd miss out on life if I listened too much to my mother. I was fortunate to have the socially aware voice of my mother tempered by the rougher realism of my father. Their advice, though confusing and often contradictory, served as a useful guide. Sometimes, though, I needed to tune them both out, and listen to my own voice.

"You, C. Lodge Piscetelli, are beyond my help until you own up to what that C. stands for."

"I'll never tell."

I recognized the rumble of an old truck approaching from the direction of my father's house. He'd found the spare keys. Destiny be damned. Sometimes you have to seize control of the moment, say yes to an opportunity that flashes as tantalizing as a firefly before it disappears into a fold of the night sky, leaving you filled with regret.

"Oh, I think you will." With eyes wide open because I wanted to drown in those green lakes, I pulled Lodge's face down and touched my lips to his. He wrapped his arms around me and I melted into another kiss. I could hear my father's truck pull into a parking spot a few houses down the street. More engines followed. Headlights winked off. Doors creaked open, then slammed shut.

I was lucky. I had a family and friends—a whole wonderful town—that cared enough to worry about me. As if Lodge and I had all the time in the world, I tucked my hand under his arm and led him toward the warm yellow light shining from my windows and a little yappy dog who would be thrilled to see us.

DISCUSSION QUESTIONS

Note: Recipes for most dishes mentioned in the novel are available at www.donnameredith.com.

1. How does Molly's view of her hometown evolve during the story? What are the strengths of Alderson? The weaknesses?

2. How is Molly typical of the "sandwich generation"?

3. Woodson Trask is a complicated man. Discuss his good points and bad points.

4. What aspects of her life does Molly have control over and what things can't she control? What events in her recent life would especially make her feel out of control?

5. On what basis does Blacks For Progress file a lawsuit against Alderson High School? Are the complaints justified?

6. Tracking students has long been an issue in public high schools. Should different tracks exist, or should all students be held to the same standards?

7. Though Molly and Liz are friends, they have never discussed any aspect of race. When Molly finally asks some questions of Liz, what does she learn?

8. Lies, small and large, form an important thread in the novel. Near the novel's beginning, Molly tells lies, one to her father's boss about why Woodson missed work, one to Mrs. Alford about her lipstick, and another to her son Quinn about the cookies she had intended to bring home to the boys. Woodson lies about his alcoholism. Woodson claims Molly's mother never lied, but Molly remembers it differently. Molly's son Graham lies to her about using pot. Her neighbor Lodge Piscetelli lies about why he moved

to Alderson. J.D. Marshall also lies to Molly at school, and in the end, she lies to J.D. about why his mother killed his stepfather. Which lies felt acceptable to you? Which ones didn't? How pervasive is lying in our culture?

9. Name several problems Molly faces as a 40-year-old widow who would like to have romance in her life again. What missteps in judging men does she make? Have your first impressions of people ever been way off base?

10. How does the recession affect Alderson High School classrooms? Are schools in your community facing similar issues?

11. Problems caused by the recession, as well as Molly's various clothing mishaps, add humor to the novel. What was your favorite humorous scene?

12. Initially Molly views Reverend Bolden as an adversary. Why do her views change?

13. J. D. Marshall challenges Molly's philosophy that no children are throwaways. Discuss the strategies she uses to work with him, what things complicate their relationship, and the outcome.

14. What successful moments does Molly have as a teacher?

15. Think back over your own school years. What were the most important traits of the teachers who influenced your life? Was there a "Miss Baker" in your school?

You might also enjoy these titles
BY WILD WOMEN WRITERS

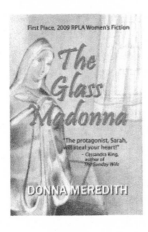

First Place, 2009 RPLA Women's Fiction

"The protagonist, Sarah, will steal your heart!"
- Cassandra King, author of The Sunday Wife

DONNA MEREDITH

THE GLASS MADONNA
BY DONNA MEREDITH

Donna Meredith's award-winning debut novel, *The Glass Madonna*, tells the powerful story of a woman's determination to create her own destiny. Coming of age was supposed to be easy in the '70s, but tradition still bans women from making glass, an art form Sarah Stephens views as part of her family heritage. And regard for virginity is not as dead as Sarah thinks when she gives hers up to a college boyfriend. Her husband, unable to get past his jealousy, isolates her in a backwoods trailer and tells her he always wanted to marry a virgin. Unintentionally reinforcing his criticism, Aunt Livvie treasures a family heirloom, a glass figurine of the Madonna. It shines with perfect purity no real woman could achieve. The novel weaves together stories of three generations of glass workers who emigrate from Germany to West Virginia.

WET WORK
BY DONNA MEREDITH

With memorable characters, a lush Florida setting, and our most precious natural resource at the center of its plot, *Wet Work* is an environmental thriller evoking a Carl Hiaasen novel, corrupt strip-mall investor replaced with crooked water-project developer. Impoverished college student Summer Cassidy just wants to earn her master's in

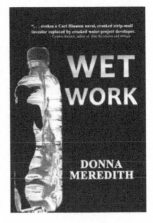

". . . evokes a Carl Hiaasen novel, crooked strip-mall investor replaced by crooked water-project developer."
- Cynthia Barnett, author of Blue Revolution and Mirage

WET WORK

DONNA MEREDITH

hydrogeology. That, and hustle some foosball, chase a Frisbee, drink a few beers. Two months shy of her graduation, a corporation's desperate efforts to suppress her research into contaminants in its ASR water wells upend her world. But nothing is going to keep her from pursuing the truth or her dreams. Not the end of her scholarship. Not the thugs who come after her. And especially not the enigmatic Ty Franceschi, even if he is hotter than the Florida sun in mid-August. Summer Cassidy prefers to shred the bad guys with science, but if that doesn't work she slings a book at a nose, whips a wrench toward a windpipe, or grabs the nearest gun. She is a bit of a bad girl, but one whose vulnerability will win your heart.

The manuscript for WET WORK won a Royal Palm Literary Award in a contest sponsored by the Florida Writers Association in 2013.

All Wild Women Writers titles are available through amazon.com and barnesandnoble.com in both print and electronic versions. Most bookstores can order them.

Made in the USA
Coppell, TX
13 August 2020